Shanghai Ruby's

Shanghai Ruby's

A Matthew Thornton Mystery

David R. Thompson

I dedicate this novel, Shanghai Ruby's, to Darquise, my sweet and loving, beautiful wife for forty-five years who unexpectedly passed away on September 20, 2021.

She was a true inspiration in my life and my writing, often featured in my detective fiction novels in various romantic and entertainment scenes.

Although the light in my personal and creative candle flickers without her, Darquise remains in my heart where she will always be with me.

—David R. Thompson

Praise for Shanghai Ruby's

"Thompson has the ability to describe *Shanghai Ruby's* characters, set during the 1940s Hollywood's Golden Age, from amorous to menacing, with equal entertainment for the reader. You can almost smell the Lucky Strike cigarette smoke wafting across the room, taste a cold brew at Shanghai Ruby's bar and admire the beautiful femme fatale's sprinkled throughout. It's filled with action, suspense and mystery. Great read." — Larry Morphew, Author of *Country Folk*

"David R. Thompson has once again proven that he's the king when it comes to spinning a hard-boiled detective yarn. His prose oozes with language that harkens back to the best of Hammett or Chandler. It's 1948, and P.I. Matthew Thornton is doing what he does best—solving crimes. In this latest novel *Shanghai Ruby's*, Thornton has his arms full, taking on a communist organization whose plans is to destroy the Hollywood film industry. He meets shady characters along the way who don't make his job easy—but Thornton is tough. Neither femme fatale, thugs, or mobsters will deter him from solving the case. A 'don't miss reading, or you'll be sorry' detective novel. Thoroughly entertaining. A real page-turner. I highly recommend it." — Tony Piazza, Author of *A Murder Amongst Angels*, *The Curse of the Crimson Dragon*, *Murder is Such Sweet Revenge*, and *Murder in the Cards*

"*Shanghai Ruby's* treats us to a wild ride that takes us back in time to the late 1940s. From Los Angeles to Catalina Island, we find ourselves in the steamy world of sex, violence, kidnapping, car bombings and murder. Thompson captures in stunning detail what it must have been like to live in the days of The House Unamerican Activities Committee and how characters from

Humphrey Bogart to Ernest Hemingway all play a role. So, pour yourself a glass of wine and sit down to an adventure filled with lively characters and a plot with more twist and turns than a rollercoaster." — Frank Grady, Author of *Mermaid Jewels*

"It's 1948 in the seedy underbelly of LA and P.I. Matthew Thornton is asked by a friend of Bogey himself to recover stolen jewelry. A task that drags him into the world of organized crime where violence, murder, sex, and a host of very dangerous characters await. Fast-paced, great characters and well-plotted. Highly recommended." — DP Lyle, Award-winning, best-selling author of the Jake Longly, Sam Cody, Dub Walker and Cain/Harper thriller series and Forensic Science series

"Tough as a nickel steak and smokin' hot. Read it wearing welder's gloves." — Rob Leininger, USA today award-winning author of Black Sun, Killing Suki Flood, and the Mortimer Angel Gumshoe series

"Like your Java sweetened with a shot of bourbon, baby? Have I got the brew for you, served scorching hot at *Shanghai Ruby's* the title of David R. Thompson's new novel. Set in 1948 Los Angeles, this cup is filled to the steaming brim with bombshell broads, blazing bullets, blackmail, and betrayals—not to mention Communist counterfeiters, exotic night clubs, and international intrigue. Cream and sugar? Maybe some sugar, at least a steamy honey trap or two from his femme fatales." — James Lincoln Warren, Award-winning author of *The 1% Solution*, *Treviscoe of Lloyd's* mystery series, *Mother Brimstone*, and *When the Wind Blows*

"It's Los Angeles in the aftermath of World War Two. Life is cheap and women are dispensable. The House Un-American Activities Committee. The looming Red Menace. Prostitution. Murder. Car bombings. *Shanghai Ruby's* has everything, with plot switches faster than a pinball machine in overdrive. Thompson captures the era so well you can taste it, smell it. In a world where the wrong word can mean a bullet, P.I. Matthew Thornton's infidelity enquiry quickly leads him into a scenario which could mean an end to everything he had been fighting for. Now, all he has to do is stay alive." — Ian Walker, Author of *Counting the Dead*

"Thompson hits this one out of the park like Joe DiMaggio on a good night in Atlanta! He captures the thrills and chills of Hollywood just after World War Two as he takes us on a fast-paced journey through the city's seedy and glamorous addresses. Movie stars and gangsters alike get equal billing as Matt Thornton P.I., takes no prisoners chasing the truth behind his client's dilemma. Everywhere from the dark alleys of China Town to the glamor of Catalina Island; from tattoo parlors to the brothels and seedy hotels, Thompson connects the dots and dispenses justice. A gripping and delightful tale with a bombshell ending!" — Donald Whitman, #1 Amazon bestselling author of *Fatal Healing*, *Dig Deeper, Dig Wider*, and *Isle of Deceit*

"The way Thompson portrays LA of 1948 is not only entertaining but draws you into the period with the language and the atmosphere of post WWII. His colorful descriptions of the events of the time are amusing and interesting at the same time. He captured the era exactly, and I got caught up in the never boring scenes as they played out in great detail. Excellent story." — Daniel Krygsveld, Author of *Internet Killer*, *The Final Battle*, *Flower on the Run*, and *Houseboat*

"It's 1948 Los Angeles. Matthew Thornton P.I. is hired to recover jewelry given to a mobster's mistress. It's a dangerous case, but he needs the money. Partnered with his assistant and sometime-girlfriend Rhonda who moonlights as a striptease dancer, he realizes what looked like a simple case has a connection to several murdered women, as well as a communist plot to overthrow the Hollywood film industry. Thornton attracts a small cadre of offbeat allies, and he and his partners descend into the steamy world of sex, violence and murder, eventually realizing they are not just fighting for their own lives, but for the fate of their entire country. A fun and exciting read. Highly recommended." — Melissa Bowersock, Author of *Lightning*

Strikes, Queen's Gold, The Field Where I Died, Murder Walk, and *Blood Walk.*

Chapter One

The war in Europe and the Pacific had been crushed. All further thoughts of conflicts were conveniently kicked under the carpet and replaced with a mood that attempted to remain celebrant … but also complacent. Meanwhile, something equally, if not more insidious, had replaced Germany and Japan's world-conquering obsession. It was burning just below the surface, like smoldering tree roots after a raging forest fire, and wouldn't be easy to stamp out. Small sparks left over from the world conflicts were beginning to ignite unrestrained in pockets from Europe to Asia. Before long, these sinister tentacles would reach out unnoticed to the untrained eye, behind the scenes of seemingly innocent endeavors in the United States as well. Grasping, twisting, manipulating, and disrupting, they'd reach deep into the moral fibers woven into the hearts of many of those unsuspecting Americans that offered minimal resistance, resulting in their personal destruction.

Government checks and balances were few but selective and would soon grow in proportion to the perceived threat. They would rapidly attack this menace with a vengeance. While devouring some participants completely, they'd chew up others and spit them out, to serve as lessons for those failing to adhere to their traditional patriotic obligations.

Life in 1948 Los Angeles was a particular target, as it returned to a prewar high, most oblivious to this lurking, crippling peril. With few exceptions, L.A., like most major cities on the home front, was now more anxious to continue the post-war winning streak than *Sea Biscuit* hauling an overweight jockey. Settling into a normal life again was an obsession. Employment was up; big and small manufacturing companies were bursting at the seams with prosperity. They'd hire anybody that walked through the doors. Tinsel town was pumping out more movies and radio shows than ever, entertaining the new and jubilant expanded families. Banks were doling out government-backed mortgage loans to ex-GI's with more abandon than playing poker with your eyes closed. Automobile sales had never been higher, and GI brides were snapping up house appliances faster than a fleet of sailors on shore leave can empty their wallets in a waterfront bordello.

Struggling through my own share of lean years, everything was also connecting in the private investigation business. After several successful high-profile cases, the caliber of my clientele had risen higher than a jungle fever. Over paid silver screen celebrities with deep pockets were stumbling over each other, willing to pay me handsomely for unraveling the scrapes and peccadillos they'd gotten themselves into. I hadn't been stabbed, shot, pistol-whipped, or hospitalized for quite a while. I'd also made a sizable bundle on the last case I was working on. I couldn't have felt better.

I told myself I was entitled to take a little time off to go deep-sea fishing with my Louisiana pal Leland Avery on his off shore tub, the *Excalibur*. He was straw boss of the dead-end Anchor Marina in a back channel section of Los Angeles Harbor, where I berthed my former live-aboard 40' ketch the *Black Swan*. Now the sleek black sailboat was growing moss at dockside when it wasn't off to the Channel Islands, frequenting the night clubs and gambling joints on Catalina or taking romantic moonlight interludes up and down the coast.

After a few too many quiet days at sea pursuing elusive swordfish with good ol' boy Leland and drinking too much tepid beer, I was itching to get back to home port and begin knocking heads again in some of my usual cases.

There were only three other things that changed in my life. A mid-sized apartment I could barely afford nestled between the Hollywood movie studios and the flesh pots dotting Sunset Boulevard. A new upscale office I could barely afford. And last but not least, a well-stacked flashy secretary with a sketchy background and non-stop curves to go with the office. She wasn't the one I thought I really needed, but maybe I was wrong, and besides, I didn't have much choice at the time.

Betty Joe Sharp, or B.J. as she was affectionately called by my old pal Nathaniel "Tex" Sharp, was histwenty-something strawberry blonde bombshell of a younger sister. This sizzling babe , who I preferred calling by her look-alike celebrity name "Rhonda ," helped him during the day with his struggling neighborhood service station business. She normally wore agrease-stained jump suit and a bandana to keep that blonde lion's mane out of her eyes. But that was before reaching to the stars for something more glamorous. First posing for several men's girlie magazines au natural and then moonlighting part-time as *"Rhonda Flame"* the *"Hotter than a Blow Torch"* exotic striptease dancer at one of L.A.'s popular burlesque joints, the *"Florentine Gardens"* on Hollywood Blvd.

There the gorgeous blonde started as a cigarette girl carting around a neck strap tray loaded with stogies and smokes. Scantily clad, her bubbling breasts poured over the top of a low cut, short black sparkly thigh-high costume. It was flared at the bottom with white ruffles, her black lace panties peeking out from underneath whenever she bent over to serve a customer. Her matching fishnet stockings were attached to a snappy garter belt. The whole package showcased non-stop legs teetering on a pair of black spike heels higher than the Ambassador Hotel. With her angel's face and that contoured figure stuffed into any intoxicating get-up, it guaranteed hustling tobacco for tips wouldn't last longer than smoking a pack of Old Gold's down to your nicotine-stained fingers.

She was more than popular with several tough characters running the L.A. night club scene. They paved the way for her thermal rise to the top. She was quickly recast in something else to take advantage of her assets by the chubby cigar-chomping club manager Nick Grant, affectionately known to insiders as "Gramps." First, in a chorus line to whet the appetites of the paying suckers closest to the stage, then as one of the feature strippers sandwiched in between an assortment of burlesque variety acts from "Senor Wences," a Spanish ventriloquist to the "Flying Herzogs" a trapeze act imported from somewhere in Eastern Europe.

For now, she also temporarily decorated my outer office part-time. How long? All bets were off as she was ambitious and anxious for real pizzazz out of life. I couldn't complain. I knew if she stuck with it, she'd get more than her share of kicks out of my business. I certainly did, but some of those she probably wouldn't like any better than I did.

She was dazzlingly beautiful and added just the right touch by politely whispering to my customers into the telephone with a voice softer than a fluffy kitten. She reeled them in faster than a siren trolling for lost sailors. I couldn't ask for more. However, she was also misfiling reports, eagerly over sharpening pencils, and typing correspondence with just two pokey fingers … all of which I tried to overlook.

I was sitting in my new private office, waiting for a few expected return callers to spark up my day and quietly contemplating where my business was going with this new addition. I thought about why I'd hired her in the first place.

Tex was worried about his sister's future and practically begged me to take her off his hands to teach her something about my growing business. Even more important, it was to keep her out of further trouble with some of the unsavory underworld characters that frequently dropped their crates off for tune-ups, and gunshot damage repair and … were regulars at the *Florentine*. I knew she'd grown up drop-dead gorgeous and liked to party, so I silently questioned the wisdom of his request asking me, of all persons, to be a watchdog over this doll.

But, he was one of my best pals from our old Army days and also helped me bust up several rough mob enforcers on my last case here in L.A., so I couldn't argue. Tex said there'd been a problem with her and didn't want to elaborate on the details. I told him I didn't think hiring his knock-out sister was a good idea. I needed someone with typing experience and more acclimated to working in an office environment. Her experience was limited to bumping and grinding in a strip joint and helping him pump gas or customers after hours. He desperately tried to assure me that eventually, she'd be just the right person and was a quick learner. I didn't think so, but only time would tell.

Aside from Rhonda's front office looks, perfect figure, and few office skills, I rationalized that at least in a pinch, she'd be able to tune up my auto. Tex had given me that steely- eyed glare that I'd seen work before on the enemy. It said if I didn't agree with him, we'd have a show down. I didn't want that. So, I told him I'd try her out for a while and see how things worked out in the P.I. business, with no promises. He said that would work for him, and we exchanged power grips on it.

In between buckling down to the secretarial tasks, I broke up the mundane office work by assigning her to routine surveillance at a few hotels, photographing cheating spouses, and a stint at a local gun range, practicing with one of my .32 cal Colt automatics. As a native Texan, she was a natural deadly shot at close range, and I let her carry the little purse gun for protection if needed.

However, she had other things on her mind. When business was slow, which it usually was, there she sat; day dreaming about an expensive once in a lifetime trip to Paris, France, visualized from a black and white photo of the Eiffel Tower posted near her desk and her strip tease costumes and other props at the Florentine.

Nevertheless, she typically divided her office time between buffing her nails, shuffling reports, and trying to appease me by acting office efficient. And, regardless of what she was or wasn't doing in my business, she was at least drop-dead gorgeous and flashed like a roadhouse neon along a darkened highway whenever I entered.

As usual, she had my attention this day, stretching out her new cashmere cream-colored sweater and poured into a pair of skin-tight dark chocolate brown leather hip-hugging pants. The whole package was wrapped tighter than a loan sharks delinquent payment squeeze. It was definitely a trendsetting departure from the usual baggy-legged costumes they were pushing on young women in swanky high-end department stores. Combined with a matching pair of double strap sky-high stiletto heels, she anxiously waited for my next customer to enter and stumble over her beauty before meeting me and getting down to serious business.

I'd moved into larger quarters to accommodate my expanding business with this dish. My office was still in the same Chrysler building on the corner of Hollywood and Vine Streets. It was higher up on another floor, but not enough to give you a nose bleed. It wasn't much different than my old one, just a steeper price tag to go with the corner location. The rent included slightly used art deco-styled desks and matching guest chairs, a well-seasoned black visitor's leather couch that converted to a hide-a-bed, coffee tables, and a water cooler with an attached paper cup dispenser. Off to one side, a standup entertainment credenza boasting a well-stocked hidden bar with a small ice box. I kept that stocked with an assortment of cold beer and sodas. There was now enough chrome trim on all the furniture to require dark-tinted cheaters upon entering, and it took me a while to get used to the flash. There was also an odd assortment of fake rubber plants, a gift from a movie prop department client, and two unidentified stuffed fish trophies from another client plastered on one wall in my office. The rest of the furnishings were equally seasoned and comfortably arranged in both Rhonda's outer and my inner offices.

Once I had a little more dough, I thought, what the hell, why not splurge a little, at least while I was still kicking. In my business, there were so many close calls that I was on afirst-name basis with most of the local hospitals. You just never knew when that faceless guy down a dark alley wearing a heavy chalk pinstripe would spell out your name with a burst from his "Chicago-typewriter." I threw financial caution to the wind and just needed a few more well-heeled clients to help keep up the rent for this show.

One thing I did need was someone to type up reports and answer the telephone. I was getting sick of "Little Miss Wind Chimes" from my answering service. She was a mumbler that was hard to understand when she collected messages. They were not always taken down correctly or decipherable. I'd keep her on part-time, but rationalized that this change with Rhonda wouldn't be too bad after all. Eventually, her typing skills might improve, and her spelling errors would be eliminated. Until then, I'd just keep my detailed reports shorter, briefer, and more focused. After all, my spelling wasn't that accurate either, and I might even type a few myself if I had to.

Rhonda and I shared a common secret, which neither one of us openly acknowledged. That seemed to work out just fine with both of us. I supposed it would only be a matter of time, though, before we'd have to discuss it, but for right now, neither one of us wanted to peek under those covers.

I swiveled in my new chrome and black leather chair and frowned at the overcast fog. It suddenly crept in from the Pacific behind me while my back was turned. Usually, it lifted, by this time in the morning. I didn't like it. My late model Buick Roadmaster convertible with a new midnight black paint job and a tan top, red leather seats, a heater that worked, a driver's side chrome spot light, plus an AM radio, was parked down below in the alley flanking the building. It was another used number with low mileage that I'd bought from my pal Tex. From this high up, you wouldn't notice where the bullet holes had been patched. I could only guess, but it was probably already covered in condensation. That would mess up the fifty cent wash job I'd just gotten on my way into the office earlier.

Groaning in disgust at the weather development, I spun back around, feeling better seeing Rhonda peek around the corner of my office door. She announced in a merry sing-song voice from across the room, accentuating with her red-lipped smile, "Matthew, sweetheart, Mr. Carson McCullen, the President of McCullen Industries, just arrived and is very anxious to speak with you."

She'd stepped in close enough for me to inhale her perfumed body, sliding a hip onto the corner of my desk in a move smoother than downing a glass of vintage Dom Perignon. If that didn't send my flag up the mast, she punctuated her delivery with more suggestive body English than was glimpsed by the front row suckers and high rolling mobsters at the Florentine.

Whispering confidentially with those pouty lips again and stretching her sweaters seams to the limit, she added, "I thought you told me you were waiting for his return phone call to set up an appointment, or am I mistaken?"

"No … you aren't, kitten. But I'll see him, anyway, just show him in." I couldn't resist grinning at this cupcake's act. I also wondered what she was wearing, if anything, under that tight teaser of an outfit.

"Okay, Mat-thew," she purred, easing off the desk top and running her hands over her hips, smoothing out imaginary wrinkles. I just shook my head, watching her tight posterior float back across the room to collect my visitor.

She motioned for McCullen to enter, partially blocking the entrance with her voluptuous body. This time I groaned to myself, watching her performance again, and thought, "She's going to be a handful all right; Tex was right on that score, but what a handful."

McCullen squeezed by, hat in hand, and gave Rhonda a practiced charming smile, eyeing her figure in that skintight outfit and not complaining either. I wasn't sure, but he may have brushed her cashmere sweater in passing. It seemed a little too close for my money. He was probably thinking the same thing I did anyway, and I didn't blame him, but studied him quickly and determined I could take him easily if I had to.

He was about my height and size; six feet or so, about 200 lbs. and broad-shouldered, but otherwise seemed to be going to pot. Somewhere in his late forties, his hair was already thinning on top and turning prematurely grey around the edges. It was cut long, parted on the side, and combed straight back, glistening with hair tonic. He carried himself with guarded confidence like he'd been an athlete in his youth, but now was slightly round- shouldered and a little paunchy from too much desk work. From the premature creases appearing on his kisser, he probably resented growing older every time he looked in the mirror. If he didn't, he should have. His desperate expression and ruddy complexion were plastered on a slightly puffy face, telegraphing his love for the bottle. His mug was a dead give-away to a man carting a heavy load of problem baggage.

I motioned towards one of my empty visitor's chairs as he advanced with an outstretched paw. His hands were unusually large, his handshake firm, and the skin was rough, like a manual laborer's. He dropped down, eager to conduct business. This overly anxious intrusion into a P.I.'s office usually meant your cash register was already on high alert. I could almost hear the bell signaling big bucks were blowing in my direction. I was anxious to start my meter running.

I hadn't met McCullen before, but I guessed from his appearance and demeanor that he was a self-made man that had worked his way upstairs the hard way. We'd only talked briefly about a possible sabotage job at his aircraft electronics factory in El Segundo. Then, I'd placed him on the backburner while I solved another pressing case in Simi Valley. He'd mentioned Humphrey Bogart as a mutual connection, and I immediately catalogued this guy as a high roller in my fee department. From the looks of his well-tailored double- breasted dark pin- striped threads, starched white shirt, hand- painted tie with a diamond- studded tie clasp, and matching cuff links, I wouldn't be wrong.

Sitting across from my desk, I couldn't help noticing the nervous, worried expression on his face. He wanted to talk and fast, like it was his final confession. What the rush was wouldn't take long to find out.

Rhonda slid quietly back into the office behind him, anxious to be helpful. I watched her technique, working our client. She whispered seductively in his ear, asking whether he'd like a cup of coffee or maybe something else a little stronger before we started. He thought about it longer than normal and settled on the Java, probably confused over her suggestive proposal. She poured out a mug full from the small pot brewing on the hot plate nestled on the low wooden credenza under the window sill. He followed her movements with fascination as she placed the cup on a coaster towards the front edge of my desk. Her captivating smile, surrounded by the wave of her blushing blonde hair casually tumbling over her shoulders, seemed to catch him off guard. McCullen would have been blind not to admire her assets. Especially that shapely posterior and those uplifted breasts stretching out her tight sweater when she bent over with the steaming delivery. He was no fool and returned her disarming air with a weak school-boy grin as if he'd just been caught peeking through a bedroom key hole. He turned slowly back towards me after she clicked the door closed behind her, let out a sigh, and reached for his cup.

Taking a quick sip and another pause to collect his thoughts, he blurted out in a throaty, halting baritone, "W-what an absolute knockout, Mr. Thornton. You're a lucky man to have such a gorgeous woman working in your office.

She looks so familiar, though. But I can't place her. She looks like ah-ah Rita Hayworth, right? No, no that's not it, but I should know. Maybe I've seen her before, no …" he hesitated, drawing a confused mental blank, and then continued. "I've seen plenty of those knockouts in the flesh at some of the charity events I attend. But maybe it was somewhere else. If there's one thing I know, it's fine wine, beautiful women, and fast race horses. And your secretary is definitely one rare beauty. Trust me, she's a carbon copy of a movie goddess, if ever I saw one.

"You should see the secretaries we have in my company… trolls, real trolls. Good typists, but God all mighty, homely as a sack of prunes with pits and ugly enough to start a cattle stampede."

His observations were meant to be entertaining, but I was getting annoyed with his digression and wasn't amused. "Yes, I can see a resemblance to someone special, but I thought that maybe it was a little closer to ah… how about Virginia Mayo?" I suggested, throwing him a curveball on purpose.

"No, no! That's not it, somebody else…" he corrected instantly, followed by a fit of coughing and his face flushing with this uncontrolled outburst.

I couldn't argue with him on that point, she did compliment my office, and we did have it wrong about her identity, but he was right about her similarity in appearance to someone famous. But McCullen was getting a little too worked up over my doll. He was clearly disturbed and preoccupied. It was leading to something serious, which I was about to find out.

I tapped a Lucky out of the pack, offering him one, which he declined. I lit mine, blew a small smoke ring toward the ceiling, and pulled out a lined pad of yellow note paper, anxious to get started and moving our conversation forward.

I made that offer again for something stronger to calm him down. This time he took me up on it without a second thought and side lined his coffee cup fast. He accepted a couple fingers full in a shot glass from my bottom drawer rye bottle without complaining. I joined him and toasted his decision, then sat back, anxious to kick start that discussion.

He now felt a little more relaxed and reached inside his coat to pull a jet- black Maduro stogie from a leather case. The cigar promised to smell stronger than a natural gas leak and was larger than a submarine torpedo. I couldn't wait. He fired it up with a gold plated lighter, probably monogrammed, blowing a cumulus cloud skyward, mushrooming across the ceiling like an atomic bomb.

Before speaking again, he glanced around the room, then over his shoulder as if he was afraid to be overheard by any interlopers. Seeing none, he scooted his chair closer and began in a low, barely audible, fast- paced, confidential tone. "That's what brings me here today, Mr. Thornton."

"The thefts or sabotage business at your factory that we talked about before?"

"No, no, no, neither!" he said and coughed a couple more times, motioning for another refill from the rye bottle I'd placed back in the desk drawer. He needed to clear his throat before he could start again.

As I refilled his shot glass, I wondered how this jitter-bug could manage a large corporation without a running booze boost to calm him down.

"That problem seems to have disappeared over the past few weeks, and I hope forever. Maybe not . I'll let you know if it returns. This is even more serious," he continued, tossing off the dregs in his glass and looking around again nervously. "It's ah… a little more… personal."

I had a vague idea where this was going, but my meter was ticking, and the longer he talked, the fatter the fee. Unfortunately, he didn't seem to be getting anywhere. So, I said, "Okay, Mr. McCullum, you can cut to the chase. What gives? You can confide in me. I'm on the friendly side, remember?"

He nodded an affirmative and continued. "It's about ah-a woman that I met at the Blue Parrot Bar and Grill. It's not far from here, in Hawthorne, not far from *my* company," he emphasized, with a slightly proud, arrogant air.

I did know it, and had already guessed correctly the source of his problem. "Ah, yes, of course, a woman. That's not surprising, and yes, I've been there. It's very swanky if I remember correctly; soft piano music, subdued lighting, quiet and romantic. It also has just the right atmosphere for a quiet rendezvous with someone you're keeping on the Q-T. A nice lounge and restaurant that serves excellent food and a small intimate hotel down the street, right?

I added, "Did you know that whole Parrot entertainment package is owned by a few underworld characters? I've had run-ins with several of them in the past, and they're a dangerous bunch to tangle with."

"Y-Yes, you're correct on all counts, especially on the last ones which I just found out about, and that's why I picked you." He nervously coughed a couple more times, waved for another short refill, and after polishing it off, cleared his throat again and continued.

"I heard you were involved with some entertainment "owners" at one time and ah- knew your way around a tough crowd," he said, fidgeting with his empty whiskey glass desperate for more and receiving none, blew a stream of acrid smoke in my direction.

I coughed a couple of times. He was beginning to stink up my new office puffing on that El Rope-O. I wasn't impressed with his matching attitude either. I got up and cracked open one of the side windows to let in some fresh smog, or I'd have to get the office ceiling repainted, and my new double-breasted suit dry cleaned sooner than I expected.

"Okay, now where are we with your problem?" I said, ignoring his hints for another refill.

I was beginning to run out of patience with this character. I dropped the bottle back in the bottom drawer while there was still some left and slumped back down at my desk. If he hadn't been one of Bogart's high roller referrals, I'd have dropped him faster than a slippery lawyer.

"It's very simple," he droned on, licking his lips and wishing my bar was still open. "I asked my wife to meet me at the Blue Parrot for a cocktail and dinner. It was right after a late meeting I was having with some of my managers about that sabotage problem. They assured me that everything seemed to be back to normal, and I was feeling relieved and looking forward to celebrating with Nora, my wife.

"I'd bought her a very nice white gold ankle bracelet decorated with diamonds. I had it gift wrapped and placed it in my coat pocket, intending to give it to her that evening at dinner.

"I arrived at our scheduled time and waited, but she didn't show up. Finally, after I'd consumed too many martinis while waiting, I grew impatient and called the house. She wasn't there, and the housekeeper said she'd left about a half-hour previously to visit a friend that had unexpectedly called. She didn't have any more to add to this excuse, so I hung up and decided that as it was getting late and I'd heard this line before, I'd stay and eat dinner there anyway."

"Weren't you worried that maybe something might have happened to her?"

"Not really. You see, Nora and I'd been having some difficulties in our relationship for quite some time, and I suspected that she had been unfaithful with someone but could never prove it. You know, disappearing on mysterious shopping trips and returning with not much. A lunch or dinner with friends, who seemed to cover her excuses, even when she wasn't with them? But I was trying to walk past that and—"

"Okay, okay, I get it. So?"

"Well, as I was getting ready to shift from the lounge into the dining room, this absolutely stunning brunette appeared from out of nowhere. She was wrapped in a mink stole , wearing a black strapless evening gown, white pearls, black stiletto heels with an angel's face and shape like Ava Gardner. She seemed to be by herself and slid comfortably onto an empty barstool across the room and ordered a martini. I couldn't take my eyes off of her and noticed that none of the other men in the room could either. After lighting a cigarette, she surveyed the room as if she was waiting for someone. I was praying that whoever it was wouldn't show up. In the time it took her to polish off her martini, she was still alone. I wanted to meet her desperately and jealously searched the room for others that thought the same thing. I knew I had to make my move without more hesitation, or I'd miss out. I was nervous but caught her eye as she continued to glance over her shoulder and received the most heavenly red- lipped smile with an "I'm yours for the evening" written all over it. It was a look missing from my life for years. My heart began pounding like a teenager on his first date, and I found myself practically dancing over, asking her to join me at my table. At first, she hesitated. Then she double- checked the crowd in the lounge one more time and, apparently still not seeing someone else there, smiled again and said she'd love to join me.

"One thing led to another, and time passed first with more cocktails, then through an absolutely perfect dinner. I was naturally anxious and in the mood that we continue to get down to a more-ah-romantic interlude. The adjacent Blue Parrot Inn down the street was convenient. She didn't object, and as a matter of fact, I think she even suggested it. I was powerless to resist her charms and beauty. Maybe it was the alcohol, but I don't think that was all of it. It just seemed right at the time, and I'm afraid I overdid it, Mr. Thornton, and that's why I'm here to ask you to help me."

"What can I do? It seems a little too late to unwind your tryst, doesn't it? You're party's over, pal. I'd say your candles have already been blown out, and the cake's been eaten too."

"Yes, you're right, but that's not all of it. You see, before we parted, I foolishly wanted to give her something as a token of our evening together. Money seemed too crass; she looked like a million bucks already, so lacking anything else, I gave her the diamond- covered ankle bracelet that I was going to give to Nora. My Ava's real first name, or so she said, was Nicole. An initial engraved inside the bracelet even matched. I fantasized that I'd selected the bracelet just for her when I put it around her ankle. At that moment, I was in heaven and foolishly floating on a sea of too many martini's, several bottles of champagne and who knows what other booze."

I groaned at hearing all this, but let him continue.

"We parted later, and I didn't see her again. That was last Friday night. We'd made no plans to meet again, and I was afraid to go back to the Parrot as I didn't want to get more involved as you'll soon find out why."

I interrupted, "What was her name, McCullum? Did you get her real name, where she lived, worked, friends, anything else to go on?"

He didn't answer, just sat there wringing his hands together in despair and giving me a vacant stare, like he had something to hide. I sighed and tossed my pencil down on the pad of yellow paper. With the exception of a few doodles, it was still mostly blank like my mush -brained client sitting across from me. I knew that if that dame had given him anything other than a midnight joy ride , it was probably just a phony story anyway … what a sap. This play had blackmail written all over it and couldn't have sounded any more phony.

I gave him time to catch up with his narrative and didn't say anything to break his concentration. He finally picked up his train of thought and droned on after a few more minutes of silent composure, sweat breaking out on his forehead, and muttered, "I-I'm sorry if I'm telling it confusingly, Mr. Thornton, but there's quite a bit more, and I don't think you're going to like the rest of this story any better than I do."

"Don't worry about that . I've heard a lot of sob stories before. Just keep going. So far, you haven't given me much to work with, but once I've seen the whole picture, maybe something will fall into place."

"Thank you," he said, wiping his damp face with a handkerchief. He'd turned ashen, his voice losing its confident tone as he continued. "She said she only wanted to use first names, you know, *incognito*, she called it. At first, I thought that was real cute and clever. It was a good way for me to be anonymous as well. I know now that was stupid. I wasn't thinking straight. Afterwards, when I'd given more thought to Nora's bracelet present that I'd given away so hastily to this strange woman in the hotel room for a one-night stand, I realized that I might have a problem. But, I decided to just forget about it and write the experience off to poor judgment. I'd go on about my everyday business as usual, until this showed up on my doorstep, this morning."

McCullen began trembling as he fumbled for a section of the *Herald Examiner* newspaper from his inside coat pocket. He handed it to me, pointing to a black and white photo of several smiling people with the caption reading *Joseph DeCosta, Majestic Movie Studio executive and party, celebrate in the winner's circle at Hollywood Park with his thoroughbred Miss Be'haven.* The story continued, extolling this high-roller's acceptance into the world of the rich and famous legitimate gambling fraternity that owned and bred horses for fun and profit. I went back and double- checked the photo again, not believing at first what I'd just read. I could see why he was trembling. I didn't want to see more and tossed his newspaper aside.

Well, here it was, a photo of a mixed bag of tough characters surrounding a horse, including a smiling dame with an Ava Gardner face and body and DeCosta's arm wrapped around her tighter than a hungry boa constrictor. Unfortunately, she was a perfect match for McCullen's description all right. This dish was the missing piece of the puzzle he'd been mumbling about and the one I'd been waiting for. I needed this case, like a slap in the face with a soggy bar rag. This now was not my lucky day. I just rolled snake-eyes, and they both belonged to a thug named DeCosta.

I threw my pencil back down on the desk and grumbled out loudly, "That was Joey DeCosta's broad. You must have been screwing DeCosta's wife, girlfriend, or some other dame in his personal stable. What the hell were you thinking?"

McCullen didn't answer, just sat there looking pale, shell shocked, and mute, praying I was wrong.

"This is worse than I anticipated," I added, wrinkles creasing my forehead. "You couldn't have picked a bigger gangster to cross. He's the new gun in town running Majestic Studios, placed there by the syndicate getting their foot in the movie industry. He's fronting for the big boys from Chicago. As you can see, he's a smooth, dapper thug with tough connections and, as you can also guess … deadly. What do you expect me to do now, pal? It sounds like you're too late to back out of this mess. I advise you to take a powder from town for a while, 'til this blows over."

"I didn't know who she was. Oh God, what's going to happen to me?" he said, ignoring my advice and pleading desperately, realizing the mess he'd gotten into and working himself up into a coronary .

I groaned and watched this toad squirm. What had started off as an overconfident business big shot was now melting down right before my eyes. This mess wasn't making my day any brighter either, but then again, what else was new in my racket.

"You've got to help me, Mr. Thornton, please," he begged, sliding forward to the edge of his chair. "Maybe you can talk to Nicole or whatever her name is, and get that bracelet back. It's a direct link to me. I-I know I'm going to wind up on a slab if Mr. DeCosta ever finds out what I've done."

I didn't want to tell him, but that was the same mental picture I also had of this fool.

"Okay, calm down, calm down. Here, take it easy. Let's have another shot or two of that rye. After hearing your story, I need one too." I poured out two more generous shots each while I tried to think about this disaster he'd gotten himself into and what it meant for me to get mixed up in it.

I cast a glance at all my new office trappings and considered all the other debt littering my life. Then after another minute or so, said, "Okay, McCullen, I'll take a crack at it, but it'll cost you plenty, as it's going to be damn dangerous for me to get you out of this scrape."

"I-I'll write you a check right now for two thousand to get you started and double it when you get the bracelet back, okay? I won't quibble. I promise," he said, shaking.

"You're damn right, you won't. It's not enough. Give me six thousand up front, and we'll call it square when I find the bracelet and no squawking, or you can hire someone else!"

"O-okay, that will be all right," he said, deflating and hesitant to part with the dough but desperate. He scribbled in his checkbook and then handed me one, relieved that I was going to run with the ball and lift this nightmare from his shoulders.

"By the way, what was your wife's excuse for standing you up for the dinner engagement?" I stuffed his check quickly in my desk drawer for safe keeping.

"She said she'd received an urgent call from one of her closest girl friends who was threatening to commit suicide over her husband's infidelities and interceded to prevent it from happening. She'd been so preoccupied with her friend's dilemma that she forgot to call me on time at the Parrot. When she'd finally gotten around to it, I'd already left the restaurant for the evening with Ava," he said, looking down, ashamed of this pathetic explanation.

"Nice story," I said, not believing a word. "Did you buy it?"

Trying to convince himself, he added in a voice barely audible, slumping back in his chair, , "It was apparently the truth, as I found out the next day."

I didn't comment further. This whole debacle seemed hopeless, but I'd already promised to give it a shot and taken his money. I didn't like anything

I'd been hearing so far and wondered if his wife was also playing him for a sap. I didn't want to scare him off by discussing that, as I needed his dough to cover my expanding expenses , so I dropped it.

After his uneasy confession of a booze- fueled one-night stand gone wrong , he was covered in sweat, his hair was ruffled, and his tie askew. He wasn't relieved at all to get it off his chest. Instead, he was still clearly upset and looked like a defeated man who'd just heard a guilty verdict read and wasn't optimistic for a retrial. I didn't sympathize with his misery either, which probably made his case worse, but this was his problem, not mine. I just hoped I wouldn't get too caught up in the middle of this mess, or I'd pay for my poor judgment in taking it on in the first place.

I gathered a few more personal facts and told him I'd contact him as soon as I had something to report. I worked up my most confident smile, and we shook hands on our agreement. His was now colder and clammier than when he'd arrived. He quickly shoved both hands inside his trouser pockets, hoping for a warm up and a dry off, but it wouldn't help.

I was relieved our office meeting was over and was left with a bad taste in my mouth about this guy. I'd go along with this case for the dough, but I just didn't like him for some odd reason.

McCullen attempted to compose himself before leaving. He straightened his tie, buttoned his disheveled suit coat, and tried to pat down his unruly hair before retreating back into the outer office like a whipped dog.

On his way out, he cast a final inquisitive glance at my cupcake. She was busy double tapping her way through a mountain of delinquent insurance investigation reports and flashed him another one of her show-stopper smiles without missing a swipe of the typewriter carriage or breaking her concentration. He just shook his head, dropped on his lid, and returned another puzzled feeble grin, hoping to cheer himself up. This time, it wouldn't work.

I ushered him over to the hallway front door and clapped him on the back as a gesture of assurance for our successful outcome. We both knew it was doubtful.

I watched a depressed man with a noose around his neck stumble into the elevator that would take him down to the street and out to a doubtful breath of fresh air and a probable necktie party.

As I closed the hallway door, I glanced back inside the office at my kewpie doll focused on hammering her typewriter keys and said to myself, "It's Rhonda Fleming, pal. It'll probably come to you later … if you have a later."

Chapter Two

I motioned for Rhonda to follow me back inside my office, helped myself to another shot of rye to steady my nerves after listening to this debacle, and handed her McCullen's check with instructions to deposit it in my Wells Fargo bank account immediately. I had little confidence that bird was going to be around much longer and didn't want to get stiffed if he didn't make it.

"Your intercom was on the whole time, Matthew. I heard the entire conversation," she said, perching her shapely behind on the edge of my desk. "McCullen's in real trouble for screwing DeCosta's dame, isn't he?"

"It's a disaster, sweetheart, if his story's even straight. Couldn't be worse. You know the mob; they usually take a pretty dim view of anyone nailing their women, unless that person has a bigger hammer. Then, they make an exception, but not as a rule." I didn't elaborate more, glancing sideways at her rear comfortably mashing a couple of freshly typed reports on the desk top. She caught my drift and ignored it.

"If I can't get this resolved quickly, there's going to be hell to pay for McCullen, and I don't intend to be caught in the middle of it."

"What are you going to do?"

"I'm going to start by dropping by the Blue Parrot and inquire about this DeCosta dame or whoever she was. I've got to see if I can find her fast and have a discrete conversation with her before McCullen gets discovered. I'm sure she's being watched, though, and that's a problem. It's a long shot that she's even there, or anybody will admit seeing her. Maybe, it would be better if you went along with me. We'd be less conspicuous as a couple, and I might be able to connect with her without drawing any suspicion."

"I'm okay with that, Matthew. We have a vague description of her from his conversation that I overheard. I'm sure we'll be able to recognize her if she's there again."

"Thanks, sweetheart. I'm sure we will, but we won't have to worry about a description. He left this newspaper clipping with her photo, or so he thinks," I said, fishing the tossed rag out of the waste paper basket beside my desk and stuffing the picture page into my coat pocket. "You don't need to change either. You couldn't look more attractive than you are."

She grinned at my compliments like a stripper with a fist full of tips and slid off the desk to get her purse from her office desk drawer.

I was already getting used to having this cutie around and noticed she'd said "we'd recognize," including herself in the business. Maybe Tex was right!

* * *

We piled into the Roadmaster, and I fishtailed onto Hollywood Boulevard, anxious to resolve this mess I decided to change course with the dough and personally deposited McCullen's check at my bank a few blocks away on the corner of Wilshire and Highland. Afterwards, I walked next door to a drug store and bought another pack of smokes. What I really needed next was a couple more shots of booze at one of the neighborhood saloons to cool me out. But not wanting to waste any more time, I headed south instead, straight towards the Blue Parrot Inn.

Traffic was still light, and the feeble mist was attempting to lift, trying to clear away the sticky cobwebs draped over the city streets. I thought about my check, sitting there waiting to clear McCullen's bank and worried that it might not make it in time. Then shoved the idea on the back burner and tried to think of something more pleasant.

I clicked on the radio, leaning close to Rhonda, brushing her shoulder. I couldn't help inhaling her perfumed body and asked, "See if you can find a station with some music on it, doll. Anything but soap operas, okay? I hate those sappy shows. They're probably all plugging up the airwaves right now anyway, with their midday spiel to housewives."

She smiled, spun the dial, and instantly found The Andrews Sisters harmonizing "Near You." She glanced over at me and grinned at how easy it was. I nodded at her choice, and she smiled back, satisfied with her quick selection, as she began singing along with the familiar tune.

Listening to her musical voice filling the car was soothing to the ear. And watching her puckered lips mimicking the lyrics was just the right antidote for the doldrums that were already creeping into my subconscious. I exhaled a sigh of relief and tried to feel better.

For some reason, an optimistic thought ran through my cabeza, and I felt like celebrating. Maybe, this McCullen disaster wouldn't be such a mess after all, as were most of my cases. Maybe, it would clear itself up sooner than I expected. But on that score, I would be wrong, almost dead wrong. I just didn't know it at the time.

I popped open the wind wing, reached for my new deck of Luckies, and offered one to Rhonda. She took the pack and tapped out two instead. Depressing the dash board lighter, she lit both and handed me one with a red-lipped grin. I had to shake my head. What a cutie pie she was. I took a drag and blew a column of smoke out the open window. I noticed it tasted a little sweet and sticky on the end. It tasted like her. She noticed the red smear on my lip and laughed. I checked the rearview mirror, ran my tongue over my lips, and smiled back, making a mental note to clear off the tasty grease paint before entering The Blue Parrot watering hole.

I took La Brea south for several miles. We drove through a seedy section of the Inglewood factory area containing McCullen's company buried somewhere in the background and shot past the airport in Hawthorne. I swung a hard right toward the Pacific on Rosecrans and slowed down to a crawl for another few blocks towards the beach.

The Blue Parrot Restaurant appeared on our left through the light mist, accompanied in the distance by the all too familiar sound of crashing surf and salt air. It was pungent enough to clear your brain and your sinuses. The unmistakable smell of fishy seaweed and kelp was as overpowering as a laundry basket full of old socks. But, the rolling ocean waves in the distance were upstaging the scene like a hand full of nature's glistening industrial diamonds.

The parking lot was beginning to fill up with a lunch crowd. I slid my heap into a convenient spot close to the front entrance. With the morning fog now almost lifted, I didn't have to run the wipers to clear away the moisture that was still clinging to the windshield. I'd just let it sit there and evaporate on its own.

A smart-ass parking valet breathlessly ran over with a wise crack about self-parking and stuck his palm out anyway as a reward for his lecture. I told him his tip would come later, and maybe without a fat lip if my car was in the same shape, I'd left it. He backed up fast and looked worried. I grinned, slipped him two bits to ease the pain from my heat, and ushered Rhonda inside for a look-see.

With her red- lipped smile, sunkissed blonde hair, and knock-out figure in that skin-tight sweater and those hip-hugging dark leather pants, she attracted more than our share of attention. We were shown a comfortable black leather booth in the lounge, on the side I'd requested. Maybe bringing this "flashing neon" along wasn't such a smart idea after all. I'd find out soon enough.

I ordered a couple of extra-dry martinis from the waitress. She was a sun- streaked brunette kewpie doll with a short shaggy hairstyle, big brown saucer eyes, and bubbling breasts bursting out of a low- cut costume. It was probably too skimpy for the lunch crowd, but she flashed me a come-on smile as well, clinching the sale. The whole package was guaranteed to pry a few extra bucks out of your wallet anytime, and I was a sucker as usual.

Rhonda and I tapped our glasses together, a toast to something, took a couple of quiet sips, and I fired up a couple of Luckies for both of us. Then I slid out of the booth and decided I'd ask around about the cupcake in McCullen's photo. No takers from either the bartender or anyone else working in this watering hole. They were either lying and didn't recognize this dish or too afraid to tell me the truth. I decided to try my luck on the other side in the restaurant.

I knew this was probably going to be a long shot anyway and wasn't easily discouraged. This was familiar territory. There were always lots of dead ends and blind alleys to chase in.

I went back to the booth and joined Rhonda. We knocked off our martinis, thinking in silence. I was about to order another round before asking several others that had just drifted in when a noisy commotion outside sounding like emergency vehicles on the roll drew my attention.

Rhonda gave me one of those looks reading my mind that said, "This place is going to be hotter than we anticipated."

I slid out of the booth and decided to investigate the cause of the sirens. As I cracked open the front door to the lounge, an invasion of squad cars descended in the direction of the Parrot Inn down the street like a swarm of locusts attacking a wheat field. They lit up the overcast with their roof deck racks flashing brighter than a Grumman's Theater Premier and, at the same time, producing clouds of dust as they jammed on their brakes, sliding to an emergency stop in the gravel parking lot. Putting on a major performance for the sidewalk gawkers was mandatory for these showboats, as they all piled out simultaneously looking official in their dark uniforms and over-armed enough for a hostile siege from outer space.

Rhonda followed me outside to investigate. I watched a coroner's meat wagon with several men pull up behind the patrol cars. They hesitated, exiting at first, as if taking a deep breath, reluctant to join the ruckus, then decided there'd be no more stalling and joined the cavalcade already inside.

"This isn't exactly the situation I was expecting around here," I said to her over my shoulder. "I'll have to find out if this has any connection to our reason for being here in the first place. I hope not, but who knows."

We quick-stepped the block in less time than it takes to down a couple jiggers of 90 proof George Dickel whisky and merged into the sideshow clustered out front of the Inn.

"Better hang back, baby, with the rest of the crowd, until I take a look-see."

She was clearly disappointed but did as I asked, anxiously peering over the heads of the others. I stepped forward to see who was in charge of this barn burner. I spotted Captain Tucker "Tank" Sherman, a big bulldog of a guy.

He was the grumpy middle-aged South Los Angeles homicide detective, bull dozing his way towards the uniforms covering the entryway to the Inn.

Tank, as was the only name he'd let anyone use since he peaked in his high school football days. He was a bulky giant built like a pro-wrestler gone to seed with a head like a watermelon, big hands like catcher's mitts, and an oversized torso. He was now stretching out a cheap dark blue suit coat and probably one belt notch away from splitting his pants. He was overweight, sweating profusely and puffing on a huge Corona. Shouting orders to the cops and the curious bystanders, as we approached, I noticed he was quite impressed with his own overbearing effect on everyone and enjoyed hogging the limelight.

He saw me out of the corner of his eye as I rushed forward and couldn't help commenting sarcastically as I jammed on the brakes, "Well now, look who's here, it's our "Famous Shamus to the Stars. What brings you down here, Thornton … slumming?"

He stuck out his paw, and we gave each other a test of strength. He grimaced with a tighter clench on his stogie as I turned up the heat on this big lug, no stranger myself, to the weight room at the Melrose Gym.

"Not a bad grip for an old man, Sherman," I said, smiling and ignoring his smart-ass remark. "What gives? Maybe it's right down my alley," I added, hoping I was wrong.

He volunteered an explanation without more wise cracks. "A maid at the inn reported to the manager that she'd discovered the body of a dead woman. It looks like a neck tie party for some bimbo. She must have been here a while. She's stiff as a board."

"I'd like to take a look. Any objections?"

He hesitated for a second, "No… I guess not. I sure as hell don't need you here, but I guess I owe you one anyway for helping my brother-in-law with that gang of bank robbers and killers over in San Pedro last year."

On that, he was more than right. I masterminded the whole trap for a gang of losers. His brother-in-law, Foster Berringer, and his goon squad with the Long Beach P.D. also helped me split the reward money. He'd taken most of the credit and was a civic hero, but I wasn't worried as my pals had come out on top as predicted, and I wasn't griping about my expanded bank account.

Rhonda became antsy and didn't want to be left in the background with the other city riff-raff. She managed to side slip the cops holding back the gawkers and drifted silently up beside me while I was talking to Sherman. He couldn't help admiring this dazzling number's tight assets in spite of the seriousness of the crime scene. He also couldn't resist inquiring with a sly grin who this dish was and her connection to me, especially after she put her arm through mine and flashed him a smile brighter than a beach bonfire weenie roast.

I introduced Tank to her as my new secretary and assistant, which were two stretchers, but fit the occasion, and he seemed to buy it. He gave me a quizzical look after taking in her linked arm routine, but like all the others, he was immediately overwhelmed by her beauty. After double- checking her figure several more times, he shook his head and gave up trying to work it out. Then, failing to relight his cold stogie, he grumbled something incoherent under his breath and motioned for us to follow him inside.

I smiled as she relaxed her grip on my arm and thought, maybe this babe was going to work out after all.

The faux Mexican hacienda- styled inn was once ritzy and expensive. It was now gloomy and depressing. The rundown lobby consisted of drab beat-up furnishings, droopy potted plants, and yesterday's decorations. We followed Sherman as he plowed forward in the direction of the suite of rooms with the body of the murdered woman. The place was crawling with cops, posted everywhere acting busy but seemingly confused by the crime scene. Most were just taking up space, trying to look official and cast inquiring glances as we paraded by, escorted like dignitaries with their boss leading the way.

The self-service elevator past the now empty lobby desk had an out -of-order sign pasted on one of the scuffed up and broken doors sitting ajar. We took the stairs to the second floor and down a darkened hallway. I thought I'd remembered this place correctly when McCullen first mentioned it, but it had gone down the drain in the last few years, no doubt from overuse by the quickie in and out nightly trade. Like the lobby, the once lavish oriental carpets were now visibly worn and dilapidated, and the walls were plastered with washed-out tattered mural wallpaper with scenes of old Mexico in what used to be vibrant shades of orange, reds and yellow. The hallway was equally dim from several low wattage overhead light bulbs, and the whole place had an odor of mold, urine, and decay. Flashy and upscale, as I'd remembered it, had been rapidly over taken by dingy and seedy.

Rhonda and I looked at each other, and she read my mind again before I said, "What the hell was McCullen thinking when he brought that dame to this dump? He must have been really smashed."

As we neared the murder victim's room, I hoped it wasn't going to be connected to my client. After seeing the rest of this dump, I had a premonition that wouldn't be promising.

A couple of uniforms were flanking the doorway protecting the crime scene. The coroner was already on site. He and his staff were confirming the cause of death. The rest of the homicide dicks were already tripping over each other, snapping photos and trying to collect evidence before it was obliterated by the look-e-loos.

"Well, there she is," said Sherman, shoving the fedora back on his head and pointing at what was probably once a beautiful young woman, his soggy stogie dropping ashes on the carpet. He flipped back the sheet covering a hell of a shapely young platinum blonde in her early to middle twenties. She must have been damn attractive before her demise and still a real looker. Except now, she was just a stiffing corpse, lying on her back on an unmade bed in this rat-hole hotel in a crummy part of town.

The quick peek told me she was as naked as a burlesque dancer nearing the end of her act, but that's where the similarity ended. This dish was wearing nothing more than a black G-string, except it wasn't where it was supposed to be. This one was wrapped tightly around her neck.

She'd been left in a contorted, uncomfortable angle, legs apart hanging over the bed side, bare feet almost touching the floor. From the bruises on her face, she looked like she'd been roughed up first to make it easier for the killer. Her tongue was out and bloated, and her glazed eyes were bulging and staring blankly at the fly specked ceiling. It looked like she was still calling for help that wouldn't come. From the other bruises on her body and the position of her arms grasping at her throat, she'd struggled for oxygen, but wasn't strong enough to fight for it. She died trying.

It wasn't a pretty sight and not for a weak stomach. I shot a quick glance at Rhonda. She was hanging back, trying to be brave, but not really wanting to take it all in either. I thought, this kid under the sheet was about the same age as Rhonda. She still had a long way to go in life. Getting snuffed out that early was another crime in itself. It shouldn't have happened.

"Who is she, Tank…any idea?" I said, stepping forward for a closer inspection. I was trying to recognize this dish but decided to keep the news clipping photo in my pocket. Sherman had enough on his plate already, and I didn't want him involved in my business, not just yet anyway.

"Don't know. Room was registered to the usual Smith couple, so that's no help. Apparently, nothing significant in here, no I.D., nothing. We'll check out the usual, you know , labels in her clothes, dental records, finger prints for any prior arrests. Other than the thrashing, she didn't have any other marks, scars, or tattoos. We'll track her down, though, but it's going to take a while." He exhaled heavily, a sour expression creasing his mug, "Thornton, my desk has unsolved cases already piled higher than a hooker's skirt. I didn't need this mess to top it off either. This factory area is turning into a real shit hole."

"Maybe you should retire, Tank."

"Don't tempt me, Thornton. What I really need right now is a strong drink. And don't push me either."

I ignored his comments. "Cause of death is obviously strangulation from the panties wrapped around her throat," I said, getting back on track. "Raped?"

"Sweet Jesus, man, most are. The one's turn'n tricks in alley's or liv'n in flops are a sure bet. In this case, who knows? Probably, it looks like it. But we'll find out soon enough."

He paused to relight his drooping stogie, took a couple of quick puffs, and caught smoke in one eye as he shook out the match. Squinting from the sting, he continued with a slight cough, "When we autopsy.

"Yup, Thornton, she's probably just another one of the usual bimbos that frequent these cash and carry flea bags and don't give it away for free, either.

"She'll make a few lousy bucks from some loser she picked up in one of the dive bars around the beach or one of these crumbs working in the factories around here. Then she'll drift off somewhere else when it starts to get too hot from us cops rousting her and her johns."

And I thought, "Yeah, she'd also probably get sick of paying off the bulls with their greasy hands taking turns grabbing her goods for free and their sticky fingers in her purse as well."

"Motive's maybe robbery, but I don't think so," he sighed at the lack of evidence, his buttoned suit coat stretching. "Her purse is missing, but she must have been entertaining somebody important from the few bits and crumbs left behind." He motioned at the bedside stand. "Something else going on here. Maybe it was drugs. We'll find out. Looks like something was left behind by mistake, if it was robbery though," he said, not explaining and getting side tracked by one of the investigators tapping him on the shoulder for advice.

I turned to Rhonda, who wasn't used to hearing this descriptive banter or seeing a murdered woman's corpse, and noted that she was still holding it together, better than I'd expected. At first, she looked a little green but hadn't fainted or thrown up. That was a good sign. Instead, she'd been observing the entire scene, not just the naked body. Stepping closer, she whispered over my shoulder, "Matthew, do you see what I see over there on the night stand?"

She nodded in the direction of the ash tray beside the headboard. I didn't at first because I'd been concentrating on the naked body, so I eased over in that direction for a closer look at what she'd spotted.

"Looks like a few stubbed- out cigarette butts, some with a bright red lipstick stain and a half- smokedMaduro cigar with the same gold band smoked by my client, doesn't it?" I whispered quietly as one of the lab boys stepped in front, cutting me off, and dumped all the contents, including an empty crushed Chesterfield cigarette package, into a couple of envelopes for evidence and analysis later.

Unfortunately for him, he'd just missed a match book packet that had somehow fallen on the floor under my shoe. When he turned, I quickly scooped it up , including a pawn ticket from Gold's Pawn Shop in El Segundo barely visible on the rug under the edge of the bed. I dropped both in my pocket.

The match book cover read *Shanghai Ruby's* with several numbers written on the inside flap. Another dump I was familiar with. It was a tough saloon converted from a warehouse, located off of Neptune Avenue in Wilmington, in the Port of L.A., a short drive from the Pike Amusement Park in Long Beach and other clip joints and bars flanking the waterfront wharfs. I'd been there before, tracking down bail jumpers and other losers. It was rough and seedy. Booze, music, dancing, and your choice of girls in skin- tight skirts, slit to the thigh in every size, shape, and color. Offering unlimited entertainment, comfort, and companionship to bolster the spirits of the homesick sailors and merchant marines that descended nightly from the docked ships in the harbor was the theme. After consuming enough overpriced booze, they were unable to say no to anything, which kept their pockets perpetually empty and the ships' doctors in business afterwards.

Shanghai Ruby's was owned by a dangerous but beautiful Chinese dame with a face and body to die for that ran her saloon like a fire breathing dragon. She used to run the action in another crummy dive up north, between San Francisco's old Embarcadero district and Chinatown. She was almost a throwback to the old Barbary Coast days; ruthless, dishonest, and deadly, with a bad attitude to fill in the missing pieces, unless you knew her, which I did, and she liked you, which if you were lucky, she did as well. We were two of a kind, she often said. I didn't know why . I wasn't Chinese. The rumor that floated around was that some of the Tong thugs in the Chinese community were reorganizing their crime nets starting up north to take over all the brothels and other gambling operations, especially those that were profitable. Ruby was fair game for big payoffs. But, she apparently didn't cooperate and decided instead to fold up shop, leave town and start over farther south, where the options were less fatal. I never believed it.

She was too tough to push around and hired equally tough characters for protection.

Ruby's hell hole usually smelled like trouble and now seemed to be calling out my name again. I'd check it out later and also trace that phone number on the match book if that's what it was.

Rhonda edged up beside me and whispered again, "It's not the same girl that McCullen described in his photograph, is it?"

"She doesn't look any more like Ava Gardner than I do, sweetheart, but then her face is a little distorted from the thrashing she took. But, here's another thing. This kid's not a natural brunette either. Notice she's a blonde up top, and also on her speed trap. Take another look," I nodded toward the girl's spread legs. Rhonda peeked closer and didn't comment, just turned away looking uncomfortable. "Unless she was wearing wigs or McCullen was completely blotto and had his lights turned out when they tested the bed springs ... it's not his dish."

The lab boys were fast but not thorough and making noise that signaled they were about to wrap up the scene. One quick glance around told me they thought they were finished and anxious to get back to their lunch breaks. Aside from the final dusting of prints, the place was pretty well cleaned out of any more signs of evidence. Except, something caught my eye they might have overlooked.

An unused Gideon Bible placed in all the hotel rooms for those that could read and were still worth salvaging sat conspicuously untouched on the edge of the night stand. As they were packing up their lab gear, I picked it up and nonchalantly thumbed through the pages. Stuffed inside, somewhere in the middle chapters, was a stack of crisp twenty-dollar bills pressed flatter than a bunch of freshly picked Daisy's. And as an added gift, they were covered with a short cryptic note written on cheap stationery that read....

Gina-

Present for my baby.

Love, Frankie

I shot a quick glance out of the corner of my eye at the commotion preoccupied on the other side of the room, then casually slipped the dough and note, joining the pawn ticket and matches, into my side coat pocket and eased the book back into place.

I turned to Rhonda, who'd been starring in the direction of the body getting collected. I whispered it was time for us to blow. Before they hauled blondie off to the city morgue, I noticed one more piece of evidence that I wanted. It was also one I couldn't obtain. Rhonda had noticed it too and stepped closer to give me a desperate jab in the ribs. There was nothing I could do and sent her only a silent grim frown.

Peeking out from below the half- covered naked body sheet was the only other thing the young woman was wearing. A diamond- encrusted gold bracelet dangling from her left ankle. It was sparkling in the seedy hotel room lights brighter than the flashing neon advertising a burlesque show.

And calling out loud and clear … another connection of my client to this murder.

Chapter Three

There wasn't much more I could accomplish by hanging around that dump any longer, especially with all the cops milling around. I fingered the evidence in my side pocket to make sure it was safe, then grabbed Rhonda by the arm and told Sherman I'd see him again soon. I ushered her downstairs, fast. He wasn't sorry to see us leave and gave a slight grunt with a hand flop and a nod that were his sum total parting adios. I knew he wouldn't be anxious to have me sticking my nose into his elite autopsy report when it was finished either. Or, snooping into any of the other findings his homicide dicks might uncover after exhausting a lot of leg work at the taxpayers' expense. I'd still pump him for more answers anyway, and he knew it was coming, whether he liked it or not. I knew he'd probably run into a dead end sooner or later and give up long before solving the crime. I'd need his pieces of the jigsaw puzzle to blend into mine if there was any connection with McCullen, and then I'd finish the job, my way.

He seemed relieved to have gotten the corpse finally secured under wraps and out the door. Now it was only a matter of questioning every person and employee in the Inn and writing out an endless stream of reports before his day was over. I was glad I was private and not a public servant fussing with all the paper work.

Under pressure from the uniform squad outside the inn, the crowd of noisy busy-bodies was already scattering in all directions. I brushed aside several grumblers that were still blocking the sidewalk, clearly disappointed in not finding out what the commotion was all about. Rhonda was a little wobbly on her feet, so I put my arm around her shoulder and let her lean against me. We took our time walking back down the crowded street to the lounge where I'd left my car. I escorted her inside, and she quietly slumped down in one of the darkened side booths. Her head flopped against the back rest, and she didn't look too chipper. I was going to fire up a smoke, then changed my mind and stuffed the pack back into my pocket. I mentioned ordering some lunch, but she looked drawn, pasty, and queasy. She didn't reply, only shook her head no. I got the hint and instead called for a cab to take her back to the office. I hoped the moving vehicle wouldn't cause her to pop her cookies on the way.

I suggested we wait outside under the entrance canopy as the lounge had an over whelming odor of spilled booze, stale cigarettes, and a moldy carpet that needed replacing. I helped her out of the booth, put my arm around her and let her lean against me again as we shuffled toward the door like a couple of uncertain lovers stealing work time on a tight noon schedule.

After a few quiet unspoken minutes watching the circus on the street dissolve and listening to an annoying overhead canvas flap in a fresh breeze blowing from the beach, Rhonda finally blurted out, in a small weak voice, "It-it's better Matthew if I leave. I'm sorry. I'm still feeling woozy after seeing that strangled young woman. This fresh air helps a little, but I need a change of scenery too."

This sure as hell wasn't it, and she gagged a couple of times, focused on the potted plant beside her as a possible receptacle for her breakfast.

"You don't need to explain it to me, baby, I understand. I've felt that way myself a few times. Maybe just grab a light meal later at the diner next door to the office. Some hot tea and toast might help settle your stomach, nothing heavy. We haven't eaten lunch yet, and it might help."

From the grimace she made, I knew it was a stupid suggestion again and dropped it. I didn't have to ask if she was covered in the financial department but slipped her one of the double saw bucks I'd just lifted anyway. I figured it would easily cover her cab fare and lunch and maybe take some of the sting out of her first crime scene. I noticed she just absently stuffed it into her purse without looking and was beginning to clam up, anxious to leave.

I still needed her to hold down the fort back at the office, as I was expecting several more important phone calls from several high-rollers and said I'd call her back in a couple of hours for any messages. She nodded yes to everything just to shut me up and gagged a couple more times, probably still thinking about my food suggestion. A wave of relief finally swept across her face when she spotted the checker cab careen into the parking lot and slide to a stop in front of us. I hustled her inside and watched the back of her head in the window as the yellow sled disappeared into the damp overcast, towards the coast road and back to work.

I flicked my lighter on a fresh Lucky, sucked in enough to get the engine running, and wondered how she'd make out in this investigation business. She was a tough character all right and seen some rough times with an even rougher crowd before this. I had to admit, she was still green, and snooping around murdered stiffs was a new experience and enough to make anybody feel sick. But I was proud of the way she held together anyway. Maybe, Tex was right after all. I'd give her a chance. This kid could take it, at least for now anyway.

* * *

I'd get started tracking down a few leads for this mess that might give me the answers I needed. Either McCullen was stupid and lying to me about that dame and his evening's escapades, or he was telling me the truth, and this case was darker than I'd anticipated. If so, that sap was being set up to take the hit for murdering that dish. If I didn't come up with some answers pronto, Sherman's investigators would beat me to the punch and begin connecting all the dots pointing directly to him that spelled out "Guilty as Charged."

I needed to know the answers to a lot of questions; what happened to the Ava Gardner looker in the photo and who was the dead blonde, and why was she wearing the same ankle bracelet. What was his stogie doing in the ashtray? If it wasn't McCullen in the room, then who was it smoking the same cigar, and why were they there? I had an idea who the dead dame was but didn't want to let on to Sherman or discuss it with Rhonda until

I was sure. If I was right, it might lead me to the motive behind her death. I liked all the pieces of a jig-saw to fall into place before I jumped to any conclusions. I'd track her activities down and find out what the hell she was doing in that dump in the first place. And then I'd find the scum that snuffed out that cutie pie and dole out a little of my own justice, just in case the system was rigged for that bird, and he was handed a free "Stay Out of Jail" pass.

What I had to go on overshadowed the start Tank Sherman was making by a long shot; a blonde that wasn't an Ava Gardner wringer, cigarette and cigar butts that looked familiar, a match book cover from *Shanghai Ruby's* with numbers written inside, an ankle bracelet, a connection to Joey D. and the Majestic Studio, my client Carson McCullen and his lust for a one night stand. And what about McCullen's wife missing their dinner engagement, the Blue Parrot's connection to organized crime, and lastly, the stashed dough with the wrapper of first names hidden in the Gideon?

There was undoubtedly more, but for now, that was plenty. The bases were loaded. It all needed to be unscrambled in my brain, and right now and I was beginning to get a short circuit with the over load. I needed to get started without wasting any more time and begin collecting the pieces, setting them down into a pattern that made sense.

I'd start with making a call to McCullen. We needed a fast conference to square away a few discrepancies in his story. I ducked back inside the Parrot Lounge and located a phone booth in the back by the cigarette machine. I fished out my notebook from an inside coat pocket, found his office number, fed a couple of slugs into the box, and dialed. I fired up a Lucky while it rang a half a dozen times.

The main switch board operator finally answered and put me through to his extension. After a couple more rings, it was answered by his secretary, a crotchety character with an unfriendly, nasal toned, snippy attitude. She was no doubt one of the efficient, indispensable, homely as a bed pan company fixtures he'd described in my office.

I politely explained who I was and that I was anxious to meet with McCullen regarding a personal matter and quickly.

"I'm very sorry, Mr.Thornton? Mr. McCullen is not available right now and will be out of the office for several days."

He'd flown the coop already, now that I had this mess dumped on my shoulders.

"Where is he, Miss…?"

"It's Clinch, and I'm not at liberty to say," she said, with a touch of arrogance.

"Listen, sweetheart. It's very important that I speak to him pronto." I was not at all pleased with the stall she was trying to feed me.

"That's confidential, sir. I don't discuss his personal activities with anyone I'm not familiar with."

I lost it and said, "Listen, sister, I told you who I was already. I'll repeat and pay attention this time. I'm a private investigator, name's Thornton. I was hired by McCullen, your boss, to help him out of a jam. Now give with the know-how and fast, or you won't be sitting on your can in front of his office with that sassy attitude, much longer. Do I make myself clear?" Not waiting for her answer, I added with emphasis a little louder this time. "Now, once more, I want to know where he is and right now. No more stalling!"

She didn't have to give it more thought and nervously blurted out, "He's spending the day at the Hollywood Park racetrack with a friend of his , Mr. Bogart, I think he said his name is."

I'm not sure she even knew who Bogart was from the way she answered, but now that I had her primed , I pumped her. "More."

"He-he told me he's planning to take his boat the *Sundancer* over to Catalina Island right after the races. H-he'll be there for a few days of fishing and will stay there at his cottage over the weekend and be back to work sometime the following week."

"That all you got? Sounds a little vague to me."

"Sorry, Mr.… ah…" She'd already forgotten my name. Some secretary.

"Thanks anyway. I'll catch up with him before next week. If he calls, tell him Matthew Thornton's anxious to talk to him about some new developments on our case and to call my office. It's important." I hoped he'd bite and hung up.

That wasn't great news. Catalina sat about twenty-six miles west in the Pacific Ocean and was connected to the mainland only by slow boat or small seaplane. That guy was in way over his head now more than ever and was already celebrating, now that I was working on his problem. Bogart was rubbing shoulders with a potential murder suspect and would also be involved in the same cesspool as McCullen unless I could unravel it before Tank Sherman's police squad beat me to it.

There wasn't any point in rushing over immediately, as McCullen would take the better part of the day getting there by boat tomorrow. I'd have to catch an early flight the following day and try to find him before he went out fishing. If that was what he was actually doing. He needed to fill in a few blanks for me and fast. His story now already had more holes than a secondhand suit stored in moth's balls.

I circled a business in the yellow pages and tapped out another Lucky. Then I fed a few more nickels into the phone slot and contacted the Amphibian Air Transport reservation office for the short seaplane flight to Catalina. It flew out of the Long Beach airport directly to Avalon Harbor on Catalina and perfect for a quick rendezvous with McCullen.

"The small Sikorsky's or the Grumman Goose," the desk clerk told me, "are reliable puddle jumpers that seat only a handful of passengers and never have accidents."

I added, "I also heard they're noisier than a runaway tractor and rattle your choppers like a dentist drill."

She ignored my comment, topping it with, "They're also fast and serve free drinks, sir." That caught me off guard and clinched the sale.

I didn't like the looks of those contraptions and just thinking about flying over there in one of those kites still made me a little nervous, in spite of the booze.

I placed a reservation for the following day and told the girl, "I'd prefer a seat near the emergency exit, just in case. Thank you."

"That won't be necessary, sir, but if you insist…."

I did and hung up.

I made one more call to my pal Doris Fillmore, a newshawk that worked in the city's dirt -filled trenches for the *Herald Examiner*. She could root out the location of a buried truffle faster than a starving pork chop, and I needed more dope on this character McCullen and now.

Hiding smoothly behind his manufacturing business façade, he was a little too secretive for my money and maybe had more to hide than he was letting on. If anyone could cut below a faux business veneer, she could. A clerk in her office with a voice like a squeaky, skinny teenager answered politely, "Sorry, sir, she's out on another crime assignment and won't be back until later. Would you care to leave a message?"

"Yeah, tell Doris, Matthew Thornton, she knows who I am, needs her to dig out the background on a local manufacturing big shot named Carson McCullen and to give my office a call when she has something." I stressed the urgency of this message, and the kid got it without backtalk, and we hung up.

I tapped out another smoke and decided I needed to grab a bite to eat at a local hash house somewhere close in Long Beach before tackling *Shanghai Ruby's*.

Whoever belonged to the packet of matches and sucking on fancy stogies was a key player in Blondie's death. If it was McCullen, what the hell was he doing in that dump anyway? That one still mystified me. Maybe at *Ruby's,* I'd find some answers, but they would undoubtedly be connected to some characters that would be expecting trouble. And if so, it was on the way.

I squeezed the S&W.357 mag. I carried in a shoulder rig under my left arm for insurance, double- checked my spare cartridge speed loaders on my belt, and climbed back into my Buick. I swung out into the early afternoon traffic off of Rosecrans and noticed the earlier mist was finally gone. A glance westward told me that somewhere in the distance over the Pacific, the sun was attempting to creep around the edges of dark cumulus thunderheads. Their next ominous move would be in the direction of Catalina Island, with a final stop on the mainland. The whole damn thing spelled a storm was brewing on the horizon. That wasn't a good sign, and I didn't want it. We'd had enough rain already this year, and Southern California was green enough.

I fumbled for my deck of Luckies on the seat beside me and fired one up. I pulled a couple of drags on the butt and considered a little light traveling musical entertainment on the radio would ease my spirits. Rhonda's ease at a radio selection earlier flashed through my mind. For some reason, maybe my antenna wasn't connected properly, I just hit static and a few fuzzy stations then gave up. I decided instead to settle back and concentrate on my next few steps in unraveling this mess with McCullen. Familiar streets disappeared in my rear view, and I rehashed over what clues I'd picked up so far. Nothing I envisioned looked promising.

Regardless of how I tried to work it out, I just didn't like the way they were stacking up against him. The guy was a dead duck anyway you looked at it.

I picked up Sepulveda and worked my way south into Long Beach and switched my thoughts again to something more pleasant… finding a joint with a much deserved square meal.

What I didn't know at the time was that it would be followed by a rendezvous with much more trouble than I was expecting.

Chapter Four

I spotted Dale's Diner, a little hash-house just off Atlantic Avenue atSeventh Street., and eagerly hung a left, bumping across the embedded trolley tracks. My brain, as well as my stomach, must have been low on fuel. I wasn't paying attention and just missed getting clipped by one of the bulky Long Beach cable cars. My heart kicked up a notch when it passed close enough to touch. Clanging only a warning, it continued charging blindly along toward the beach like a blind folded six-ton stampeding elephant. A load of happy tourists and sweaty shoppers clinging to the overhead hand straps were oblivious to my close call.

I jerked the steering wheel over sharply and careened into the diner's postage stamp- sized gravel lot. After sliding to a stop between a dented Ford pickup truck and a faded blue Hudson sedan, I sat there for a few minutes, replaying the close call in my mind. I wondered how in the hell I could have missed seeing that behemoth in the road and exhaled a sigh of relief that nothing had happened. After settling down, I thought again about getting something tasty for lunch inside.

I rolled up the windows and squeezed out cautiously, without bumping my door into the adjacent crate, and hoped the other owners would do the same when they left. I didn't have much confidence they would, but went inside anyway and said good bye to my dent-free chariot.

What was once a proud five-star dining experience on the Southern Pacific railroad line, the old car now sat propped up on a bed of cinder blocks disguised by a makeshift boarder skirt. It now occupied one end of a downtown Long Beach dusty parking lot and converted to a twenty-four hour eatery that had seen better days. It was sporting a broken neon sign inside a dirty front window advertising the dump like an over the hill boxer with a perpetual black eye, that would spend his declining career mostly on the canvas. I'd eaten there once or twice before without getting sick, so decided the risk was minimal. I'd tackle it one more time.

Except for the owners of the two jalopies outside and a couple of walk-ins, the narrow diner was almost empty. I slid into a tight booth next to one of the windows and tried to visualize my heap outside through the hand-splotched window. It was still there, undisturbed.

I retrieved the one-page menu stuffed beside the mini table top juke box and selected the hot pastrami on rye with sour kraut and a cup of java. I didn't have to wait long to get noticed. I easily caught the attention of a bored waitress fussing with some condiments on the counter, and she hustled over, anxious to be more useful. She was a green-eyed cutie pie with a pouty angel's face, somewhere in her early twenties chewing gum and impatiently tapping her pencil on a small yellow pad. She was wearing a small homemade name tag pinned to her white blouse that said "Candy" written in neat bold capitals with smudged ink. Her forearms were decorated with several tattoos of cartoon characters I'd seen in the funny papers, suggesting a childish and "tough as nails" seamier side of life. Hers also backed up with a slightly sassy attitude for extra confidence. The kid's captivating smile of square white even teeth on a sassy little face would melt the heart of any Hollywood casting agent. She just needed to be discovered, but this was no Schwab's in Hollywood. What a waste the kid was in this Long Beach dump. Her mop of bubble gum pink dyed hair was chopped off short and clean but left fluffy and shaggy. A style you'd want to ruffle with both hands. Cutie stuffed it under an oversized white bow with the edges peeking out like feathers escaping from an overstuffed pillow. She reminded me of a full-sized kewpie doll in a short skirt and waitress apron getup that you couldn't resist squeezing.

She flashed me a non-stop persuasive smile, snapping her gum anxiously in time to some nervous rhythm playing in her head, anxious to speed up my order. I told her what I wanted, but she attempted to talk me into a couple of fresh, just-caught off the Long Beach pier today, fish tacos with homemade salsa. No dice on the harbor fish, at least not today. I knew what usually floated by my boat in the marina, and it never looked edible. When that failed, she pushed a combination plate of greasy home- cut fries and a cheeseburger with the works, apparently another staple at Dale's, she said, working the gum overtime and popping a blown bubble. I almost fell for the greasy burger but held firm and insisted on a pastrami sandwich with a side of sauerkraut. She scribbled down my choice shaking her head in disappointment, and stuffed the pencil behind her ear, almost convincing me I'd made a mistake.

I tossed the menu aside and watched her sashshay over to the counter to collect the coffee pot. You couldn't help notice her suggestive walk. This doll already knew how to throw a mean curve you couldn't catch without trouble. She fumbled around with a tray of freshly washed cups stacked next to the cash register and finally made a selection. I'd find out soon enough that the one she'd drawn contained a small chip and a lip stick smudge, maybe hers. She didn't seem to notice, and I didn't mention it. I let her retreat back to the kitchen area to place my order and just wiped it off instead. The Java was predictably harsh and too hot to drink. I let it cool down for a few minutes and then blew off the head of rising steam and took another sip. It wasn't any better the second time around and still too hot to drink. I grimaced, set it aside, and lit a Lucky to dull my taste buds.

While waiting, I glanced around at the four characters, silently concentrating on their meals. Two withslicked-back hair eating at the counter appeared to be workers from across Ocean Boulevard at the Pike Amusement Park. One guy was wearing a uniform that advertised the Cyclone Racer, a rollercoaster ride on rickety wooden scaffolding that was a high-risk gamble by any insurance statistics you'd dare to read. Another wore a war surplus brown leather bomber jacket with *Wall of Death* printed on the back. That numbskull was a motorcycle daredevil that rode at top speeds around and around inside a gigantic woodenbarrel-shaped tub inhaling exhaust fumes until he couldn't stand up. He didn't look too bright from where I was sitting, but after a few dizzy spins in his washing machine, I guess it would be enough to scramble anyone's brain. The other two, stashed at the far end in a booth by themselves, must have been the drivers of the crates flanking my Buick. All in all, it was a rough crowd. At least they had enough sense not to eat the junk they served at the concession stands on the midway across the street.

I took a chance on another sip of coffee and only partially scalded my tongue. Glancing over at the Wurlitzer juke box sitting in one corner, I was thankful it was still silent. I wasn't in the mood for some jumpy numbers and didn't find anything amusing with the cornball faded wall signs plastered around the room with the cute slogans: *Help keep Long Beach clean, please wipe your feet before leaving- Courteous service is available on request- Tip us or Die of Thirst.* They were far from hilarious, as the owner of this hash house must have thought.

My meal finally arrived. Maybe a little sooner than I expected. It was hot, and I was hungry. I polished off the pastrami sandwich, which was actually corned beef, but when you're hungry, who the hell cares. It was also a little tough but still edible. I would have liked a beer, which they didn't serve. I settled for a road tar refill instead.

After finishing, I tossed my napkin aside and lit another smoke. I called over the doll with the pink mop and asked her if she'd ever seen either the Ava look-a-like in my folded newspaper clipping or the blonde from my description with the possible name of Gina. At first, she hesitated. I shoved a fin in her direction to grease the wheels. She stuffed it inside her uniform pocket out of sight, glanced over her shoulder around the room, and quietly began to remember. She drew a blank on the brunette but opened up about a platinum blonde.

"Mister, if there's one thing around this beach and amusement park, it's blondes. All shades, whatever you want, and whatever the bottle color says. Say, what's this about anyway? You a cop?"

"Why? Don't like cops?"

"They can get kind of rough, you know? You ain't a cop, are yah?"

"I've had a few run-ins with some tough ones myself, kid," I said, brushing off the question. "They can be a pain where the sun don't shine."

"Yeah, You're right there, mister." She paused, thinking about it, fingering the fin in her pocket, then working up a little conspiratorial grin, like we were now mutual pals. She glanced over her shoulder again at the crumb in the leather jacket with his back still turned and continued in a lowered voice again. "You got more to go on?"

I mentioned the ankle bracelet. She gazed vacantly over my shoulder for a few seconds, tapping her pencil on the order pad. Lights flickered upstairs.

"Yeah, I did see one." She turned on a warm smile, and hearing this news, so did I. I reached for another Lucky and let her continue without interrupting her train of thought.

"A platinum- haired blonde wearing one a few weeks ago came in here. First time I seen her she was with my friend Chester. Then she was kind of trashy. Yellow stringy hair, chipped nail polish, thrift shop clothes—you know, try'n to be pretty but, not much class. He told me she worked somewhere over at the Pike. I think her names yeah, that's it, Gina ... or something. Then, I don't see her for a while with him, and he says he dumped her. But I ain't so sure about that. Then she shows up again with another guy, and now she's all fancy. You know, all dolled up... real flashy; expensive clothes, hair dyed real nice, perfume strong enough to smell across the street, lips a bright and shiny red you could see in the dark, new high heeled shoes, matching purse- the works. That's when she was wearing one of them small gold ankle chains with plenty of sparklers surrounding it. She kept dangling her leg off the counter stool like they was maybe real diamonds or something special to look at.

"You couldn't miss it. I wished I had one too, when I seen hers, but thought ... oh, what the hell, they was just paste anyway."

I didn't want to spoil the kid's illusion, but the diamonds were the real McCoy, if they were on the same ankle bracelet given by McCullen.

"She was act'n kind of stuck up too, like she was now too good to be eat'n in our hash house. She tried to act like a lady, but she wolfed down her food like she hadn't eaten a solid meal in a month, just like I seen her do before. They didn't talk much either, just kinda whispered secret like, to each other. She had plenty of dough in her purse though. When they finished eat'n, she pulled out a stack of double sawbucks thicker than a phone book, paid and left a fat tip for me. With that kind of loose dough, I think she must have been hook'n somewhere around here, probably at the Pike, the beach hotels, or maybe had connections with some high rollers in some of the private gambling joints in L.A."

"What makes you think so?"

"Cuz, I just said, she used to come in here once in a while with that other one over there," she said, jabbing a thumb over her shoulder at the loser sitting at the counter shoveling in his meal with his back to us advertising The Wall of Death on his jacket. "He's usually broker than a beach panhandler. I should know; I usually stake him to a free meal here once in a while … like today.

"That other crumb that picked Blondie up here one night for dinner? She must have started screwing him instead of Chester cuz she dropped Chester like a hot fry'n pan afterwards, and I never saw either one of them other two again. Too good for us at Dale's, I guess."

"I doubt that. Maybe more to it than you know about, sweetheart."

"That other guy, he works over on Pine Avenue in one of them tattoo shops. He looked more like a pimp or gambler than a needle pusher. That's the funny part. I mean him too— new suit, snappy tie, new hat, shined shoes. You know the type, like he was work'n the angles instead in some saloon, gambling or something crooked."

"Think she got the dough from him?"

"Certainly not from a geek like him."

I think she was wrong on that count, but let her continue with her theory.

"I think she even paid for both dinners then, too. Typical of the pimps I know, always take'n, never give'n."

"Good observation, kid. Don't fall for it."

"You know, lately, I been see'n some new customers eat'n here, carry'n bigger rolls than I ever seen before. Don't get it. Big tips, though. Can't complain."

Maybe something there too, maybe not… otherwise, I'd hit a bonanza with this kid. She was actually a smart cookie. I needed as much information as I could get out of her before she ran out of steam or got sidetracked. I worked up my best smile and sweetened the pot with another fin to keep her talking. This one she shoved inside, down the front of her bra. I wondered where she'd hide the next one if offered.

"Where, sweetheart? On Pine? What's this shop called? Got his name?"

"I know most of the tattoo artist's around here, as you can see from my arms," she said, proudly showing me as if I hadn't noticed before. "That guy's new in town, I hear. Don't know his name for certain. Maybe Fred or Jake, I don't know. I think he just started at Archie's Tattoo Shop over on Pine, as I said before."

"Could it have been Frank?"

"Yeah, maybe. I dunno," she said, scratching her head under her bow with the pencil point and glancing around nervously.

"What's he look like, sweetheart?" I asked, sensing she was about to lose interest in my third degree. I'd have to work faster before the well ran dry.

"Nobody special. Kind of short and weasely. You know; pinched face, narrow beady little eyes, kind of yellowish teeth like he don't like to brush, dark Bryl creemed hair combed straight back, ugh!" She shivered a little. "Just thinking gives me the creeps."

"Not bad, kid. You got more?"

"Not sure of his name as I said, but noticed he's got a funny tat, like a flag or something on the back of one of his hands and some other crazy designs on his arms. I didn't pay much attention to them."

"Think he was a sailor?"

"Maybe, but I don't think so."

"Why not?"

"He was too pale for a sailor and looked weak. I go out with lots of sailors off the ships in San Pedro. Mostly bigger guys with good tans, like you." She smiled. "They know how to spend their dough and treat a lady right. They always pick up the tab at a restaurant too. Not that guy, he was as pale as a ghost, like I said, and she paid. I don't think he's broke, maybe just stingy and must have spent a lot of the time indoors, you know?"

"Like maybe in jail?"

"Could be."

"You're alright, kid. You should be a detective. You're smart and observant."

"Thanks, but I hate cops, remember?"

"Yeah, I do. Maybe you'd like a private investigator, better?" I grinned.

She'd guessed already and said, "Yeah … maybe I would," and grinned back.

"Thanks for the know-how, sweetheart. You've been a big help. I'll be back sometime," I said and slid out.

She smiled again at my compliments and was about to continue when the greaseball in the leather jacket looked over his shoulder and snapped his fingers, signaling for a coffee refill or something else and pronto. She shut down our conversation and drifted off in his direction to see what the punk wanted.

I'd wrung out more than what I'd expected from this kewpie doll anyway and tossed another generous tip on the table covering my bill and her extra information. I grabbed my hat from the seat and decided to shove off. It was time to follow up on what I'd just learned. *Shanghai Ruby's* would have to wait.

I yanked the door open and, glancing back, caught another sweet smile from Candy before she disappeared behind the counter. I thought about some of the so-called Hollywood phonies that without their shoe lifts, false teeth, and wigs had nothing on that kid.

But I didn't like what I was hearing or seeing. The punk in the leather jacket wasn't too happy about something with little Candy. From where I was standing, it looked like he was starting to get rough. I didn't think it was a complaint about his meal either. His hand was squeezing her tightly around the forearm, and she was having trouble pulling away. Their voices were argumentative and getting louder.

I changed my mind, stepped back inside, and swung the door closed. I decided it wasn't time to leave after all. At least not right then, anyway.

Chapter Five

Grease ball didn't see me approaching. I was halfway across the room before he picked up my reflection from the stainless-steel grill behind the counter. Candy managed to wrestle her arm loose, backing up fast to stay clear of the trouble she spotted brewing.

Dangerous Dan wasn't going to get tagged from behind for his roughness with the little cupcake and armed himself for attack instead. Before I could reach him, he spun around on his counter stool, a contorted expression on his face. He'd grabbed the sharp and pointed steak knife off his plate, hoping to take me by surprise. It was a mistake he'd soon regret.

Attempting to make the first move, he stumbled upright from the counter stool a little off- balance, swinging the blade in a desperate waist- high slashing motion that was out of reach for its intended target. I'd seen the move coming and whipped out my .357 S&W mag. from the shoulder holster. Instead of retreating from his threat, I dodged his first swing. Then took a couple of quick steps forward and moved inside the swinging arc of his knife, faster than he anticipated. I was prepared for destruction.

Smashing the revolver straight across his face, I easily crushed his nose and opened a bone- deep gash along the cheek with the sharp edges of the cylinder. He fell back in pain, dropped his blade, and grabbed his face to feel what damage had been done. The blood poured through his fingers. Just for added insurance, I pistol-whipped him again across the top of the head several more times, opening up a flap of skin across his scalp. He grabbed there with the other hand and sank to the floor in a sobbing heap. I stepped out of the way, trying to avoid the blood spatter from this crumb staining my suit. Candy, who'd crouched down behind the counter, peeked over the top and let out a sharp shriek at seeing this bleeding mess already staining the floor.

Dangerous Dan was finished for the day, attempting to hold his face and head together with wads of paper napkins desperately pulled from the counter dispenser that had fallen beside him. The other Pike character decided he didn't want to offer any assistance to his pal and looked like he was about to lose his lunch after seeing the carnage. Holding his gut with one hand and covering his mouth with the other, he made a one-way trip out the door faster than a rat with a bellyful of arsenic. The other losers, sitting at the far end just kept quietly concentrating on their meals with their heads down like good boys, as if nothing important happened. Minding their own business and staying out of trouble was a wise decision.

Someone must have called the local P.D. or maybe it was just time for another fresh sinker and Java break, as a squad car pulled up smartly in the parking lot outside. From where I was standing, I didn't recognize the two young rookie lugs seated inside. They weren't in any hurry to get out, so I knew it was just another routine stop.

I figured it might be better if the little waitress wasn't involved and took the initiative. I grabbed junior by the collar and dragged his limp, bleeding carcass over to the front door, and tossed him outside in the gravel, just as both cops were opening their doors to get out and enjoy a nice quiet coffee break.

"What the hell is this mess?" bellowed the one closest to the moaning bloody heap, vomiting at his feet. He looked up at me standing in the doorway grinning.

"Welcome to Dale's Diner, Officers," I said, introducing myself and flashing my P.I. buzzer discretely.

"This punk just pulled a knife on me inside, and I had to cool him out. Hope I didn't interfere with your java break."

"We know who you are, Thornton. You can put away your tin shield, and we don't need none of your wise cracks either."

"Touchy, boys. Better hurry. The sinkers are getting stale with all this chatter."

"Yeah, okay smart ass. You may be a pal of Foster Berringer's all right, and he may be Captain of homicide here in Long Beach, but you're just a private peeper to us. And, don't you forget it."

"Afraid I might get the drop on solving another one or two of your cases?" I said, prodding the overly serious rookies.

Ignoring my comments, the one with the biggest belly continued, "We heard over the radio a little while ago about the dead dame at the Blue Parrot and understand you was just there, too. What gives with you, Thornton? You a magnet for trouble or something?"

"I'm not afraid, if it comes my way. I can take care of myself, that what you mean?"

"Ah, nuts," said the one closest to the moaner in the gravel, slapping the air in disgust, not wanting to push me and giving up. "Now, we've just got a whole lot of damn paper work to do because of this trash," he said, nudging him sharply in the ribs with his toe and smirking when the loser groaned.

The other cop circled around behind the punk on the ground and jerked him to his feet, grumbling under his breath about not being able to take a break without something always screwing it up. He snapped on a pair of cuffs, cinching them tight enough to make him wince, and pushed him roughly into the backseat of the squad car, bumping his head on the way in. Then, he slammed the door in disgust, violently enough to shatter the glass. I noticed the blood-soaked paper napkins were still stuck to the side of the kid's face and across the top of his scalp. That seemed to have stopped the blood flow, but his eyes were now flicking back and forth like a pin ball machine nearing tilt. He was probably going to pass out next, not that it was any concern to the two cops.

"I'll drop by the station and give my official statement later," I said, grinning pleasantly, as both lugs piled back into their squad car, disappointed they'd chosen Dales as a nice quiet place to hide for a while.

They didn't seem to care when or if I showed up either, as the one on my side said, leaning out the window, "Take your time, Thornton. This guy's a pain in the ass around here anyway. Always getting into fights, gets drunk as a skunk or trouble of some kind, and got a rap sheet a mile long. Tossing his ass in the can again will be a pleasure. Hope the judge throws the key away this time, but I know he'll be out on bail in a couple of hours, get patched up, and we'll just have to do it all over again. He's got friends higher up than you think, pal. Thanks for nothing!"

"Don't mention it. Always anxious to help Long Beach's finest. Oh, and don't forget to give my best to Foster when you see him," I said, with another grin. I gave them a small half-assed salute as they pulled back onto Atlantic Boulevard in a spray of gravel and dust.

I decided to see how Candy was holding up after this fiasco and went back inside. An overweight slob in a greasy apron with a soup strainer mustache and grumpy expression on his kisser was putting the finishing touches on the bloody cleanup with a dirty mop. After a few more sloppy swipes, leaving behind several puddles of dirty water to slip in, he shuffled off to the back dragging his bucket, mumbling something about "God-damned punks from the Pike."

Candy was sniffling quietly at one of the tables by the window and looked up with red -rimmed eyes when I entered. I sat down across from her, reached for an ashtray, and flicked in a spent match for my cigarette. She dabbed her eyes with a paper napkin and muttered, "Jeepers, mister. I-I don't even know your name."

"Just call me Matthew, baby, okay?"

She nodded, sniffled again, and continued, "Did you have to beat up C-Chester so bad, Mister ah-Matthew? He was only twist'n my arm. I can take it. He's done that before, you know? It don't hurt so much anyway."

"You go out with that bum?"

"Yeah, sometimes … and sometimes he's real nice, too."

"Well, he wasn't today. You got anybody else that's better?"

"Not really . I've been on my own since I left home at seventeen."

"Watch out for that loser, kid. He's trouble with a capital T."

She gave me a blank stare, and I sensed she didn't care much what my opinion was, so I dropped it.

"What did he want, sweetheart?"

"H-he wanted to know what you was ask'n me."

"About the dames?"

"Yeah, that's it. I told him I don't know nothin and don't tell you nothin. That's when he started getting rough. Called me a liar and started twist'n."

The tears flowed again and she stabbed at her eyes and cheeks with a fresh paper napkin. I felt sorry for the kid and didn't like what I'd just heard. That loser named Chester knew something that I'd have to dig into, and the little pink-haired doll was now right in the middle of it and didn't know it, yet. I did and was worried for her, but there wasn't much I could do about it. I hoped I was wrong.

"Next time you see that bum, tell him I let him off easy. And, next time, he won't be so lucky, okay, sweetheart? Now dry your eyes. I'll see you again. I'll be back and maybe have those tacos next time. What do you say? Good idea?"

"Yeah, I guess so," she said and blew her nose a couple of more times, stuffing the napkins into her uniform pocket next to her order pad.

I got up to leave and gave her one of my P.I. cards. She didn't look at it, just absently folded it in half and shoved it into her pocket next to the soggy napkins, mumbled "thanks," and gave me a weak smile trying to perk up. I wasn't convincedthat everything was going to be all right with this kid, and I think she sensed it.

I closed the door behind me on the way out and didn't look back. I should have, but I didn't. I'd continue where I left off, starting with Archie's Tattoo Parlor a few streets over. But, the thought of Chester and his pals looming in little Pinkie's background left me with an uneasy feeling that would be hard to shake.

Chapter Six

I hopped into the Buick, deciding it wasn't smart to leave it in the diner's crummy parking lot. I'd take my chances along the street a few blocks over on Pine Avenue. I cruised around the block slowly until I spotted the tattoo shop on my left and pulled into the nearest empty curbside spot across the street. I locked the doors and crossed to investigate, dodging a couple of crates going too fast towards the beach. My lucky day, so far.

Archie's was still several miles from *Shanghai Ruby's* and squeezed in between a small empty used furniture store and a dental office. According to the chipped overhead signage pointing up, Doctor Pain's gloomy unpopular door-less entrance led to a darkened stairwell and a second-floor probable horror chamber.

According to the crowd of potential customers nervously peering inside through Archie's dusty windows, the little tattoo shop typically manned by an ex-sailor or a high school dropout seemed to be one of the more prosperous businesses on that side of the street. I wondered what the "Tooth Puller," with his fancy college degrees or more likely correspondence school diploma, terrified customers and an empty patient chair most of the time, thought about that irony.

I entered andside-stepped a smiling couple just leaving with small bandages taped to their arms in what must have been an enjoyable afternoon. The whole place smelled like disinfectant and my boxing gym on Melrose. The walls of the room were painted a crimson red, bright enough to wake the dead, and covered in once colorful and now yellowed designs with matching prices affixed to each underneath. They were mostly traditional nautical themes from anchors and ships to mermaids, pinup nudes, and everything else patriotic in between. A large flickering neon sign overhead advertised "Design Flash- Pick your Poison ." Nice sales pitch, I thought.

Two husky, bare-chested young Marines with serious expressions and their uniform shirts tossed over an adjacent coat rack were sitting stoically on kitchen chairs on the opposite side of the room. Both were getting something memorable inked on their chests they'd later regret. A couple of wiry guys, one wearing an old sailor's hat upside down and one bare headed, both with rolled- up sleeves advertising their own share of skin art on skinny, sinewy arms were hunched over their victims with buzzing machines in rabid concentration. The one with the dirty hat puffing a droopy cigarette must have sensed me enter and turned to see who was next. I nodded and smiled. He gave me a blank stare, then turned back around and blew a cloud of smoke out his nostrils across his customer's fresh art work. He was now more than anxious to finish on the Marine and begin work on another sucker.

I fired up a Lucky, tipped my hat back, and waited, drumming my fingers on the counter, anxious for information from one of these two lunkheads. My anxiety wouldn't speed up the process. I tried to settle in, glancing around again at the dingy design choices plastered on the walls. None looked appealing, and all looked like they'd been tacked there since before World War I. I thought about the cartoon designs the little pink- haired Candy had inked on her forearms and couldn't find them on the wall. I wondered if she had more hidden underneath her waitress uniform. That crumb Chester must have seen them all from the familiar way she talked. What a loser. She deserved so much better but didn't know it.

I double- checked my watch several times and noticed I wasn't making much progress. The sound of the small electric tattoo machines whirred in the background, accompanied only by inaudible chatter from the brave customers in the chairs trying to bolster their own courage and the loud music blaring from a Philco radio on a side shelf. I noticed the lighting seemed to be a bit too subdued for performing these intricate operations, but nobody seemed to be complaining, so I guessed it didn't have much effect on the accuracy of the design anyway.

I checked my watch once more and thought about *Ruby's* down by the waterfront. I decided I'd let this ride a little longer and question whichever one of the tattoo clowns finished first. The little weasel Candy had described was important. I'd keep waiting. That little crumb was suddenly part of the big picture starring me in the face, but his description didn't match with either one of the two with coat hanger arms working here today. At least not right now anyway. I'd have to be patient a little longer, something not in my nature.

The one with the cigarette smoke in his eyes finished up first as predicted and finally glanced around again, squinting to see if I was still there. He wasn't disappointed on that score, but would be once we'd talked. I wasn't there to get branded. He began hastily straightening up his workplace, putting his supplies neatly away, and shook hands with the grinning Marine plastered with a fresh bandage across his chest. Spinning around in his chair, he exited, anxious to hook another sap, before I'd lost interest.

"What can I do for you, mister?" he said, showing a mouth full of crooked teeth and desperately sweeping his hand towards the fly speck- stained designs on the walls like an exhibition of newly discovered Picassos. "Yeh got something picked out yet, friend?"

From the no-nonsense look on my face, he knew without a further pitch it was going to be a no-sale. He was overly eager to line his pocket with some of my dough, but it wouldn't work. He pushed once more, hoping to influence my decision with a more aggressive angle.

"Come on, come on, buddy, I ain't got all day. Which one? You must have decided by now, you been stand'n here awhile. Let me make a suggestion for you, ah-how about, ah…" He picked out something that looked like a rodeo cowboy on a bucking bronco. I winced and cut him off.

"Sorry to disappoint you, pal. I'm not here for ink. I need some information. Let's cut out the sales crap, okay? I've wasted enough time here already."

"But…" he interrupted.

"Just shut up, and I'll do the asking," I said, holding up my hand to prevent further interruptions.

The ex-swabbie looked more than disappointed, probably wondering why he'd rushed the last job. No telling what shortcuts he'd taken on his last design, but the Marine wouldn't notice until he'd removed the bandage, and by then, he'd be out to sea anyway.

I continued, "I'm looking for a little guy that I heard works here." I described the little runt Candy had seen and watched his face lock up. "He goes out with a platinum bimbo from time to time. You know him and the girl or not?"

"What you want him for, friend? Who told you he works here?" he said, becoming defensive and taking a step backward, not sure if he wasn't going to regret his smart mouth.

His partner, overhearing our loud conversation, set his tattoo machine aside and left his customer unfinished, who was anxious to join his friend with the bandaged chest who'd already gone outside.

"I've got a message for him that I'd like to deliver personally. And tell me about the blonde, too." I gave the two stooges a look that meant my patience was wearing thin, and I expected answers and pronto.

I decided to sweeten the deal and reached for my money clip and added, "Here's a couple of fins for not giving me the needle, okay? Now let's talk."

"Yeah, yeah okay, thanks. I-I guess that sounds fair enough," said the one with thestill-smoldering cigarette clouding his kisser and the well-worn sailor hat with *Spike* written across the unturned edge. He turned to get a confirming nod and a snaggle- toothed grin from his partner. They both decided to cooperate, stuffing the dough in their pockets.

"He works the second shift here sometimes if we're busy."

"Name?"

"Frank Murphy. He's alright."

"You know him long?"

"No, not us. We just met him a few weeks ago. He's a friend of Archie's."

I shot him a puzzled glance. "I need more."

He caught on without more prompting, "You know, Archie … Archie Bates, the guy that owns this shop." He pointed over his shoulder to a partially faded black and white photo stapled to the wall showing a tall, well build mug with arms heavily plastered with tattoo's giving the needle to another sucker grimacing in pain. "Archie said, he and Frank are old pals, did time together. Frank just got out of stir and needed a job, so…."

"What about the blonde, Spike?"

"You mean Gina?"

"Yeah, that's her," I said, that piece fitting together conveniently with the scrap of paper in my pocket.

"I think it's his girl, a real classy dish too. Her name's Slade, Gina Slade. She stopped by here a couple of times and they talked kind of quiet, like they had something they didn't want us to hear. A real looker she is. We was jealous too, right Benny?" he said, jabbing his friend in the ribs and grinning. "He spends time in the slammer, you know, and then gets a dame like that when he gets out. What a lucky guy, ain't he?"

"Yeah, real lucky," I said, thinking back to that once beautiful babe, naked and cold as a fish on ice, sprawled on a rumpled bed in that dump that I'd just left a few hours ago. I just shook my head.

"You know her, mister?" he said smiling, watching for confirmation of his opinion.

"I've seen her, pal. She was some dish all right."

"W-what do you mean *was*?" he said, catching my slip. He wasn't so stupid after all. I lied my way out of it. "I mean, ah- the last time I saw her."

"Oh, yeah, you're right."

"Frank going to be here tonight?" I said, changing course to lighten the message by sounding like I was familiar with the guy.

"No. Benny here," he said, pointing to his pal, "he come in late so he's go'n to run the show instead. You might try Shanghai Ruby's on Neptune Avenue, maybe later this evening. Frank said he knows someone there and likes to stop in for a drink sometimes to shoot the breeze. Helps him settle his nerves, he said."

I was going there anyway. I wondered what his connection there was, but these punks wouldn't know. I said, "That's reassuring for your customers, isn't it?"

"W-what do you mean? He ain't no jitterbug, mister. He's clean and sober."

"It's nothing. Forget it, pal. I didn't mean anything. Just ah-Ruby's a popular place around here, right?"

"Oh yeah, sure."

He didn't get it. I let it pass, but sensed he was coming out of his stupor and might wise up this Bates character before I had a chance to grab him.

"You know where Frank lives? Maybe I can catch up with him there?"

"He lives around here in Long Beach," Spike continued, blurting out on a winning streak, my dough already burning a hole in his pocket and thinking maybe more on the way. "I think he said it was somewhere off of Pacific Avenue, the Argosy Court apartments or…"

"Nix, nix," Benny mumbled out of the corner of his mouth, jabbing him sharply in the ribs to clam up, but it was too late. He'd already blabbed too much. I salted his comments away, noting the crumb lived only a few blocks from the shop. If I played my cards right, I might be able to nail him at home.

Spike nervously grinned, showing off his yellow choppers again. He ran a dry tongue over the two in front stuck under his upper lip and then tried to backtrack over his faux pas by changing the subject.

"Say, mister, what did you say this is all about?"

If the little shop hadn't been filling up with more dopey customers, I would have throttled the little bastard right then to get what I needed. I'd already waited longer than I'd planned on and was starting to build up a head of steam with the stall, but I'd let it ride to see if I could squeeze more out of either of these losers.

"I'm delivering an important message, re-member?" I was wrong. They'd run out of answers and were getting nosey.

I unbuttoned my suit coat and let them catch a glimpse of my holstered .357 mag. persuader. They glanced at each other and got the picture fast.

"Oh ye-ah, I guess so. Y-you look like somebody connected too," one of the dim-wits mumbled, deciding to shut up with the questions.

I fished out a couple more fins, slid them across the counter, and said, "I suggest you two clowns keep our conversation under your lids. I don't want to return and repeat my request, comprende?"

They both nodded nervously in tandem like a couple of attached Siamese twins and pocketed the extra grease equally fast with only a smirk. I had enough to go on and didn't have to say more to clam them up. I slammed the door on my way out.

It was too early for Shanghai Ruby's. I'd pick it up later. That joint was becoming more and more of a focal point in my investigation, and I was anxious to collect more information, but I didn't want to miss that little punk Frank Murphy either. Fresh out of stir, Spike said. That was a new twist, and what did he have going that was connected to the dead blonde back at the Parrott. Did he even know she was dead already? I'd work on that angle soon enough.

I'd spent too much time at the tattoo shop already. I decided to check back with Rhonda at the office and see how she was doing and to inquire about a couple of calls I was expecting. I had a feeling that this case was going to crack wide open with something that was going to sail right past Sherman's astute police department investigators. This was also much bigger than what I'd originally anticipated with McCullen. He might very easily be the next victim to turn up cold as a tomb stone, if I didn't get the pieces into place soon enough. On that, I would also be wrong.

Chapter Seven

I left the Buick curbside and walked across the street and down about half a block to a Rexall pharmacy. The small counter up front serving ice cream sodas to some rowdy teenager's killing time after school was packed and noisy. I bought a backup deck of smokes, collected the change, and asked the harried druggist for his phone booth. He motioned towards a back corner where it was hidden behind several shelves of overflowing merchandise collecting dust. Hopefully it was a little quieter. I slammed the folding door closed and fed some coins into the slot, connecting with Rhonda on the second ring. She announced my investigation business in a cheery voice sweeter than a hot waffle smothered in melted butter and Log Cabin Syrup. I was pleased in the way she answered and, also she'd recuperated from her earlier shakeup at the Blue Parrott Inn.

"Hi baby, it's me, Matthew. I can tell from your voice you're feeling better."

"Mathew, darling, I am. I was just thinking about you too," she purred into my ear.

God, I loved that voice. What a treat to hear that response instead of my usual answering service, grating in my ear with an impersonal salutation.

"I laid down on the couch here in the office for a while and felt better. Then I went down to that little restaurant next door you suggested and had some toast, coffee and a couple of scrambled eggs. I'm okay now, good idea. What a relief. I started feeling better and even read one of the newspapers some customer had left behind."

I let her ramble on and just listened, smiling at that beauty's enthusiasm, almost forgetting why I'd called.

"Did you know that several actors, screen writers, and a few other executives in the movie business are beginning to get hammered by some Washington congressional committee about something? I didn't get it, but it seemed important. Oh, and two FBI agents were found shot to death, somewhere here in L.A. Their bodies were just dumped in an alley. I think it was not far from our office over by Gower Gulch. Isn't that tragic?"

She exhaled into the phone, a little out of breath and all excited to tell me everything that she thought I'd missed so far today. I could almost see her sweet face, relieved of the day's tensions earlier. Just as well she'd gone back to work. My day had been a little more turbulent, a minor disaster, to say the least.

"You're right on top of the latest scuttlebutt, sweetheart. Especially about the politicos getting involved in the Hollywood business. That killing sounds interesting too. You're right. That's just off of Gower and Sunset, right down the street. It's where most of the out of work wannabe extras hang out waiting to be cast in one of the low-budget one-reelers, serials and oaters. I wonder if they're connected. Maybe some of that trouble will translate into business for Thornton Private Investigations. I'll have to look into it, if I have time."

"I thought you should know about it anyway," she said, happy to be involved.

I cradled the phone under my chin, dug out a Lucky, a pack of bent matches that refused to light first time and thought about what a smart kid she actually was. After coughing once or twice from the enclosed fumes, I cracked open the booth door to let the smoke escape and continued, "I've been making some headway around the waterfront here in Long Beach, which I'll tell you about later, but first, any callers?"

"Yes, ah-a Mr. Ernest Heming-way," she said, fumbling over the syllables. "He wants you to meet him tomorrow morning at the Majestic Studio where they're filming the movie *Duel at Dawn* He said it's very exciting and based on one of his novels. Said he's been offering advice on the script as it stinks the way it's been adapted for the big screen. I don't think I ever heard of him and never read any of his other stories either, but didn't let on."

"Smart move, baby. That's one of the calls I've been waiting for."

"Oh, who is he?"

From her comments, I knew she had no idea who the hell Hemingway was and said, "I'll fill you in, baby. In addition to being a big shot writer and international sportsman, he's also a focal point for newshounds when he's in town. He usually frequents all the ritzy night clubs, fancy restaurants, and famous watering holes, sometimes more drunk than sober. Usually his evening ends in a publicized brawl with one of the other customers."

"Like how some of your evenings end, too … right?"

"Sort of, the difference is, he's a celebrity in a select circle. He usually hob-knobs with an A- list of actors, actresses, producers, and directors. And in spite of his querulous personality, they're all anxious to grab onto his popular big as brass balls."

"Oh, oh!" I heard her snicker in the background.

"I figured that would get your attention. You'll probably get to meet him. We talked a while back about this assignment, last time he was in town on another matter. I didn't think it was anything more than celebrity name-dropping and hot air at the time."

"Sounds like you're lucky you were wrong, doesn't it?"

"No doubt about it, angel."

Rhonda didn't miss a beat. She continued on with her report, regardless of the client or what it was about. "He said it's very urgent. He thinks someone is trying to sink his intrusion on this picture and needs 'some muscle pack'n iron' as he said to back him up. Does that make any sense to you?"

"It sure does, and it sounds too good to be real, sweetheart. Want to go over with me, now that you're feeling better?"

"I'd love to."

"I think you'd learn a little more about this private detective business if you tagged along. If it's not too involved, I might even assign you to stay there in the shadows to find out what's going on. It'll also give me an excuse to nose around Majestic regarding that dame in the McCullen case."

"Okay, I'll get right back on this stack of overdue insurance reports right now. They'll be finished before I lock up today. I'm excited, Matthew."

That would be soon, and I knew it wouldn't happen with "Little Miss Hunt and Peck" on the keys, but tried a little encouragement anyway. "Give it your best shot, baby. Also, call up the answering service and put Miss Wind Chimes back on duty for a week, starting tomorrow, okay? What else?"

"Doris Fillmore at the *Herald Examiner* newspaper called and said she has a very interesting scoop on Mr. Carson McCullen and wants to know when you can meet to discuss it."

"Call her office and tell her I'll connect with her tomorrow after the Majestic appointment and maybe meet with her at Rico's Seafood Grotto across the street from the studio. That's maybe, if I have time, okay? That it, baby?"

"Yes, for now. Ah… I'm scheduled to be dancing at the Florentine Gardens Club tonight. You remember, don't you?" she said, almost apologetically.

"Yes, I do. Maybe I'll stop over later if I have time. On second thought, I don't think I will, as I've got several more things on my list I need to tackle before the evening's over. Meet me back at the office in the morning about nine and we'll ride over to the Majestic from there, okay?"

"I'll be there," she said, hearing the slight annoyance in my voice and added, "I'd like you to see my act if you have time, Matthew."

I wasn't crazy about her working late and then trying to catch enough shut-eye to focus on my P.I. business the next day, but I'd considered that when I first took her on. So far, she was burning the candle in both directions and could handle it. Neither of us was complaining, so I'd let it ride until it was a problem.

"Thanks for the invite anyway, baby. I'll try to make it, but no guarantees, okay?"

"I'll see you tomorrow then," she said softly.

She sounded disappointed I wasn't going to watch her act, but there'd be other opportunities in the future. Strip tease acts, I'd seen before. And Rhonda's act, I'd seen before too, but not on the stage.

I could already hear the typewriter clicking its way into the delinquent pile of paperwork spilling across her desk when I hung up. For now, that was good enough.

Shanghai Ruby's was on my list, but according to the time on my watch, it was still a little early for the typical bar crowd or anyone else that might steer me in the right direction. I'd drive over to the Argosy apartments first instead. One way or the other, I'd track down this Frank Murphy creep, as he was the only live lead I had to work on, for now anyway.

Chapter Eight

I t was later than I wanted it to be. Walking back to my parked heap, I could feel the sun beginning to weaken, and several of the shops were already snapping closed signs on their front doors. I sat inside my crate for a few minutes, thinking about so many of the unconnected pieces I had yet to collect on this mess but knew it would only be a matter of time before I'd figured it out.

I unwrapped my fresh pack of Luckies, treated myself to one, and then reached outside to adjust thedriver-side mirror, which someone had knocked out of kilter in passing to close. I needed to get moving. After a couple more drags on the butt, I stubbed it out in the ashtray and swung out into the late afternoon traffic. Workers impatient to get home were rushing, driving carelessly, and plugging up the streets. I didn't need a traffic accident to slow me down. I cautiously cut over to Pacific Avenue in search of the Argosy apartment building, anxious to zero in on Frank, the "little weasel" Murphy, as Candy described him.

Because of the vague location description from those two knuckleheads back at Archie's, I'd have to make a clean sweep beginning at Ocean Boulevard and work my way up the streets from 1st to who knew how far inland. Long Beach was a big city, but maybe I'd get lucky. Scanning both sides of Pacific's narrow two-lane street and avoiding the trolley car tracks in between was easy. But, not wanting to miss the building, I was frustrating the other cars piling up behind me as I trudged along at a snail's pace. If I didn't find it within a few blocks, I'd have to pull out of traffic, find a phone book and track it down that way. It didn't take long to cover half a dozen blocks, and I decided to try a couple more before giving up. I got lucky and spotted the Argosy off to my right on the corner at Eighth Street.

I pulled a U-turn and swung into an open spot across the street about half a block away. I decided to approach it on foot as discreetly as possible. It was still day light, and I didn't know if Murphy was home and didn't want to scare him off if he spotted me.

I darted across the street, dodging a busy stream of traffic, and slipped into a light crowd on the sidewalk. They were walking in my direction towards the raised trolley car boarding platform further down Pacific Avenue. Squatting under a shade roof in the middle of the street, the waiting benches were already overflowing with cranky shoppers and unruly children. Some were clutching packages, and all were anxious for the next car to take them back inland to their neighborhoods after a busy afternoon of shopping in the downtown heat.

The Argosy apartment building was a four-story faded red brick affair that had seen better days but fit right in with this shabby neighborhood also going to seed. It was centered on Pacific Avenue and wrapped around Eighth Street hogging about half a block. A water -stained decorative cornice ran around the top like a dirty ring in the bathtub. A rusted iron fire escape crawled up to the roof at the center next to the covered front entrance. Every floor was dotted with red anchor plates keeping the exterior load- bearing walls from bulging out like a fat man losing the battle with a tight belt.

From the number of windows, the old building must have contained fifty apartments. The corner units were covered with sun- bleached, tattered, red canvas awnings, and the ones down below street level were only half exposed and covered with vertical metal security bars. I wondered which apartment my man was hiding in. A dimly lit basement number with the iron bars was something he'd be familiar with and probably the cheapest. That was a sound bet, but I'd have to ask before I threw my money away.

I searched the corroded brass mailboxes by the entrance, spotted his name, and depressed the chipped call button. I'd play fire department building inspector if he answered and fingered my stack of phony business cards selecting the right one. After several more tries with no response, I selected another box labeled Lynette Tatum, Super. I leaned on that button to get some attention and hoped she was home and in a better mood and more sober than most of the building superintendent's I'd run across in similar dumps like this.

I was in luck, I guess. A woman's voice that sounded as smooth as a metal rasp caressing a freshly minted horseshoe, shouted into the squawk box with a scratchy voice demanding , "What the hell you want?" and adding for emphasis just in case the intruder wasn't paying attention, "You interrupted my supper. This better be good."

She was obviously home, not in a mood for timid souls, and didn't sound sober, as I'd already predicted.

After a little bantering back and forth with another phony story and a vague promise to sweeten my visit with a liquid present she couldn't resist, she reluctantly buzzed the entrance door open. I entered the dingy world of the Argosy and made my way down a darkened hallway reeking of moldy carpets, soiled diapers, and urban decay. I stumbled over a stack of yellowed newspapers, empty milk bottles, and an overturned baby carriage with a busted wheel before finding her apartment door.

I knocked and was greeted by a short, fat, greasy-haired woman of dubious middle age. Her puffy face, with a droopy left eye and a serious case of high-octane halitosis, hit me like an atomic blast. She timidly peeked out from behind her door, not certain about her visitor, and insisted on breathing heavily in my direction. From what I could see, she was wearing a faded house dress covered by a matching dirty apron. She smacked her lips with a look on her kisser that said she was overly anxious for the sauce I'd mentioned. Her one good eye lit up when I flashed the promised pint from my hip pocket, and I didn't have to say more. The old bag was hooked. She belched once in my face, excused herself by covering her mouth afterwards, and hiccupped. Before I changed my mind, she motioned me inside quickly, slamming the door behind me hard enough to make the wall pictures jump.

One look around was more than enough. Her dump was furnished in a combination of dilapidated late Victorian and contemporary flop house. The smell coming from either a pot of boiling cabbage and soiled laundry or something equally odorous elsewhere, was overpowering. Maybe it was coming from her. I couldn't tell and didn't want to find out. I reached for a smoke to mask the stink but changed my mind and decided it would be safer to keep my cigarette lighter closed and, in my pocket, away from this booze hound.

After a few more vague words of explanation for my intrusion, I handed over the pint of cheap whiskey as promised. I usually kept a stash of cheap booze in my heap's glove box for just such emergencies. She immediately rewarded me with her pass key to explore Frank Murphy's basement apartment at my leisure. Said she thought she'd seen him leave the premises earlier with a large valise and had no idea where he was going, how long he would be gone, or when he planned to return. The valise in hand though, was a good sign he was going somewhere special for a while, so I could explore without interruption.

I left her struggling to uncork her dessert and rapidly descended down the stairs to inspect Murphy's chamber somewhere in the catacombs below. The hallway leading to his dungeon was decorated by cobwebs and dust clinging to a series of low wattage bulbs protruding from the ceiling at random intervals. In spite of the lighting, the basement appeared gloomier than the upper level, if that was possible, and smelled worse. Several exposed pipes running overhead dripped something on the bare concrete floor, a musty odor from the dampness adding to the unpleasant ambiance. This dump was a rat's playground, and this crumb must have fit right in. His cave number was at the end of the tunnel furthest from the stairwell. I approached as silently as possible, tiptoeing around the puddles, and surveyed both sides as I advanced to spot anyone else aware of my presence. If they were inside their dens, they were equally quiet and didn't hear me coming. I thought I heard a radio playing behind one of the dumps doors and listened outside for a few seconds. But I was wrong. I didn't hear voices or anything else stirring inside, including Murphy's. Satisfied with all the tenant's doors remaining closed, I eased the key into his lock, silently opened the door, and slipped inside.

Across the room, the dirty half window studded with the security steel bars was covered by a cheap motheaten lace curtain and backed up by a tape patched roller window shade pulled part way down. Enough daylight still penetrated through the bottom of the curtain, so I didn't need the lights on. But the sun peeking inside was too weak to mask the moldy, damp odor that clung to everything. I could see the sidewalk outside was still active with the foot traffic I'd been part of earlier. But from inside, it was visible only from the knee down, if you were lucky. It was a depressing view through the jail house bars unless a shapely dame wearing a loose skirt in a sudden tornado just happened to be passing by when you were looking outside.

I wasn't sure how long I had to survey this dump, so didn't waste any time and began to investigate. A quick scan around this small one-bedroom fleabag told me it was sparsely furnished in early Salvation Army, but in spite of the vintage of his used junk, everything appeared to be clean, neat, and organized. He'd learned to keep his possessions in order, almost military ship-shape while in the slammer. From the Spartan lack of possessions, Frank wasn't the sentimental type either. He obviously traveled light and was used to being on the run. The furniture was temporary at best.

At first, there didn't seem to be much to go on, but what was there was still telling, as I'd soon find out. Several well-trod oriental carpets were scattered here and there across the floors in the tiny four rooms. I decided to check out the bedroom first and save the small living room for last.

A single bed in a chipped black metal frame took up most of the space. Across the room sat a scuffed- up five- drawer wood highboy dresser. It was topped with a framed mirror on a stand, a clean hair brush with a comb stuck in the bristles, a white ceramic ashtray from the Wave Crest Hotel on Catalina Island containing an odd assortment of change, a couple of tokens for public transportation, a small, well-worn bone- handled pocket knife, a couple sticks of Beemans Clove chewing gum and a half deck of Chesterfield cigarettes with a pack of matches labeled *Shanghai Ruby's* stuffed under the cellophane wrapper. I pulled out the matches. There was nothing written inside. I shoved them back. Crimped under the edge of the mirror frame, a small grainy black- and- white photograph of a couple in their late teens or early twenties held my attention. A smiling youthful blonde and a skinny serious rat-faced young man, both standing like stiff boards in baggy bathing suits, glared back at the camera. They were holding hands at a beach, somewhere I couldn't identify, and trying to have fun. I thought she looked familiar. He didn't, not yet anyway.

All the dresser drawers contained newer, slightly damp clothes neatly folded and stacked, nothing else. I looked around for more and opened a corner closet reeking with an overtone of mothballs to disguise the damp odor. It contained a new dark gray fedora, size 6 3/4 placed on a shelf, and two new double-breasted pin stripe suits with the price tags still attached. One was in charcoal and one in slate gray. Both were well- tailored from an Izzy's Haberdashery in Long Beach that I'd never heard of, and both carried a size 38 label. He wasn't a big man, and I'd bet my last C note that he was a cocky little bastard, too. Beside them , several stiff starched dress shirts on hangers with paper covering the shoulders, half a dozen flashy hand-painted ties drooped over another rack, a couple with dancing girls, I would have liked myself. Two pairs of lightly worn black Florsheim shoes in size 8 1/2 that were sitting on the floor caught my attention. I noticed the leather was already sporting a light hazy coating of mold inside.

The guy's taste in clothing wasn't bad for a newly released jailbird. From the unworn condition of these threads, he must have been holding out for a special occasion. Maybe someone's funeral … maybe his.

There was also something else that all the best dressed thugs were wearing, a well-oiled handgun. His was a .38 cal. Colt police special revolver with a 6" barrel. It was loaded, ready for action, and hanging in a right-handed shoulder rig, next to a box of spare ammo also parked on the back shelf next to the hat. Now that was a nice piece to come up against. Not in the same league as my .357 mag. but in the right hands would still punch a man-size hole in your gut. This guy was itching for a repeat visit to either the big house or a long rest in a pine box. I wondered what other cannon he was pack'n right now. I turned to close the door when I caught something else out of the corner of my eye that I'd almost missed. The two shoe boxes neatly propping up his new shoes. I decided to see if they were empty or, did he have a fetish for more footwear.

I brushed the shoes aside and took a peek. And what do you know? Each was jammed with stacks of neatly arranged bundles of twenty-dollar bills. I riffled through a pack and noticed they were as fresh and crisp as the day they'd arrived at a bank teller's window. What the hell had this guy been up to? I slipped a couple out of the stack into my coat pocket for evidence. Then returned the boxes of dough back into position and decided to keep looking. This was getting interesting.

An equally distressed wooden nightstand next to the bed was stacked with well-thumbed girlie magazines scattered across the top. An ashtray lifted from the Franklin Hotel in San Pedro was filled with cigarette butts, some just stubbed out and some with a shiny red lipstick that looked familiar. Inside the only drawer, a deck of playing cards labeled Starlight Casino, Catalina Island again waited for another game of solitaire and a pack of condoms ... opened and bragging, now that several were missing. Well, that was more like it. At least now I knew something specific that he'd been up to.

I shoved the drawer back inside, but noticed it didn't want to slide in all the way. I pulled it back out again. Hidden behind the drawer was another bundle of those crisp unspent twenty-dollar bills taped inside to the back, acting like a door stop. I helped myself to several more of the double sawbucks, slipped them into my pocket to join the others, and returned the rest to their hiding place. That must have been his backup stash, just in case the other was discovered first and left as a decoy. I looked around for a telephone with a matching phone number to the one in my Ruby's match book, nothing. He must be using one somewhere else in the building. I'd look for it later.

Back in the living room , aside from the odd table lamps, faded tapestry sofa, a matching easy chair and a window table holding a Philco radio, a half bottle of Old Grand-Dad whiskey, and a couple of water tumblers, there wasn't much else to bother with, unless...

The table stationed underneath the window was round. Just maybe there was another side to it that you couldn't see. I pulled aside a straight-backed wooden chair that was shoved underneath, grabbed the edges with both hands, and gave it a quiet spin. I wasn't disappointed.

The other side facing the wall contained another drawer. This guy was one surprise after another. I slid it open. It contained a pad of cheap news print paper, a fountain pen, and a bottle of blue/black ink. I scribbled a couple of sample sentences on the pad with his pen, tore off the page, folded, and shoved it into my coat pocket, underneath the pad of paper, something else, a copy of a recent scratch sheet from Hollywood Park race track. Mr. Murphy not only liked to bet on the ponies, he'd also gotten a tip and circled his favorite … Miss Be'haven. According to the news clip I was carrying from McCullen, that nag turned out to be a clear winner for the same race. And, next to that, a schedule of seaplane flights to Catalina with one leaving today underlined.

Well what do you know ? I'd hit a home run in this dump. I turned the table back around the way I'd found it and took one fast tour of the small kitchen and bathroom. Finding there only the usual accouterments and nothing more, I decided it was way past my time to leave. I had plenty to go on already.

I searched the long hallway for a house phone and found one near the base of the stair well. The telephone number on the face of the wall mount was the same as the number on the inside of the matches I'd found at the Blue Parrott. Things were starting to shape together, but that would be only one of them. I'd keep looking.

I stopped back by Lynette Tatum's apartment on the way out to drop off the key. She was already half in the bag when I knocked. This time, I held my breath. It wouldn't work. The door flew open, followed by another wave of fetid aromas, foul enough to curl wallpaper. Droopy eye slumped against the door frame and tried to refocus on my kisser to identify who I was and drew a blank. After I'd refreshed her memory, she mumbled she didn't remember either me or loaning me a key in the first place, then hi-cupped a couple of times and absently stuffed the key back into her apron pocket. Edgy to continue her evening buzz, she ended our chat by slamming the door in my face. I wasn't insulted … just thankful.

By the time I hit the street again, the sun had disappeared, and the foot traffic was well on its way home out of this crummy neighborhood where the air was hopefully fresher. The street lights were already on, casting gloomy shadows across the vacant sidewalks. Ominous thoughts flashed by of what lurked within the darkened portals of the surrounding buildings and the damp, litter- strewn alleys in between.

I glanced around, didn't see anybody important, just a shabby bum aimlessly pushing a cart of junk across the street. I climbed into the Buick, reached for the dashboard lighter, and touched off another weed. Sitting there on the deserted street, I thought about what Frank Murphy meant in my picture so far. Who the hell was this character, and how did he fit in? He left behind a trail of clues that all pointed to one thing, at least a definite connection to the dead bottle blonde at The Blue Parrott, and that spelled trouble, big trouble.

I stared vacantly ahead through a dirty windshield in a daze. The jumbled pieces collected so far danced across the top of my dashboard, like cardboard marionettes and all out of sequence. Clouded by the cigarette smoke curling out the side wing window, I tried to piece them into some semblance of order that made sense out of this mess; same cigarette brand and butts with same colored lipstick stains, Joey DeCosta and his winning horse selected on a racing form, a trunk load of new clothes, plenty of stashed dough from somewhere and matching note paper. From the stolen souvenirs, I knew he was no stranger to Catalina Island, the black and white photograph of some young couple, and finally his matchbook connection to Shanghai Ruby's. I shook my head. Maybe nothing but cobwebs so far … and then maybe not.

I had more to go on than usual. But I wasn't any closer to the brunette in McCullen's story than I was when he first walked into my office, or was I? I'd continue to muddle it over later.

The dashboard clock signaled it was time to visit Ruby's for more information on McCullen's dame. Following up anymore tonight on Murphy, the ex-con, would have to wait. He was already on his way to an offshore island that I was also scheduled to visit in another day anyway. I'd track him down then, if he was still there.

I instinctively squeezed the .357 under my left arm for assurance, snuffed out the butt in the ashtray, and fired up the black beauty. Slipping into a light stream of early evening traffic, I headed towards Shanghai Ruby's and further entanglements.

Chapter Nine

A cool evening fog straight off the ocean was finding its way ashore as I worked my way over to Anaheim Street. in fading traffic and on into the port area. Docked merchant cargo freighters, a Navy ship repair yard sporting sky-high heavy lift cranes, and an assortment of decommissioned military battleships waiting for the wrecking ball loomed in the distance like marooned ghosts. I slipped past the old Terminal Island Fleet Air base and continued creeping through the misty curtain at a slow and cautious pace until I hit Avalon Street.

Ruby's would be off the next turn on Neptune Avenue, right on the waterfront docks. It was a former cannery warehouse, still with an unpretentious orange-tinged , rusted galvanized roof over a matching rustic metal siding with Shanghai Ruby's painted in large red weathered lettering outlined in black on the sides. It stood out amongst the docked ships and adjacent storage warehouses like a flashy beacon trolling for lost sailors and slumming couples. I circled past the barely visible winking entrance sign several times, still mulling over my findings so far, then gave up and whipped into the surprisingly well-lit parking lot. Tossing out a half-smoked Lucky , I braked next to a parking valet. He stuck out his hand automatically. I reluctantly tossed him the keys to my heap and dug out some dough for his trouble. I crossed my fingers and watched him squeeze my sedan in between a couple of late model high end autos , a light-colored Cadillac Fleetwood sedan and a dark Lincoln Continental. I noticed some of the others in the lot were also late models with plenty of flashy chrome, probably freshly washed and now covered in condensation. The numerous Packard's and a few Chryslers or two were outflanked by the other jalopies also vying for equal space and relegated to another self-parking section towards the back, that I didn't know existed beforehand. My Buick with the patched up bullet holes fit right in here someplace, probably closer to the self-parking area.

Several slumming couples crowding together ahead of me dressed stylishly, not formal, but probably well-heeled, were now rubbing elbows with the regular customers also jockeying for the post position at the entrance. Most were an odd assortment of characters dredged up from the various merchant marine and military ships at dock and an assortment of lowlifes from blue-collar neighborhoods in and around San Pedro and Long Beach. They were the usual backbone in dives like this. But something was now different. From my past recollection of Ruby's, this appeared from the outside to be a fancier layout. Quite a departure from the rough-cut saloon I'd seen here before and expected to see again tonight. I wondered where she'd gotten the dough for this set up.

Before entering, I stood in the parking lot surveying this new joint and sucking in some of the damp salt air commingled with the fresh smell of the ocean and the surrounding wharf. Barnacle encrusted creosote coated pilings, fish, and the usual odor of decomposing seaweed typically accompanying waterfront dives like this assailed my senses and recalled numerous pleasant times spent at sea on board the *Black Swan*. This probably wouldn't be one of them.

I glanced upwards. Lots of neon flashed above the multi-story galvanized sided building, illuminating the exterior and the interior through a long bank of partially open sliding paneled windows running lengthwise across the front behind the entrance porch. From where I was standing, Ruby's was remodeled in a South Pacific style with oriental overtones. It was reminiscent of a decadent Chinese opium den or a dilapidated, darkened warehouse containing an assortment of wooden cargo crates bearing mysterious inscriptions, low ceilings with hanging kerosene lanterns, shady characters packing weapons, and speaking confidentially at candle lit tables. They'd be drinking watered- down booze, eating overpriced meals, and making shadowy transactions. Desperate dames of every nationality, size, and shape wearing too much makeup, skin-tight dresses, and costing you a week's wages for their company would treat you roughly in a back room. And you'd return for more after next payday.

It was the current theme in nightclubs, bars, and restaurants popping up around Los Angeles. But in this rundown port located along the gloomy, damp docks close to the harbor cities, Ruby's was a natural. The decadent location just added to its appeal to both the high and the lowbrows, now crowding to get inside and blow their hard-earned dough.

Numerous blazing torches stood like sentries marking the entrance under the galvanized tin roof. Serious security was posted outside and seemed prepared to slug or shoot their way out of any tight spots if necessary. For some reason, I felt trouble was brewing and wasn't far removed from this joint. Several nervous beefy oriental thugs wearing tell-tale custom suit coats hiding heavy iron were stationed near the front entrance and pretending to act nonchalant with the arriving customers. But they were also keeping a close eye on activity around the parked vehicles.

The parking valets, who also appeared to be pack'n heat, were casting nervous glances toward the goons on guard and were a tip-off. I felt something was in the wind and would be blowing soon, maybe tonight. I didn't need to be part of it but wouldn't shy away if confronted.

After the crowd thinned out, I edged past the entrance and glanced around inside. It was large, smoky, and noisy, filled with couples dining and drinking something sprouting small umbrellas at candle lit tables. A long overflowing bar flanked one wall on the right, and a kitchen door next to the bar flopped back and forth continuously. Off to one side, a stairway to heaven beckoned for the high rollers, a darkened hallway to somewhere in the back called out for the low rollers. A Negro dance band on a raised bandstand towards the back blared through the din. It featured a wailing saxophone no one was listening to, competing for attention with several other instruments. I thought I recognized the well-dressed sax soloist and tossed him a grin and short wave. He continued to play, and I wasn't sure he spotted me. I'd catch up to him later.

Sheets of plaited bamboo covered the unfinished industrial walls, and dried stuffed fish dangling from the ceiling were plastered everywhere, trying to act tropical. Private booths, mostly occupied, were sprinkled along the side opposite the bar, now jammed with sailors and other locals jostling for a stool or standup elbow space and working on an early buzz.

Several intriguing hustlers wearing colorful tight satin dresses short enough to reach under,fresh-cut flowers in their hair and makeup no thicker than waffle batter , circulated around the suckers pushingwatered-down booze, over-priced champagne, and a shoulder to dream on later.

The joint was maybe a little more polished than before, but not that much had changed. It was still fronting for a waterfront whorehouse from any angle you looked at it, except now it had a dining, dancing, musical twist to reel in the slummers. There was still too much incense, too much- spilled booze, too many fights, and the floors were still too sticky. Anyway you looked at a dump like this, you still couldn't mask the stink, regardless of how hard you tried. In spite of the trappings and depending on which side of the room you were standing on, it still smelled like tired construction laborers, disinfectants, and trouble. I'd seen it all, too many times before. I'd find an empty spot, order a drink and ask around.

I smiled at one of the circulating cupcakes wearing a red hibiscus behind one ear, a mini sky blue satin number and a slippery kisser plastered with enough fire engine red lipstick for a dozen sailors and said, "I'll just sit at the bar for now, sweetheart. I want to talk to Ruby, if she's here. I'm an old friend of hers from Frisco. Tell her it's Thornton, Matthew Thornton."

She looked disappointed I wasn't there for the booze and a tumble later. It didn't take her long to recover after I slipped her a fin, followed by a firm tap on her rear to get moving with my message. She tossed me another "maybe later" smile over her shoulder and evaporated into the crowd with my dough. Hopefully it was to find Ruby as I'd asked, but I wouldn't bet on it.

I slid onto an empty barstool between a sweat- stained stevedore straight from the docks and nattily attired businessman in dark double-breasted threads, both probably planning to cheat on their "sweethearts" and ordered a beer. The bulky oriental bartender looked familiar. I couldn't place him.

I usually never forget a face or a head shaped like a block of cement with a personality to match. There was something about that guy I didn't like. He was the missing link all right, and I knew if it came back to me, we'd probably clash.

I lit up a cigarette and didn't have long to wait for my suds. Blockhead deposited an ice-cold mug in front of me with a shark-eyed grin like he recognized me too and then returned to his other customers towards the far end of the bar. I didn't like his look any better up close and continued to think about it as he drifted into the background.

* * *

The first pull on a cold brew is always the best, and this was no exception. After a couple more to wet the pallet, I felt better and settled in to wait for Ruby. The background music had died off, and I noticed in the mirror behind the bar, the couples dancing were returning to their tables. A bulky fellow wearing a dark tux with shoulders wide enough to touch both sides of a door frame at the same time threaded his way through the crowd in my direction. His gleaming smile, plastered on an inky black glistening face could only belong to one person.

"Joshua Keys," I said with a grin, turning around. I slid my stool back and grabbed his out stretched paw for a firm shake.

"Mr. Matt. I wasn't sure it was you when you come in, but now I knows it's you," he said, his smile widening further than the Grand Canyon.

We both sat down at an adjacent table, and I caught the attention of the blockhead glaring at mypal from behind the bar. I motioned to him to hit us for another cold one and still didn't like the sour look on his ugly mug when he turned to pull the tap.

"Joshua, don't you think it's time you dropped the Mr.? Just call me Matt, okay? We've known each other long enough." I tapped out another smoke and snapped open my lighter.

"Okay, that's just fine with me, too," he said. "Miss Sam she say I should, but I say, I'm not going to unless Mr. Matt say it's okay. Nows you do."

I smiled at that.

A full- figured cupcake waitress spilling out of a peek-a-boo top arrived with his beer, bending lower than necessary over our table with the delivery. Josh shot me a conspiratorial grin, shaking his head from side to side, mumbling something incoherent under his breath. I didn't catch it but understood what he was thinking anyway. He then smacked his lips and emptied half the cold draft in one swig as his eyes followed the cutie pie melting into the background.

That first cold taste generated a confirming nod from him as well, and he grinned again like an overstuffed kid on his first trip to a big city restaurant.

He quietly took another pull on his frosty mug and, working himself up to something serious, said with a frown, "I gots only a fifteen- minute break here, Matt, but I'm glad to sees you again."

"Me too, you play a mean sax, Josh. Your band?"

"Yes, sir, it sure nuff is. And dat's my brother Moses ober dere, too," he said, proudly pointing to the young, slim drummer in a snappy tuxedo that I'd heard on a solo riff that could give Gene Krupa a run for his money. "Dat's who I wants to ask you abouts."

We both now had something to discuss, and with only his short break, we'd have to work fast before we were interrupted. Watching him savor his suds, I thought back to those days he was a contender for the Army middle weight boxing championship. He was a good strong puncher, could take the punishment as well, and came equipped with all the right credentials; big, strong, and tough, but not good enough to clinch the title. After getting defeated too many times, he was washed up in the Army boxing game and reassigned for the war's duration as a cook, truck driver, and grave digger. He returned to civilian life no better than he'd left it and picked up the pieces with menial jobs; janitor, dishwasher, stockyard laborer, before he caught on permanently working as a bouncer, bartender and all around helper at Sam's Saloon on Melrose Avenue, right around the corner from my office.

Samantha Malone, a knock-out platinum blonde with a heart of gold, a face that rivaled Jean Harlow's, and a soft body that you couldn't get enough of, gave him a jump start on a better life. Her show-girl legs that kept her in the movie chorus line musicals until she retired allowed her to become a well-off saloon owner, and that's where I caught up with him again. It was a step up, but now he'd added a musical side to his ambitions as well. I'd heard he played the sax part-time, in a jazz band at the black and tan Alabam Club situated next door to the Dunbar Hotel on Central Avenue's colored section in L.A. Now, here he was again in another mixed color joint on San Pedro's waterfront, pouring heart into his music and hoping to kick start his life in another direction with his own band.

"Okay, Josh, what gives?"

He'd finished his beer already and was looking around for a refill, almost ignoring my question. Maybe he was stalling, but he seemed to be more worried and apprehensive about something else. I caught our waitress by the waist as she cruised by and told her to bring two more cold ones. I checked my watch for the time. It was running out.

"Josh, you said you wanted to ask me something about your brother, right? I'm all ears."

"My brother's the one that knows about this place we play'n in now. He say he know a man when he's in jail, and they talk'n about this here Shanghai Ruby's. Dat man he tells, Moses, dat he got connections here and if he wants to play his music here, he go'n to arrange it. Moses been tell'n him about my playing jazz at the Alabam and that him and me we make'n our own band when he gets out."

"Okay, so where's the problem? Sounds like that's what you're doing. Didn't know you had a brother or one in jail, but so what? Is there more?"

"They sho is." He grabbed the latest cold draft almost before it hit the table, helped himself to a generous swig and continued. "We get's us in here, but I don't like what I been hear'n about this here Ruby's or Moses' fren. He's no good, Mr. Matt. Moses, he say to me..."

He was starting to get worked up, sweating a little, and caught himself talking louder than he should have if he had something confidential to say. He nervously glanced around to see if anyone was coming our way or had overheard him so far. I noticed his brother was still busy talking to someone by the bandstand and I didn't think anyone had been listening or was interested in our conversation, but the same thing crossed my mind. I nodded for him to grab his beer and follow me over to another empty table with more privacy closer to the wall in one corner. We dropped into place and I pumped him for more.

"Okay, that's a little quieter. Now, what's the other guy's name and what's his connection to this joint? Maybe we can get to the bottom of this before we both run out of gas tonight, okay?" I said, taking a fresh pull on my own brew and anxious to move the conversation into my territory.

"He calls hisself Frank sumpin and he been say'n Moses and me and the brothers in this band, we need to join some organization that's for our own goods. I don't like what I been hear'n, It don't sound right. We jus like playing our music, Mr. Matt, but Mr. Frank he say, that's not good nuff, if we want to keep playing here or somewheres else. What's I going to do?"

"What's the organization he's talking about, Josh?"

"I don't know, but he show me a card with some writ'n on it I don't unnerstand. I don't read so good, you know. It's my eyes. They not see'n so good like befo my boxing."

It wasn't his eyes. I don't think he was ever much of a reader, before or after his Army boxing days, but during the war they drafted anybody that would follow orders and keep their mouth shut. Somebody higher up would do the thinking. I didn't press the issue, just listened.

"He say dat's going to cost us sumpin to joins too. I talks to Moses and he say we needs to join, if'n we wants to keep work'n, but I's not so sure."

"Don't get pushed around, chum. Don't sign up for anything unless someone you trust reads it first."

"Dat's why I's talk'n to you Mr. Matt. Miss Sam, she say she trusts you and me too's."

"Okay, pal, thanks. I'll look into it."

He sat back, smiled and took another relieved swig, pleased that he'd unloaded his worry onto my already loaded shoulders . It was one more thing I didn't need, but this sounded like either a union squeeze or something worse. Maybe they were connected. I'd dealt with local union goons in the past, but this might be bigger, if I was right. From what I'd been hearing from the city undercurrent and reading in the local rags, it was spelled out loud and clear to those that could read between the lines. In spite of the upsweep in the country's prosperity, there was an odor creeping out from all the dusty farms, smoke- stack factories, mines, and labor work camps spread across the country. Ever since the war was over, all the cracks and crannies from New York to Los Angeles harboring clusters of dissatisfied men and women feeling entitled to a bigger share of the action than they'd earned, were targeted and easy pickings for the troublemaking Communist agitators spreading the manure of social control and domination by a higher authority for the betterment of all. It was stinking in the wind and smelling worse than a brick of Limburger cheese on a hot engine block. This membership pressure for musicians and other entertainers to join something for their own good sounded like just another layer of the disease, those rats would be spreading next.

Joshua's disclosure played right down my alley, and now I knew I was on the right track, but it was more complicated than I originally imagined. I just had to fill in the missing pieces, sort out the deck for the jokers, see which cards fell into place, and place my bet on a winning hand before the whole house of cards collapsed around me.

"What's this Franks connection to this joint?"

"He tell Moses, dat he connected to da club owner."

"What? Is he oriental? I thought that guy was white?"

"I don't know? Maybe, he both. He sure nuff looks white to me, but his eyes dey do look kinda funny?"

"You mean, a little slanted like the Chinese?'

"Yes, maybe dat's it. Like dem Chinese eyes, kinda squinty.

"You sure about that?"

'No, I coulds be wrong," he muttered, unsure of what he'd just given me for a description. I dropped it.

I pulled out the newspaper clipping of Joey DeCosta's twist and laid it on the table, pointing to her. "You ever see this Frank character with either a good-looking dame that looks like this brunette here or maybe with another well stacked blonde that wears a flashy ankle bracelet?"

He polished off the dregs in his beer glass, touching the picture, thinking about it and said, "The blonde, she been here befo. She sits wid dat Mr. Frank ober der," he nodded toward a private booth off in one corner. "De sometimes talks for awhile and den leaves together. De woman's in dat picture wid dark hair, she show is fine look'n too. Dey bof is, especially dat blonde. One time I sees dat one wid da dark hair sit'n together wid dat blonde and da mens. They talk'n like fren's."

"Another man, too?"

"She usually sits at da bar, talk'n to a man ware'n a nice suit. Not likes dem," he said, pointing to a couple of rough-cut blue collar characters sitting at one end of the bar, probably locals that worked in the ship yards.

I glanced over his shoulder at the musicians gathering over by the bandstand, getting into position to begin playing again and knew his information bank was closing shop. "Okay, Josh, thanks for the scoop. Looks like we're through for now, pal. Time to get back on that honk'n goose."

He smiled, slid his chair back with a squeak on the floor, shook my hand again with that iron grip firm enough to rattle your choppers and ambled back to continue playing another set, relieved I was going to settle his problem.

I sat back down, tossed down the rest of my suds and lit another Lucky while I digested Josh's comments. This Frank character was connected to Ruby's nightclub all right and seemed to be a key number in this mess. He was pushing something on the colored musicians and I already knew what it was, even if Josh didn't. He also knew the blonde cutie that was snuffed out at the Blue Parrot. The Ava Gardner clone was a player here also, but where did she and McCullen fit in? Was he the other man in the nice suit?

The real question now was, what did they all have in common if anything and how did they all fit together into this scheme muddling around in my brain. It was still far from enough to go on.

Chapter Ten

ood was being served all around me and in spite of my overall impression of this joint; the smell streaming past on the steaming trays from the kitchen was making me hungry. I stopped another circulating cutie wearing a yellow orchid in her hair, ordered another beer and a menu. She snatched a loose copy off the bar and I scanned the choices, while I waited for my next cold round. I didn't intend to eat here, especially a full course dinner, but the pork dinner combinations appeared to be a sure bet as a house favorite from what I could see others were eating. Maybe I'd grab something here after all, before I left tonight.

I tossed the menu aside, took a sip of my fresh beer and glanced at my watch. It was later than I expected. I was startled by a shadow crossing my table and glanced up. This dish had silently floated over from somewhere in the main dining area and stopped in front of me. I slid back, stood up and was greeted not by Ruby as I expected, but another smiling oriental knockout. She was unusually attractive, more so than Ruby or any of the others I'd seen drifting around this room tonight. She looked more Eurasian than pure Oriental. A beautiful light olive skinned combination of something exotic that you couldn't classify and didn't want to.

She appeared to be in her mid-twenties, sophisticated and from the way she approached my table, carried it off with a touch of arrogance. Her shiny raven black hair was swept across her shoulders, cut off straight above the eyes and left loose and lively in the soft candle light when she moved her head. Her sparkling eyes and gleaming white teeth were set in a face meant to fall in love with. After one look, I was halfway there. This doll wore no over the top makeup like all the others. Slightly oval almond shaped dark eyes, gently arched accented eye brows and flaming red lipstick on a puckered mouth, hinted at a tantalizing dame that knew how to use her assets, possibly as your worst weapon. Her well-proportioned body was intriguingly packaged in a skin-tight black oriental silk dress custom designed to discretely expose her breasts. Decorated with embroidered full-length golden dragons entwined from front to back, it was slit to mid-thigh on one side, exposing perfectly proportioned legs. She was balanced on black stiletto heels high enough to give you vertigo just looking. From whatever scent she was wearing; maybe sandalwood or lavender, she was intoxicating.

Before she'd even spoken a word, I knew this was one dangerous dame. She had a hint of everything imaginable; every mystery of the orient, from tantalizing sex, to anything illegal, immoral or toxic. It was all wrapped up in one ravishing package, including your trip to the city morgue … if you weren't careful.

She was balancing a black slender cigarette holder like an ice pick with a dab of shiny red lip stick on one end, the other tipped in gold, contained a smoldering cigarette. When she spoke, her mellow seductive voice took me by surprise. It drifted in my direction like an unexpected ocean fog rolling across the deck of my boat at sea after dark, foretelling a disaster lurking … dead ahead.

"Mr. Thornton? I heard you were in town tonight. I'm so glad you decided to stop at *Shanghai Ruby's*," she said, then breathlessly continuing without a pause. "I've heard so much about you. We finally meet. I'm called Jade, Black Jade, but my friends call me Noir. Please do."

"Just call me Matthew. That's black in French, isn't it? Nice, I like it … suits you."

I offered her my hand. She shot me a guarded smile, not sure how I meant the compliment, and extended hers for me to grasp. It was smooth and cool to the touch, like a reptile in the grass and I didn't hold onto it for long. I had a strong feeling this babe would be a challenge to connect with. Her dark eyes under those arched eyebrows were locked on mine like two Cobras on high alert and made me feel uneasy, especially her comment about knowing ahead of time I was coming here tonight.

I pulled out the chair and she sat across from me, tapping out the ash on her cigarette in the ashtray, never losing her composure. This Noir babe was a smooth almost bloodless character all right and knew how to hold her cards. I glanced over her shoulder toward the bar and blockhead was locked onto both of us like a magnet, watching and waiting for our next move. I'd have to be cautious around here; there were too many eyes and ears following me tonight starting with him.

I tapped out a Lucky for myself and snapped a light from one of the courtesy packs on the table. It was a mirror to the match pack in my pocket that I'd picked up at the Blue Parrot. "I was hoping to speak with Ruby. We were very close at one time. Is she here tonight?"

"She told us about you many times. So sorry to tell you, Matthew, but Ruby is no longer with us."

"Oh, I'm sorry to hear that, Noir. Maybe I'll speak with her another time."

"I do not think so. She died in San Francisco. I am her daughter."

I was shocked and disappointed with this news of Ruby's death and had never heard her speak of this dish before either. This evening was already taking a strange turn, and I began feeling uncomfortable.

I blew out a stream of smoke towards the ceiling and said, "I-ah…a didn't know she had a daughter."

From the surprised look on my face, she read my mind and decided to fill in the pieces, no doubt selectively. "Actually, I am her adopted daughter, but that is another story for another time. My sister and I were brought back to the states from China several years ago when we were young. Now I own Shanghai Ruby's. My sister Pearl is called Apricot Blossom. She also runs a massage parlor and curio shop not far from here in Chinatown, where they sometimes play Mah Jong in the back parlor. You might like to attend?"

I nodded, smiled politely, lied and said, "I might," and tossed off the last of my beer.

I wasn't the least bit interested in getting my rod oiled by a masseuse, shopping in an Oriental junk shop, or penny-ante gambling at board games with old-timers. It was probably a front for illegal activity anyway, which

I'd uncover when I had more time. However, it did sound intriguing.

I could see this wasn't going to be easy obtaining the information I needed. I didn't want this lead to dry up before it even started, so just played along. I had a feeling it would be difficult to get her to open up with something I could use without a lot of foreplay in the diplomacy department. I hoped I was wrong. I might have to escalate my persuasive tactics.

"Would you join me for a cocktail? I'll have another beer, also."

She didn't hesitate and said something serious to a passing oriental waitress in Mandarin. I'd been to the Orient and knew enough to understand that what she ordered was straight forward. No funny business with loaded drinks, at least not yet anyway. Instead of the flowered waitress delivering the drinks, blockhead quickly appeared at our table with a deadpan expression, delivering some concoction for her in a tall glass covered with one of those miniature bamboo umbrellas and a brew refill for me.

I watched the way she sipped her drink slowly and deliberately. She quietly observed me at the same time, like she was sizing me up for something I wasn't planning. My beer was a safer drink than one with alcohol and tasted okay. She moved very cautiously with calculated gestures measured just enough to throw you off balance. She held her sleek black cigarette holder poised like a weapon in a pale slim hand of red lacquered nails sharper than talons. On the index finger on her right hand, she wore a black jade ring large enough to bust down a door. That I didn't trust and had seen smaller, that contained enough poison to drop a charging bull. Those deep dark snake eyes of hers darted back and forth across my face like a serpent's tongue testing the air to find out what I wanted. She was playing the smooth Oriental game of forcing me to show my hand first before divulging too much information herself. I'd played that game before with Ruby, so was onto her. First, I'd order some dinner and then work my way in slowly from there.

She suggested we move into a side booth reserved for VIPs that was quieter and more secluded, where she would join me for dinner. She directed me to the one with a semitransparent bamboo bead covering over the opening, adding to the illusion of privacy. Once settled inside in the semicircular booth, we were just as private and comfortable as if we'd nestled into a private room of our own. She sat close but preferred an angle facing me, close enough to allow her leg to casually touch mine.

In between courses of dinner, Black Jade presented a vague history of Ruby with her involvement in the Tong takeover in San Francisco's Chinatown and her death from an explosion in a friend's restaurant that she was visiting about a year ago. She and her sister's rise to power afterword's in L.A., and this Shanghai Ruby's supper club was then set in motion. Both girls were originally bought from a Geisha training temple where they learned the subtle arts of pleasing gentlemen. She alluded again to her sister's business, the Full Moon House of Pleasure, in Chinatown L.A., if I was interested. It became apparent that they were offering illegal gambling, probably also selling dope as well as prostitution, and who knows what else.

What I really wanted to know was about the elusive Frank Murphy and what he was doing at Shanghai Ruby's with his blonde girl friend and the brunette Ava G. look-alike. That was still a mystery. She knew nothing about the subjects and clammed up when questioned.

We'd finished eating, and I realized I'd struck out with this dish. Her well of information was vague at best, and only if it concerned nothing, I was really interested in. I was planning to call it an evening when she made a final proposition, which I suspected was on her agenda right from the beginning.

"Matthew, I think it's time for us to get a little better acquainted, don't you?" she said, giving me a sly, coy smile with a raised eyebrow and stubbing her after-dinner cigarette out in the ashtray. She'd kicked off one of her stiletto shoes sometime during our meal and punctuated her suggestion with a raised foot planted firmly between my legs, her toes manipulating my responsive … her intended objective.

Naturally, I rose to the occasion, but didn't trust this babe. Especially after the sketchy background details, she'd reluctantly fed me about Ruby's demise and the particulars concerning her sister's probable illegal operations in Chinatown. I'd let it ride. I knew where this latest play was going and had to be cautious. I might wind up as a side order of chop suey for ignoring the warning signs.

"I have my own private apartment located upstairs. I know we can be more comfortable. You can explore Noir's most intimate pleasures in harmony. You see."

It wasn't spoken so much as a request but more as an assumed decision that would be mutually agreed upon without question. She expected me to follow blindly, but I wasn't falling for it. I noticed she'd cast a sly deliberate glance in the direction of blockhead the bartender when we exited the booth. He nodded back to her that he understood the meaning of her gaze and reached for a telephone sitting on the counter behind him to make a call.

I was prepared myself. Something unexpected was in the wind as we threaded our way through the crowded main dining room towards the back. She led me down a private, darkened carpeted hallway that had an overpowering odor of pungent incense. Other closed rooms of possible pleasure were situated on either side, and I envisioned the action going on inside. I walked close to the doors listening but couldn't hear anything from inside the rooms as we passed. Maybe it was too early, or maybe they were just storage rooms after all.

She led the way. I held a hand rail ascending a steep dimly lit stairway. It was covered in a plush red carpet deep enough to get lost in. Other than some muffled rhythmic clicking sounds, like a hidden metronome mirroring her ascending footsteps, we moved silently upward, unspeaking. The sway of her shapely hips and posterior from my position below was intoxicating. It was a maneuver she'd undoubtedly practiced, guaranteed to lure the unsuspecting, blindly into a spiraling vortex with the possibility of no return. Each stair step upward was executed with calculated precision, knowing her shapely legs in high heels and tight slit skirt held my attention without question.

I glanced behind me numerous times as we proceeded and squeezed the heater in the shoulder rig under my left arm. I was relieved we hadn't been followed, stopped or interfered with, but that didn't mean my eyes were closed. We reached a second-floor landing with a darkened unfriendly hallway leading to what looked like adead-end at the other end. The whole place was gloomy, quiet and cool as a morgue on a Monday morning. We passed several closed doors painted a shiny lacquer black before reaching another closed door, this one painted in shiny red lacquer. I cast a momentary look upwards. For some reason, maybe the height of the ceiling, I felt there was another floor or an attic crawl space above. Black Jade ignored my observation. She unlocked her private apartment entrance with the red door and stepped inside. I cautiously followed. Turning on the lights from a side wall switch, it illuminated a room decorated in colorful Oriental imported furnishings, both stylish and expensive. An over-powering smell of jasmine or other incense permeated your senses upon entering. Carved jade knick-knacks in a variety of colors, ivory in abundance, blue and white glazed jars and other intriguing pottery,hand-carved statues, and other trappings in every size, shape, and colorful design were neatly arranged everywhere. Semitransparent lanterns in orange, reds, and yellows hung from the ceiling. Multicolored tapestry chairs and a sofa with a black lacquer coffee table inlaid with abalone shells with matching end tables and lamps were arranged neatly around the room. The main living room was larger than my entire apartment in L.A. And more lavishly furnished. An ebony-colored standup bar embedded with decorative dragons of abalone shells and matching lacquer stools sat off to one side, waiting for a visiting guest. A teakwood dining set sat off to the other. An assortment of other teak furniture sprinkled in between glowed in the warm ambiance and mood of the room. This place was too opulent for an over-saloon apartment. It must have been set up for a professional business of some kind and gave me the jitters.

She offered me something a little stronger than the beer I had been drinking downstairs as an after-dinner aperitif. A snifter of cognac sounded right for the occasion, but I wasn't fooled by it either. I decided to take a chance. I watched her hands carefully pour out two snifters from the same bottle. It was a relief she didn't pull any funny business when she took a sip from hers first. We made ourselves comfortable on the couch, smiling, chatting amiably about nothing, and sipping our drinks. I was still prepared for foul play on her part and playing it cautious.

After another round, raven hair suggested we'd be more comfortable in her adjoining bedroom. I took a look behind her. More teak, dresser to night stands. The walls were plastered with oriental dragons. This time, inlaid mother of pearl set in panels ofhand-carved teak. The subdued lighting from the surrounding night stand lamps was quickly replaced with numerousincense-laden candles she lit while floating around the room.

I watched as she methodically removed her jewelry and placed it in a hand-carved jewelry box. Then she slipped off her high heels and slithered out of her black dress, followed by her bra, black lace panties, and stockings with more practice than a snake losing its skin. She arranged them neatly on a side chair and turned slowly towards me, proud of her body. She was a beautiful eye-full, all right. I set my cognac snifter aside on a night stand and stripped off my own clothes just as fast, tossing them onto another chair near hers. She slipped close and wrapped her arms around my neck, pressing her warm naked breasts against my chest. Looking up into my face with her dark, dangerous eyes was like peering into a crystal ball and seeing the other side.

Her body was a vision of perfection from her firm, full tilt-up breasts to her body's smooth lines in exact proportions. She was built like a sleek thoroughbred without an ounce of anything extra out of place. Her tongue darted deep into my mouth like the serpent she was. We backed up to the bed, anxious for the main event to get started. She didn't want it tomorrow, and neither did I. I glanced skyward again and didn't like what appeared to be mirrored reflecting tiles situated in the ceiling. There were more around the room walls, maybe for an audience. I didn't think so, but from where I was standing, I couldn't tell for sure.

"Ruby say you like Shanghai Squeeze, yes?" she whispered in my ear. Her hand slipped below my waist and, smiling coyly with raised eyebrows, gripped my throbbing egg roll. "You lie down on back. Noir show you best, okay? I be back in minute," she said, moving away behind a decorative screen, not waiting for my response.

She stood in front of the adjacent dresser mirror, where I could observe her movements. After admiring her reflection, she ran both hands slowly and sensuously over her body as if self-stimulating foreplay. Then, parting her legs, she retrieved two intimately placed shiny spheres, carefully dropping them onto a circular glass jewelry tray. They made a familiar clicking sound as they rolled together, touching the inside rim. Satisfied with her preparation, she returned, smiling. Anxious to continue her way, she faced me with my back to the bed.

I had other ideas. "How about we take another direction on this, doll?" I said.

She looked disappointed and wanted to object but didn't argue. This dish was no novice to any mattress scene. She'd be able to cover the bases regardless of which direction we took, but sunny side up or down was not an option I wanted to debate. I wasn't going to face upwards towards the reflective mirrors under any conditions. Maybe just an old con game, but I wouldn't fall for it.

I spun her around, facing away from me, and bent her over the edge of the bed with my hand firmly placed on her back. She didn't need more instructions. She grasped the covers in tight handfuls, eagerly spreading her legs and cheeks wide. I stroked her slowly and deliberately with my extension. She felt smoother than a piano's keyboard, and I was anxious to tickle her ivory. She purred with my touch, undulating side to side in anticipation. Her love nest was moist and an anxious target for my field cannon. I moved my troops forward.

She rotated her hips several times, anxious for my deep intrusion, moaning with that deep, lusty voice I'd first heard tonight and groaned, "Ride me, Matthew, and hard."

I entered her smoothly and carefully, taking it slow at first before working her up into a passionate rhythm. Twisting and pumping, we were soon both on fire. She grasped and regrasped the bed covers, desperate for a sprint to the finish line. Once I rounded the final turn, I drove her faster and smoother than speed shifting a super-charged Cord into top gear.

"Yes…yes, that's it," she groaned in another gritty tone of ecstasy. "Harder and dee-per."

Her hips and pelvis gyrated smoothly in time with the thrusts I was generating like a primed oil well ready to strike the promised load. Little drops of perspiration beaded on her back, blending with the pool of sweat dripping from my forehead.

This dish was a thoroughbred all right. She knew what she wanted right from the beginning, and so did I. She'd obviously seen plenty of action in the past and been ridden hard at some of the major tracks but still rated the winner's circle. The only thing missing for this filly was a riding crop for that extra push over the edge. She might have liked it, but she wouldn't need it. I had something else in mind.

She was now breathlessly racing for the home stretch in a passionate frenzy. As we neared the finish line, I reached forward and grabbed a fist full of that black mane with one hand and with the other, slapped her firm silky buttocks, producing a startled yelp and instant red welts. The sharp, stinging, cracks were loud enough to drive her into another level of raw, unfettered ecstasy. She didn't flinch or back off. Instead she reached back, digging her claws into my thigh, rough enough to draw blood. She was relishing the punishing ride. I responded, grinding against her naked buttocks, hammering harder than a ten-ton trip hammer banging out license plates in the big house.

That was just the edge she needed, "Now, now … I want now," she pleaded, gripping my stallion in her vice-like snatch with that one final, well-practiced, over the top *Squeeze* she'd been saving for a photo finish. It was good, very good, anyway you looked at it and we both knew it.

After uncoupling, we collapsed on the bed, hot and sweaty. She crawled forward and slipped halfway under the cool sheets. Leaving her tantalizing body partially exposed from the waist up, she reached for her cigarette holder. I lit one for both of us. Instead of sliding in beside her, I reached for my clothes and began getting dressed.

"You like, Matthew? I make best, don't you think? I learn very special," she said, puffing on her smoke and caressing one breast sensuously trying to sell me on an encore. She began working the other hand below stimulating herself again under the sheet. To sweeten the offer, she rimmed her cherry red lips with a wet tongue hoping I'd fall for it.

This dish was tantalizing and she knew it … but, I wasn't buying more. It was time to move on.

"You not going to lie down on bed beside Noir?" she said in a little girl voice pretending to frown and tapping the sheets beside her, trying for a replay.

"Sorry, sweetheart, got to go."

"You hot? You like to take shower instead with, Noir?"

"Not now, baby. I'll get cleaned up later."

I took a final sip of my Cognac and fired up a Lucky. She sipped her Cognac and laid back against the pile of pillows her tousled, black mane of glistening damp hair sweeping across her shoulders, dark eyes sparkling in the flickering candle light.

Maybe she was anxious to have my hands running over her body again or was she just stalling for time? I gave some serious thought to planting another smoldering kiss against those puckered lips and caressing her breasts peeking over the top of the covers, but I resisted. After seeing another bulge in my pants, she was clearly disappointed to see me planning an exit, but seemingly contented with our brief encounter anyway.

"Ruby was right about you, Matthew. It's not exactly the way I planned it, but we were good, weren't we? Will I see you again?"

"I'm not sure, baby. Depends on a lot of things blowing in the wind right now, maybe."

I exhaled a cloud of smoke from my cigarette, blanketing the shiny tiles on the ceiling, then stubbed the butt out in the nightstand ashtray and finished my necktie.

I was purposely vague and wasn't comfortable hanging around here any longer. The setup wasn't right, and her answers to most of my questions earlier were purposely evasive. The jury was way out on this dish, and I had a lot of digging to do for the right answers to match some of my suspicions before she and this Ruby joint were in the clear. But one thing was right on target, she was one "sizzling dish" in the sack in spite of my reservations. A return engagement? Maybe, if I only got lucky here tonight. What did she really have in mind for me? For that, I'd eventually have to wait for the right answer.

I said, "Adios" to this cupcake and kissed her once more. In spite of her frowns and moans that I was bailing out so soon, it was time to head back down to the *Black Swan* at the Anchor Marina in San Pedro for a little serious shuteye. I had another big day planned and needed an early start from this side of town. I left her lying back in bed, closed the door quietly and entered the darkened hallway.

I hadn't reached the stairwell yet, when blockhead unexpectedly exited one of the adjacent rooms to Noir's and approached me with his usual scowl, crowding my path.

"You took her from behind, didn't you?"

"None of your business, blockhead. Ah- ha … I was right. You must have been peeking through those mirrors," I said with a grin. "Disappointed I didn't fall into your photo trap, too?"

I gave him a nudge to shove him aside, but he was big and bulky. I also remembered this moron was one of Ruby's faithful enforcers in the old days.

He mumbled a confused excuse about observing our bedroom performance and added something about how he never liked me when I was with Ruby either. He was close enough to observe the battle scars creasing my face and wasn't intimated. Stubbornly insisting in crowding my space in the narrow hallway, he wasn't finished letting off steam either.

I'd had enough of this lug and dropping the grin said, "Back off dog breath … out of my way." I gave him a push on the chest up against the wall.

He was still closer than I liked. From the way he'd been looking at us downstairs, I knew he'd been jealous of Noir's interest in me and wanted a showdown. It wouldn't work out the way he planned.

He didn't say more. But, from the determined look on his mug, I knew he'd take a swing and try to take me down. It was a tight hallway and I couldn't get out of the way in time. He tossed a short throw and I stepped aside, catching his glancing blow on one shoulder. We grappled. After deflecting his next telegraphed punch, I drove a sharp knee upwards into his groin, smashing his balls as hard as I could. He dropped his arms and grabbed his crotch instinctively with both hands to prevent another blow. I followed that up with a two-handed clap to both ears, ringing his chimes loud enough to hear back in China. He screamed in pain. I could almost hear his eardrums blow, but this loser was a big lug and far from finished.

He was partially out of commission and going to need another round of softening up before I was done. I had to work fast. Instead of pasting him with a round house swing like he deserved, I gave him a short-range elbow smash across the bridge of his nose. It snapped his big head backwards, smashing it into the wall hard enough to dent the plaster. He collapsed down the wall like a deflated gas bag, spattering blood on the floor from his busted nose, obscuring his vision. I stepped over the bleeding loser, cupping his ringing ears to silence the bells and groaning in pain from the smashed snout.

I still wasn't finished with blockhead. Before leaving, I dropped another well placed knee into his ribs to remember me by, then grabbed my hat off the floor, adjusted my tie and took the stairs down and out to pick up my heap in the parking lot.

Chapter Eleven

The fog and light mist had turned into a weak but steady drizzle while I was inside drilling for oil. I stood on the front porch and lit a cigarette, watching the falling rain drops glisten in the parking lot lights through the blown smoke. I tossed the match out into the rain and thought about this joint tonight and was still amazed there were no knockout drops or any other funny business from that broad. Other than a jealous bartender getting in my way upstairs and maybe his fruitless attempts to snap a few compromising blackmail photos of one of Noir's customers, nothing else happened while I waited. I flicked the smoke into the downpour and contemplated the shortest route to my Buick through therain-filled pot holes in the parking lot. A couple of drunks stumbled off the front steps blindly in no particular direction, hoping their buggy would suddenly appear and whisk them away before getting totally soaked.

Mine was off somewhere I couldn't see, hidden in the back by the parking lot valet. I'd let him find it for another few bucks and wait on the front porch under the roof. They'd moved the portable umbrella covered valet station closer to the sheltered overhang entrance. I shouted at the guy on duty, now wearing a yellow rain slicker and hat pulled low over his collar and got his attention to go get my heap. He motioned that he remembered me and, without a squawk about a ticket stub matching his board of auto keys, raced over to the other side of the lot and returned faster than jackrabbit on Peyote. I dashed outside, greased his palm with more dough and slid in behind the wheel on a damp seat, tossing my hat beside me.

He'd left the engine running and the windshield wipers were flopping overtime against the drizzle. I ran my hand over an already steamy window, twisted my defroster switch on and slipped her into first gear, spinning the tires on a slippery patch exiting the parking lot. I swung left on Neptune Avenue bumping over a couple of hidden gopher sized pot holes deep enough to jog your fillings loose and swore at the city politicians responsible for road maintenance. After that round with Black Jade, I was anxious for a good night's sleep and headed in the direction of the *Black Swan*, closer at the Anchor Marina in San Pedro than my apartment in Hollywood several long miles away.

I reached for the radio dial, pausing in midstream. One glance over my shoulder told me another story I wouldn't like. The glint of something in the rearview mirror caught my attention and give me a start. Maybe, I wouldn't be doing any resting on the boat or anywhere else for a while, possibly a long while … unless it was permanent.

A face that I didn't want to see right now was staring back at me from the back seat with a twisted grin that spelled trouble, big trouble. I started to reach for my .357 mag. under my coat, then put on the brakes. I wouldn't be able to get it out easily and if I did, I was in an awkward position to do anything effective with it sitting behind the steering wheel facing the wrong direction. I was trapped like a rat in my own trap.

"Well, well, well… out so soon?" I said. "What rock did you crawl out from under Chester? You want another lesson in manners?" I watched his arrogant reflection pointing the barrel of a large caliber revolver towards the back of my head, and added, "And watch that heater, you might shoot yourself."

"Shut up you bastard," he mumbled, slapping me on the side of the head with his gun barrel. I mumbled under my breath trying to absorb the stars and didn't elaborate on his cheap shot.

"Take a left on 8th street and I'll tell you when to turn again, got it? And don't try driving fast or nothin else smart. I'm on to those tricks, smart ass. We're going to have us a little party and guess who's the guest of honor?"

"Yeah, I'm looking forward to it, punk."

"We're have'n fun already, ain't we?"

He didn't wait for a response, just grunted a sickening laugh and slapped the side of my head again, this time harder. He followed up with a couple of sharp prods to the back of my neck with the gun barrel, reminding me who was in charge of this joy ride, at least for now anyway. He growled with a rasp, "Now, get moving."

I winced again after the last tap and this time saw a kaleidoscope of shooting comets, but stayed focused on the rain-soaked road, swerving around a pock marked section of pot holes. I was going to make another crack about the bandages wrapped around his noggin, but decided against it. I just said, "I got it, pal. Anybody else going to this shindig I know?"

"Yeah, you and that little big mouth whore cotton Candy that you were so cozy with at the diner. She's on our list too. If you don't spill faster than a rusty drain pipe, she's gonna be the centerpiece of our party tonight and you can watch while me and the boys take turns hitch'n a ride on that bitch. You got it, pal? It'll be up to you."

"Yeah, I'm catching on."

This cockroach was starting to get worked up about something he thought I knew about and I definitely didn't like hearing what he had in store for the little pink mop-headed cutie either. The guy was a real psycho all right and was released immediately from the slammer by someone, as predicted. Some justice system; it worked just fine for the criminals. Especially those that should either be locked up permanently or exterminated. They were all running loose. Everyone else…well, the hell with them.

I was looking forward to getting an edge on this crumb before this hay ride was over so I could kick his carcass into a deep, dark sewer somewhere it wouldn't stink up the city and slam a nice tight manhole cover over the top.

One glance in the mirror at his agitated face told me it would be better to calm down too and shut up. This jitterbug was waving that hardware around a little to carelessly for my money. I hoped he didn't have the hammer back on his heater, but couldn't tell from my angle.

I steered straight, slow and careful, avoiding some of the larger water filled holes that would produce a nice, nasty trigger tripping jolt, if we slammed into them. That I didn't need. I'd just have to play it smooth and calm until I could make my move, if I lived that long.

"Okay, take Earle St. and just take it nice and slow until I tell you to stop," he ordered.

In spite of the heavy downpour, one glance around through the foggy windows, told me where we were. I knew this Los Angeles Harbor like the back of my hand and where we were going wasn't the best place to be late at night. We'd bypassed the heavier traveled areas and were now in a desolate section of Terminal Island. Quiet old storage warehouses, many empty, lined both sides of the damp streets. Overhead lighting was minimal to none. The busy port loading and unloading docks were over a few streets and unless there was a freighter or two waiting to be serviced, this was a mighty lonely stretch to be stuck in with a gun shoved in your back by a thug with revenge. I slowed way down to get my exact bearings and anticipated one of these old vacant wooden warehouses was our intended target. If I wasn't wrong, I wouldn't like it any better. This was a crummy area with limited options for outside help. I spotted only a few burned out homeless bums, sleeping off a booze jag in an alley, to count on … great.

Grease-ball was a man of few words. He signaled with another heavy gun barrel rap on the right side of my head again and grunted more directions under his bandages. "Pull in over there, smartass, stop and shut the engine off."

He pointed with a waving motion of his gun that I was to park next to a dark colored empty Hudson sedan in front of the last gloomy building on the right, the one with no lights in front.

The multistory slightly dilapidated and weathered wooden building that he'd picked, like all the others in this section, had seen better days before and during the war as fleet military storage facilities. They were now just hanging on to avoid the wrecking ball. Some of these old shells still housed some merchandise. Most were abandoned, useless until they'd gotten torched to collect the insurance value or sat empty, crumbling and moldy, save a stiff rodent or two decorating the abandoned traps. This one was no different.

I slid into the gravel lot, killed the engine and cut off the heaps running lights. There was only the sound of a moaning fog horn somewhere in the harbor trying to break through the silence for company. While I sat there waiting for our next move, I unbuttoned my suit coat and squeezed my .357 mag. under my left arm for assurance. It was still there and too soon to unleash with this jitterbug still somewhere behind me in the shadows. I'd wait for a better opportunity.

Grease-ball slid over and unlatched his back door with the gun still pressed firmly against my skull and said, "No time for tricks, buster. Get out and put both hands on the back of your head and I'll tell you when to get moving."

I didn't argue. We both exited carefully and smoothly into the driving rain. If I couldn't get my .357 out in time, at least I needed to get my hands on his revolver. But he wasn't stupid enough to get that close and lingered back in the sheet of gray rain. He waved the gun again towards a solid sliding wooden door in the front and said, "Move it, Thornton, and open it slowly and stay in site where I can see you."

I moved forward at a snail's pace, stalling for time and searching for an angle. I glanced back once or twice and noticed his bandages must have been getting soggy. He'd stopped to wipe the downpour from his face and was falling further behind. Maybe this was the opportunity I'd been waiting for. Quickening my pace as I approached the building, I noticed the padlock was dangling and the door open a crack. A shaft of light glowed from inside. I could hear muffled voices. Others were already inside waiting our arrival. This wasn't getting any better. So far, I still had my gun. I just needed the right opportunity to unleash it before whoever was in there would make it impossible.

Not sure what or who was waiting for me inside, I gave another quick glance back at Chester, now just an outline in the downpour. He was stumbling in the puddles of water and still fussing with his waterlogged bandages. I decided to make my move. Dropping my arms, I grasped the sliding wooden door handle with both hands. Instead of pulling it slowly as expected by dum-dum behind me, I flung it along its rusted rails with a surge of adrenaline, spinning out of the lighted doorway and using the sliding door as a shield as it opened. It slammed against the opposite edge of the door frame with a bang, startling the occupants inside and exposing whoever was waiting with my surprise party. I flattened my back against the wall and reached inside my coat, grasping the .357 mag. prepared for a firefight with Chester, but it wasn't necessary. A fusillade of gun fire instantly erupted from inside the warehouse, blasting through the exposed lighted doorway out into the darkened rain streaked night. The unexpected volley from automatic weapons struck only the darkened figure of Chester standing way back in the rain drenched shadows, blowing him backward in a crumpled heap behind me near the Hudson.

His arrival, unfortunately for him, surprised his pals who were waiting for both of us, but not that suddenly. Their immediate reaction was to blast the unannounced intruder, who was only silhouetted outside in the darkened building parking lot in the rain. I now had two choices; make a run for it to the Buick parked close by, if I had time to get there and hope to get away, or move forward and bag whoever was gunning for me.

I chose the latter, spotting my best approach. I slid along the outside wall towards a metal fire escape ladder situated near the corner of the building. I climbed up on a stack of abandoned shipping pallets, grabbed the bottom rung of the sliding steel ladder and yanked it down to my level. I glanced back towards the open doorway and seeing no one emerge to investigate the body outside in the rain, scrambled up to the landing on the second story. It led to another door with a dirty chicken-wire encased glass window in the top half. I had to move fast to get inside and off the exposed balcony. I knew busting through the double pane safety glass would be noisy and difficult and hoped the old building management hadn't been too diligent in securing the premises. I tried the door with a prod and a silent prayer. It paid off. It opened reluctantly with a broad shoulder nudge. I squeezed inside as quietly as possible around the opening. It was partially blocked by wooden crates full of something heavy with stenciled instructions written in Chinese characters. Aside from the light creeping in from outside the half-opened doorway, I found myself in a semi-darkened room. I was somewhere above the thugs who'd just plugged Chester by mistake and now surrounded by dusty packing crates of abandoned merchandise and a few prying eyes from some four-legged creatures.

Why had Chester brought me here? What were they doing down below and what did they want me for, revenge? I didn't think so. I knew something or they thought I knew something. Or maybe I was onto something and they wanted to know how or who I was connected to. Was little Candy already involved? What a mess McCullen had gotten into.

I pushed the door gently so that it would appear closed from below, but it wasn't and would still be a viable escape, if necessary. It was time to begin hunting. I snapped open my lighter, scanned the room quickly for an inside door leading to somewhere else. I spotted it at the far end of the room and navigated a serpentine route through a maze of unknown industrial merchandise, a few dusty desks, empty metal shelving and a few dusty work benches. This too wasn't locked, the knob turned easily with only a slight squeak. I moved it inward an inch or two and peered outside, anxious to spot my attempted assailants somewhere down below. Unfortunately, it wouldn't be quite so simple. My room opened up on a short balcony which ran around the building inside in a horse shoe shaped pattern with a stairway at the far end leading to the first floor. Other similar offices or smaller storage rooms were adjacent to each other, all looking down below into a central assembly or work area intended for production of some type. It reminded me of a prison cell balcony looking down into an open courtyard.

The area below was dimly lit and from where I was standing, I couldn't see who was down there. I could hear agitated men's voices talking together, but not clearly enough to distinguish what they were saying. I needed to view it and hear it from the balcony railing out front from where I was hiding. I slid past the storage room door and crept forward across the dusty balcony closer to the rail. Down below two men wearing cloth caps and work men's clothes were pacing nervously back and forth, next to several work benches with three kerosene lanterns throwing off weak light and flickering shadows. They were nervous and unsure of their next move after gunning down the vague figure that might be their pal, possibly lying outside in the rain dying or maybe already dead. From where I was standing, I might be able to take out one of the thugs, but the other one would jump out of sight immediately and have me trapped upstairs. He'd also be able to get away before I could get closer. I could hear they were contemplating bursting out into the rain to retrieve their fallen comrade, who they'd possibly gunned down by mistake, but were worried they might possibly get blasted themselves by persons unknown. Maybe they'd beat a hasty retreat through another exit. One of them mentioned something about a pink haired party doll, but I couldn't see her. It must have been Candy. That was just what Chester had mentioned on the way over.

It was time to act. I'd put a stop to these rabid dogs before they collected her for their next victim. Unfortunately, my position was far from advantageous. I needed to maneuver into another location closer and take them both by surprise. The open wooden stairwell was located opposite from where I was watching. It was far from an optimal way of descending closer. I'd be exposed, but I had no other choices. I cautiously maneuvered in that direction and began a heart pounding decent into a cauldron of sub-machine guns in the hands of two jumpy lunatics. The way the stairs were situated, I'd be out of site and hidden until I hit a landing halfway down. Then I'd be out in the open and fully exposed. I began slowly, trying to avoid any loose steps that would creak or make noise signaling my presence. Before I reached that midpoint, a quick survey of the room layout presented several possible alternatives to a full-frontal suicide attack. One idea looked more promising than the others and would set several chain reactions in motion at the same time.

Not far from where I was standing, several large canisters labeled flammable printers ink sat piled on top of each other near an open section of the railing. An overhead block and tackle arrangement, used to haul them up for storage was connected by a sturdy length of rope and lay neatly coiled up beside the stack. I retraced my steps and lashed one end of the rope under the top lip of one of the barrels, unhinged the lid disconnecting the clam clamp attachment and set the cover aside. Then I quietly worked my way towards the far side of the balcony with the free end of the rope and wrapped it several times around one of the large building columns, snubbing it off and slipped behind it for cover.

I focused on the two below who were still debating their next move. I contemplated mine which was a little shaky at best, but it was all set and just needed to be executed. I felt confident anyway in spite of my setup. They were still confused at not seeing any opposition yet to their presence and had tossed over a couple of tables facing the open door prepared for a frontal assault, guns facing in the direction away from my intended entrance down the back stairwell. I noticed they'd relocated their kerosene lanterns, which were now sitting atop a short stack of wooden shipping pallets, as targets directly below my hoist arrangement.

My timing had to be perfect for this maneuver and I'd only get one quick chance to exit safely before the whole building burst into smoke and flames. They could be heard mumbling incoherently in something other than English. Maybe it was Spanish, I wasn't sure from that distance, but it didn't matter as they were headed for oblivion anyway. I was now prepared to unload a barrel full of flammable liquid in their direction, pour on the lead and then get the hell out of there, when I noticed something that I hadn't seen before. That hit me in the stomach with a sickening blow. Over in a far corner, another table and a couple of chairs, one of which was occupied by someone I didn't see before and would be a serious problem with my plan.

A little pink haired mop-head was just visible next to a stack of packing crates. "Damn it," I mumbled under my breath. They already had her and it looked like their party had already begun.

She'd been stripped and tied to a chair with tight ropes coiled around her naked body. A gag that she'd worked loose, dangled around her neck. She should have been pleading with the thugs to turn her loose, but from what I could see, she was silent. Her head was slumped down on her chest and she was either drugged, unconscious or worse.

With her in the picture, I'd have no choice now, but to ambush them straight out. Get in as close as possible and hit them hard and fast. I slipped down the stairway quieter than a second story burglar, avoiding a couple of steps that didn't look secure. Flattening out on the midpoint floor landing, I was prepared for a rodent extermination. With as low a profile as possible,

I steadied my .357 with a two fisted grip, took careful aim at one of the two thugs crouched behind the overturned table, brought his head into clear focus in my sights and squeezed off a well executed round. His cabeza exploded like a Halloween pumpkin dropped from a fifteen story high-rise; blood and brains decorated his pal crouched beside him. The scared survivor unleashed a startled reflex round from his Tommy gun, blasting nothing in particular in a circular arcing motion upward and around behind him as he panicked trying to trace the source of the surprise ambush attack. His rounds missed me, but punctured the open container of flammable ink upstairs over his head, dumping the contents below on the kerosene lanterns sending them crashing to the concrete floor. The stack of wooden pallets piled next to the broken lanterns, burst into flames fueling the fire. I dished out several more rapid rounds towards the lone fleeing kidnapper, and maybe missed as he escaped out the open front door concealed by the rising smoke and spreading flames.

Dashing down the splinter covered stairway was worse than leaping over a den of rattlesnakes with your shoes tied together. I tripped and stumbled over the few remaining cracked or missing steps until I hit bottom. Then leaping over the puddles of spreading flammable liquid and avoiding the side of the building now succumbing to the encroaching flames, I finally reached the frantic Candy struggling to get free. The noise and odor of the burning building had aroused her out of the tortured thrashing she'd endured from those thugs and she was desperate to escape from her rope bonds. Recognizing me trying to release her bindings, she pleaded, "Help me, help me Mr. ah- Mr. ah…." she couldn't remember my name in her stupor and began a fit of coughing from the acrid smoke.

"Save your breath, sweetheart. We'll be out of here in a flash, hopefully," I said fumbling with my pocketknife to cut the tight ropes away and began coughing myself. The hot flames were now spreading at our backs and the stifling smoke was beginning to overtake both of us, but I kept sawing away at her bonds, sweat pouring into my eyes.

Her wide-eyed terror and now seeing her surroundings in peril after she'd regained consciousness was agonizing. She continued coughing and was in a mild state of shock. After I'd hacked through the last knot, she desperately reached up and grabbed me around the neck to pull her up and out to safety.

"Please get me out of here, m-mister," she pleaded, her fingers frantically reaching towards my shoulders for escape.

"Hold your breath, baby. We're on our way."

I grabbed a bundle of what looked like her dress and panties they'd dumped next to her chair and also spotted something else I'd need later. I grabbed that off the floor too, then scooped up the naked cutie in my arms and raced for the open sliding door, desperate for some fresh oxygen myself.

Hesitating for a split second in the door way before exiting, I braced for retaliation from the escaped thug, probably waiting outside. I noticed the rain had stopped and from where I was standing the entire parking lot now appeared to be deserted. The big Hudson sedan parked next to me earlier was long gone, and with it apparently the thug from inside and Chester.

I rushed outside and ran towards my Buick, the black noxious smoke pouring out behind us, covering the front of the old decrepit warehouse like a dirty veil on a homeless bag lady.

"Mr. ah-ah…," Candy blurted out unable to finish, tears of relief streaming down her slightly battered face at seeing she'd escaped her traumatic ordeal, her arms hugging me tightly.

"Matthew Thornton … your hash house earlier today, remember? We're outside the warehouse now. Just take it easy. Take some deep breaths. It's going to be all right, okay? They're all gone. You're in safe hands now, doll."

She didn't say anything more, just continued sniffling with her head on my shoulder. She was still shaking like a mixed cocktail in mild shock and not even aware of her nudity, as I held her close in my arms. I slid her gently on the autos front seat and handed her the fist full of her clothes I'd snatched from inside and nodded for her to put them on. She starred at them numbly for a few seconds, wrapping them over her exposed breasts and the rest of her body. And then began fumbling into them, anxious to cover herself completely. She mumbled something about her missing bra while still coughing and trying to inhale a little fresh air at the same time. I tried to inhale some cleaner oxygen myself, but it didn't help much with the deadly stench spreading in our direction and felt rotten from sucking in those noxious fumes inside.

I was used to the rough stuff. Plugging this trash and dumping it in the nearest garbage can was a pleasure I usually enjoyed. But the more I thought about what had just happened to this little cupcake, the madder I got. She wasn't playing by the same rules as the gutter rats that kidnapped her. She couldn't fight back and just had the wind kicked out of her, and hard. I looked down at the little pink-mop slumped in the front seat trying to compose herself after her ordeal and thought what a tough kid she was, a real survivor. She'd been roughed up, but after close examination, I didn't think any of her bruises looked serious. It could have been worse, much worse. With Chester's arrival, they were just warming up for some real fun with this dish. My timing at throwing those punks into a tail spin was to close for both of us, but effective. I'd get even, I always did. I also had a surprise souvenir I'd unleash, when needed. The cowardly thug that escaped my wrath dropped his .45 auto Tommy gun in his hasty retreat. I smiled, thinking about that. It was now safely wrapped up in my auto's trunk for future retaliation. The other one was still inside, turning into charcoal along with its owner.

As I slammed the lid closed and locked it, two yellow headlight beams appeared down the slick street, penetrating thru the damp misty fog that had replaced the earlier rain fall. I wasn't sure who it was or what they wanted, but standing my ground with my sidearm instead of using the automatic, now bundled up in the trunk, was my only option.

I slammed the door shut on Candy's side, told her to get down on the floor as close to the firewall as possible for protection and stay there. Crouching down behind the front fender, I reached for my .357 mag. and braced for trouble. I glance over my shoulder at the black greasy smoke pouring out the open warehouse doorway. Flames were visible in the background, licking the buildings remaining contents and I knew it would only be a matter of time before the port fire authority and police, would be arriving on high alert also.

We both had to get the hell out of there and pronto, as a holiday turkey was also cooking inside and I didn't want us involved.

Chapter Twelve

An older model Ford coupe with a single wiper struggling to clear away the mist pulled directly up in front of my heap and slid to a stop with squealing brakes. It wasn't a replay with the Hudson as I'd expected, but I held my ground anyway, still crouching behind the heavy Buick's fender with my revolver, poised for retaliation. It wouldn't be necessary. The driver's side door snapped open without hesitation and my pal Joshua Keys, stepped out into the dim glare of his headlights and recognizing me, gave me a cautious wave.

I shoved the magnum back into the shoulder rig and stepped forward, feeling like the cavalry had just arrived. He was a little late for the showdown, but better late than never and arriving unarmed earlier, would have been fatal anyway.

"What the hell are you doing here, Josh?" I said, smiling and shaking his hand. I reached back and opened the side door for Candy to unwind, who was still huddled inside waiting for my "all clear" before appearing.

"Mr. Matt, I ober hears dat bartender, Charlie Loo. He tak'n on de phone to someone abouts you and dat you's in a heap a trouble wid dem. Dey goin to take you to a warehouse fo some kind of a party. I don't like what I'm her'n so I writes down de a-dress he talk'n about and decide to leave after my last break and here I is. Looks like you sure nuf in a heap a trouble with dis burn'n building and all."

He looked at me with scared bug eyes surveying my soggy clothes and holstered gun prepared for battle, a young woman with pink hair climbing out of my auto and the smoke pouring out of the burning warehouse behind us. He wasn't sure what he'd gotten himself into, but knew it wasn't good. He looked shaky. I could tell he wanted to leave and fast, but I needed some help and he was it.

A plan ran through my mind that I thought might work and I had to convince him…and fast. "Josh, here's the setup. You've got to help me. I'll explain briefly, but we've only got a few more minutes to get the hell out of here, so listen carefully, okay?"

He nodded dully and didn't question my authority. Just stood there sweating nervously and rocking back and forth, anxious to return to the safety of blowing his horn back at Ruby's.

I laid out a brief version, leaving out most of the salient details that didn't sound encouraging. "Little Candy here was kidnapped earlier tonight and held at gunpoint in the warehouse by a couple of thugs. I was next on their agenda. I had a visitor in my car with a gun at my head, when I left Ruby's and couldn't get away. We drove here, but I outsmarted them, released this little gal, torched the building and silenced a couple of the punks before I was finished. One or two got away, but this kid's got to go into hiding for a while until I can unscramble the motive for this mess or she's not going to be so lucky next time. I can take care of myself, but I don't want to see her decorating a slab in the city morgue, okay? I need her stashed someplace safe until then."

He didn't like one damn thing I said, his eyes popping out of their sockets listing to this disastrous chain of events. He knew full well that getting involved in my scheme might backfire if he didn't play his cards right and wasn't looking forward to hosting his own necktie party.

He began stammering, "Oh L-Lordy… Oh, no, n-not me. Ah- ah pink-haired white girl in my auto-mo-bile dis late at night around here and I don't even knows her? And- and, it looks like she done got herself a shiner or two tonight. Oh-no Mr. Matt, it don't look good. No, no, no… I ain't go'in to get mixed up in dis. You knows what happen to us black folks like me, if'n I gets caught wid her, and like dis wid dat beat up face?" he said, backing up slowly with his hands flopping up and down in despair and shaking his head side to side as he fumbled for the door handle behind him trying to escape.

"Josh, Josh stop, stop! Give me a few days to unscramble this, but take her someplace safe. Didn't you tell me one time you had relatives living in that little town called- ah, Val Dosta, or something? No, no that's not it...that's in Georgia. Ah, Val Verde, right? That's it...north of L.A, right?"

He just stared at me, not responding, contemplating this situation spiraling downhill faster than his jalopy with a busted brake line. With Rome literally burning right beside us, I had no other options. So, I poured on the gasoline.

"Look, it's just for a couple of days. I'll make it worth your while, okay? Here..." I peeled off a fist full of McCullen's C notes and stuffed them into his sweaty palm before he could change his mind.

That nailed down his attention. But he was still trying to weasel out of it, "Dat town's blacker than the backside of yo mama's fry'n pan Mr. Matt and you know's it. My Aunt Juba and Uncle Cuffee been liv'n dere, peaceful like for years." He pointed at Candy clinging close beside me, "A young white girl like her, and-and wid dat, dat pink hair … un, uh, no suh." He shook his head negatively again, hoping I'd give up and think of something else. "She'll stand out in dat town, like a rabbit in da turnip patch. Maybe lot's of trouble fo me and dem both. And you knows it, too."

He held out the dough, but I didn't take it back. I just turned up my sales pitch. "Josh, just disguise her for now. You know, cover her head with something and keep her out of sight when you get there."

He shot me another uneasy stare like I was nuts with this whole idea. I suggested, "How about a-ah do-rag or something. And, maybe some hair dye tomorrow or anything else you can think of; just get her out of here fast before it's too late. It's only for a few days. We're wasting time. Do you hear that?" I said louder this time and pointing in the direction of Long Beach. "That's the port fire department. They're on the way here right now, probably accompanied by cops and who knows what else." I added a couple more C notes to his stash.

He took another final last look at the fist full of money I'd handed him. It was more than several months' worth of pay for tooting his sax at Ruby's. Cash is king and he wasn't 100% or even closely convinced, but I knew he'd cave-in. Sometimes even just 51% is better than nothing.

He finally sighed and said, "Okay… okay. I'll do it, Mr. Matt, but I's awful nervous abouts it. I gots to avoid the traffic, carry'n her wid me in dis ol jalopy on da back roads, too. I still don't likes it."

I ignored his doubts, smiled and clapped him on the back, as he reluctantly stuffed the money into his coat pocket. He scribbled down the telephone number where I could reach him or speak to his aunt about the girl. It was a place called "Shampy's", a saloon next door to his folks who he said didn't have a phone yet. Great, nice setup I thought…it would have to do.

We'd done enough stalling. I motioned for Candy to get into his jalopy. Josh opened his side and slid in under the steering wheel, still shaking his head. He wasn't happy and damned rightly nervous about this chain of events he'd become involved in, but would do as I asked with no more complaining.

Candy had been listening to this entire conversation and was equally uneasy about this plan. Before they drove off, I fished out another bundle of dough, leaned in through the open window and pressed it into her little hand. "Here's some traveling money, sweetheart. I'll call and let you know when it's safe to return, maybe by bus in a few days."

Her chin quivered like a dish of jello, and her brown moist eyes met mine. "T-thanks, M-Matthew…for saving me. I-I guess, I'm going to be all right. For some reason, I trust you and him and I don't even know either of you, but I guess I have to. I still have your card in my pocket you give me at Dales today, see?" She touched her side pocket for reassurance and produced the crushed card like a kid with a favorable teacher's report.

She tilted her face up and puckered up her swollen lips and gave me a tender kiss on the cheek. I touched her bruised face with my hand softly and kissed her forehead.

"Hang onto the card, angel. It's always your ticket out of hell if you need one, okay? Go with my friend for now. He's a good man, and don't worry."

A weak smile passed by her worried face and I said turning to Josh, "Take good care of her, chum. She's a diamond in the rough and worth every cent of a million bucks. I'm counting on you."

I assured her that Joshua Keys was an old and trusted war buddy, that this was in her best and safest interest and that I'd connect with her again, soon. I hoped she felt a little bit better about what was happening and my solution. It wasn't good, but it was the best I could do, for now.

As the two trusting souls pulled out of the parking lot, I watched Candy tie a small bandana over her head. It was probably just a cleaning rag pulled out of his glove compartment, but they both laughed at something humorous Josh must have said about my suggested masquerade. That made me feel better. Then her head slumped down beside him out of sight.

It would be a long slow ride to Val Verde, proclaimed by the community leaders as the "The Black Palm Springs of California". An all African American vacation village developed in the middle of no-where, north of Los Angeles sucking up the dry desert, proudly promising a retreat from the Los Angeles smog, heat and oppression for those of color. Anchored by an Olympic sized public swimming pool and funded by black entertainers struggling themselves for identity in show business, it was surrounded by a scattered collection of ramshackle houses, a school and church, numerous false front shops and general stores, saloons and a promise for their future. Some folks in L.A. referred to it despairingly as "Tobacco Road."Maybe they were right, but I didn't think so. It didn't appear to be much in the beginning on the surface. But below, it was just enough to get started and eventually it would be someplace to be proud of.

I followed them for another few blocks, both of us avoiding the screaming fire trucks, police, and other port vehicles plowing through the light fog past us in the opposite direction. After we hit Neptune Avenue, we split up. I lost sight of their taillights as Josh turned north towards the coast road and I spun off toward the Anchor Marina, only a short drive away and a much deserved night's sleep on my ketch the *Black Swan*.

As I drifted back to my boat in silence, I wondered if I'd made the right decision about setting those two on that track. But it was too late to change direction on them and only the future knew the answer. I sure as hell didn't and wasn't going to guess. I reached for my dashboard lighter, torched another smoke and let it cut in deep, and kept my eyes peeled through the light fog and cigarette smoke for the turnoff to my marina.

Chapter Thirteen

Sleep didn't come easy. I flopped and turned all night on the cold, damp boat and couldn't get comfortable. It was something I was used to, didn't like, didn't need, and the more I thought about my new unoccupied apartment back in L.A., the better that sounded. I couldn't clear out the cobwebs and kept turning over everything from the warehouse fire and my last sight of the pink-haired doll peeling out of sight down that misty port road with Josh, to the conversation I had with the Black Jade about the mysterious demise of Ruby and her involvement with the Frisco Tong gang, including that mix of miscast characters that hung out at Ruby's. Nothing at that joint added up either. That was just another jumbled bowl of hot Chop Suey, in addition to that mess with McCullen and his dames. I just wasn't sure how to unravel any of it, yet. One thing was certain, the more I became involved with his case, the worse it was turning out...for me. Maybe I had more on my plate than I was prepared for, and this was only the beginning.

By now, I was totally awake. I needed to jumpstart my day and clear up my thinking cap. A cup of fresh, hot Java and a good breakfast would be the right start. I'd find a friendly hash house closer to my office where the food was hot, the service fast and the atmosphere subdued.

I glanced at the bulkhead clock, noticed I was running late already, grumbled about the time, and stumbled out of the forward V berth. I'd been too tired to get cleaned up after the warehouse debacle and smelled like burnt toast. I tossed on my bathrobe and slipped into a pair of deck shoes. The rain had stopped overnight, but the docks were still slippery, as they were most mornings. I worked my way up cautiously to the marina head and shower stalls for a major spruce-up.

On the way back, I glanced toward Leland Avery's wood-framed dockmaster shack by the front gate and found it empty. The heavy-handed, two-fisted, ex-detective was usually manning his forward post early and was probably passed out on board his tub. Guarding the entrance gate like "Custer on his Last Stand" usually found him most mornings holding instead of a brace of smoking pistols, a steaming cup of black Joe, heavily spiked with anything over 80 proof and perusing the classified section in the *Herald Examiner* for his latest money-making scheme. He threatened to retire any day soon, spending his days at sea fishing further south of the border. Ensenada, Mexico, was his threatened destination. There the fishing waters were clean and still clear, the booze was cheaper and the senoritas, hotter than a plate of habanero chilies, or so he said. I figured a friendly contact in Mexico might be beneficial to me someday and salted his plan away for future reference if it ever came to fruition. As I retraced my steps back to the *Black Swan*, I noticed his tub the *Excalibur* was still tied up at the dock, so he was still around here, someplace. We'd celebrate before his departure, if and when the next time I saw him.

Back on board, I tossed on a reasonably well-pressed suit of clothes; knotted one of my favorite hand-painted ties from Sid's Haberdashery, strapped on my .357 mag. hardware including two-speed loaders and checked myself out in the closet mirror. I grimaced at what glared back, snapped on my lid, and locked up the *Swan*.

Yesterday, I'd been planning to stop off at the Long Beach police department this morning and file my statement on the incident at Dale's Diner with that punk Chester. But, after last night's gunfight, it didn't seem like such a good idea...more likely a waste of time. I'd hold off on that paperwork for now as he'd probably just turn up in an alley, a floater in the ocean, or on a morgue slab anyway. I doubted it would be in a hospital or a reputable doctor who was required to report all gunshot wounds. First, I'd check the morning papers at breakfast and see if his body turned up, before doing anything more.

I shot across the Badger Street Bridge towards Long Beach, hung a left on Ocean Boulevard, and gunned the Buick north on Pacific Coast Highway back in the direction of Los Angeles. I felt positive about my day's fact-finding agenda at the movie studio and was anxious to pick up Rhonda and get started. I fired up a Lucky, watched the smoke curl out the open wind wing, and dialed up a radio station for company. Unfortunately, I hit some announcer babbling boring morning news about; congested street traffic and multiple fender-benders, a layer of dense yellow smog obscuring everything including the Hollywood Hills sign and the usual political corruption scene in Washington with Senate hearings attacking the movie business. That wasn't what I was interested in or wanted to hear, at least not yet anyway. I snapped off the depressing events of the day and decided I'd continue without being informed.

I continued north picking up Sepulveda Blvd. and merged onto La Cienega Boulevard. I checked my dashboard clock, snapped it a couple of times with my fingertips to see if it was still working and decided it was either time to stoke up my furnace and fast, or just grab a sack full of sinkers and a container of Java somewhere and head directly back to the office.

After a few more traffic-choked miles in silence and still thinking about something more substantial to eat, I spotted *Blinky's Diner* on the corner of Pico Blvd. It was apparently a popular hash-house, but for some reason, maybe I'd heard something negative, one that I'd avoided numerous times in the past. After eating there, I might find out why. The parking lot was always overflowing with crowds waiting outside. This morning the lot was only partially full and no one in sight waiting to be seated. I was anxious for that hot meal before picking Rhonda up at my office and our meeting at Majestic Studios with Hemingway so wheeled in and parked.

In spite of it already being past the usual breakfast time for dining, the little restaurant was still overcrowded inside. I sat at the only empty stool around the corner of the L-shaped counter. Not my favorite position, but I didn't have much choice. Glancing around I noticed that even though the waitresses were rushing, many customers were still sitting with tilted up menus, waiting. I scanned a counter menu for my selection, anyway.

Their "Lumberjack Special" of ham, bacon, sausage, three eggs, a stack of buckwheat pancakes, and coffee looked perfect, but I groaned after a disappointing glance at my wristwatch told me to forget it.

I desperately motioned for a passing waitress. "Miss, I'm running out of time. Just prepare a cup of Joe to go and bag of four of those hockey pucks I see sweating under that counter dome behind you." Not a response. Maybe I didn't get through. I sweetened it up, "And thanks, sweetheart. Please step on it, okay? Big hurry." Now she gave me that irritated look for the rush request, scribbled down my order on her pad, shoved the pencil over her ear, and began fumbling with the sack of stale sinkers first.

I drummed on the countertop anxious to make tracks and glanced towards the stool next to me at a quiet big guy with broad shoulders and a deeply tanned face. He looked broke and familiar. He was wearing a battered fedora pulled low enough to obscure his features and a faded brown thrift shop mismatched pant and suit coat combination that was shinier than the eyes of dead trout. Flipping through the morning edition of the *Herald Examiner*, he looked like a guy that really needed the "Lumberjack Special" more than I did. I thought about giving him a treat but changed my mind. He seemed to be content just nursing his cup of boiling Joe and letting his cigarette smolder in the counter ashtray. I waved off the smoke drifting in my direction and asked if I could take a look at anything he wasn't reading while I waited for my order. He didn't look up at first, just grumbled something. Folding up what he'd been reading, he turned and gave me a broad white-toothed smile and said, "Sure friend, I've finished most of it already anyway," and slid the front section in my direction.

"Burt, Burt Lancaster," I said, now recognizing him. I blurted out his name louder than I should have, but the noise inside the restaurant masked my faux pas. He ducked his head down, tugging on the brim of his hat, obviously trying not to be recognized. I'd almost blown his cover.

"It was, the last time I looked, but don't broadcast it, okay pal?" he said, whispering behind a sip of his raised coffee cup. A frown crept across his face annoyed at the interruption, as his penetrating eyes tried to place me.

After another moment of staring, his eyes narrowed into a squint and he said, "Say, didn't I meet you not too long ago at the, ah-ah-Santa Anita race track, right?"

"Yeah, that's right, names Thornton, Matt Thornton."

He gave me a hardy handshake warming up and flashed more teeth. "Yeah, I remember you now, Thornton. You were with a hot blonde and I was with a couple of stunt pals from the studio. They'd dropped quite a bundle that day on some nags that barely made it out of the starting gate. They recognized you. Told me you were a private dick and pulled their nuts of the fire several times, right?"

"That's the way I remember it," I said, without elaborating more about the two losers he was with. They were both a couple of bums and heavy gamblers. Always in debt way over their heads with the wrong guys in town and were lucky to be walking around on two sound legs. If he was playing their same game, he'd also need my services sooner than he expected.

I handed him another of my P.I. cards to jog his memory of my expertise. He glanced at it, snapped it with his index finger twice, maybe testing the paper's tensile strength, and casually dropped it into his coat pocket.

"I'll hang onto this. Who knows, I might need your services someday."

"That's my guess too," I said, grinning.

He didn't get it and explained, "We're shooting down the street at Paramount today. Don't let the outfit fool you."

"Wouldn't fool me, Burt," I said, my stomach beginning to rumble.

He glanced down, a little embarrassed at his disheveled second-hand suit, and brushed off a few imaginary stray crumbs from his coat lapels.

"I'm in costume for a few rough and tumble fight scenes," he went on, bragging. "I used to be an acrobat in the circus you know, and this will be second nature for me. I'm looking forward to it."

"Thanks for the update. Didn't know you got your start under the *Big Top*. Nice. Hang onto that hobo outfit. It would fit right in for riding the rails if the movie business ever falls flat."

He ignored my frivolous comment and just kept smiling, but had read my mind on that crummy outfit he was wearing and I'd read his mind on his gymnastic skills as a necessity to supporting his film career. I handed him another card for safekeeping, just in case the other one disappeared back to the costume department when he turned in his disguise.

He returned to his coffee and classified section in silence. I began scanning briefly through my pages, looking for any article concerning the demise of that punk Chester from the Pike in Long Beach or anything else on that disaster at the Port. There was no news so far on finding his corpse anywhere. I didn't like it. That rat should have been exterminated and tossed in the city garbage dump already, but was apparently either still kicking, or else they just hadn't discovered his carcass yet. I guess I wasn't finished with him and was right about putting little Pinkie on ice for a while.

I continued flipping through the rest of the rag and found another headline hard to miss. That one was more like it. I optimistically reached for a sip of the Joe the waitress had bagged and uncapped it. It was too damn hot to drink. I burned my tongue and shoved the steaming container aside, slopping some on the countertop. I reached for one of the donuts and continued reading.

The headlines flashed in bold type at the top of one of the inside pages covering Long Beach exclusively, *"Port of Los Angeles Fire Destroys Abandoned Warehouse & Claims Life."* Well, there it was. I read on, hoping the authorities had gotten all the facts confused as usual. They hadn't, just didn't have all the details pieced together yet. The burned corpse was still unidentified, the bullet that had blown his cabeza apart, and wasn't recovered yet and his machine gun wasn't even mentioned. He was the prime suspect in the cause of the fire along with a possible vague connection to an organized crime hit. So far I wasn't involved and that's the way I wanted it. I scanned further.

A smaller article with scant details mentioned, *"Two G-Men Killed in Hollywood Shootout"* that were found dumped in the alley near the Gringo Gulch section and was equally vague. Police were apparently on the hot seat for dragging their feet with the investigation and Washington Agents had been dispatched to take the lead in solving the crime. Who were those guys and what were they doing to get themselves bumped off?

Another smaller story on the *"Blue Parrot Inn Mystery Woman Found Dead."* Police were following up leads to identify the body and cause of death—

strangulation? No…possibly poisoning. What the hell? Where did that come from? They must have done a quick autopsy on that dish. That one, I'd have to follow up on, too.

One more article caught my eye and jumped off the page, *"House Un-American Activity Committee Cracks Down On Hollywood Movie Industry.".* Right-wing Washington congressional crusaders were getting ready to lynch the careers of left-leaning Communist-inspired ring leaders connected with the movie entertainment industry; writers, producers, and directors all working for some of the major studios, at least for now. The lefties had been singled out to testify before the anti-communist politicians and would be held accountable for their actions and skewered as examples for their membership in the communist party and their affiliations with other members. Those saps would be just the tip of the iceberg to testify before congress. They'd apparently been infiltrating and affecting the movie industry for years with sympathetic propaganda scripts and left-leaning philosophy, indoctrinating the public through their storytelling on the silver screen. They'd been accused of attempting to influence and control the minds and actions of John Q. Public citizens by government takeover and control whether by peaceful or violent revolutionary tactics.

That congressional crackdown would turn the movie-making business upside down. I wondered which movies were on the hot seat and who else was connected to those Reds and next on the chopping block. I didn't want to glance sideways.

There was nothing more I was interested in. I returned the rag next door to Lancaster, thanked him, and got up to leave. He shook his head and said keep it and slid it back.

Before I left, there was one more thing I'd thought of that might help with my McCullen case. I decided to give it a shot and said, "I have a case I'm working on that you might have an answer to."

I had his attention and aroused his curiosity, so I continued. "You and Ava Gardner were in that last picture "The Killers" together, last year, right?"

"That's true and she is some woman. I hope this isn't going to be personal."

I assured him it was strictly business nothing else, "I have something here that maybe you can identify, as you know her better than I do."

He smiled at that. I pulled out the newspaper photograph of McCullen's so-called Ava standing next to Joey DeCosta at the track and pointed to her.

"Does that woman look like Ava Gardner in your opinion?"

He took one look and said, "It does, sort of, yes. But, if that's the Ava I know, then I'm Fred Astaire. She's close and very attractive too, but uh-uh. See, she's standing next to Joey DeCosta?"

I nodded at the obvious.

"I've seen him before from a distance at the track with Sinatra. They're about the same size, except DeCosta's heavier and smokes cigars."

"Okay…so? Did it stunt his growth?"

"No of course not," he said, pointing to the clipping again and frowning at my flippant remark. "I'm over six feet tall. I know Sinatra personally and he's more than half a head shorter than me. That would put them both not more than five and a half. That women standing next to DeCosta you think might be Ava is wearing maybe 3" high heels and is approximately his height, so that makes her about 5'3" or less in her bare feet. She's the height of Lana Turner. Ava Gardner is much taller at least 5'6" in her stocking feet, and that I know. So, with high heels on, she'd be at least 3" taller than DeCosta. Therefore, that doll in your picture could not be the real Ava G." Proud of his simple deduction, he flashed me a smile broad enough to eat a watermelon sideways and handed it back to me.

"Well, what do you know? If that acting business you're in doesn't pan out, you might consider the private investigation business. It doesn't pay as well, but there are certain fringe benefits that are hard to beat." He grinned again flashing me another big mouthful of his shiny white Chiclets.

"Thanks," I said, flashing my own choppers. "That's all I needed to know for now. You've been a big help."

I shoved the clipping back into my coat pocket and changed the subject before he got interested asking more questions. "Looks like I won't be eating my breakfast here after all. No time. I'm running late, and thanks for the help with the I.D. Don't forget, I'm in the phone book if you ever need my P.I. services."

Taking in his secondhand suit one more time I couldn't help adding, "You know, I was going to suggest that maybe you could use something more substantial than that cup of road tar and it was going to be on me. I thought you could use it."

He let out an over-the-top boisterous laugh and said, "Thanks anyway, my friend. That would have been generous, but unnecessary."

"Oh, why is that?"

"I already ate a "Lumberjack Special" before you arrived.

"Oh…okay, glad somebody had a good breakfast today."

He laughed again, this time louder, now that he was leaving and maybe a little too theatrical after seeing the expression on my face. "Maybe I'll take you up on that another time. I have to go now, too," he said, shoving his empty coffee cup aside, double-checking his reflection in the mirror and the wall clock mounted over the cash register, before shoving off.

I grabbed his newspaper off the counter, including what was left of my sack breakfast, tossed some dough on the counter and we both walked outside.

Climbing into my shiny, but bullet-hole patched Buick; I couldn't help noticing Lancaster's serious expression in his suit of costume clothes as he slid behind the wheel of the largest silver-gray Cadillac sedan on the lot. He peeled out into the heavy mid-morning traffic onto Pico Blvd. without even looking over his shoulder at the oncoming traffic and disappeared back to a make-believe fight scene at the movie studio. I had a strong feeling I was going to see that guy again, and real soon.

Chapter Fourteen

y stomach continued to grumble, as I tooled back north on La Cienega towards my office. I stuffed another stale sinker into my mouth and washed it down with the tepid cup of Java cradled between my legs. It was already much later than I'd planned, but said, "The hell with everybody. They'll just have to wait."

At least the weather had cleared, but I wouldn't have that as an excuse. I thought about McCullen's newspaper photo and wondered who that dish really was. If he was that confused over the looks of his Ava that still didn't mean that DeCosta's doll wasn't the same one he'd been banging at the Blue Parrot Inn. Lancaster's I.D. only proved that the one standing next to DeCosta was not the real Ava, just a body double with a similar resemblance and maybe still DeCosta's bimbo.

I torched the last Lucky in the pack, sucked in a lungful of nicotine to quell my nerves, coughed a couple of times to smooth them out, and tossed the match out the window. I almost followed it with the crushed empty packet when I remembered I'd slid that pawnshop ticket I'd nicked at the Blue Parrot under the cellophane wrapper for safekeeping. I stuffed it into a side coat pocket with a mental note to follow it up, maybe later in the afternoon.

Glancing at the dashboard, I also noticed I was already exceeding the posted speed limit. One thing I didn't need was a gung-ho motorcycle cop with a fresh ticket pad to slow me down. I let up on the gas pedal.

As soon as I hit Sunset Boulevard., I hung a right, ticking off a few more miles. I began tapping on the steering wheel in concert to some unknown rhythm in my head to speed things up. It wouldn't make any difference. I continued cruising through the morning layer of smog and traffic-heavy streets surrounding the movie studios, scattered around the Hollywood neighborhoods like so many well-dressed warehouses hidden behind fancy front entrance facades. I passed several youthful starlet wanna-bees cruising the streets near Gringo Gulch trying to look dazzling and hoping to make it as an extra in anything glamorous off the sidewalks. Then again, I could have been wrong. Maybe they were just hookers trying to reel in a few early-bird suckers for a luncheon date and a quick spin in the sack before returning back to their nine-to-five's.

Picking up Vine Street, I zipped around a few straggling pedestrians lingering in the crosswalks. Sid's Haberdashery caught my attention with his flashy new store front sign and I stopped only long enough to drop off my smoke-infused suit for a major dry cleaning. After a couple more blocks, I finally spotted my Chrysler building, found an open spot in the alley bordering the building, and shared the elevator up to my office floor with a well-dressed older couple with a nervous leashed poodle cowering behind them.

Rhonda was seated at her desk buried behind an overflowing stack of unfinished reports and two-finger tapping away with enthusiasm at her typewriter when I walked in. I broke her concentration when I closed the door and she looked up startled. That face and body were more beautiful every time I saw them, I thought. She was wearing a matching beige cashmere sweater and thigh-high skirt combination with brown stilettos. Her hair was neatly arranged on top and a yellow pencil with a well-worn eraser protruded over one ear. This kid was a genuine knock-out that I was lucky the movie business didn't have their mitts on, yet.

"Where have you been, Matthew? You look terrible and we're late, you know," she said, first glancing at my disheveled appearance and then pointing to the wall clock.

"It's a long story gorgeous and I also had a rotten sleep last night, too. I'll tell you about it later."

I tipped my hat back on my head and dropped into the chair beside her desk. "Want a sinker?" I said, waving the sack in my hand. "I have a couple left over from a breakfast joint on Pico where I almost got a decent breakfast, for once." I helped myself to another and tossed it on her desk over the stack of reports she'd been typing.

She gave my choice of suits the once over again and shook her head. "No thanks, sweetheart. I already ate this morning; you know my usual two poached eggs, two slices of toast and coffee. I have to keep my trim figure in tip-top shape. You know I don't eat that junk." She moved it aside closer to the edge over the trash can.

"Yeah, I know…saving yourself for the mugs at the Florentine."

She just smiled and started shuffling the mess on her desk into neat piles, anxious to leave.

I couldn't blame her. The hockey pucks were stale and lousy anyway. I tossed the one I'd half eaten into the trash can beside her desk followed by the sack and my container of left-over cold coffee. "What time did you say we were supposed to meet over at the Majestic Studios?"

"At 10:30 P.M. and it's almost that time now and don't forget you were going to meet with Doris Fillmore from the newspaper someplace afterwards. You had to call her when you finished up at the Majestic, remember?"

"Oh yeah, I'll have to find out what she's got on McCullen. Nothing surprises me about that character, either. I have a gut feeling he's in on something bigger than I first suspected, up to his ears in Buffalo chips, too."

I produced the newspaper out of my coat pocket and tapped the Blue Parrot Inn story with my finger, "Take a look at this Rhonda, and tell me what you think. This does not add up to what we saw yesterday."

She scanned the article and gave me the same startled expression I must have had when I'd first read it too and tossed the paper aside.

"Poisoned? What about those black panties wrapped around her neck?"

"I know. Either someone's trying to cover up the murder angle and make a suicide out of this or there's something else going on. It doesn't make any sense. If I have time, I'll drop by Tank Sherman's office when I get through at the Majestic today and see if I can get some straight answers. I might have to call Doris and postpone our get-together.

"I noticed you have your hair in a- ah…what's that called? A French twist? I like it. It's on top of your head, perfect…especially for today. Makes you look more ah- serious? Yes, that's it."

"What's so special about today, Matthew?"

"I want you to hang around the Majestic and gather information. Just tag along with Hemingway and keep your eyes and ears open. You'll need to blend in, okay?"

"That sounds good. What do I have to do?"

"Just pretend you're on Hemingway's personal team. The regular movie staff is always busy fussing with scripts, taking notes, running errands, and in general, just looking busy. But in actuality, they are really not doing much at all. I'll brief you on the drive over."

"Okay, I can do that, sounds like fun," she said smiling, getting excited and not having the faintest clue what this was about, yet. Neither did I, but would soon find out.

"This is serious," I reminded her. "With your looks and shape, you'll fit right in, but first you'll need a little more of a disguise to tone down the glamour."

I pulled open a file drawer and fished around inside for a few props and handed them to her. "Here's a pair of horned rim specs with just plain window glass that I want you to wear. Makes you look studious and here's a clip board with some typed notes on top over a yellow pad for taking notes and bring along a couple of freshly sharpened pencils, your specialty." She didn't get the crack about the pencils, and I shouldn't have said it as she'd finally tapered off destroying all the office pencils once she'd settled down to normal clerical routines.

We closed up shop and rode back down to the lobby and stopped at the front desk. My pal "Fast Eddy" Simpson the concierge, was busy handicapping the day's races at Santa Anita and Hollywood Park, a stubby pencil jotting down facts and figures. His connection to "Gimpy" the bookie, a small timer with big ears who ran a lobby cigar and newsstand over at the Woodruff Hotel, usually produced the best pony tips in town.

"What's cooking today at Santa Anita, pal? Anything running out of Joey DeCosta's stable with good odds?"

"I like this one, Captain," he said looking up, eagerly pointing to "Princess Gina" in the third race at the same time startled by beautiful Rhonda standing beside me, giving her the once over with an envious gleam in his eyes.

I practically swallowed my cigarette when I saw this entry's name, but salted it away. I introduced her as my new private secretary and confidant. He whistled, a sly grin plastered across his kisser, and said, "Wow, Captain. I'm sure glad I'm work'n this lobby instead of the track stables, like before. The scenery here just went first class." He whistled again and followed that up with another face-splitting smile in her direction.

"No doubt about it, pal. She's a keeper, so far, aren't you, kitten?" I said glancing sideways at my cupcake.

"If you say so, Matthew," she said, sliding her arm through mine, adding a little extra squeeze for assurance.

Eddy glanced at both of us, just shook his head, exhaled, and continued where he left off, "It-it's a six-furlong purse of $100,000. I was hoping you'd stop by, great odds at 10 to 1. That DeCosta's sure been have'n good luck lately, too." He gulped for more air still thinking about Rhonda gracing his lobby.

"I think there's more behind it than luck, Eddy." I peeled three C notes off my money clip for a win and told him to collect his usual cut if he was right and added another couple of fins for some extra skinny, I needed from Gimpy.

The last bit brought a quizzical wrinkle to his brow. I fleshed it out for him. "I want you to ask him to I.D. the broads that usually accompany Joey DeCosta at the track. You know…names, descriptions, and anything else he thinks important to throw in. It's important to a case I'm working, so I need it ASAP, too. And if you get something and we don't connect, just drop a note with his findings in my office mail slot, okay?"

"I got it, Captain. Gimpy being an ex-jock, he still has connections at all the tracks. He'll know, if anybody does and can keep his mouth shut, too."

"Thanks pal. I knew I could count on you," I said, clapping him on the shoulder. I'd just tossed another chip down on the table and would just have to wait and see what that one yielded.

He grinned at me and now thoroughly smitten with Rhonda's beauty, gave her a glazed parting smile. She returned it with one of her heart-melting puckered specials, as I steered her towards the front door. I knew Eddy's eyes would be focused like magnets on her shapely derrière. He couldn't resist it. No red-blooded male with a normal pulse could. For a brief moment, I knew "Fast Eddy" was in heaven as he watched her trim figure glide across the lobby on her sky-high heels and soft, tight skirt. She was floating like a puff of cumulus clouds on a warm summers day; beautiful to behold and soon to disappear from sight.

At least he didn't have to pay for a front-row seat at the Florentine Gardens for his private floor show.

Chapter Fifteen

Fifteen minutes later, we rolled up to the Majestic Studio's front gates on the corner of Santa Monica Boulevard and Formosa Avenue. It sat across the street from one of my favorite seafood restaurants and watering holes, Rico's Seafood Grotto. The entrance into this movie studio's cardboard Valhalla, where you thought dreams were made and your soul was sold for maybe a chance to be famous for a flicker of time. It was similar to Paramount's with overhead sweeping signage flanking the gated and guarded front pillars. The Majestic Studio's lettering was in raised oversized fancy scroll script and lit with a hundred lights after dark. It was less pretentious than some, but still caught your eye, night or day when you drove by and it signaled to all comers, they were an active player in the movie business.

The studio was at least twenty acres of executive offices, writers, editorial, prop and costume buildings, a commissary, and numerous false front villages designed to replicate everything from urban to a variety of historical settings. All were surrounded by cavernous warehouse sound stages many of wood construction built in the 1930s. It was an entire square city block, fronting on both main streets. Some also whispered about a secret tunnel for VIPs running underneath Santa Monica Boulevard connecting the studio side to *Rico's* restaurant and bar across the street. It was supposedly frequented by major player Errol Flynn and other "A" listers when they supposedly needed a quick belt between scenes. I wondered about that one, but could never find the entrance from Rico's side and just wrote it off to another Hollywood myth…or was it.

I'd briefed Rhonda again on the way over with her assignment. It was simple. I leaned in close enough for her to hear me over the traffic noise and repeated, "Remember, just look inconspicuous, if that's possible," she smiled at that, "and take notes for a few hours on all suspicions characters connected with Hemingway, okay?"

"I can do that, easy," she said and eagerly dug out her steno pad and fake specs from the bottom of her purse to convince me she was prepared. I shook my head, grinned, and continued, "Perfect, but what about the clipboard you brought laying in the back seat?"

"I have both, just in case I need more paper."

"O-kay…good idea. Then ah- take a cab back to the office, pick up your auto and begin tracking down that item left at a local pawn shop from the ticket we lifted from the Blue Parrott."

"What do you mean we? That was you—"

"Well, you know what I mean. After you've figured out what was pawned, return to the office and continue to tackle those overdue reports … please? I'm going to get canned by those insurance companies I've been working for, if I don't send them in some status reports- and soon."

"Can do, boss," she said snapping me a small cute salute attached to another sweet smile as we approached the Majestic Studios.

Unfortunately for us as we arrived, the place was crawling with police cars waving traffic away and several fire trucks hosing down something smoldering beyond the entrance inside.

I recognized the security guard on duty, Elmo Bates, and waved as he stumbled out of his guard shack acting disorientated. I knew him from the days when I was still scratching for work before my P.I. business caught on and I was just a part-time bodyguard for some of the tinsel town big shots. He had a nervous, distressed expression and was wearing a sweat and dust-stained uniform. He also didn't look friendly as he approached, clipboard in hand to take names as duty called.

"M-Matt Thornton, thought it was you," he said, adjusting his cap and coughing from some of the smoke drifting in our direction. "You picked a hell of a day to visit, my friend. We've got problems, as you can see," he said, sweeping his arm in the direction of the chaos behind him.

"What's going on here, Elmo?"

"A bomb went off outside one of the film stages, just a little while ago. Number 36, it's about halfway down the main drag." He pointed straight down the central thoroughfare at what was now a jumble of confusion. From where I was sitting, I could just see fire trucks still pouring water on what was left of a parked white convertible that had been destroyed by the blast and still smoldering from the sabotage. Film crews and actors in an assortment of last century costumes were everywhere, milling about and getting in the way of police and firemen. Several were being questioned by the police, but probably only adding more hysterics to an apparently otherwise tragic and chaotic situation.

"Any injuries?"

"Couldn't say, Matt. Yeah, sure…probably, I guess so. I'm not getting involved. That's police business. Somebody must have triggered it though, but from where I'm standing it's just a mess and everyone's still shaken, including me. I-It was one hell of a blast…let me tell you. It rocked my guard station and damn loud. M-must have been a trunkload of dynamite." He slumped against the fender of my Buick, pale and still stunned by the close ordeal.

"Elmo, I guess from the looks of things you're not taking in any visitors right now. I was supposed to meet Ernest Hemingway here this morning. You got anything for me about that meeting?"

"Yeah, yeah it's here someplace." He fumbled underneath his clipboard of notes and lists, his hands still shaking. "He told me to give you this when you came around," he said, finally producing a sealed envelope with the words *Confidential: Matthew Thornton, P.I.* typed in bold lettering on the front. I glanced at Rhonda, who slid closer trying to peer over my shoulder to see what I'd been handed. I kept the engine idling while I ripped open the envelope, quickly reading the contents.

Shamus,

Studio turning into a powder keg. The scriptwriters for my story, "Swords at

Dawn" have butchered the plot. So far, the movie's a disaster. I personally hate it and told DeCosta. He's bought the story and insists it's his to tell on film. He seems powerless and is letting them get away with it. If he doesn't, I think they are going to mastermind another strike like the blood bath a year or so ago at MGM and shut the whole god-damned place down, including my movie.

I am not popular around here with scriptwriters. Think they're a tight group of Commie sympathizers. I have too many objections and suggestions to make it more like originally envisioned in the novel. Both actors playing main roles, Wes Canyon and Evan Rude, especially Wes, are OK in my book.

DeCosta's been trying to appease me by invites to some of his boring charity fundraisers. Mostly fronts for investing in his movies by other attendees ... hi-rolling businessmen, producers, directors, a few wealthy "A" list actors and actresses, several other saps like yours truly, and a few studio "B" list bimbos for window dressing.

Have had enough of tinsel town for now. Clearing out later tonight for a little fresh air back east. Will meet with publisher Lester Cartright in N.Y. about plan for next novel already in progress- til this mess blows over. Can be reached there if necessary. Wes to explain more details- our situation here.

There's something more sinister and dangerous to this situation than on surface. After private conversations with Wes about his Army "undercover operations" during the Big One, am convinced you two could work together and handle any rough stuff if necessary. Have enclosed check for $200. Should more than cover your expenses for any inconvenience my sudden departure has caused your schedule. Have changed meeting to Rico's Grotto across street. Wes to meet you there. Have several belts on me.

P.S. Studio loaned me flashy white Oldsmobile convertible. Mucho chrome with red leather seats to use while here. Hate color and feel like pimp driving it. Use if you want til I return. Battery going to be dead anyway sitting there (keys under floormat)...

Will return when things cool down, if don't get bumped off in meantime.

E.H.

"Lucky you didn't meet here earlier or you would have been right in the middle of that explosion when it went off," Elmo said, jolting me awake from

Hemingway's letter and anxious to get back inside his shack and sit down.

"Yeah, yes you're right, Elmo," I said, stuffing the letter back into the envelope and shoving it into my inside coat pocket. I tossed him a wave off and shifted into reverse to spin around.

I glanced at Rhonda and she didn't like what Elmo had just said and cringed. I couldn't blame her. This place was a mess and Hemingway had predicted trouble was brewing when he'd made the appointment for our visit in the first place. And now that this place had completely unraveled, he'd cleared out and had sent a substitute to help me unscramble his assignment which was vague, at best. Smart. I wasn't sure what he expected me to do, but picking my own partners was something I didn't need any help with. I would soon find out what this was all about after talking with Canyon, but I knew before I met him, it wouldn't be good.

As I spun the heap back toward the street, Rhonda turned in her seat towards me and asked, "I take it we're not going into the Majestic? I know it's a mess right now, but—"

"Sorry, baby, after reading this letter, Hemingway's changed the plan. And I'd say it wasn't any too soon for anyone involved, either. Especially him.

"We're going to meet an actor you may have heard of instead, a guy by the name of Wes Canyon. He's starring in Hemingway's new movie, *"Sword's at Dawn"*. We're just driving across the street to *Rico's* restaurant, okay?" She looked confused. "Hemingway already flew the coop last night and I think that bomb blast may have been meant for him too."

"How do you know?"

"That car that just went up in smoke looked like his studio loaner."

"Oh, oh, Matthew, this is getting dangerous, isn't it?"

"Scared?"

"No...not actually. I-I kind of like the excitement, don't you?" she said with a nervous grin, giving my leg a warm nudge with her thigh.

"Yeah me too, sweetheart," I said, reaching to tap her knee, but stopped short to spin the steering wheel. "Okay, here we are." I spotted an open parking space near the restaurant's front entrance, killed the engine, and set the parking brake. "Let's go in and meet Mr. Wes Canyon and hear what he has to tell us about this mess around here."

Chapter Sixteen

When we entered, Rico's always smelled like old money from its traditional, quiet, upscale nautical atmosphere to the snazzy staff in formal white stiff waiter's attire, efficiently circulating in the background. Rhonda squeezed my arm in awe, as we both adjusted to the half-light and I surveyed the crowd inside wondering where Hemingway's pal was hiding. I'd been there before, but never on my own dime, sometimes with a client or two or with a client's money only, as was the case today. That was even better.

The maître'd said to follow him for my rendezvous with Canyon. He'd already arrived and was waiting somewhere in the background. Rhonda was fascinated by the stuffed fish of every variety from Mako Shark to Wahoo looming over us from the mahogany paneled walls as we passed. Framed celebrity black and white photos adorned all the walls in between the saltwater trophies. We hurried past most without closer inspection, except for the one of Ava Gardner that I gravitated to automatically and paused for just a brief second to admire her beautiful smiling face. Red leather covered booths flanked both sides of the deep navy blue carpeted main dining room and starched white cloth covered tables dotted the middle. Most were empty this early in the day, but would soon be overflowing with well heeled, pleasantly lubricated customers.

Off to one side, a long ornate, mahogany bar sporting red leather high backed stools faced a mirrored background with indirect overhead lighting, illuminating a selection of booze tantalizing enough even for a tea-totaler. Behind it, a slim bartender wearing a starched white short jacket, a snappy black bowtie and a well-oiled hairdo was busy giving a Martini shaker a workout for some lucky customers sitting towards one end of the bar. From the way they were nuzzling in the semidarkness, you could tell they probably weren't married to each other and were anxious to jumpstart their luncheon buzz and something else more tantalizing afterwards.

We were led into the private backroom normally reserved for quieter, confidential dining. It was typically available, if you had reservations and liked to pay for a more exclusive dining experience. I wasn't concerned today about that.

"I think I've heard of Wes Canyon, but I'm not sure what movies he was in though," Rhonda whispered, gripping my arm, as we approached. "What do you want me to do now, just sit there and listen?"

"I guess, he's in the "B" pictures and pot-boilers. Maybe this is his big break. Who knows? Let's just see how this goes, first. Just follow my lead, doll and jump in, if it makes sense and take notes. Who knows what he's going to say. Listening will tell us more than talking, get it?"

She nodded an affirmative and I knew this beauty was smart and would be all right to have as a shadow on the wall. I watched her adjust the phony secretarial eye glasses, smooth out her hair and invisible wrinkles in her outfit as we were shown to a darkened booth towards the back.

A well-dressed middle aged man, wearing a navy blue blazer and dapper multicolored ascot over an open white shirt collar was sitting there by himself nursing a cocktail, puffing on a cigarette and from the overflowing ashtray next to him, waiting impatiently. He slid out to meet us as we approached. An automatic smile creased his sunlamp tanned face. His heavily lidded, slightly glazed eyes seemed to refocus when he thought he recognized my beautiful strawberry blonde partner.

Wes Canyon was movie star handsome in the traditional make-believe sense, if you liked them that way. He was a carbon copy of what you'd seen on the big screen, if you could remember ever seeing him. Closer inspection disclosed that he was shorter than usually projected, no battle scars, a slim almost weak build, glistening even white teeth … probably capped, closely cropped hair graying at the temples and from a light shining overhead, his noggin was already thinning a little on top. He was all wrapped up in studio polish, including a Ronald Coleman pencil thin mustache, attempting to disguise a weak long upper lip. For a second, he reminded me of the accountant keeping the books for my detective business. His well-staged manner and appearance naturally included a practiced smooth mellow baritone delivery. The whole persona was fabricated for capturing the unattached hearts of the front row bubblegum set on Saturdays and the blue-haired spinsters taking in a midweek matinee … from a distance.

He had nothing that would normally grate on your nerves unless you looked beneath the surface veneer … which I would, soon enough. Rhonda just stared and I needed a drink after meeting this showboat.

Canyon and I shook hands guardedly and introduced ourselves. He had a surprisingly firm grip for an actor. I introduced Rhonda as my personal secretary, who'd be taking notes and not Rhonda Fleming as he might have thought or maybe the Florentine gardens "Blow Torch" if he'd frequented that dive, which he probably had. Much to her surprise she was rewarded with a toothy smile and a warm Hollywood kiss on the cheek and a hug, instead of a handshake. She pretended she was enchanted immediately with his charming introduction and intimated that she was another fan and admirer of his movies. I nudged her to snap out of the nonsense, as we all slid back into the oversized semicircular booth. Canyon sat on one side Rhonda closer to me on the other. I didn't want her sandwiched next to the studio "Don Juan" like a warm muffin stuffed in a baking pan and oven ready for consumption. I needed this meeting to stay seriously focused in spite of my attractive companion.

Our waiter appeared and I ordered; a seafood platter of hors d'oeuvres, a George Dickel whisky and soda for myself, a very dry Beefeater Martini for Rhonda, who whispered it was too early for her to drink and Canyon not wanting to be left behind, didn't object to another refill of whatever he was already drinking, first polishing off the dregs in his glass before the waiter disappeared. No one else admitted wanting any food, as it was still early, but I was starved and with Hemingway paying for it, why not.

While we worked on our drinks, both of the non-eaters helped me polish off the platter of finger food anyway. Canyon and I first sparred with a few similar war time experiences in the European theater, while Rhonda worked on her Martini, listened and scribbled down a few things of interest. We finally hit common ground … our connection with the OSS and underground partisans, his in France and mine in Spain that included Rhonda's brother Tex. Then, we got down to the business at the Majestic that Hemingway was worried about. For openers, I produced the envelope with Hemingway's letter that he'd left for me and slid it across to Canyon.

"Take a look at this and then fill me in on what's going on around here, especially right now across the street. Isn't that convertible that just got torpedoed, Hemingway's loaner?"

"I heard that's the one. I was here having a drink when it happened, so don't know much more."

"Close call for Hemingway, eh?" I said, digging deeper.

"N-no, I don't think so. That could have been meant for anyone, maybe even me," he muttered in a nervous staccato.

"What makes you think so?"

"DeCosta loaned his crate out to a lot of people at Majestic, besides Hemingway."

"Well, somebody must have tripped the explosives. Any idea who bought the farm and why?"

"N-nope, sorry. No idea."

He was probably lying, as he looked down, avoiding my stare. In between several more, short belts, he sucked on the ice cubes in the nearly empty glass to calm his nerves. It didn't seem to be working. He signaled a passing waiter to hit him again for another refill and then slammed his glass on the table, impatient with the service.

Rhonda shot me a startled glance and nudged me with her knee under the table. She'd also observed his nervous smoking gestures, agitated speech pattern and rapid booze consumption.

This guy was a derailed train wreck about something. He'd chain smoked a carton load before we'd even arrived. And he continued, torching and snuffing one right behind the other, filling our end of the restaurant with more smoke than was legally allowed by the local fire marshal. I also wondered how many drinks he'd already polished off before we arrived.

"So, what gives around here, Canyon? And by the way, what was your real name before you went Hollywood?"

"You are a detective and direct too. It was Marvin Mumford, what difference does it make?" he said, fidgeting in his seat.

"I just like to clear the air with who I'm really talking too, okay? Marvin Mumford, eh? Let's just stick with the new moniker … good choice. Now, what makes you think someone could be after you, Wes?"

"You must have heard of the House Un-American Activities Committee that's been turning up the heat on the Hollywood set. Some are already going down the drain."

"Yeah, I read the papers, so?"

"Several years ago, the theatrical carpenters union, and others were threatening a big strike for more pay, benefits and everything else with all the studios, big and small. The teamsters, who handled all the studio transportation, were against it and with all their muscle and connections it fizzled out, but it was still simmering below the surface. Last year it surfaced again at MGM over in Culver City."

"Yeah, I know all about it, I was there. I'd been hired by the big boss, to help restore order for the studio. Picked up a scar or two on that day," I said, pointing to my forehead. "It wasn't good, turned out to be a real bloodbath. Movie industry trade employees, communist sympathizers and members of the communist party united on one side against law and order and the moving picture business management on the other. It was finally settled, but not a pretty sight and could have been done with less bloodshed. Social upheaval and revolutionary revolt was the order of the day. That stinks in my book."

He didn't waste another breath on his speech, before polishing off the last drop of his vodka, desperate to receive another immediately by our now hovering waiter.

"Okay, I get it, but how does that affect you or Hemingway? What's the connection here, fella?"

"Maybe it affects me, not him. Especially if they thought I was going to use DeCosta's auto, which he also told me I could to do when we were on one of the sound stages shooting a scene a couple of days ago. Someone must have overheard him talking to me."

"Does the studio own that car or is it just a rental? Do you know?"

'I think it belongs to Mr. DeCosta personally. Hemingway told me he had DeCosta "by the balls" as he put it and DeCosta was trying to get him to cooperate with everybody working on the picture so he could wrap it up. He lent him one of his cars to drive around town while he was here. I guess trying to get him to spend more time off the lot when they were shooting. But what Hemingway was talking about, I have no idea."

"More. Where do you come in? Why would somebody be after you?"

He shook off imaginary cobwebs fogging his memory and paused after another short pull on the sauce, searching blankly for an out to his confession somewhere across the empty room.

Rhonda paused from taking notes and tapped me again with her knee, noting his hesitation to go on. I reached under the table cloth to touch her warm thigh for concurrence and instead felt the outline of her garter belt snap attached to the top of her stockings. She glanced sideways, smiled as I played with the covered clasp. Then she reached under, patted my hand warmly, squeezed it between her legs and then removed it slowly and whispered-

"Easy, big guy … not now." Her promise followed by a cagey grin.

I smiled back at her tease. This kid was good all right. She'd interrupted my brief flight into a mid-day fantasy and I squirmed a little in my seat, adjusting my shorts into a more comfortable position.

The fleeting thought about a continuance later with this doll quickly evaporated, as Canyon picked up the threads of his story again and droned on. "It's about testifying before the committee and probably worse … I-I'd have to give names," he muttered.

This came as a shock and caught me off guard. "What the hell are you talking about, Canyon? You aren't a Red or a Commie sympathizer, are you?"

"Well n-no, not exactly. This whole thing was a mistake right from the beginning and I regret it, believe me. You see, Mr. Thornton, I was indirectly connected to one of the local partys right after I returned from the war. I'd met this young woman working on one of the movies I had a small part in and just got sucked in with her. Maybe you've heard of her, Sheila Perkins?"

I drew a blank and shrugged no connection. He'd struck out on that one and frankly, I didn't give a damn anyway as his whole story was starting to stink. I glanced at Rhonda and she just stared back at me also registering no recognition either. I had a feeling this guy's story was going straight down the sewer and him with it. I'd just listen, but I knew it wasn't going to turn out well and right now I had more important things to do. I checked the time on my watch and motioned to a passing waiter for a final refill on my drink, Rhonda's was still half full.

He didn't care that we didn't know his girlfriend, just wanted to get his dirty laundry out there for all to smell and droned on. "She was a real cutie. Had stars in her eyes for show business and even bigger dreams for humanity. She wouldn't hurt a fly, but got swept up in a movement that sounded like it had good intentions, but was actually just a front for a gigantic propaganda machine that as you've been probably reading about, didn't take long to establish a foothold with our liberals in the entertainment business. And, I got swept up into her misguided trash can as well and now I'm afraid, I might be doomed. Now, being a Hollywood producer, director, actor or writer associating with the Reds is a catastrophe. You are either banished from the entertainment and movie business in this country when you rat on your friends in the party, if you're lucky or you are held in contempt receiving a stiff jail sentence for not cooperating followed by banishment as well. Either way, I'm a pariah and either way I'm on a Black list or a list of some kind that seals my fate from making money in this business in the future. I'm screwed and don't know what I'm going to do."

I detected a slight tremor to his hand, raising his glass for a quick sip. He absently rotated the glass on the coaster. Clinking the ice cubes against the inside in a swirling motion, a frown crept across his face, as he thought about what he'd just confessed.

What a mess this guy was. "You fool, you joined the party. You are a Red, aren't you? How in the hell could you fall for that party line crap-ola, Canyon? I stay as far away from politics as humanly possible. Always have. Most of its bullshit anyway."

"I know, I know, but it was easy and I fell into the trap. I never went to any local party meetings though. My only real connection was knowing Sheila, that's all. When I worked with the partisan commie sympathizers in France against the Nazi's, I thought I was doing something at the time to help their cause. They thought they were doing the right thing too, but many were caught and executed for their actions. You must have connected with some in Spain?"

I stubbed out my cigarette and said, "Sorry, pal. I fought on Uncle Sam's side in the big one. Any of my connections and Rhonda's brother fighting right along beside me, were with our own troops which sometimes connected with Spanish Freedom Fighters, but that was all. They knew we were there to stamp out the Huns and not get wrapped up in anything Russian. I'm afraid you got swept up in a lost cause here afterwards and should have left that European war and all the crap politics behind when it was over. You didn't and instead you're now going to pay a steep price for your mistaken judgment.

"What happened to your girl Sheila? Still seeing her?"

"No … she's dead. Car crash off of Laurel Canyon Boulevard, a while back."

He looked down, depressed at having tossed out everything and was now "left without even a pot to piss in".

"Sorry, Wes, how did it happen?"

"Police said it was faulty brakes, but I don't believe it. Her Nash was always tuned up and in good shape. I suspected foul play connected with the party, but could never prove it."

"Who have you told this story to, Hemingway?"

"No, he only knows about my OSS work behind the lines in France and was only concerned that his troublemaking on the set was annoying the "big money boys", as he liked to call them. A strong arm and a hired gun was all he wanted from you to watch his back, but now that he's left town, that doesn't matter. But, only because of what's just happened today with that car bomb, have I realized that this now is going to crack wide open."

"Who else, knows this commie connection of yours?"

"I only told Mr. DeCosta a few days ago, hoping to save my job on this movie project as the studios are beginning to slam the doors on even those with connections. He seemed to be sympathetic with my situation, except my conversation must have leaked out. Or, maybe they're just sending a message to anyone planning to testify sometime in the future."

"Any way you look at it, sounds bad to me, pal. I'd say the party's got your number already for crying on DeCosta's shoulder and you're not too popular. I suggest you lay low for a few days. I don't think they'll resume with your picture right away after that mess across the street. I'll nose around DeCosta's side of the tracks alongside my own business and see what turns up. If there's anything concerning you, will get back … can't promise more."

I thought he'd perked up a little with the bone I'd tossed, except he just shrugged it off when he said, "I'm not going into hiding, Thornton. I'm in no more danger than anyone else around here connected with the party. I can take care of myself."

I thought, what a fool and said, "Okay, suit yourself, pal. Give Rhonda some phone numbers where we can contact you again. Oh, and one more thing, take a look at this." I pulled out the newspaper clipping of DeCosta and his friends at the track and pointed to the Ava Gardner clone in the photograph. Canyon slipped on a pair of reading glasses and lost his tan.

"Ever see that dame standing next to DeCosta. She's a real looker," I said, pointing to the dish with the big smile and DeCosta's wrap around hand cupping her breast.

He shook his head slowly, double checking the dated photo and mumbled, "I'm not sure I know who she is, why?" He gulped what was left in his glass as a refuge from the truth. From his reaction, I knew he was covering up something that I'd eventually find out.

I probed once more, "She wouldn't be hard to miss, Canyon. Maybe works on the studio lot somewhere?

"She must be one of DeCosta's usual bimbos. Several have been in a few low budget "B" numbers to get their feet wet and tail seasoned by some of the studio big shots. Apparently that one's worked her way to the top … fast. You know how it goes?"

"Yeah, I get it, anything more?"

"I already told you, I haven't seen her before," he replied. "Sorry, you'll have to ask around."

That was about it for this guy. I'd pumped his well dry for what it was worth and I didn't like either his answers or his attitude. Hemingway was wrong on this bird. He wasn't okay in my book and would probably deserve all that he had coming. I stuffed the clipping back in my pocket as he dug out something of his own inside his coat and silently handed it to me to read.

"What's this?" I said, flipping through a professionally prepared multipage newsletter entitled the "Progressive Leader" printed in bold lettering across the top. A quick perusal of the well written and persuasive articles answered my question.

When I looked up, Canyon caught my glare and elaborated, "I thought you should see that in case you haven't already. It's the latest commie propaganda spiel that's been circulating around all the movie studios recently and maybe even to some of the other entertainment joints around town … that I don't know. It's clearly slanted at promoting communist party membership, agitating for leftist social issues and inciting members to take action by infiltrating and subverting all levels of business and government. This commie, studio, union mess is all connected isn't it?"

"You could be right, Canyon." I tossed it back on the table. A trashcan would have been more suitable. "Keep your eyes peeled and ears waxed. Maybe we'll uncover who's involved in financing, publishing and distributing that rag. Know anyone in the Screen Writer's Guild? From what I've heard, that seems to be the central hot bed."

"I know a couple of guys. I'll nose around from this end, okay?"

He was in a precarious position and knew it. Only by cooperating with a stranger that Hemingway had chosen, could he dig himself out of this hole he'd fallen into.

I nodded and said, "Be careful, Chum." He offered a clammy hand to shake before we left.

As we slid out of the booth, he gave Rhonda another once over. A recognition finally clicked and he blurted out like a Boy Scout in a bordello with a big grin plastered across his mug, "Say, a-aren't you that striptease dancer "Torchy" over at the Florentine Gardens nightclub? I-I thought I recognized you when you walked in, but just couldn't place it 'til now. Am I right?"

Rhonda shot me a quick sideways glance, smiled sweetly with that "eat your heart out" kisser and shot back in a soft purr, "I'm sorry Mr. Canyon, you must have me mixed up with someone else. I'm only a private detective's secretary. But, thanks for the compliment … anyway."

"Oh, I'm sorry. I must have confused you with someone else," he mumbled an apology. Then he bent closer and offered her another Hollywood kiss on the cheek, as a consolation prize. We left him there in the darkened, empty booth; filling his overflowing ashtray, polishing off more booze and contemplating a dismal future.

Chapter Seventeen

A yellow checker taxicab pulled smartly up in front of *Rico's* and unloaded a well-dressed couple, eager for a lobster luncheon. I was going to send Rhonda back to the office in that crate to pick up her coupe and begin tracking down that pawn ticket in El Segundo, but changed my mind. That could wait. I'd keep her with me for something to eat. After spending so much time listening to Canyon's doubtful depressing story line in that gloomy cave, I needed some fresh air and a change of atmosphere. I knew my sexy partner probably did too. When I mentioned another plan, her eyes brightened and she perked up. I didn't have to say more.

We'd both had it with *Rico's*, for today, anyway. I whipped the Buick convertible east onto Santa Monica Boulevard with Rhonda glued by my side. My suggestion for lunch at the Brown Derby near my office on North Vine Street was just what we both needed before continuing and I felt elated to be outside in the sunshine. Even moving through the midday traffic was a relief from that dark mausoleum where we'd left Canyon.

I popped out the dashboard lighter for a smoke and glimpsed Rhonda as she began to drop her secretarial disguise, which would have only fooled a blind man anyhow. She shoved the cheaters into her purse and turned that blonde mane loose in the wind, letting it whip around her beautiful face in the warm sun. Turning towards me with a puckered smile she said, "Wasn't it ironic where we were sitting in that restaurant?"

"About what, baby?"

"I mean the "Red" colored booths and all the black and white photos of

Hollywood's elite plastered around the restaurant on the walls. They might be "hot shot movie stars" with the public, but now they're on the "hot seat" with the Federal government." She laughed at her joke and so did I.

"That's cute, baby and a smart observation. I thought the same thing as we were leaving."

"And what about that phony story from Wes Canyon? Didn't that sound a little rehearsed? I mean, he even had the glum expressions and all to go with it. If he was that worried, why was he still in town?"

"You read my mind again, sweetheart."

Tex was right. This kid was sharper than a freshly cut diamond and catching on so damn fast, I might cut myself trying to unwrap her tight package later. That cabeza had more than just a beautiful face. She had brains as well as a showgirl's figure.

"I think he's not telling us something, Matthew. Don't know what, but he's at least hiding behind that excuse of a girlfriend. Doesn't that sound weak to you?"

"Yeah, his whole story stinks, especially hiding under a woman's skirt. But, Hemingway's no fool. He may like this guy for his movie, but he wouldn't like what we heard today and would dump him faster than a plate of green cheese. Maybe Canyon's not in trouble with that commie congressional committee after all and has something else going on.

"Like what?"

"Don't know yet, but will find out, if I have time. We've got more iron's in the fire than getting involved with that guy, angel. Let's just concentrate on those first. I'll snoop around at the Majestic after lunch on McCullen's dame, while you track down some of those other clues we picked up on the crime scene, okay?"

"Sounds good to me, Matthew. I'm getting hungry. Look, there's the Brown Derby," she said pointing to the famous restaurant across the street, as I slowed to enter the parking lot.

* * *

It was midday and the Derby was packed. After greasing the palm of the maitre'd up front, we were escorted to a private, comfortable booth half way towards the back. My strawberry blonde partner garnered the usual admiring smiles and nods, including a few envious raised eyebrows, from some of the tinsel town celebrities seated at the surrounding tables. She tossed them her most captivating smile, leaving them guessing her unknown identity, as we slipped into the booth, warm thighs touching again underneath the starched table cloth.

I ordered two very dry Bombay Gin and Noilly Pratt Vermouth Martini's to get us in the right mood and wasted no time placing our order. We both gravitated to the Derby's "Daily Luncheon Special"- *Calf's Liver & Onions with Bacon* paired with a tossed salad, a small side of fried potatoes, fresh garden peas and a glass of Burgundy wine for me and chilled Chardonnay for Rhonda.

I glanced around and noticed it wasn't the first choice for many in the restaurant. Several preferred what I'd noticed listed on the luncheon menu as the *Trout Amandine*. However, what they were eating looked strange and smelled worse. Whatever it was, appeared to be smothered in something like cornflakes, maybe an attempt to mask the offensive odor. From the gagging sounds emanating from the surrounding tables, I was convinced it was something else, but wasn't sure what and tried to ignore it.

Rhonda caught the scent too, sniffing the air several times. She leaned in closer and said, "M-Matthew, I-I don't know what those other people are eating, but I'm beginning to feel queasy."

I suggested holding her nose while sipping some wine to coat her palate. I had my doubts about that remedy and from her pale and sweaty countenance, I knew she wasn't lying. I was feeling slightly nauseous myself. But what I really thought about saying would have been far less effective, but more entertaining....

"If you're feeling faint Rhonda, just bend over; put your head between your legs and … yodel."

She'd shoot me a startled expression and mutter, "The tabletop is in the way and, and … I don't know any alpine songs."

Naturally confused over this suggestion, I'd mention an alternative solution and say, "I'll help. I'll put my head between your legs, if you'll do the musical bit, okay? Just, make something up. Trust me, it will work."

She wouldn't be confident with my plan, but would shrug her shoulders with resigned reluctance and acquiesce. I would follow with self-doubts of my own, especially after listening to her practice a couple of times. She'd sound more like a strangled cork getting jerked out of a wine bottle than a Swiss miss in heat.

I'd bump my head a few times adjusting my own position and get ready. When all was finally in order, a sweeter and purer Alpine aria would never grace the wooded valleys and mountainous peaks in all of Bavaria, like hers during that wonderful unique following moment.

The Derby would come alive with "the sound of music" and all the surrounding tables and booths from front to back, including the waiters and bartenders would join in harmonizing and humming along. Her melodious voice would echo off the walls and reverberate as far and wide, as the parking lot outside.

I sat there, chuckling at this daydream, when Rhonda broke up my reverie. She said, "Matthew, what were you thinking about? You were smiling for once, at something funny?"

"Ah- yes, just a passing thought about you, sweetheart and a very pleasant one, too."

"Oh, thank you. I'm feeling better now, too. That sip of wine seemed to work and I don't smell anything unpleasant anymore either."

After we finished our lunch, I couldn't resist asking my waiter about our neighbor's luncheon choice. He pinched his nose and whispered something confidential about another spicy Derby creation, *Creole Macaroni & Cheese Fish Casserole*, substituted at the last minute to cover a gap in the menu. Just the thought of that combination was enough to make you nauseous.

Ours was a hit though with both of us anyway and after a few more glasses of wine, I left a healthy tip for the excellent service, as usual.

As we neared the front door, Seymour Swartz, one of the Derby co-owners that I'd helped squeak out of a connection in a local murder case was delighted seeing me again, this time under less strenuous circumstances. He pumped my hand vigorously while ignoring me and staring at Rhonda, "Who is this beautiful young lady, Matthew," he fawned, grinning like a movie star pervert, holding her out stretched hand, longer than she wanted. "Please bring her again soon to grace our humble establishment. You look so familiar, sweetheart," he said, casting a glance at some of the black and white photos plastered on the walls, trying to spot someone that he'd forgotten was there. Haven't I seen you in something recently?"

He'd probably seen her out of something recently at the Florentine, which I was sure he attended, but didn't comment other than, "Sy, we've got to leave. We're already late for another appointment, especially after this morning over at the Majestic Studios, so-ah-."

He looked confused; another one still trying to place my cupcake and just smiled not certain that he understood what I was mumbling about. Just to cinch our return soon, he threw in a complimentary free pass to cover the valet parking, good anytime. That made my day.

We left arm in arm. On the walk back through the parking lot, I envisioned Rhonda chattering about a return engagement as the Derby guest soloist and me, performing an encore in our office to investigate the tensile strength of my new couch hide-a-bed.

But instead afterwards, I just dropped Rhonda off at the office, where she picked up her Ford coupe to play detective at a local pawn shop. I could double back to the Majestic and maybe the crime scene, hopefully picking up a few threads on the McCullen dame. But first, I had one more delinquent item on my agenda.

I stopped at Schwab's drug store on Sunset Boulevard, dropped a few coins into a rear-booth telephone and caught my favorite newshawk Doris Fillmore at the *Herald Examiner*, working at her desk.

"Hi baby, Matthew here," I said, sounding upbeat, while my thinking cap was working overtime to concoct a plausible excuse, she'd buy for stiffing her on the luncheon meeting date I'd promised.

"Matthew, I'm so glad you didn't call me earlier for lunch," she said in a cheery, breathless voice, taking me by surprise.

"Oh, why was that? I thought you'd be a little disappointed that maybe I'd, uh- stood you up," I mumbled.

She didn't complain, instead said, "No, not at all. I just returned from another crime scene and was writing up the story for the late edition and wouldn't have had any time for us anyway."

"Oh?"

"Yes, I barely had time to eat. I just grabbed a sandwich at the corner deli, on the way back to the office."

"I see, well- ah-"

"Matthew, why don't you drop by my office building instead and I'll give you a quick rundown on what I've uncovered so far on McCullen, before I finish my article. Sound good?"

"Perfect, I'm on my way, angel," I said, relieved as she squeaked out a kiss good bye and we hung up.

Chapter Eighteen

William Randolph Hearst's Herald Examiner newspaper was an unusual and excessively ornate Mission Revival styled building on West 11th Street. It was only a short distance away and not far from the Chinatown district, maybe another item on my unfinished agenda today.

I parked around the corner in a curb-side red zone, the only available empty space on the busy street. No cops in my rearview mirrors, so I slid out and locked up. I entered the massive, opulent, cavernous two-story-high lobby that seemed as large as the equally overly ornate similarly styled Los Angeles Union train station.

The *Herald Examiner* building was decorated in exaggerated Spanish Colonial-influenced styled architecture with mile-high beamed lobby ceilings, drooping crystal chandeliers, curved multistory windows flanking the front, over polished marble floors, cornices, and cast gold-infused wall figurines stationed throughout this 100,000 square foot five story extravaganza. A two-story bronze railed staircase protruding at the far end of the lobby, led to the sky-lit reporters' desks and editorial offices on the second floor. A caged elevator with an attractive female operator dressed in a bell-boy outfit was stationed in the middle, for those that preferred a slower, swankier ascent into the pulse of the working minds driving the newspaper.

As I worked my way forward, I spotted Doris waving from the far end balcony outside her office area and I waved back. I quickened my pace, hastening to meet my old flame and the best inside information source in

Los Angeles. I was anxious to collect anything she had on my mystery client, McCullen, and knew she was never a letdown with reliable information.

As an ace crime reporter, she covered the trench warfare faster and more accurately than anyone else pounding a journalistic typewriter in the city, to root out the crime, corruption, and political graft. She was usually the first one to uncover a dead body at the city morgue and wrap a story around it, the first one at a bloody street murder, the first one on the crime scene from outside tips, the last one to leave the police station when a suspect was being questioned and the last one to leave when the coroner's meat wagon had hauled away another corpse for autopsy. She was next in line for the city editor slot and a well-deserved promotion, if she wanted it. Which she probably didn't as working a daily and sometimes nightly crime beat was still what made her tick. She knew that getting wrapped up in the business of selling tabloid-styled newspapers recycling other reporter's stories was not really her forte.

I took the trip upstairs the fast way and two at a time, removing my hat on the way up to let off the steam. Doris was waiting at the top with a big red-lipped smile, her cobalt blue eyes glimmering like the ocean on a warm summer day, as I approached. She clutched a manila folder close to her breast, that I assumed was the McCullen report, but she didn't comment on what it was. She was wearing a light grey tailored business skirt and matching suit coat, a white blouse with a string of grey pearls, and black medium height shoes. Her brunette hair was neatly swept up on her head with a French twist in the back accentuating her graceful neck but expressing the serious business composure necessary for her next high-level role she was trying to avoid.

"Beautiful as usual, baby and ve-ry business-like in that sharp outfit," I complimented, followed by a low whistle and my broad smile.

"That's nice of you to say so, Matthew," her plump kisser an invitation.

I added, "Your Chanel No.5 perfume still gives me a hard-on. Reminds me of some good times we had together, remember?"

Her eyes glistened with a silent answer only, because she knew I was sincere in spite of my phrasing and had said it all. She glanced around to see if my ribald comments had been overheard, yet from her sly grin, I could tell she wouldn't turn down another chance, if it was offered.

I had a feeling this meeting with Doris would be another positive offset to some of the negative situations I'd been subjected to recently and was looking forward to spending time with my old flame, as well as getting down to business.

I put my arm around her and said, "Baby, you're always in style and always attractive, in spite of that mean beat you walk. Sometimes I worry though, after I've read some of your crime expose's. You write some of the most informative and often lurid stories in tabloid print today. But, it's dangerous stuff to collect where you go, angel."

"I know, but someone's got to get into the gutter to do it and you know who's the best don't you?"

"I do…you, babe."

"Yes, that's me all right."

She smiled, gave me a warm and prolonged kiss on the cheek and an affectionate hug as once old lovers do when surrounded by strangers in a public place. She felt good standing close to me. After we exchanged a few more familiar pleasantries, she took my arm and steered me to a small private empty conference room at the end of the corridor, anxious to get started.

A large walnut table surrounded by a dozen matching chairs filled the center of the light beige room. Potted parlor palms filled in the corners. A long built-in walnut credenza containing only a hotplate with a steaming coffee pot on top flanked the side opening into the hallway. The outside far wall was floor-to-ceiling glass windows overlooking street traffic several stories below, crawling around each other like ants on dropped food. The other three walls were decorated with framed news clippings, headlines boasting of the newspapers more sensational stories in journalism. One, in particular, caught my eye, Doris's famous coverage of the "Mulholland Drive Lover's Lane Murders". I scanned the tragic story, shaking my head in disbelief again, as I recalled some of the gruesome details that Doris had captured so vividly in black and white print. Her award-winning coverage included city maps, gruesome photographs of the victim's dismembered bodies, and the retelling of their unsolved deaths in copious details. It brought Doris instant almost celebrity status within journalism circles and would prompt senior Herald executives to give serious consideration to elevating Doris out of the gutter crime beat and into the hallowed circles of executive editor status. I knew she'd been avoiding the promotion for quite a while, but it would only be a matter of time before she succumbed to the wishes of the William Randolph Hearst organization and accept her just reward…whether she liked it or not.

"Fascinating story, isn't it Matthew?" she said, reading my mind and sliding her arm through mine as she proudly reread several passages of her descriptive award-winning prose, over my shoulder.

"That case is now getting colder than an Eskimo's pizzle, baby." Doris was no virgin to salty language and just chuckled at my expression as usual. "Too bad the local P.D. still has it open on their books and couldn't pull it together. I might have been able to help at the time, but I was out of commission, remember?"

"I remember. I've saved several juicy stories in my files that you did help solve though; the "Indian Bend Hotel Murders" out in Palm Springs, the "Malibu Beach Slasher" case and one of my favorites, the "Murder of Actor Kirby Lamont" at the Flamingo night club in West Hollywood."

She was on a gutter newshawk's memory dream roll, but I grimaced, after hearing that last one. The only thing that stuck with me about the Lamont stabbing case was that I'd wound up in the hospital full of bullet holes. "Yeah, that Flamingo killing had the P.D. baffled didn't it, and I almost bought the farm too, didn't I?"

"Yes, you did, sweetheart," she said, tightening her arm through mine and glancing up with sad eyes. "Sorry I mentioned it."

"No, I don't think I want to read about them again, Doris, even if my name was plastered all over your newspaper." I smiled and added to lighten the mood, "For me, once they're closed, they stay closed, but you're free to keep those stories to wrap fish or paper your birdcage if you like, okay?"

She understood and grinned. We moved away from the old news clippings on the wall and helped ourselves to a cup of the boiling Java from the pot on the credenza. Then seated next to each other at the conference table, she presented the manila folder of information compiled on my client, Carson McCullen. She slipped on a pair of horn rim spectacles and adjusted them closer to the tip of her nose. I slid an ashtray between us and offered her a cigarette. After we both paused to fill up the room with a little smoke and in between sips of the steaming coffee, she flipped open the folder and began disclosing the details.

"This Carson McCullen file is quite interesting, Matthew," she said, jabbing a forefinger at the top sheet. "As you know, I enjoy working on stories that have a hazy background with possible underworld connections. I think you have a client here that has a checkered past and is possibly more dangerous than even you might realize. He presents himself locally as a reputable businessman as a successful founding executive of a large, local manufacturing corporation, specializing in aircraft instrumentation and other electronic products. His core business was and still is apparently built around his machine shop business. He specialized in forging and metal works in the old country, before he became an American citizen."

"Sounds bland, so far, where did he come from?"

"Not so fast, lover. Let me tell it my way, okay?"

"I'm listening, baby. Go on."

"It's what his real expertise has focused on that might be of real interest to you. From what I've uncovered, there is possibly another side to this character than is generally unknown in the conservative circles he socially revolves in. I'll lay out what I've uncovered so far, and you can fill in the missing pieces after you hear them."

I smiled and was going to interrupt again with another thought, but she gave me a raised "not yet" stop sign, so I said, "Okay, okay I'll shut the trap and just keep listening."

She grinned and continued, "Because I'm in the newspaper business, I've been able to uncover more about this guy than I originally expected. When you hear about some of these details, I'm sure you will have plenty to work with, on whatever your involvement is with this character."

Doris didn't know this was already turning from a possible blackmail case or possibly just drunken bad judgment on a pickup date gone wrong to a possible murder rap. I'd keep that part confidential, at least for now.

"His name was changed from Carl Muller to Carson McCullum when he arrived in this country in the early 1930s. His trade while living in Switzerland or Austria and that part is vague, but my guess connects him with the Swiss banking system, where he was a successful machine shop and forge owner. Why he left is unknown, other than he must have gotten wind of a war brewing and decided to leave before it heated up around him...or maybe something else. After he arrived here, he established a small machine shop again which expanded into a manufacturing foundry in the town of Syracuse, New York of all places."

I stubbed out my cigarette, looked puzzled, and said, "Why there?"

"Who knows, it's in upstate and is an odd location. Maybe it was just a foothold in the states somewhere obscure? Or, maybe he knew someone in the Germanic population that settled around there? Anyway, his foundry business grew and was apparently quite successful and profitable. He focused on supplying the various growing newspaper businesses around the country building and repairing paper-making machines. It's a very specialized niche business and he was apparently one of the best."

"That's the connection with your newspaper and how you were able to collect as much on him as you have, isn't it?"

"Yes. Let me continue. It's involved, but I think you'll agree that it leads to a place we should all be concerned about.

"As a wealthy man, he apparently returned to Europe several times by the late thirties, for supposedly business purposes, doing what or seeing whom, we don't know exactly, but my guess is he was in contact with high ranking Nazi's who by then were flexing their muscles for the big one. While there, he married a woman whom he'd known for years, prior to his immigrating to the states. Then after they returned to Syracuse, he made another change. He decided to leave northern New York. He abruptly sold off his foundry business and he and his wife moved to sunny Southern California. With the profits from his paper printing machine business, he set himself up in a new venture, an electronic manufacturing business in El Segundo. Then, with contracts garnered from various high-level contacts in business and government agencies in Washington, he was one of the first to get in on the ground floor manufacturing aviation instruments for the United States military that was building up support for the pending world war."

"What's the history on his manufactured instruments? Were they legit or defective?"

"That's information I found to be all wartime classified, so I guess we'll never know. I have my own suspicions, knowing his background and probable pro-Nazi connections. In any event, he made another mint on that operation courtesy of Uncle Sam and probably a handful of slippery politicians. And that brings us up to today and what Mr. McCullen/Muller has been up to recently that concerns us? I think he's either getting bored or it was an old dormant plan from the beginning, and he was just waiting for the right opportune moment to execute it. From what I've heard unofficially from several high-ranking Washington sources of mine, there's a big socialist-communist conspiracy plan in motion to overthrow our governmental system and democracy in general. As you already have heard in the news recently, the Red Menace is gaining a foothold by infiltrating everywhere, especially here in California; politics, government, the educational system, and the entertainment industry. As a matter of fact, the story I'm working on right now concerns, just that and it's another shocker, too."

"Care to share it with me before it hits the press?

"Why not, but let's not digress too long, okay? I've got to get back to it or I'll miss my deadline" she said, glancing at the wall clock over my shoulder. I followed her gaze and thought about my convertible parked illegally next to a fireplug down below and wondered how much it was going to cost me to get Doris's inside dope on McCullen.

She took a sip of her Java and continued, "You must have heard of Lowell Phillips, one of the big screenwriters over at Olympic Studios? He was found dead this morning from a self-inflicted gunshot wound to the head."

I didn't know who he was, but whistled and frowned at this disclosure after hearing his profession. I had a good guess where this one was probably going.

"He was 39 years old and apparently had just recently bought a small bungalow off of Fairfax in West Hollywood to celebrate his newfound status in tinsel town. He was obviously on a roll with some of his latest screenplays. You remember "Revenge at El Dorado Creek" don't you?"

"Yeah, I think so, wasn't it a western last year? The one about struggling cattle ranchers in southern Arizona killed by a gang strong-arming property owners out of their ranchland? The ranches are all supplied by a connecting creek of water that holds the real lands value- gold. One young widow contacts her dead husband's best friend for help. He's out of the country supplying stolen U.S. Army guns to Pancho Villa across the border in his support of the Mexican War. With the U.S. Cavalry hot on his tail trying to recover the stolen arsenal of weapons, he slips back across the border with Villa and his men to help the ranchers. All hell breaks loose when he arrives. It's not a bad picture either."

"You've got a good memory, Matthew. That *was* one of his. Now he's just another dead sap caught up in the latest congressional testimonies and hearings. From what I could find out, he was scheduled to appear in a few days. I found out, it was rumored that he was planning to rat on his friends belonging to the party, but was wracked by guilt and talking suicide ever since his name had been linked up."

"You sure his suicide wasn't coaxed?"

"What makes you say that, Matthew?"

"I just returned from the Majestic Studios where another Red mess is brewing. A convertible in the parking lot was blown to pieces and it wasn't just an overheated battery either.

"So, it looks like we're on the same page with this Phillips business as well, Doris. But what's that got to do with this McCullen character?"

"He may be a key linchpin in the commie takeover around here."

"I don't get it."

"He's a mastermind when it comes to fabricating certain types of machinery, isn't he?"

"If you say so, go on."

"What do you think those two government agents were doing in town that were just murdered a couple of days ago?"

"The FBI agents I read about? No idea."

"Matthew, they weren't FBI agents. Their exact titles were purposely left out of the newspapers. They were treasury agents."

"T-treasury agents?" I stammered. "You mean they were investigating…"

She cut me off and then finished without stopping, "Yes, that's it. They were in Los Angeles investigating apparently one of the best counterfeiting setups ever unveiled. I heard that the money uncovered so far is about as perfect as what is produced at the U.S. mint…maybe even better. This is such a hot story, we're not even allowed to write about it, until it's been cleared by higher-ups in the government."

She slid in closer, glanced around the room once to verify no one else had entered or was listening, and said almost in a whisper, "Matthew, it could only have been produced on paper producing machinery manufactured under the highest government standards. And there is only one person here in California that knows how to make quality printers like that. I think it's our friend Muller or McCullen…and that makes him one-dangerous guy to be around."

"And I'm right in the middle of it, too!"

"If you say so, sweetheart."

"What's the connection to the commies?"

"According to my sources on the police blotter, several hoods, a strange mix of whites and Chinese that were arrested recently around here in L.A. had something in common. All carried wads of new uncirculated crisp twenty-dollar bills. Their money was suspiciously printed with a similar range of serial numbers and upon closer examination; all their currency was determined to be superior quality … *counterfeit.* That's when the Feds were called in. But listen to this, that's not all."

"Oh?" My ears were practically on fire now that she had my full attention.

"This gets even better. These characters were also card-carrying "Redder than a Boiled Lobster" commies, as well. And by the way, that's another confidential…off the record story, Matthew. It has yet to be written and printed, so keep that one under your hat too, okay?"

I nodded in agreement, polished off what was left in my cup of cold coffee, and thought about the connection to the bills I'd lifted from the Blue Parrott crime scene. Several were still stuffed in my pocket along with a few samples from the stash I'd uncovered from Murphy's seedy basement apartment in Long Beach.

I said, "Give me a list of the numbers Doris. I think I've run across some of the same slick dough around town in the last 24 hours that might also be connected to this ring."

She slid a columnar sheet of paper in my direction. I copied down the series of numbers on my note pad and said, "So, you think that McCullen's an ex-Nazi and still trying to undermine our system by using the commie sympathizers and their organization taking root everywhere, to begin flooding the market with his bogus money?"

"That's about it, in a nut shell," she said, whipping off her glasses and tossing them onto the dossier.

"I think there's more than that. What does he get out of it? There must be something in it for him? There's got to be more behind it than just a disgruntled Nazi left adrift in the states, right?

She looked puzzled. I offered a thought.

"What's the financial shape of his business right now? Any idea?"

"I have something here that will give us the answer," she said, sorting through the stack and producing a financial statement.

She scanned the page, smiled, and then slid it towards me. I read it from top to bottom. After noting the highlighted numbers and footnotes, I handed it back with a grin and said tapping the bottom of the page, "Well, there it is, Doris. He's going down the drain in his electronics business since the war ended. Instrumentation for military aircraft is no longer in big demand or profitable like it used to be, is it? And, I'll bet if we were to check out his personal finances, we'd find out he's way over his head in personal debt too; big house, fancy fishing boat, expensive trips, jewelry he can't afford, racehorses, high-end automobiles and who knows what other expenses. His sudden association with the celebrity Hollywood set must be to help bolster his status in the community and hopefully garner more lucrative contracts with other high-profile connections for his sinking business. Doris, this "show boat's" in big trouble and probably broke. He's probably selling his bogus printed dough to anybody interested in turning a quick profit, including the Reds, who also have their own disruptive agenda, just to offset his personal financial debacles."

"You might be right."

I tossed it back to her and she smiled pleased with our analysis and discussion. I said, "Now all I have to do is tie it all together and connect all the missing pieces. Find out where the printing presses are located, blow the whistle on everything connected to the commies, and see where my client fits into this jigsaw puzzle. Without getting injured or killed in the process."

A quick thought raced through my cabeza about the dead body of a young woman in that seedy Hawthorne Hotel room and another dead body or two connected with the warehouse disaster and the flaming drums of what looked like black flammable printers ink. I muttered out loud, almost more to myself, "I already witnessed a few samples of that the other night."

She didn't catch that last thought and I didn't elaborate. She just said, "What? Oh, that sounds easy, Matthew," then shook her head in disbelief, knowing I'd be lucky to get through this one unscathed. "But I know you and I know you'll get to the bottom of it, even if it gets rough. I'm like that too. That's why I like to stay on the outside of the news business myself. That's where the real action is…on the streets, I mean. Not behind an editor's desk buried somewhere here in this stuffy mausoleum."

She swept her hand around the room with a sigh, resigned to her ultimate newspaper promotion destiny as we slid back in our chairs. She collected her papers, methodically shuffling them into a neat pile. Shoving them back into the folder, she said with an affectionate parting smile, "Good luck, Matthew. I'm always here to help, if I can. Please give me a call. I would love to see you again; before this job has me so tied down, I won't have time for anything else."

"Thanks, sweetheart, I will. I feel better with what you've uncovered. It's starting to make some sense now. I'll call you, as soon as I wrap this one up, okay?"

She sent me a weak smile at my offer, and we parted with a tighter embrace, an affectionate kiss, and an unwritten promise to resume sometime soon. As I watched her attractive body melt through an inside conference room door, back to her desk and her unfinished story, I wondered if she'd stay married to this newspaper job forever or she'd find the right guy and eventually share her life with someone else. I knew the answer before I'd already asked myself that question. I tossed my empty paper coffee cup into a nearby trash basket, dropped on my lid, and clicked the door closed on my way out.

Chapter Nineteen

Outside, it was just beginning to rain again. I double-timed it back to my Buick, now sporting a pink parking ticket flapping under the windshield wiper. I was relieved it hadn't been towed yet. I gave the scrap of paper a quick glance, scribbled a change to the license plate number, and slid it under the wiper blade of the jalopy parked behind me. Then, put up the top and mopped off the wet seat with a rag retrieved from the glove box. Before leaving, I sat there a little longer and compared the list of the counterfeit serial numbers Doris had given me to the dough in my pocket. They all matched. My old girlfriend was plenty smart and onto something. And now, I was also carrying around a wad of illegal currency myself. After listening to her expose' on McCullen, I was convinced more than ever, that this case was not just a simple affair by a cheating husband gone wrong.

I decided to pick up the scent back at the Majestic Studio disaster later after things had cooled off. Instead, I swung east to investigate Black Jade's sister, the Apricot Blossom's connection to this mess. She was located somewhere in Chinatown, only a few miles away and closer. I had a hunch her House of Joy was much more than just a massage parlor. It was probably a Tong connected front for everything from prostitution and dope peddling to money laundering, gambling, and whatever else was illegal and could turn a healthy profit behind the hidden bamboo screen of questionable respectability.

For many years to come, Chinatown would remain a rat's warren of nefarious activities, always one step ahead of the law with its narrow, dusty, secretive, and sometimes ominous streets and alleys. Poised like a crouching Tiger, Chinatown was a world unto itself, always prepared to pounce and devour the unsuspecting and unprepared intruder that ventured off the path, attempting to unravel whatever misdeeds were in play at the time.

It had been reluctantly relocated to the west side of the encroaching Union Train station in the late 1930s and was still struggling to get acclimated to its new surroundings. I'd been there numerous times before and was sure I'd drive around in circles and crisscross the tight little crowded alleys between the streets again until I'd found the place I was looking for. Nevertheless, because of my curious conversation with Black Jade back at Ruby's and a connection to several clues I'd picked up at the Blue Parrott murder scene, I was now drawn there like a moth to a hot flame. I also had that old familiar feeling again that I would probably get my butt burned…if I was lucky and possibly worse…if I wasn't on my toes. I felt confident though with my familiar persuader, nestled under my left arm and a coat pocket full of spare ammo. Nevertheless, I gave it a squeeze anyway, just to be sure it was still in place.

There was always something sinister in Chinatown that I wasn't prepared for lurking just below the surface. And my suspicions told me that if that beautiful but deadly Black Jade was anywhere involved … it wouldn't be good.

Chinatown was a quagmire of plugged up streets full of mostly Asian, old world humanity still clinging to the time-honored ways. Some still insisted on carting passengers in old-fashioned rickshaws hauling customers to colorful restaurants decorated in paper lanterns serving traditional food from recipes originating in China containing cryptic ingredients. Narrow alley incense-laden curio shops crowded each other, pushing imported junk from hand-carved trinkets and Tigers Balm to soothe tired muscles and eliminate constipation to overpriced faux ivory carved Mahjong and chess sets. For those more adventurous, back alley brothels and drug dens with private entrances sold everything illegal. They were hard to get into, unless you had the right connection's and even harder to get out of, than a pair of western boots. The whole little exotic, unassuming world was surrounded by innocent appearing open street market vendors with fly encrusted produce, meats, poultry, and sweets all displayed in open wooden crates in the still-hot afternoon sun.

Automobiles of mostly older vintage were chugging volumes of eye-stinging exhaust in the mostly narrow sometimes unpaved streets and alleys. Some of the old-timers were still clinging to the old country ways in dress, customs and all cultural manners. For others, the odd queue and skull cap were still present as the old-timers shuffled in hardwood sandals and baggy silk pajamas up and down the narrow streets, looking poor, isolated from the 20th century and out of step with the progressive United States. Many though, had already smartened up and succumbed to the new modern lifestyles of the typical Southern Californian in western dress, inappropriate behavior and for the juveniles…sometimes disrespectful manners. Comingled with them on the teaming, overcrowded streets were the occasional tourist from somewhere else, looking lost and inquisitive as they search for the latest overpriced trinket or a festive meal in one of the safer high priced restaurants. If they were daring, maybe in one of the bargain out-of-the-way alley restaurants frequented mostly by the blue-collar oriental on a family outing or one on a work break.

Many though, brought with them their unsavory underworld connections and practices and this was without a doubt, where I would become involved.

I swung the convertible down Spring Street, one of the main arteries, noting the wooden Hop Sing Tong Association character sign attached to an older building on my left. It was fronting as a benign blue-collar, workers union organization, but still had the earmarks of an influential strong arm, enforcer of the local labor movement. Nobody worked in Chinatown unless the Tongs helped themselves to a cut of the action.

I snaked my way west over to Hill Street and as predicted, circled in search of the Golden Pagoda, a local restaurant famous for its dim sum. That sounded inviting, but as the contents would be questionable, you were always guaranteed a surprise ingredient and not necessarily to your liking. I'd pass. Maybe another time and then again…probably not.

At five stories, the Pagoda was the highest building in Chinatown. It was shaped like a narrow lighthouse bulging at the base for additional ground floor dining space and consisted of five levels with reverse cascading upswept roofs, a traditional design intended to ward off evil spirits. It was a familiar landmark that would guide me toward the Apricot Blossom's *Full Moon House of Pleasure* located somewhere within its radius of narrow streets and alleys marked in Chinese characters on improvised signs, many tacked to the sides of buildings.

Once I'd spotted the tall pinnacle with its multiple graceful roof lines, I proceeded north a few more blocks. The street indicated as Bamboo Lane written in characters on a weathered signboard, appeared on my right. I wheeled into the only curb-side empty space I'd spotted since I'd arrived within the oriental borders. It was near a dilapidated building with a side loading dock occupied by two-day laborers dressed as coolies stacking wooden crates of live chickens, ducks, and a few squealing pigs, destined for the restaurant kitchens. This didn't look like the safest place to park, but the pickings were slim to none. A couple of street beggars were lurking in the shadows hunkered down out of the rain, up next to the building. I crooked a finger to get their attention and dropped several coins into their outstretched palms and motioned for them to keep an eye on the Buick. I think they understood, but I just received blank stares and a glimpse of two gaping mouths with discolored teeth that were no stranger to chewing betel nuts. I said so-long to my crate, flipped up my coat collar, and decided to take my chances, exploring on foot.

The narrow, partially paved street I'd been seeking was gloomy and sandwiched between double-story high wooden buildings, many with overhanging balconies and most in a distressed state of neglected, weathered disrepair. The muddy alley was already crisscrossed with puddles littered with overflowing trash bins, empty packing crates, other odds and ends of refuse, and unpleasant to walk in. I had a vague idea where I was going, but the recent addition of rain showers wasn't in my original plan.

In searching for Apricot Blossoms body shop, I passed several soaked and mute Orientals, casting furtive glances at the foreign intruder they didn't recognize. Clinging close to the sides of the buildings and dodging the trash piled under the few overhangs fronting several small empty shops, we silently brushed shoulders, mutually attempting to ward off the increasing drizzle. I thought about asking for help from one of those I'd passed or darting inside one of the open stalls to make an inquiry. But aside from a break out of the rain, it probably would only produce another unknown response. I dropped the idea and just kept looking for the character sign I'd memorized at Ruby's and hopefully find it before I was totally soaked.

Out of the corner of my eye, a character sign over a doorway across the street from me indicated the *Full Moon House of Pleasure*. As the downpour increased, I hesitated. Huddling under the protective cover of the overhang afforded by the small empty curio shop behind me, I observed a small crowd of men gathered out front, about to enter. Something told me to put on the brakes. A well dressed, man near the front was carrying a satchel and looked damn familiar from a photograph I'd seen recently. In spite of the low visibility, I managed to identify little Frank Murphy. He was older and heavier now than when he'd posed for the grainy black and white photo with the girl on the beach, but there was no doubt in my mind...I would recognize that ex-con punk anywhere. He was the same loser that lived in that dump in Long Beach.

"What the hell is he doing here?" I muttered out loud. "I thought he'd be on Catalina Island by now. Either he didn't go or he was over and back faster than a homing pigeon with a tailwind."

Murphy was surrounded by three dapper and tough-looking Caucasian hoods that would normally be out of place in Chinatown. They wore fedora hats pulled low obscuring their features and appeared serious and nervous about something. They glanced furtively around, like they were searching the darkened damp street, corners and shadows for trouble. I blended back under the eaves and appeared motionless. They missed me and anyone else they might have been expecting and decided it was safe to enter. I wondered if some of those late-model autos sucking up several street-side parking spaces I'd just passed, didn't belong to some of those thugs.

Murphy must have been delivering something to someone inside or was he selling something? There was no way I could find out unless I could peer inside. From the front, there were no other building windows, only one solid door with a speakeasy grated window for confidential identification prior to admittance. Not exactly the entrance you'd expect for a massage parlor. There was no other front access to the rest of the building which was connected to another on either side. There must have been another entrance, but it would be all the way around to the backside and only accessible from the end of the street.

I retraced my steps back to the beginning of this street and splashed around the corner curious to investigate from another secluded entrance. Running through the puddles, I ignored the misty drizzle, which by now was subsiding, but had already thoroughly soaked through my suit and shoes.

The alley behind this block of ramshackle buildings was darker than the front side, with no street lights. It wasn't illuminated by even a few dimly lit back doors, as all were solid. Instead, the path was marked by only weak shadows from several flickering building lights threatening to short out in the downpour. There was more litter as obstacles than I bargained for and in spite of the wet weather; the trash gave off a nauseating stench. I stumbled several times over the refuse, trying to identify exactly where the back door to Blossom's joy joint was located. In the gloom, it was confusing. I'd counted off the paces from the front side and hoped I remembered correctly and would be able to pick out the right door. But they all looked the same without more light. Naturally, there was no signage to identify the shops and I wouldn't be able to read them, even if there was. I spotted a steel fire escape ladder that ran up the back of the building to the roof, but some fool had placed a padlock over the raised sliding rail connected to the building, preventing its usage even in an emergency.

I finally arrived at what I determined was the right door, the one I'd been pacing out beginning at the alley entrance. I crossed my fingers that I'd selected the one opposite the front, that it was unlocked and unoccupied directly inside…a damn tall order.

I was one soggy customer entering a strange place from the alley, uninvited and considering the cast of characters that I'd seen entering from the other side; hopefully, I wasn't stumbling into a hornet's nest that was going to blow up in my face.

Grasping the knob, I gave it a firm, confident twist and was relieved to find the door unlocked, but stuck on its hinges. With a little effort, I pried it open a couple of inches and was immediately repelled by an overpowering scent. An excessive odor of pungent incense wafted in my direction. I held my breath, worked the door loose, and slid inside. It appeared to be a darkened storage room, not more than a few hundred square feet, containing mostly stacked crates of some merchandise from overseas possibly waiting for display in this shop. Before I could close the door, something brushed past my pant leg and slid over my shoe top disappearing inside the room with me. I jumped back and caught my balance without making any unnecessary noise. Because of the darkness, I couldn't tell what it was. I hoped it wasn't a rat, but I couldn't be sure. It was something creepy and I hated rats, both two and four-legged. I tried to settle my nerves in the inky black darkness and concentrate. Except for the water squishing in my shoes, I crossed as silently as possible to the other side of the small room and listened with my ear pressed against the door panel.

A ribbon of yellow room light glowed beneath the door. Muffled voices speaking in English could be heard from within but weren't decipherable. I took a chance and cracked the door open a sliver. Holding it firm to prevent it from swinging further and without peering inside, I could now make out several voices discussing what seemed like a serious negotiation of a business transaction.

A female voice with an oriental accent, speaking with authority was apparently driving a harder bargain about something, than had originally been proposed. One of the English speakers was upset and arguing, "The big boss ain't going to like you changing your mind on this deal, baby," he said, slamming his hand down hard on something.

But she sounded smooth, smart, and had another ace up her sleeve to sweeten the pot and cinch her offer.

"I also give four best girls for tonight. You get first-class massage and many extras afterwards. Make you happy. You like very much, you see," she said, her voice rising politely to match her sales pitch.

"Uh-uh, I don't think so, sister," the man in charge said, but from his hesitation, he was a little unsure of his decision.

"Maybe you take one with you for later and return in taxi cab?" she tossed out her last and most persuasive card with a sinister smile.

One of his thugs standing closest to where I was listening bought that last pitch and attempted to be convincing. He whispered, "Boss, boss, go ahead. You saw those cupcakes out front in their see-through, short nightgowns. It's just a whorehouse anyway. Why not get some for free?"

The man whispered back, "Nix pal and keep your shorts on. I don't like this setup. It's a trap if we get separated and we don't want none of them with us to spy for that broad either. We'll be lucky if we get out of here with our dough in one piece. I've got to close this deal now, without more stalling. Maybe we do this joy joint another time, but not now. Just shut up and keep your hand on your heater."

"O-oh, hell, okay," the other guy groaned, disappointed.

There was a long silent pause on both sides. I listened for footsteps withdrawing from the room, signaling a dissolved negotiation. But, after considering his take-it-or-leave-it position, the man caved-in and mumbled, "Okay, okay, sweetheart. You give me the three hundred thousand and I'll give you the six hundred in mixed denominations. We'll take a rain check on the kewpie dolls. Maybe another time…deal?"

"Yes, good. I like, we make deal…first we look-see," she said in a severe monotone, now in charge.

"Okay, agreed. Go ahead and inspect," the man said and I also detected an exasperated sigh.

I stepped back away from the door edge, blending into the storeroom shadows attempting to see who the occupants were and what exactly they were negotiating. One quick peek told me I'd stepped into a nest of pit vipers. I froze, barely breathing, and unleashed my .357 mag., prepared for trouble. From where I was hidden, this couldn't have been worse.

I wasn't surprised to see little Mr. Murphy with his valise, open and placed on a table situated in the center of the room. His partners, the three losers from the tattoo parlor were standing firm and stiff around one side of the room still appearing nervous. One look on another side told me why. A wall of unsmiling oriental Sumo-sized thugs with crossed arms the size of tree trunks and packing large gleaming blades stuffed under their belts, glared back as the territorial guardians of this establishment of pleasure and masters of the situation.

The oriental female voice belonged to another raven-haired beauty, wearing a steel blue silk dress decorated with more full length, golden dragons breathing fire. It was cut low over her breasts and slit to the thigh, showing off lots of well-turned leg. This exotic dame had that same no-nonsense face as Black Jade and probably that same hypnotic effect on men; heavenly to yum-yum in the sack and no doubt, deadly to cross in a business transaction. I guessed that doll was the Apricot Blossom.

I also guessed that in spite of Murphy's tough guy partners packing heat, he knew he was outmatched in this setup, and whatever deal was on the table with this babe it was going to be her way, or else they'd join the trash piles in the back alley with their throats slit ear to ear.

I watched as the oriental dish placed her matching valise on the tabletop next to his and after examining Murphy's contents, and he'd examined hers, she nodded and they made an exchange. Murphy looked relieved at the decision. Apricot Blossom showed no emotion at the final agreement and didn't comment more.

The merchandise was just what I'd expected to see. She'd handed several sample packets of treasury bills from Murphy's valise to a small, frail, bespectacled, well-dressed Asian in a non-traditional dark business suit standing beside her. Her little advisor examined them minutely for details, turning them over several times; holding them up to the light, snapping them vigorously and finally returning them back to her with a smile. Then after riffling thru the stacks in the valise to insure, a correct count, he smiled and gave her a small courteous bow of final approval.

They were exchanging Murphy's counterfeit dough with the real stuff and this dish had just bought an oversized valise full to peddle to her partners in Chinatown at a very healthy profit. It was only the tip of a gigantic iceberg. This transaction would probably repeat itself and an avalanche of phony dough would soon spread like a busted damn flooding throughout Los Angeles and the surrounding communities. No one would be able to trace the origin, especially in the oriental community, as no one ever talks there.

Now that the deal had been completed it looked like they were all planning to leave. I decided to get the hell out of there too. One final pause for a glimpse inside through the slit in my open door though was a mistake.

It wasn't a noisy or squeaky door closing or my squishy shoes that was my dilemma. It was a damn alley cat that had slipped inside behind me when I'd first entered. At that moment it was down by my feet, wetter than a soggy bilge mop and determined to get its paw into the small cracked door opening in search of food and a dry bed in the adjacent room that for me was only loaded with trouble. I attempted to give it a quiet, gentle push with my foot to discourage it from announcing our presence, but it didn't work. One nudge and it spooked, jumping backwards, knocking over a janitor's broom leaning in the corner.

A quick glance back inside, told me I'd better be prepared for real trouble and now.

Apricot Blossom tensed and said in an alarmed voice, "What's that?" and signaled to one of the behemoth oriental goons to investigate the source of the noise.

With nowhere else to hide in the crowded little room, I slipped behind the door, using my foot as a stop to prevent getting crushed and held my breath. As soon as the door was shoved open wider, I gave the critter another swift nudge. This time the wet mop burst forward past Bluto's feet faster than a streak of lightning and probably straight into the nights stew pot. The giant let out a high pitched, shriek like a frightened school girl with a mouse up her dress. He stumbled backwards, much to the amusement and relief of all those inside, including myself. Then he slammed the door shut in embarrassment and I exhaled a sigh of relief in the dark.

Before someone thought wise about the wet cat coming out of a closed room, I waited only long enough to let the noise subside from the other side, then holstered my heater and quietly escaped out the same way I'd entered.

Chapter Twenty

I decided to wait in my car as Murphy and his pals would have to pass my way to get into theirs too. Unless they were going to be sidetracked by Apricot Blossom's kewpie dolls or they had more business to transact, I wouldn't have long to wait. Sitting there in a damp, cold suit wasn't pleasant, but I'd been in worse situations. I lit a fresh Lucky from the deck in the glove box and thought about observing Murphy passing the counterfeit dough to that dame. It was just the lead I was looking for. Now all I had to do was determine who his other connections were, particularly those commies in the movie business, find out where the printing operation originated, who else was involved and determine how the blonde corpse at The Blue Parrot figured in with McCullen.

The rain had finally subsided, but my windshield was still coated with droplets partially obscuring the interior of my vehicle when I spotted Murphy and pals moving in my direction. He was carrying the satchel of dough, surrounded by his three body guards with their hands inside their coats, probably gripping their pistols and prepared for trouble. They approached the autos parked near me and from the gesturing and arm-waving Murphy was doing, he wasn't happy with the way things had transpired.

I slumped down in my seat unnoticed and listened as he passed by grumbling something about, "That god damned oriental bitch, she-".

His voice trailed off and I picked them up again in the rearview mirror. Murphy and one of his tough guys climbed into a dark late-model Mercury sedan, he sat in the front passenger side while the other two thugs piled into a late model dark two-door Hudson coupe.

I started my crate and left the head lights off until they'd pulled into the steady stream of congested traffic on the two-lane, street. I was prepared to follow at a discrete distance and would let another vehicle get between us for cover.

Murphy's Mercury pulled into the lead first, followed by the Hudson, glued tight behind. Smart move, nice and cautious I thought. That prevents the money car from being overtaken from the rear. This would normally be a tough tail, but I was good at this. Especially with the Mercury's one busted rear tail light, making it easier to follow if they tried to shake me. That also included one on the Hudson and several others still parked near the street of Bamboo Wind Chimes. I'd seen to that as preliminary insurance.

We wove a crazy zigzag course throughout Chinatown until they were convinced that all was clear behind. When we finally hit the main L.A. drag on Alameda Street, both vehicles continued straight south. They seemed satisfied they still weren't being followed and became relaxed and careless. My shadow couldn't have been easier. I settled back with another couple of smokes, turned on my heater attempting to dry my damp suit, and waited to see where this ride was taking me.

I left my radio off and thought about Doris's comments concerning her unfinished story about the commie screen writer from the Olympic Studios. He'd supposedly blown his own brains out. That part bothered me. Was this the latest trend in the commie circles? Or was he nudged over the edge by his pals in the writing game for letting his plans leak about ratting them out to the committee? I made a mental note to ask Doris for more inside dope on this chump and see where his connections would take me.

Letting various cars slip in and out between us, we held a steady course for about twenty-five minutes past South Gate, Compton and finally Wilmington and the harbor docks. I noticed the rain I'd left back in L.A. was now replaced in the distance by a light misty fog. That would probably work in my favor, if it didn't thicken. Continuing for another mile or so and we finally arrived straight into the barnacle-encrusted Los Angeles Harbor, my old stamping grounds.

This had all the earmarks of a previous plan and I was tight on their tail to find out who else was involved. I had a good idea, but I didn't want to guess. I'd just hang back, play it smart and let the cards turn over at the right time, in my favor.

Murphy and his pals seemed to know where they were going and worked their way over toward the streets separating the commercial piers and marinas normally reserved for pleasure boaters. I dropped back in the thinning traffic, so as not to be noticed to see which direction they'd choose. There were only a few marinas in the harbor, but if that was where they were going, it would be easy to lose them down the finger spurs of wooden docks more entangled than a hooker's bird nest. And that I didn't want to do, especially after this wild goose chase through Chinatown and L.A. I hoped they wouldn't stop there, but keep going toward the commercial side where I'd be less conspicuous in my surveillance.

I hung far enough behind so that I could park and still identify their final destination. I watched them turn at the last moment and make the right decision, at least for me. It wasn't toward the Royal Palm Marina, or any of the other snazzy numbers in the harbor with expansive well lit, parking lots and absolutely no cover for my tail. The Mercury and the Hudson continued toward the other side of the harbor towards the docks on Terminal Island.

After a few more minutes, they pulled up parallel to each other in a dimly lit section of the commercial docks facing the ocean, shut off the engines, lights and sat inside their vehicles, hesitating and observing. Aside from an offshore freighter sitting idly tied up at the docks hundreds of yards away and probably manned only by a disgruntled security team left behind on shore leave, the docks were deserted…with one exception.

Directly opposite where Murphy and his gang had parked, a white hulled 40' Matthews sport fisherman powerboat was tied up stern to the dock. It was being loaded by two men in working men's attire. "Now that's a nice fishing rig," I thought. "Must have cost a bundle."

Stacked up on the dock were heavy crates of something, maybe paper and barrels of what appeared to be the same printing ink I'd uncovered here in the port and salvaged after that warehouse fire. Another man was standing on board the boat, dressed in a turtleneck sweater, rough pants and a Captain's cap pulled down low. From his gestures I determined he was the boss, giving directions as to how he wanted everything loaded.

I parked in a shadowed area and hung back for a moment to chart my bearings for the best route to collect the information I needed from a closer vantage point. In case I was spotted in the gloomy fog, I slipped out of my still damp suit coat and replaced it with a working man's jacket, sailor's watch cap, and rubber deck shoes. It was a partial change of clothes from the back seat of my crate that I was taking down to my boat anyway and would fit right in with the harbor merchant marine surroundings. One disadvantage I had with Murphy and company though, was his pals knew what I looked like. That didn't make me feel too comfortable. However, depending upon who they were meeting; that party just might recognize me as well. I decided to proceed forward cautiously anyway, until I could identify everyone, despite my nautical appearance.

Because of the incoming inclement weather and the usual array of containers and other obstacles usually left piled up around the docks, I was able to slip in close enough to identify the party connected to the Matthews fishing boat and overhear some of their conversation without being spotted.

Not to my surprise, it was my client, Carson McCullen, and the Matthew's was the *Sundancer.* The same guy who was now possibly involved in a murder case and who was also afraid of getting whacked by Joey DeCosta's goons for screwing his mistress. Right now, he was supposed to be staying over on Catalina Island on a fishing trip, and instead here he was back in Long Beach, the boss of this crooked setup. I guess I'd hold off on flying over there first thing in the morning. Also, his two deckhands were none other than the two losers that worked at the Pike amusement park in Long Beach and were no strangers to playing rough with a young woman and starting warehouse fires. Chester was one of them and seemed to have nine lives. He'd survived my beating at the diner, his gunshot wounds by his pals, and aside from a bandage here and there, he was probably still the same smart-ass, arrogant punk that I'd encountered the other night.

I noticed Murphy's gang wasn't rushing outside their vehicles. Then after they decided to exit, each made another cautious scan around the docks before proceeding. McCullen approached them on the dock and was apparently pleased to see this cast of characters. He shook hands with Murphy, before taking charge of the valise and motioned for him to accompany him back on board. As they could see no intruders up and down the docks, they sat out in the open in a couple of deck chairs in the stern cockpit.

Now I knew what Murphy had been up to when he went to Catalina. He'd flown over and collected his phony newly minted loot from McCullen. Then, flown back, pawned off the worthless paper on their pigeon in Chinatown and met him afterwards back at his boat with the proceeds when he'd returned to restock his printing supplies. Maybe another swap was in the wind. For that, I'd have to wait and see.

McCullen was drinking a can of beer and offered one to Murphy from a deck cooler. Murphy nodded his head yes, but looked stiff, ill at ease, and out of place, sitting there on the boat in his business suit and fedora hat. He was probably thinking about what McCullen was going to say when he told him that the Chinatown deal did not go as originally planned. I was waiting for that myself and watched for a reaction from Murphy's men, who were chatting, but edgy and smoking with the two punks from the Pike, now taking a break from loading the supplies.

McCullen seemed to be in a buoyant mood as he took a couple more swigs of beer as if to delay the valise opening ceremony, like a kid with a surprise birthday present that he'd already seen hidden before receiving it. He glanced up at Murphy's stoic face, smiled to break his icy mood, and asked, "Everything go okay in Chinatown, pal?"

"They're a rough bunch, boss," Murphy said, moving in his deck chair a little and tipping his hat back to let out the rising steam.

"So, what's new? The Blossom dame give you a hard time on the deal?"

"Well, uh-actually it ah…"

McCullen suspected something wasn't kosher and snapped, "Well what Murphy, spill it. Did we or did we not clear the three hundred and twenty-five G's that I expected?"

"N-no, not exactly," he muttered, glancing over at his pals for support who were now paying attention to this heated conversation and poised for a showdown if Murphy was in trouble.

"How much, Murphy? How much did you agree on?"

"Uh-uh."

"Give me an answer!" demanded McCullen between clenched teeth, his tone rising.

"Three hundred grand even, boss. It was uh…"

McCullen cut him off almost shouting, "What? Only three hundred G's? You got stiffed, Murphy! That's not what the agreement was and you know it. What happened?"

"Ah-ah-I can explain…"

"You're not skimming on me, are you Murphy? Because if you are, I'll spread the word and you'll be sucking wind at the end of a rope for that murder you're behind in Frisco at *Shanghai Ruby's*. Or better yet, shark bait on my next fishing trip offshore, capisce?"

While he'd been chewing out Murphy, McCullen flipped the valise catch open, releasing the flap, exposing the contents, and peered inside. Glancing back up again, his face relaxed. Easing from anger to satisfaction at the sight of the real dough replacing the worthless counterfeit paper printed up only recently, he grinned like a sly greedy fox. Then, helped himself to a handful, held it up to the weak light cast from one of the cockpit lanterns, and laughed.

Murphy attempted a weak smile too, realizing the pressure was off, and offered a plausible excuse to support his decision. "N-no boss. I ain't lying. It was either that or no deal. The sister of Black Jade's that runs that "joy joint", that Blossom bitch, started to back out on the whole deal. So, I figured we was close, and three hundred G's was better than nothing. That whole damn whorehouse was surrounded with heavyweights all pack'n iron and we was lucky to get out of there in one piece and with the dough."

McCullen sat there listening and didn't comment, just let the silence compel Murphy to continue making excuses.

"And besides, "Murphy continued, grasping for something solid, "I figure we could always stiff her next time around once she gets hooked on turn'n a profit with her Chinaman friends."

That was the something solid he'd been searching for and McCullen seemed to buy it.

"Yeah, you know, maybe you're right there, pardner. I, uh guess you're pretty clever after all. Yeah, that's exactly what we'll do, and we'll also pick another place to meet when and if there is another next time. Good idea," McCullen continued mumbling absently and then snickered; thinking about all Murphy had just told him.

Then just to let him know who was still in charge, he added, "And you're also going to get even with that Black Jade bitch, too. Right? She's the one that set up this deal in the first place. I don't like to be double crossed…by anybody."

Murphy and his gang looked relieved at the boss's acceptance of his answers, but McCullen had more bad news on the table that he was about to spill.

"You're going to have to learn to drive a harder bargain next time though Murphy. I'm going to take the loss out of your cut."

"B-but boss…I helped put this package together with my engraved plates and all."

"I don't give a damn. Any good tattoo artist could have done that right?"

"Well, ah-maybe…and maybe not."

"Well- no buts on this or any other time, got it? It's my plan and my equipment that's doing all the intricate printing so, you'll just have to suck it up. If you don't like being the bag man now, I'll drop you and your boys and get somebody else. What's it going to be?"

He didn't have to think about it longer and glancing over at his pals on the dock who were in a standoff with McCullen's two punks, nodded a confirmation and said, "Yeah, we're still in and we'll collect our share out of Black Jade's hide, too."

"All right, Murphy. That's more like it. Now, let's count out your shares, and then we'll talk about the last drop for now, while the boys get back to loading up this tub with more supplies."

Murphy had exaggerated his risky position back in Chinatown to save face with McCullen, but Black Jade was going to pay for her sister's double-cross and it wouldn't be a pretty situation. Maybe she'd planned it that way, right from the beginning and maybe she didn't, never the less Murphy still fell for the loss and was fleeced. She probably deserved what she was going to get by pulling a fast one on these crumbs and if she wanted to do more business with them in the future, she'd have to take it or else.

I listened for more details about the next delivery and it wasn't more phony dough, but preprinted copies of an underground commie news rag that McCullen had printed up on some of his other machinery. This guy's printing presses didn't need to be large for this volume, just efficient and reliable. The printing operation must have been located offshore, no doubt on Catalina and probably at McCullen's place.

McCullen told him, "Fly over to Catalina right after you've finished and packed tomorrow. We'll be cruising south later in the afternoon after I'm fully loaded, so don't be late." Did that mean Mexico or just another location in the states?

I managed to make out, "The delivery of that rag's, at the Majestic Studios tomorrow morning at 10:30 A.M. Ask at the gate for Milo Demitrius from the screenwriters' office. He'll also give you another series of articles they want printed up in the future. I don't really give a damn about that, but take it anyway, even if it's not printed up right away as promised. I'm planning to take a break out of town for a while anyway. At least until any heat from that phony dough cools off and then maybe we'll try another round, when it's safe."

I tried to pick up more, but the rest of the conversation was blanked out by noise from the Matthews' big twin Chrysler V-8 engines warming up to leave soon. It wasn't much to go on, but would be good enough for now.

Was this Demitrius one of the commie ringleaders at Majestic that was on the Washington hot seat? Tomorrow I'd discover the answer.

McCullen's punks handed off several heavy cardboard boxes full of what no doubt was the underground commie newsletter to Murphy's losers who deposited them into the trunk of Murphy's Mercury.

With McCullen's helpers back on board, they prepared to cast off. I assumed he was heading back to Catalina, after he shouted out loud to someone on board, "Got to get both tanks filled up tonight. We'll gas up over at the fuel dock on Pier 36. It shouldn't be closed. Cast off, but stand by to dock again, soon."

Before leaving, McCullen double-checked that his two sorry excuses for a crew had cast off properly. Then taking the helm, he pulled the big Matthews smartly away from the dock, bow first, and once safely clear, opened up the throttles on the big guttural twins. I watched his cascading wake fade away as he easily navigated out into mid-channel swinging between the marker buoys, the throb of those well-tuned synchronized engines purring into the night. Once past the neighboring docked freighter, I lost sight and sound of the big sport fisherman as it rapidly disappeared into the inky black night. It crossed my mind about what would happen to that beautiful *Sundancer* once McCullen's house of cards collapsed and I worried about it for a few seconds.

Murphy and his goons weren't interested in standing around to watch the big power boat blast off. They already had what they'd come for. I ducked further back into the shadows before their two vehicles spun around, both heading back toward the city. Murphy was by himself in the big Mercury. The other three goons from the tattoo parlor were stuffed into the small coupe and looked uncomfortable when they passed, but were smiling, pleased with their cut of the profits. The dough they'd just collected for their efforts would probably just get squandered and it would only be a matter of time before they attempted to fleece more pigeons again.

Nothing could be gained by following those crumbs anymore tonight. I'd pick up the trail tomorrow. I checked my wristwatch. It wasn't too late to make phone calls and set several plans in motion for the next day. Afterwards, I'd grab something to eat on the way back to my apartment in L.A. and then catch some shuteye before another ball-buster day tomorrow.

Chapter Twenty-One

I cut back through the port entanglement of crisscrossing streets and across the embedded freight train tracks, leaving the warehouses, slippery docks, and merchant freighters behind me. The city lights of Long Beach winked ahead in the distance as I shot down Ocean Boulevard, a slight detour coming up next on my agenda. I spotted the sign for my turnoff, cut across the Badger Street Bridge, and entered the Anchor Marina for a stopover on my sailboat the *"Black Swan."* I didn't waste any time exchanging my damp clothes and shoes for another change into some dry duds stored on the ketch. Afterwards, I planned to use the phone inside my pal, the dock master Leland Avery's office, to call everybody I could think of for the next days' party.

Leland's tub the *Excaliber* wasn't tied up next to my boat, as usual, so I figured he'd taken her out for a short cruise for a few days somewhere, maybe even a dry run to Mexico, but that I doubted. His sign "Gone Fishing" I noticed plastered on the front office door, when I'd first arrived, was possibly a good clue as to what he was doing, but not a guarantee. Whenever he was indisposed; fishing, drunk, or headed to jail, he'd leave me his key in one of my deck equipment boxes, just in case I was around to cover his ass should the marina owner inquire, "Who the hell is running my marina?"

Leland's small squat wooden framed building fronting the marina was dark and quiet when I approached. From the few advertising circulars stuffed in the door frame, it looked like it hadn't been occupied for a few days. Once inside the damp little office, I flicked on the lights, cracked open one of the side windows to let in a little fresh salt air, and made myself at home, sitting at his beat-up single pedestal oak desk. I'd brought along a half bottle of George Dickel whisky from the boat to ward off the blues, starting to creep in. I'd been thinking a lot lately about seeing the beautiful Lola for the first time. She was dancing at "Pandora's Box" strip club in San Pedro and it brought back old memories, some pleasant and some dangerous, but all memorable. I poured out a tumbler full of booze, took several, man-sized sips to shake off the cobwebs, and fired up a Lucky before starting with the phone calls.

The first one on my list was Wes Canyon. Rhonda had made a copy of his phone numbers for me and I tackled the first one on the list, which according to her note, was his apartment. I let it ring several times and just before I hung up, a depressed voice that sounded like he'd been trying to wipe out a few memories himself answered.

"Yeah, who is it?" He grumbled.

"Canyon, Matt Thornton, here."

"Oh, yeah…Thornton, ah-Hemingway's private shamus. Got any ideas how I can unravel this nightmare I have hanging over my head yet? Or is it something else?"

"Yeah, maybe, but it's not exactly what we talked about. It's something else that might help though, interested?"

"Damn right, shoot," he perked up and probably reached for a refill of whatever he was drinking.

"Okay, here's what I need you to do. We're going to do some surveillance tomorrow morning. Are you available? Want in?"

"I guess, so. What gives?"

"This may help dig you out of that commie connection, you were talking about at *Rico's*. Here's the plan. First, meet me at my office at 8:00 A.M. and then we'll drive over to Majestic Studios. There'll be three cars; me, Rhonda and you. With your lot pass, you're going to take us on a tour of the studios. We'll only be there on the lookout for someone that's going to lead us to the "Golden Goose". The tours just an excuse, got it?"

"I guess so, sounds simple enough. Care to elaborate?"

"I'll give you more details when the right time comes. You'll have to trust me. This is big, Canyon. Very big and will probably, blow the Majestic Studios right off its foundation when it explodes. You want to be on the right side, when it does…believe me."

I didn't trust that guy enough to fill him in on the commie-counterfeit connection. Not just yet anyway. So, it was up to him, if he wanted in on the bus ride with me or fall under the wheels when it rolled forward. His decision. One way or the other, things were in motion.

"Count me in, Thornton." He sounded positive and eager to join forces with me.

"Okay, then."

"I don't get in on the big picture?"

"You will, as I said, when the right time comes. Good enough for now?"

"I guess, it'll have to be."

"All right then…I'm running late. Have a few more calls to make. See you tomorrow eight a.m. sharp. And don't be late, Canyon. I'm depending on you. Adios."

I hung up fast. Didn't want to waste time with more idle chit-chat. The calls had to keep rolling. I poured out another couple of fingers full of Tennessee's finest sip'n whisky, recorked the bottle, and tossed off a healthy amount, satisfied I had one piece of the team lined up. I kept my fingers crossed when I dialed up Rhonda. Hopefully she was back from her snooping assignment and still at the office. If I missed her, I'd stop by the *Florentine Gardens* later and catch up with her after her strip tease act.

After letting the phone ring, half a dozen times, I was disappointed to hear a substitute for the usual sweet-sounding "Little Miss Wind Chimes" from my answering service picking up my call. This one announced stiffly that my office was now closed and not recognizing my voice, suggested I call back tomorrow. I refreshed her memory of who I was and that I was paying for this setup and then asked her about Rhonda's whereabouts. I was formally prompted like a memorized robotic message from outer space that I could reach her at her apartment, if I called before 7:00 P.M. I shook my head in annoyance at this impersonal character and told her thanks for the advice and hung up.

My watch read 7:15. I'd chance another call, but wasn't optimistic. It looked like a visit to see Rhonda's act was probably in the works as a backup plan. After we visited the Majestic tomorrow, my three-car surveillance caravan was necessary during daylight hours and I needed her to be part of it. She just didn't know it yet.

I took another hit on the Dickel, dialed Rhonda's apartment phone, and let it ring more times than normal. I was about to hang up when Rhonda's breathy voice answered sweetly. I said, "Hi baby, it's Matthew," relieved she hadn't left yet for her evening performance.

"Oh, Matthew, I'm just about ready to leave, can it wait? I'm rushing right now putting on my makeup here to save time at the club."

"This won't take long, angel. I'll stop over to see you after your show tonight and fill you in on the details. What time do you go on?"

"I have two shows, One at 8:30 and one at 10:30, I think. That's why I have to be there early. They change the times and order of the acts, depending on who's scheduled. Last night the strip tease acts were sandwiched in between Orson Wells and his magic act sawing a woman in half. That was very scary, the woman screamed. You know who she was?"

"No idea." I sighed. The conversation was going off the rails.

"Rita Hayworth, can you imagine?"

I laughed, "You show-biz people will do anything to get attention."

She ignored my comment, continuing, "And following our strip tease, Uncle Oscar a funny ventriloquist with a wooden dummy. Who knows what's scheduled tonight?"

I said, "That's nice. Look, Rhonda, I need you to be at the office tomorrow at eight, okay? We've got some very important surveillance work to do in the morning." I held my breath this wasn't too tall an order for the show-stopper.

"Uh-okay. I'll have to leave right after my last set though to get some sleep, if I'm going to be at the office…that early."

She sounded doubtful, but I knew once she'd put on her deerstalker cap again, she'd be okay. I changed the subject, to squeeze out a little more.

"What did you find out today with that ticket from the El Dorado Collectables Pawn Shop. Any luck?

"Plenty," she said, sounding chipper again.

"It was a rare gold coin collection worth over $100,000 dollars and the man that sold it used a phony name on the register, but he matched the description of McCullen."

I whistled and wanted more details, but would let it ride until we could discuss it in person.

"That's more like it, baby. Anything else, happening in the detective business, I should know about?"

"Um- ah- oh yes." Her thinking cap was now starting to heat up. "Ah- your friend in the lobby, Mr. Fast Eddy? He stopped me on the way back up to the office this afternoon."

"I'll bet he did."

"He told me to tell you that Gimpy's friend, the jockey at the Santa Anita race track? He'd seen Joey DeCosta squiring around, as he put it, several women."

"Okay, now we're getting somewhere. Is that it?"

"No, of course not. He said it was usually just a couple of hot blonde bimbos, that he didn't know anything about."

"Great!" I interrupted, disappointed.

"No, no…there's more, listen to this. He'd also seen him recently with another real beauty, the one that looks like that Ava Gardner woman in the newspaper photograph. She's supposedly an actress at DeCosta's movie studio."

"Did he give you a name?" I swallowed hard, waiting for more.

"Certainly. Her names ah-ah-ah…"

She drew a blank and couldn't remember.

I began sweating and said as calmly as possible trying not jinx this fountain of glad tidings. "Y-es, sweetheart? Her name, got a name?"

"It's ah…oh, it's…ah … Sherwood. Erika Sherwood," she finally blurted out.

"Bingo! That ties in. Good work, doll." Now, all we have to do is nail her down at the Majestic, but it might not help McCullen though."

"Oh, why not? You're on the right track, now aren't you? That's what you were paid to uncover and solve, wasn't it?"

"Originally yes, but now it's too late for just that. McCullen's got much more serious baggage hanging around his neck that I've uncovered. An infidelity charge by his wife is the least of his worries now. I'll explain more on that later to you after your show tonight, okay? Anything else?"

"One more thing, then I've got to get ready for my show. Oh, you know who's going to be the feature stripper tonight?"

"No idea, who?" I wasn't interested.

"Lili St. Cyr."

That dish was a glamorous statuesque beauty and one of the biggest names on the strip tease circuit. She was also intimately connected with gangsters controlling all the major night clubs from coast to coast. They helped pave her way to the top and most of the other, big-name strippers in the business as well, by personally owning a piece of the action. That, Rhonda didn't need. And, I didn't like.

"You're in with some big shots now, aren't you, sweetheart? Be careful. I know you're a big girl and ambitious, but some of those connections can rub off like rat poison. You don't have to fall into that trap again."

"Thank you for the concern, Matthew. I'm okay though. I know what I'm doing and besides, I like working with you during the daytime, I really do."

I wondered how long that would last. I didn't want her with those crumbs again. I lied and said, "Okay, that makes me feel better, too. Now, you were about to tell me about one more thing. Shoot, I'm listening."

"I'm making progress on that stack of reports you want me to type up." That wasn't important and not on my list of anything I was really interested in, but I let her tell it anyway. "I called a couple of those insurance companies and told them you'd be sending them status reports soon. When, I didn't say exactly, but they were happy I called and thanked me for keeping them informed."

I could practically see her smiling face, proud to have taken the initiative to help me stall off those insurance bean counters with that growing stack of busy work piled up on her desk. I'd probably still have to hire another temporary typist anyway, just to reduce the overflowing pile into something

I could see over, but didn't mention it.

"Okay, baby. That's all wonderful news, I just heard. I'll meet you right after your act tonight and we can talk more. I'll reserve a quiet table off to the side at the Florentine. See you later."

"Okay, Matthew. I'm anxious to have you see my act. We have some new props the boss just bought. You won't be disappointed."

She sent me a kiss over the phone and we hung up.

I wondered what the new props were as I fumbled through my notebook for another phone number and took a pull on an empty glass.

My next call was to Doris at the *Herald* newspaper. I knew she'd be out, but left a message anyway. I wanted to know if there was any connection of the so-called suicide victim, Lowell Phillips with the Majestic Studios writers' group. I'd call her back when I could.

After another couple fingers full of Dickel down the hatch, I made a long-distance connection with Captain Dan Blair at his sheriff's office on Catalina Island.

"Thornton, Matt Thornton? Haven't seen you in a while," he answered in a friendly, but authoritative tone as usual. "Planning to sail that beauty of a ketch of yours the *Black Swan* over our way anytime soon? I'll tell'm to reserve you a good anchorage if—"

"That's not it, exactly, Dan," I said, cutting him off. "I'm expecting Carson McCullen to be on Catalina soon, maybe even later tonight. You know who he is, don't you? I was told he has a cottage somewhere on the island, probably Avalon and is right now on his 40' Matthews sport fisherman called the *Sundancer*."

"Yeah, sure. Know him well. Nice guy. Lives in a secluded section near the old Zane Grey estate. Always stops by when he's on the island. Big member of the Tuna Club. Nothing but high-rollers belonging to that fishing fraternity, you know. What's cooking, shamus?"

"Dan, he's a client of mine and I think…a hot potato with the law. Could be wrong, but don't like what I've been collecting on this bird so far and don't want to jump to conclusions too fast either."

"Care to fill me in? What's that got to do with Catalina Island? I should know, if it's serious."

"He's tangled up in several situations that I can't divulge without legally breaking the confidentiality agreement I have with my client, but I'll tell you this much. If you'll call me back at my answering service as soon as he arrives and with some more information, you'll be the first one I contact if and when more action is required. I'd like someone to do a confidential surveillance on him and find out what he does with the load of supplies he's carrying. I'm not talking about boating supplies. These are sealed cardboard boxes or crates and several small barrels. That's very important and he also has two crew members with him. Find out where they're staying too."

"Okay, Matt. Can do, but if it's anything that looks dangerous or illegal remember, I'm responsible for upholding the law over here on this little slice of paradise and I don't want anyone and that includes you, to mess it up. So, the minute you have something that substantiates we have a lawbreaker holed up here, I want to be informed…immediately. Clear?"

Dan was another ex-GI drill sergeant and was just as serious about his authority in the Sheriff's department on Catalina as he was kicking the behinds of Army recruits headed off to World War II. I liked and respected that. I said, "Agreed, Dan, and thanks."

Before we rang off, he said as an afterthought, "You know, Thornton, I just remembered something. Someone told me a while back they'd seen McCullen drive through town in a small rental pickup truck hauling several wooden crates that must have been shipped over from the mainland. They were also heavy, as the truck was struggling up that hill, you know the one behind the casino that leads to his estate near the top. Wonder if there's any connection to what you've been telling me?"

"Possibly and if there is…that explains even more."

"Okay, we'll watch his moves when he arrives."

I gave him my answering service telephone number thanked him again, told him I'd probably be seeing him sooner than he expected, and hung up.

My clock was ticking off the time for my evening and I wasn't finished with calls.

Joshua Keys needed to be brought into the loop on some of this business connected with Shanghai Ruby's. I dialed up the number to Shampy's Saloon in the town of Val Verde that he'd nervously scrawled on a scrap of paper outside a burning warehouse. I hoped it was correct and had no idea who was going to answer, where he was or how the little pink haired Candy was doing.

Someone picked up after the sixth or seventh ring, mumbled something that sounded like, "Ahh-ah-who der?" And before I could answer, they must have dropped the phone as it crashed in my ear.

I repeated the call, "Hello, hello, I'd like to speak to..." but all I could still hear was talking and laughing in the background and then a fumbling disconnect as the line went dead again. I sighed, glanced at the time on my wristwatch and decided to give it one more shot.

Third time around, the pickup voice sounded a little sharper in spite of the music, chatter, laughter, and background noise, "Shampy's Sa-loon, Juba speak'n." I could hardly hear her but thought, now we're getting somewhere.

"Juba, Aunt Juba? My name's Matthew Thornton." No response. "I'm a friend of Joshua's?" Still no response. Obviously, Joshua hadn't mentioned me. "Joshua Keys' friend?"

"I knows who Joshua is. He my nephew." Then with her hand partially over the speaker, she suddenly shouted into the background, "Hushup, you fools. I talk'n wid an im-portant fren a Joshua." From the authoritative booming voice shouting into my ear, I envisioned a barrel-shaped heavyweight and felt sorry for *Shampy's* customers in her line of fire. Then she continued back in my direction, this time much clearer and with less interference. "What's dat you wants wid him?"

"I need to tell him something. Is he around there right now?"

"No, he ober playing to-night at dat Alabam club on Central Ave-nues. You know's where dat is?"

"Uh, yeah, sure I've been there a few times before."

"Dat's good."

"Christ, I guess I'll have to go over there tonight to see him then. I just don't have the damn time though." I muttered that more to myself than to Juba, but she caught some of it and let me have a broadside volley as well.

CHAPTER TWENTY-ONE

"What's dat you say'n? You swer'n?"

"Oh- uh, no. It's nothing. I was just ah- that's a nice club he's playing at, isn't it?"

"I su-pose so, I ain't neber been der," she said, cooling down fast and launched into another subject without stopping. "You know dat skinny lil white chil wid dat funny color hair, dat Joshua bring here? Cookie or Candy or sumpin else you eats, I fo'gets."

I held my breath and said carefully, "It's Candy. Yes…what is it, Juba? A problem?"

"No, Joshua he been tak'n real good care a her. They laugh'n and hav'in a good ol'time. She doin jes fine."

What a relief that was.

"That's good to hear, now Juba…"

She plowed on ignoring me and started talking louder to overcome the escalating background racket. I moved the phone away from my ear and winced. "She been eat'n my cook'n and get'n fatter. Likes dem collard greens an fatback, wid cornbread and some fri-ed chicken. Um, um, umm. Jes tink'ing about dat soul food make a body warm all ober, don'it?"

"Yeah, mouth, watering. Juba, listen I called…"

She cut me off again, muffling the speaker, but I could still hear the noisemakers in the background getting another blast. "You ain't listen'n back der? You sees who talkn'n on de phone ober here? Keep dem mouf shuts or I slaps you up aside yo head!" After a little laughter followed by more dead silence behind her, she continued where she'd left off. "Dat lil chil she been staying quiet, Mr. uh- uh-" I didn't help her out with my name. "She mostly hid'n indoors, listen'n and sing'n wid de radio and wear'n dat ol'do-rag Joshua give her. She kinda shy, ain't she?"

I wasn't surprised the kid was still wearing a masquerade. By now she must have been thoroughly fed up being stashed away in the middle of nowhere with these characters, anxious to return back to her normal life again.

But now, even more important, I needed to hold my ground on this call or I'd never finish. I tried not to breathe as I shoved my way back in with the purpose of my call.

"I suppose so, now listen Juba, tell Candy to hang on a little longer and I'll call her back in a couple of days when it's safe to return home okay?" I took a breath.

"Dat fine wid me. I tells her later dis eve'n after *Shampy* close."

I poured on another non-stop, "I have another message this one's for Joshua tell him I said not to go to *Shanghai Ruby's* for a couple of days it might be dangerous for him got it?"

"I got's it, but why you talk'n so fas? You sound like some uh *Shampy* customer dat been drink'n heavy Mr. ah- ah, what's dat you called again?"

"It's Thornton. Matthew Thornton." I sighed, telling her for the last time.

"Okay, I wrote bof a dem message down, Mr. ah- ah-Tor'ton."

What a miracle that was. I wondered if they'd ever get delivered.

I let Aunt Juba get back to the bar business and after that conversation, I definitely needed another couple of hits on the Dickel myself. No wonder they got plastered at Shampy's.

I made my last call to the big Irishman, Capt. "Tank" Sherman L.A. police detective in charge of the Blue Parrot murder case.

The P.D. operator connected me with the homicide department and as my luck was still holding, Sherman hadn't left his office. He was probably nodding with a soggy stogy in his kisser as usual, his feet propped up on his desk covering a pile of overdue paperwork. He'd also be predictably grumpy as usual when he answered.

"Tank? Matt Thornton here. Got something important I need to run by you, got a minute?"

"Not really, shamus. I'm very busy. But I suppose if I don't agree, you'll pester the hell out of me or worse, you'll come down to the station and I'll have to see your ugly mug. What is it? Trying to find out about that blonde stiff over at the Blue Parrot?"

"I wasn't calling about that, but what about her?"

"Damn it," he muttered. "Her fingerprints indicate she's a small time, hustler and sometime prostitute by the name of Gina Slade. Short rap sheet on minor stuff. Been working at the Pike amusement park in Long Beach in one of the concession stands. Apparently hangs out with a tough bunch.

Her ankle chain's still a mystery. Must be a thousand jewelry stores in Los Angeles County alone. That's going to take more time."

"What's with the poison, I read about in the paper?"

"Arsenic. Small traces found in her system. Someone's been trying to kill her the slow way with rat poison. Gives you a hell of a stomach ache."

"That it?"

"No … God damn it. The cigar butt in the ashtray? She was entertaining a high roller. It's an expensive commercial brand that we're still tracking down."

"Was the cigar band on or off the stogie?

"What? Who the hell cares?"

"What did he light his cigar with?"

"God, more stupid questions. I dunno. There weren't any matches, just a couple of spent cardboard tips left in the ashtray along with her cigarette butts. Maybe the killer dropped the matches back in his pocket. Who the hell knows."

"Okay, okay…sex?"

"Yes, another big surprise, Thornton? According to the autopsy she had sex before she was killed and from the bruises on her body it was rape."

"What's your theory on the motive?"

"Simple. It was rape and her purse was missing so it must have been robbery, too."

"From a high roller she was entertaining? He's just sitting there relaxing, puffing on his cigar in a room they registered in earlier and she's enjoying a cigarette, too. All of a sudden, he jumps up and decides to rape, strangle and steal her money?

"That doesn't make any sense, Sherman. Must be more to it than that? Was she tied up or restrained in any way? Any witnesses remember what the person looked like that she registered with?"

"No rope burns or any other restraint marks and not much help with witnesses either. The Blue Parrot's turned into a "cash and no questions asked" joint in the past few years, so most everybody keeps their mouth shut and their eyes closed as to who comes in and who goes out. Except another couple we questioned, shacking up in the next room for the weekend. Each mentioned seeing somebody go in and out of her room, but each was vague on the description and refused to say more."

So far the police were still way off base with my client's involvement in the murder, but McCullen was in over his head on everything else, so it was only a technicality as to what was his more serious crime, anyway.

"Anything else?"

"That's where we are so far, Thornton. There are still a lot of empty holes on this case. We're not done yet, so don't push it, okay? That's enough. Now, what the hell did you call me for? I hope it's important."

"Thanks for the info on the blonde, Tank. I know you're going to like what I called for and it's getting late, so I'll keep it brief."

"Just give me the facts, will yuh, Thornton. I've got more God-damned reports to write up before I leave and I'm already falling asleep over here, so make it snappy or I hang up."

"Are you sitting down?"

"Of course, I'm working. Step on it for Christ's sake."

I was right on all predictions.

"Okay, here it is. I need you to connect with the Feds in town that are working on the case with counterfeit dough being circulated."

"How in the hell did you know about that?" he shouted into the phone, his chair making a screeching sound on the hardwood floor.

I guess I had his attention now.

"Can do?"

"That's supposed to be confidential, Thornton. That counterfeit case is under Federal wraps…not street knowledge for peepers like you. My department only got involved when those two agents got bumped off on my turf. You're getting ahead of yourself, shamus. Better watch out."

"Yeah, yeah. Look, I know the two stiffs weren't F.B.I. as the papers led you to believe. They were Treasury Department agents, right?"

"Jesus, you've got more ears to the ground than a family of gophers."

I laughed, "I get around. Listen, I'm working on a case that I think exposes who's doing the printing and who is buying and peddling that junk. Interested?"

"Damn right I am. You better be on the level with this, Thornton, or I'll have your head stuffed and used as a soccer ball, got it?"

"This is big Sherman. Very big. It may be even too big for you. I'm giving you some straight dope, so pay attention. You might just get a promotion if you follow what I'm saying."

"Okay, okay. Shoot, but I don't want no promotion. I'm close to retirement. I just want to disappear from this damn sewer I wade in every day, collect my pension, and relax my final years in a nice quiet little cabin in the woods somewhere up by Lake Arrowhead."

"Great. I'm still working on the printing part of this operation, but the sooner you alert the T-Men to a local buyer of a load of the counterfeit dough the sooner they'll nab them before it's distributed."

"Where is it?"

"Chinatown…"

"What the hell?"

"Don't interrupt, Sherman. It's a joint called the Full Moon House of Pleasure on Bamboo Lane off of Hill Street. It's a joy house masquerading as a massage parlor and probably connected to the Tong."

"What's the Tong?"

"What a dumbbell," I muttered to myself. "It's an oriental Mafia that goes back to the old country, still controlling everything that isn't nailed down in Chinatown. A *Dragon Lady* nicknamed the Apricot Blossom is the slippery owner and the one that made the buy tonight."

"Hmm- I like some of them China dolls too, Thornton."

"Don't let her name fool you, pal. You couldn't handle that one. That dame's a beautiful Cobra that would kiss you deadly with her forked tongue and you'd probably want more, but wouldn't live long enough to brag about it."

"Yeah, I guess I'm getting too old for some of them spitfires anyway."

"Look, forget about that. Just focus on what I'm telling you, okay? The drop just took place earlier tonight, so the Feds. still have time to wrap this one up, before the phony dough hits the street and the trail gets cold.

"Where do you get this shit Thornton? Don't you ever sleep?"

"I'm beginning to wonder myself."

"Who's that dame buying from?"

"I'm still working on that end. Maybe the Feds have a handle on that part already."

I doubted they did or they would have been in place to nail those crumbs already. I purposely left that vague until I had more information. My client McCullen's involvement in the printing end was clear and if all went as planned for the next day, I could finally connect all the dots.

"Ah- ah, all right, I guess so. This sounds too good to be true, but I'll take a chance and make contact and see what they want to do about it. But, that's the best I can do, shamus."

"Look, I'm sticking my neck way out on this one too Sherman, but let's do it before the dough slips through everyone's fingers back out to the street, okay?"

"You better be right, Thornton, or I'll be in the shit so deep, the Feds will be able to bury me alive with just another spoon full." He sighed. "I sure hope my cabin in the pines, ain't just a picture on the wall," he mumbled, his voice trailing off as he dropped the phone in the cradle with a clunk.

* * *

I was getting tired and decided I'd had enough planning, phone calls, and conversations for one evening. Maybe that big Irish windbag Sherman was right. A good night's sleep didn't sound like such a bad idea after all.

I decided a good hot shower at the marina's men's room and a quick meal afterwards from my boat's galley was better than driving back into L. A. at this time of night anyway.

So, I dropped the near empty bottle of Dickel into Leland's desk drawer, wiped out the tumbler I'd been drinking out of, closed the office side window, flicked off the light switch, and locked up his office door, before heading back to the boat for my toilet kit.

But after a cool bracing shower, my batteries were recharged again. I was starved and looking forward this evening to seeing Rhonda's striptease act at the Florentine Gardens as promised.

Chapter Twenty-Two

After dressing in record time, I locked up the boat and rushed into Long Beach, treating myself to a steak dinner at the Rusty Pelican restaurant on Ocean Boulevard. An attractive blonde waitress in a skimpy nautical costume with a face and shape you'd want to remember; flirted her way throughout my meal and collected a healthy tip for her efforts. Afterwards, I cruised north along Pacific Coast Highway, before swinging east toward the famous nightclub on Hollywood Boulevard. The late-night burlesque show was already in progress when I arrived.

I hadn't been to the Florentine Gardens in at least a year. The building hadn't changed. Same blocky architecture styled from a nondescript sized warehouse into a building resembling a Moorish palace with miniature minarets, Ionic columns propping up the front entrance, and plenty of glowing neon to attract the suckers. On the inside, furnishings in hyper garish bright flashy colors and a formally dressed nightclub staff to part you from your dough before you complained. The whole package was rolled out by the new co-owner, a fast-talking, little showman named Nick Grant an import from New York City with deep mob connections and a flair for show biz. The nightclub's business had been slipping since the war ended and Grant was brought in as the answer to boosting business. At least it would work that way for a while, anyway. "Gramps" as he was called by his few friends, redecorated the joint with new carpets, fresh paint, replaced the tables and chairs, and hired a better-looking, staff to appeal to a wealthier upscale clientele. He promoted a newer variety of talented acts from fresher comedians and flashier scantily dressed showgirls to popular singers, jugglers, and acrobats all to the accompaniment of big-name, bands. It was an indoor circus, one gigantic floor show that seated hundreds of customers, treated to reasonably priced entertainment accompanied by overpriced food and watered down booze.

I was running late and expected the joint would be packed and I'd have trouble finding a decent seat. I was right. The crowd was far from thin. "Gramps" was the antidote, a P.T. Barnum for distressed nightclubs. I had to drop a couple of fins to get the seat I wanted at a small table to get to see Rhonda, but it would be worth it.

After polishing off several rounds of cheap booze, I sat there patiently listening to the Mill's Brothers harmonizing "Glow-Worm" and several other favorites, followed by a short comedian named Red something. The little guy was damn funny, in spite of the fact that he was dangerously irreverent with his comments directed towards a couple of local mobsters seated close to the front who weren't amused. Just as I was losing interest in these acts, my beautiful *Rhonda "The Hotter than a Blow Torch Flame,"* finally appeared.

She was billed as the evening's feature striptease headliner in the variety acts glass-encased playbill advertised outside and in spite of all the others scheduled to perform that evening; she was the one everyone was waiting for. I caught a glimpse of Grant standing off to the side beaming at his showstopper and watching for the audience's reaction as she was introduced. Big money dreams danced before him as she floated on stage, the joint erupting in applause, whistles, and shouts from the ringsiders.

When I entered, I practically tripped over the lobby marquee featuring this dazzling strawberry blonde. She was wearing nothing more than a red-lipped smile, a G-string, stilettos, and a red feather boa wrapped loosely around her luscious body. The same sign was also plastered outside at the front entrance. Once I saw that, I knew her days in the P.I. business were numbered.

I thought about that as I polished off the last of my drink and sat back to enjoy the show and witness the rise of this beautiful star. Grant was a master at producing memorable acts and I'd witness from the beginning to the very end, Rhonda's beautiful face and body holding the audience's attention. They were on the edge of their seats and I couldn't help it, so was I.

Rhonda's unique act was no doubt the predecessor to another act Grant would promote, the other big-time, stripper Lili St. Cyr, who apparently wasn't appearing tonight. Rhonda's performance was more of a complete fantasy floor show than the usual gyrating striptease bump and grind on an empty stage, performed at most other clubs in town to the beat of a gritty band.

The audience tonight would instead be treated to peeking in on Rhonda intimately stripping off her clothing within the privacy of a room resembling a bedroom boudoir. A dressing table with a mirror, a couple of ornate upholstered chairs, a fancy French recliner lounge, and a full-sized clear-sided bathtub were carefully arranged in a semicircle around the stage awaiting the dazzling star to appear.

As the curtain opened to the accompaniment of romantic and suggestive music, the stunning Rhonda entered, the audience enraptured at this vision of dazzling beauty. She floated across the room fully dressed in a long red evening gown, including, opera gloves, pearls and other fashionable attire suitable for a formal evening out, which we are led to believe has now concluded and she is preparing for bed.

She slowly begins removing articles of her clothing one at a time. Beginning with her shoes, followed by the slow and sensuous unzipping and removal of her evening gown. Stepping out of it, she draped it with care across one of the side chairs, leaving on only her black lace undergarments and stockings. Moving onto the sofa lounge, she reclined unsnapping her stockings from the garter belt and sliding them down one at a time, stretching and caressing her long, shapely legs as she collected and tossed each one onto a side chair.

The audience loved the moves and were twitching in their seats and nudging each other, smiling anxiously for the lingerie to disappear. But there was more to follow...much more.

She moved across the boudoir like a floating cloud, the black lace lingerie clinging and touching her body, begging to be removed. Instead, she slipped into a white transparent dressing gown, before removing everything else underneath, one after the other.

The music and tempo changed in intensity to match the progress of the strip. She danced gracefully back and forth across the boudoir leaving a trail of panties, a garter belt, and a black lace bra each delicately draped over the furniture for all to see with every sensual movement.

The audience strained to catch more than just a glimpse of the darkened shadows of Rhonda's forbidden treasures, veiled beneath the folds of her moving transparent dressing gown. For the moment, they'd have to settle for what they couldn't see … yet.

But there was more and they wouldn't be disappointed.

After the last few articles of clothing were removed beneath the gown and discarded, she turned sideways from the audience and in one swift motion, dropped the dressing gown and settled into the clear tub bubble bath, and began an eye-catching body wash, soaping and sponging, beginning with her breasts and working down to her endlessly long legs. The audience was unable to hold their enthusiasm; clapping, whistling, and desperate for the grand finale, they'd been promised.

With the audience now at her feet and the music reaching a pleading crescendo, she concluded her tease with the last and final act. Flashing that radiant smile, she slowly turned, rising out of the bath to the throbbing beat of the music and the applause in the background, facing the audience. Her statuesque body was now fully exposed … except for her luscious breasts and silken triangle left covered only by a handful of still clinging wet and dripping bubbles.

While the applause and audience acceptance continued, she rewrapped her damp nakedness into the transparent clinging dressing gown and flashed them a final smile and one last quick glimpse of her treasures. The curtain slid closed to another round of thunderous applause.

From the audience's reaction, Rhonda's classy act was easily the high point of the evening's entertainment. From cigarette girl to chorus girl to feature stripper and headliner at one of the most popular entertainment clubs in Los Angeles. The kid was on a roll and who was I to stop her. I motioned for another whiskey and soda and lit another smoke, while I waited for Rhonda to appear. She would probably be a while getting dressed again, so I decided to just sit back and enjoy the next few acts, which after hers would have a hell of a time following.

Alistair Greystone, a British magician in top hat and tails was next. I'd seen him before and was bored. He managed to dazzle the audience with several well-crafted, but stale sleight of hand and a few illusion tricks. It was a definite change of pace; barely passable for those that didn't know where he hid all the props. Not in the same league as Rhonda's flashy striptease performance, but then there wasn't much that could top hers anyway.

Rhonda was fast at changing into a provocative, sparkly, clinging, low cut black silk backless evening dress and definitely more appealing to see than Greystone's cheap parlor tricks or pulling stuffed animals out of his hat. She showed up at my table unexpectedly halfway through the magician's act. Her smiling radiant face lit up the room, beaming and happy with her performance. Her alluring body was wrapped up into another flashy outfit, capturing all the attention from the admiring audience sitting near me. I glanced up at Greystone. He appeared uncomfortable seeing her down below in the audience stealing the attention. I'd already lost interest long before he began bungling his patter and card tricks while failing to direct the audience's attention away from Rhonda upstaging his act. I ignored the rest of his performance as did the others now focused on the seductive Rhonda, mingling in the audience near them.

Before she joined me, she circulated around many of the nearby tables, smiling and laughing at their compliments as she autographed the programs thrust in her direction by a wave of fans and admirers of her last performance. She was floating on a cloud of newfound success and it suited her. Soon she'd be going places and the *Florentine Gardens* was just the beginning.

Joining me was one happy woman. We exchanged kisses and several servicemen in uniform at a nearby table couldn't resist this glamorous beauty, shouting out, "Hey, baby, what about another one over here?"

She just turned and blew them a sincere puckered red-lipped kiss off the tips of her fingers, which was blown right back by the admirers with appreciation.

"Sweetheart, that was one hell of a performance," I said as she settled down beside me at the table. "That was nothing like the usual striptease act at these other clubs around here. Who came up with the clever fantasy skit?"

I motioned a passing waitress in a skimpy outfit for a couple of Bombay gin martinis to celebrate her performance.

"Gramps, wasn't it great? He'd originally bought all the props for Lili St. Cyr who was scheduled to go on tonight as the headliner, but she called in sick. So, he told me to take her place and from the audience's reaction, they seemed pleased."

"No doubt about it. You were a hit tonight, baby."

"He says, I'm headed for the stars. Can you believe it? It wasn't too long ago, I was just helping Tex in his garage business and now, here I am."

The Martinis arrived, and we toasted to her newfound success.

She asked, "Did you like the show so far?"

"I arrived late. Only saw Greystone the magician. Not bad," I lied.

"You missed an earlier act with the chorus girls. I started there too, you know."

"I'd heard that and you were so beautiful they plucked you right off the chorus line and here you are now." I smiled, raising my martini glass again in salute.

She mentioned a couple of the chorus girls that she liked, Yvonne DeCarlo, a brunette with an hourglass figure that was just getting started, and another friend, Jean Spangler, who was also a no-show again tonight.

"Jean's been missing from the chorus line for several days now and I'm getting nervous. I called her apartment, but the phone just rang. I didn't have time to find out where she is and I don't like it."

She frowned and took a couple of dainty sips of her martini, sucking off the olive from the skewer and chewing it, worried wrinkles creasing her forehead.

"I'm sure she's okay, baby. Maybe you can check on her tomorrow?"

"I guess so. She's renting a room from Grant. He owns an apartment building not far from here where several of the chorus girls, room, so ... I guess she's okay."

Rhonda wasn't firmly convinced herself and from what I'd heard about Grant's reputation with young women, I wouldn't trust him either. I was glad Rhonda had her own apartment somewhere else.

Plowing in our direction and glad-handing the patrons at the crowded tables as he passed, Nick Grant the P.T. Barnum of the west coast worked his way over to our table. Smiling like he'd just won the Irish Sweepstakes, he snapped his fingers for a bottle of Champagne from one of his waiters and bent closer to kiss the cheek of his popular headliner. After we exchanged greetings, he insisted on joining us in celebrating Rhonda's successful show. I wondered how much he'd already been drinking, as he seemed unsteady on his feet and anxious to take the load off his little short legs.

Rhonda was the center of attention and after Grant planted his fat ass in one of the empty chairs at our table, he showered her with excessive compliments. He launched into a suggestion she follow up her performances at the Florentine with a tour around the states to build up her name at some of the other night clubs owned by his friends and business associates. It sounded like sweet music to her ears. She looked at me, bewildered at the suggestion. I thought it was a little too spontaneous and didn't like the tune he was playing. It grated on my teeth like fingernails on a chalkboard. I'd bet my last dollar at the track that if he was serious, most of his associates at the other night clubs were mob connections and this kid would be handed from one to the other until she was wrung out. My expression must have registered those concerns. She said with a captivating smile that was hard to refuse, "Gramps, that's all a little overwhelming to even contemplate right now. Why don't we talk more about it later, okay?"

"That's okay with me, sweetheart. I just wanted you to know, I've got big plans for my biggest star," he said, smiling like the Cheshire Cat.

He sat back satisfied at the business proposition brewing in his head and took a big swig from his champagne glass, polishing it off. After helping himself to another full glass, he sucked on his stogy, contented that Rhonda's act was in the bag and already one of the major tickets to his club's financial solvency.

He followed that announcement up with another big idea that was his original intention in joining us in the first place.

"Rhonda, I'm throwing a private bash at my place tonight right after we close. It's to celebrate the recent success the club's been having lately. It's close, just off of Laurel Canyon Boulevard. I'm inviting several people that you know from the show; Alistair the magician, Senor Wences, the ventriloquist, several girls from the chorus, those acrobats from Hungary, that new comedian with the red hair and several others, plus a few friends of mine. And Mr. Thornton, you're welcome to join us if you like," he said, turning to me afterwards with an over-confident grin, blowing cigar smoke toward the ceiling.

I declined his offer as I had to get up early for my surveillance at the Majestic, and Rhonda knew it. I guessed she'd probably not want to miss out on Grant's party when she turned to me with pleading eyes that said, "I'm sorry Matthew, but I can't be with you so early tomorrow morning. I'd really like to go to Grant's party."

I smiled, easing her out of my plans, and said, "Have a good time tonight, baby. We'll talk later in the day."

She understood and we didn't have to say more.

Grant slid back restless to continue glad-handing his customers and said to Rhonda, giddy as a truant schoolboy at the circus, "That's all settled then? I'll give you the address later, but you probably won't need it as we'll all be leaving in one long caravan up to my place. I'll be in the lead car. You'll just have to follow the others along. It's only a few miles from here anyway."

The only thing missing from that vision were a few giraffes, elephants, and a brass band. He gave her another peck on the cheek, shook my hand with his warm, soggy mitt, and tottered off towards the back of the stage.

"Rhonda, before I leave, I'd like you to do me a favor," I said.

"Anything, Matthew, just name it."

"I'd like to borrow your little coupe for tomorrow. You can take mine." She looked puzzled. "I've been doing a lot of tailing tonight from Chinatown to San Pedro and my Buick could have been recognized. I don't think so, but in tomorrow's surveillance in the daylight, my car will stand out like a black eye. Your dark blue Ford coupe hasn't been used yet and should blend right in with the other traffic."

I didn't have to say more. She left and returned from the dressing room immediately and we exchanged keys. The next act was about to be introduced and I didn't want to see another. It was time to leave. We walked together over to the front lobby. She kissed me softly on the lips, happy that I'd finally seen one of her performances, and floated back inside for her final show later. I located her Ford in the parking lot and before I drove off, picked up the gun case from my trunk, switching it into the coupe.

The short drive back to my empty apartment on Western Avenue was filled with thoughts of beautiful Rhonda in her bubble bath. I had that sinking feeling I get sometimes that tells me to be extra cautious. But this wasn't about me. When everything seems to be going along smoothly, something unexpectedly tragic always seems to spoil it. I didn't like what I was thinking and almost turned back to the *Florentine*, but I didn't.

When I arrived at my apartment building, I noticed all the street lights were out. "There's a power failure in the neighborhood, use the stairs," suggested one of the other tenants I met in the underground parking garage. That must have been it.

My furnished apartment seemed cold and unfriendly when I entered. I tried the light switch- nothing. I groped my way around the living room, becoming familiar again with the strange furnishings, and stumbled toward the kitchen cabinet where I stored the booze. After seeing Rhonda's dazzling performance tonight and again personally afterward, my place was a real letdown. I couldn't get her out of my mind.

I rummaged around in a counter drawer full of odds and ends until I found the candle stub, I was saving for just such an emergency. Once lit, I secured it to an empty ashtray in a puddle of melted wax and looked around at the bare walls. What a gloomy setup. I followed that up with several shots of George Dickel to relax. That didn't seem to make any difference. I finally gave up and retreated to the bedroom and decided to go to bed early. Undressing in the shadows of a flashlight with a weak battery didn't do anything but deepen my murky disposition. I crawled under the covers, my feelings sunken to a level of anxiety and depression.

I tossed about most of the night and awoke too many times, just lying there staring at the ceiling, thinking. Something still gnawed at my gut and just wouldn't let go. Maybe I'd find out in the morning.

Chapter Twenty-Three

My place didn't look any friendlier in the daylight, just brighter. The Art Deco-styled furniture that came with the rental tag, was colorful and shiny, but still looked sterile and boring. I'd let that ride, until I could find someplace else, I liked better. At least it was close to my office.

The electricity seemed to be working now, so I switched on my small kitchen Emerson radio and dialed up the Andrews Sisters singing "Near You" again. The thought of Rhonda's sweet face humming that tune, made me feel better. I wondered about her late-night, party at Grant's. She was just a young woman with big dreams. I hoped they'd treated her with respect. I'd call her up later and find out. If they didn't, I'd chop that little bastard Grant's carcass into bait and feed him to the sharks.

I shut off the radio, I'd heard enough.

A quick glance at the wall clock told me to stop daydreaming and step on it. I'd already dressed and followed that up with a hasty breakfast of scrambled eggs, toast, and coffee. Before shoving off to meet Wes Canyon at my office for our surveillance beginning at the Majestic, I needed to call my answering service.

"Little Miss Wind Chimes" was back on duty early and said there were only two messages ... the first- Captain Blair from Catalina…"McCullen's boat docked early in the morning." The second Doris Fillmore… "Lowell Phillips was a former Majestic scriptwriter, before falling out with the other writers and getting fired from the studio."

I thanked her for the good news, hung up, and dashed for the parking garage.

I was running a little late again by the time I spotted my office in the Chrysler building. I swung Rhonda's little coupe into my usual spot in the alley, bumping one of the overflowing metal trash cans from the diner next door. I checked the bumper for damages and didn't see any. For some reason, I had a compulsion to firmly kick one of the tires that appeared soft. It was actually more solid than a block wall and I only accomplished hurting my toe.

I limped into the lobby, wincing at the pain in my shoe from my stupidity. Not seeing "Fast" Eddy's happy face at his usual concierge station to greet me or riding the elevator up with me, spouting the latest track gossip, was a first and I didn't like that either. Instead, I shared the trip to my floor with grumpy Randall Cleveland and never liked seeing him or his face that early in the day. He was an annoying middle-aged tax accountant, always carrying a bulging leather briefcase, wearing an olive drab overcoat buttoned up tightly to his throat, an olive drab fedora crammed snugly around his ears and with a complexion and personality to match his outfit. As usual, he was anxious to start recording monetary transactions and could only spare enough time for a nod and a smirk, before slinking off to his office at the other end of the hallway.

I just shook my head and grimaced at the sight of that character, as I was about to unlock my own office door. While fumbling in my pocket for the key, I noticed it was already ajar and the lights were on inside the front office. Voices were talking in hushed tones. I slipped it open slowly and standing near Rhonda's desk, were both Wes Canyon drinking a container of coffee from the diner next door and "Fast Eddy" keeping him company. They were both wearing gloomy expressions on their faces and seemed to have been discussing something serious. Their heads swiveled in my direction when I entered, but neither spoke. I was about to find out about something unpleasant bothering them both.

"What? What's going on? You two look like you know something I should know about? Give!"

Eddy blurted out first, "I let him in, Captain. He said you'd be along any minute, okay?"

"Yeah, yeah, that's fine, Eddy. Why the depressed kisser's?"

"I-It's all in here," said Canyon, thrusting the folded newspaper in my face, annoyed at my late entrance.

"What's this all about?"

"Read it," he said, his voice grating and louder. "Your phone out of service or something, Thornton?"

"As a matter of fact, my area's been in a power blackout overnight. Some jackass must have clipped a power pole or something. Service was back on this morning though."

He wasn't happy with whatever was in the early morning edition of the *Los Angeles Herald Examiner* newspaper and from the glum expression on Eddy's face, neither was he.

I unfolded the section Canyon directed me to and read. The story was like getting an unexpected kick to the stomach and I had to sit down, suddenly feeling sick.

"Popular exotic cabaret entertainer at the Florentine Gardens nightclub in Hollywood- Betty Joe Sharp, stage name Rhonda Flame was hospitalized with serious injuries at L.A. Central early this morning. According to reports her automobile plunged off a darkened stretch of Laurel Canyon Boulevard and tumbled down the ravine. She was on her way to a late evening party at the home of Nick Grant, owner of the nightclub when the accident occurred. Witnesses say her Buick convertible was overtaken and sideswiped by a speeding dark blue or black late-model Mercury sedan- California license plates beginning with 3K.... Los Angeles Police Department is asking for any information leading to the arrest and conviction of the hit and run suspect."

No one said anything while I read, the seriousness still sinking in. I was too damn stunned to say anything either, slumping in my chair. I reread the whole damn article, again and again, finally tossing it aside and looked up at both of their faces for answers.

"Did anybody call the hospital? What the hell does serious mean?"

Canyon said, "I called, but they wouldn't give me any information. I'm not a relative."

"Jesus Christ, I'll get some, if I have to drive over there right now and tear that damn place apart to find out."

I was mad. I knew something was wrong when I left her last night. I should have gone back and told her not to go, damn it. I dialed up the hospital, lied, and told them I was her uncle and needed to speak to the section where she was at the moment. I crossed my fingers. I was directed to the intensive care unit where the nurse on duty told me her brother Tex was already waiting there and would I like to speak with him?

"Tex, it's Matt. What the hell's going on? I just found out."

"It's bad, Matt. She's covered in cuts and bruises, no broken bones, but lucky to be alive after the crash."

"Jesus!"

"But that's not all. She's in a coma. Took a bad hit on the head."

"Oh, no…but, she's not going to die, Tex. She's a tough little fighter!"

"Doctors told me, if she pulls out of it there's a chance she could suffer from s-some disabilities, but they're optimistic she'll make a good recovery."

He started to break down telling me about it and I didn't press him for more details. B.J. was his only sister and they'd weathered a lot of storms together over the years and were very close. He wouldn't want to lose her and neither did I.

"Nick Grant was here for a while last night as well as the others on the way to his party. They all witnessed the Mercury that ran her off the road. What the hell was she driving your car for anyway, Matt?"

I explained my reasons for switching cars and said, "I'm sure I was the target and it was intentional. I didn't know I was followed to the nightclub, Tex. It's my fault she's laying there. I feel just as bad about this as you do."

"I won't blame you. Do you know who it was?"

"The vehicle matches the one I was tailing yesterday and I know where the guy lives."

"I have to stay here at the hospital for now, but you know what you have to do, don't you, Matt?"

Tex's voice had that gritty edge to it like a busted beer bottle that could cut you into shreds if you didn't agree. It wasn't a question. It was a contract he'd just put out on that crumb, but it wasn't necessary. We already had an unwritten pact since watching each other's back during the Big One.

"I promise you, Tex, I will find that bastard and exterminate him and it won't take long."

I think Tex was comforted by that thought and didn't say more, so I said, "Give her a kiss for me, will you?" But he'd already hung up and didn't hear me.

Canyon and Eddy stood there listening to the entire conversation and didn't interrupt or comment. I sat there for a few moments longer, collecting my thoughts, shook them off, and told Eddy, "Go back downstairs, forget what you just heard, chum, and mind the store." He didn't argue. I slipped him a C note to seal his trap and he left.

"Wes, you also heard what's going to happen next. I'm going on a scalp hunt and pronto. I don't know you, but Hemingway trusts you, so maybe I can too. You can either go along, but if you want out, that's okay, too. Solo's all right with me with what's going to happen next, but keep your mouth shut. I won't say it twice.

What I just said didn't faze him. Instead, he gave me the strangest expression and said seriously, "Matt, there's something we need to discuss, and now is the time to do it."

"Another commie confession?"

"No, let's talk about it in the car on the way to the Majestic Studio."

"We're not going to do any surveillance work today as I'd planned, Canyon. Plans have obviously changed and we might be running out of time already. Let's get going somewhere else. I'll fill you in on the way there. And … I can hardly wait to hear what you have to say."

Chapter Twenty-Four

Canyon's dark Ford Sedan was parked not far from Rhonda's little coupe. My watch indicated 8:15 a.m. I needed a vehicle with more horsepower to get where we were going and fast. I suggested we take his. I'd give the directions and he didn't argue. Before we left, I picked up the case containing my backup hardware and shoved it on the floor behind the front seat.

Canyon wasn't nervous and even smiled as the Ford careened out into early morning traffic on Hollywood Boulevard and then south down Vermont Avenue toward Long Beach. I told him to floor it and he speed shifted into high gear, the tires squealing as we swerved around several slow vehicles. For some odd reason, he seemed to be enjoying this trip and didn't question anything. We zig-zagged through L.A. streets unconcerned with stop signs, street lights, slow cars, or even the police, which we didn't see. He was oblivious to the fact that we were on our way to the immediate demise of someone he didn't know and he would be part of it. Maybe I was wrong about that guy. Maybe he'd be all right after all.

I thought it only fair to give him a brief explanation of what we were doing, who was involved, and why we were doing it. I explained the combination of McCullen's counterfeiting scheme I'd uncovered, its accomplices including our immediate target Murphy, the rest of the gang connected to Shanghai Ruby's, and the commie writers, producers and directors working at Majestic Studios. After listening patiently to the magnitude of what he was getting involved in without interrupting, I had a feeling he was going to bail out, when I saw the serious expression on his face.

Instead, he said looking over at me with a smile, surprising the hell out of me, "Matt, this couldn't have worked out any better than if we'd been working on this together, right from the start."

"What? I thought there for a second after hearing where this was going, you wanted out."

"Out? I am 100% in, friend. I've been working on my case for too long now and not getting nearly as far as you've done already."

"I don't get it. What case?"

He broke in, "Matt, I guess you've been honest with me, it's time I let you in on a little secret that so far, no one in town knows about."

I wasn't sure where this was going or that I was going to like it and maybe, I'd regret taking this guy along.

"You know that commie business I told you about before when we were at *Rico's?*"

"Yeah, so? You're in over your head. I get it, you already told me that."

"It's a cover."

"Cover? Cover for what? What the hell are you talking about?"

"I'm a Federal Investigator!"

"A what?" I coughed on the drag from my cigarette.

"I'm a "Special Agent" with the Federal Government!"

"Jesus Christ, just what I don't need," I said out loud, fuming at this twist. And, I was also now trapped in his car on the way to eliminate somebody, with him as a witness.

"Take it easy, Thornton. We're closer together on what you've been talking about than you realize. The agency's been trying to get the goods on those commie bastards that are setting up the movie industry for a complete shakeup for quite some time. Washington's been planting agents inside the movie industry ever since the H.U.A.C. committee began their investigations of the trouble makers in Hollywood. We just needed more evidence before prosecuting them and we move like snails to get it."

"So?"

"You're running way ahead of the pack with your leads and thanks to your efforts, that now includes additional criminal activities laundering counterfeit money for a profit with subversives; I might be able to get my arms around additional solid evidence sooner than expected."

"And I thought you were just an actor."

"I am…I was. I'm also an undercover special agent that was recruited just for this movie industry job and unless I'm exposed, I will continue to be."

Glancing toward me he said, "I have a couple other confidential pieces you can also store away. Shelia Perkins, my old girlfriend, that died in the car accident? She was also an undercover agent, as was the occupant of that toasted white convertible, they loaned Hemingway."

"Jesus, what was her name?"

"Sherwood, Erika Sherwood."

"Oh no! I've been on her trail and could never locate her…until recently."

"It's too damn bad. She was a good agent, tough on the outside, with a soft heart. She didn't deserve to die that way and so soon. An unusually gorgeous woman…resembled Ava Gardner. Fit right in with this movie crowd, actually better looking than most. She'd been gathering information through some of the same sources that you've also been investigating, the commie ring of subversives at Majestic, including DeCosta and recently that Carson McCullen. Looks like both women's covers were blown and they were taken out before we could nail things down. Either the commie connections or DeCosta and his mob behind his movie studio would be a sure bet behind the death of either or both of my Federal Agent partners."

"I'll be damned."

"There's more. Those two Treasury Agents dumped in the alley last week? Witnesses say the killers were heavily tattooed. Could be connected to this guy Murphy you're going for right now."

"They probably were his pals from the tattoo joint in Long Beach they all worked in. They're all connected to McCullen's counterfeiting ring."

"There was another article in this morning's newspaper you must have missed about a raid in Chinatown earlier by the police department and Federal Agents. Know anything about it?"

"I set it up. A counterfeit sting."

"Well, well, well…now you see how I fit in, don't you, Thornton? And I've got a few scores I'd like to settle privately myself. It looks like we're in the same boat on this whole mess, whether we like it or not. Doesn't it?"

"I still have my own agenda though, Canyon. Just don't get in my way."

"Okay, okay…let's just see where this takes us with what you've told me so far, fair enough?"

I shook my head and didn't like it and he knew it. I had a partner with shadowy connections to the Feds who were conducting undercover criminal investigations of his own. I wondered if Hemingway knew anything about this. For now, though, we were stuck with each other. What a hell of a mess this was turning into. I really didn't need or want this guy tagging along with me gumming up my plans, but it was too late now.

I glanced at the dashboard clock. It was just past 8:30 A.M. I steered him in the right direction to Murphy's apartment and had my fingers crossed the Mercury was still there.

Chapter Twenty-Five

We slowly cruised past the partially empty parking lot. I noticed the Mercury was missing and told Canyon. Instead a tall, sturdy figure with his back towards the street, was preoccupied loading cardboard boxes into the trunk of a dark blue Hudson coupe.

"Who's that?" asked Canyon, pointing. "Is that Murphy, the guy you've been telling me about?'

"No, I think he's gone already. That's one of his pals, a guy named Archie that runs the tattoo shop. They're all in this mess together anyway. He'll do for now. Let's have a little chat with that crumb before he leaves. Murphy's still my prime target and this loser's going to give us some answers."

Canyon reached over, opened the glove box and helped himself to a couple of brass knuckles, and shot me a small grin, nodding with raised eyebrows. I had my own persuader and shook my head no, I didn't need another. He selected one and cranked the steering wheel over hard. The Ford shot into the parking lot, pulling up tighter than a shrunken head beside the Hudson and we flew out to grab the punk.

Hearing the squealing tires and the commotion behind him Archie spun around and bumped his head on the trunk lid as he tried bolting. His timing was no match for both of us.

Canyon was closer and grabbed him from behind. He gave him a quick shot to the kidneys with a surprising right hook with the knucks that would have floored Jack Dempsey. The tattoo artist, collapsed in a world of pain, moaning and grabbing his lower back. Tears dribbled down his face as I kicked him over on his back. He looked up into a couple of faces he didn't recognize.

"W-who the hell are y-you guys? W-what did I do?"

"We know you pal and you're going to answer some questions."

"Ah- ah-let me go, I ain't done nothin." He squirmed and I stepped on his hand. He shouted in pain. Then I dragged him back up to his feet.

"Where are your partners?"

"Who?"

"Your two skinny pals that work at your tattoo shop."

"Oh, them. T-they should be work'n later this morn'n ink'n, customers… why?"

"Never mind. We'll deal with them soon enough. That was easy, chum, wasn't it?" He looked relieved and a little dopey, massaging circulation into his fingers, but it wouldn't last. "Now let's get down to some real business. I want Frank Murphy. Where is he?" I cuffed him several times across the face to wake him up.

Something clicked in his small brain and he muttered, "M-Murphy? Ah-ah, y-you're not the guy that drives that black Buick convertible a-are you?"

"Good guess, punk."

"I-I was afraid that's who you were. L-look, mister, I ain't got nothing to do with trying to k-kill you. T-that was all Murphy's do'n. M-me and the boy's been busy over at *Shanghai Ruby's* late last night. We wasn't with him, honest. Let me go."

"I'll bet you were. Get what you were after?"

He must have been working Black Jade over for stiffing them on the money exchange. He blurted out that Murphy told him I'd been killed in the Laurel Canyon hit and run. From the frightened shock on his face, he knew his days were numbered if he didn't give with what I wanted to know. But I could also tell, he was going to be stubborn and make me work to get what I wanted.

Pointing towards a darkened, litter-strewn rat hole separating the two multistory brick apartment eyesores propping up this corner of the rundown neighborhood I said to Canyon, "Let's drag his carcass back into that vacant alley over there. I need some faster answers without any interference from passersby. Several are starting to get nosey." I nodded in the street direction.

Archie squirmed and groaned trying to reach back to rub his damaged kidneys with his busted hand as we dragged him begging toward a certain confession.

I shot a quick glance over at Canyon and had to admire the way he'd stepped up to the plate on this. He connected and wasn't the pantywaist actor now, mincing his way around a Hollywood movie set. His whole personality had changed since I unfolded my story, even throwing in some strongarm tactics of his own. Especially with his admitted vendetta for the killings of the two female agents he'd known. It was now personal with him and he knew that if justice was ever going to be served, he'd have to step outside the circle into the shadows, as I usually did, and take some necessary deviations from the prescribed legal channels. He seemed to be okay with it. For how long? I didn't know.

The alley was empty and the few apartment windows overlooking the trash down below had either been painted over or covered up a long time ago to ward off the view and the smell of garbage.

Archie was now right at home. He fit in with the dirty trash and scum that normally inhabited this filth. I had no idea where Murphy was or when he'd left, but his hourglass was running out of sand and so had this loser. It was time for answers and I wouldn't be polite.

"Prop him up, pal. Time for some straight talk."

We shoved him up against an overflowing trash can and I whipped a black leather-covered lead sap out of my back pocket.

"Murphy told you he tried to kill me last night so you must have talked to him afterwards, right? Now, where is he? That's what I want to know." He just stared at me stupidly. "Okay, have it your way." That was followed up by sharp rap to the side of his head with the sap. Not enough to knock him out, just enough to knock some sense into him.

"He-e's not here," he mumbled, shaking his head and trying to remember and talk straight before receiving more blows. "He give me these boxes here and told me to deliver them to a M-Mr. Dimetrius at the Majestic Studio in Hollywood at 10:30 today. I don't even know what's in there. Tha-at's all I know, honest."

"You're lying. More! Where the hell was he going, after he gave you the God-damned boxes?" I shouted close in his face and then gave him a swift shot to the groin with the sap as an incentive.

He folded up faster than a single pair poker bluff and just lay there sucking air, mumbling incoherently what should have been his last rights and still not planning to cooperate.

"Nothing to tell me, yet? Okay, let's try again, tough guy."

I hauled him up again. From the roll of his eyes, I knew he was about to either spill or pass out. So, I nudged him over the edge.

Turning to Canyon I said, "Our friend needs another reminder that his kidneys are about to burst inside with another shot from your brass knucks. What say, we bust him up good? This time harder, huh?"

That did it.

"No-no. I'll tell you, okay? No more," he begged, grimacing as another wave of pain crept across his face, reminding him that his kidneys were already on fire from the knuckle sandwich he'd just been eating. "M-Murphy's on his way to Catalina Island right now. His seaplane was leaving Long Beach airport at 8:00 A.M. and then he and Mr. McCullen were leaving for maybe Mexico sometime later today on McCullen's boat. H-he thought you was dead, he told me. It's true, I didn't know nothing about it. You got to believe me."

I told him to shut up, I'd heard enough. I turned to Canyon and said we had to leave right now. We decided to wrap up this damaged trash and stuff him into the trunk of the Ford along with the boxes of his commie newsletters Canyon needed for evidence and make tracks to the airport. The other two punks that worked at the tattoo parlor would get picked up later and join their pal Archie in jail sooner than they expected.

It was now 8:45 a.m.

Chapter Twenty-Six

The trail behind Murphy was now on fire. I vowed he'd be in my gun sights before sunset and told Canyon I didn't care how but burn rubber with that Ford. In the fifteen minutes it took us to race over to the small Long Beach Municipal airport off Lakewood Boulevard, we broke every law from driving on the sidewalk around slow vehicles, to bypassing a woman pushing a baby carriage and other pedestrians scurrying in a crosswalk. Canyon's maneuvers were guaranteed to attract attention by the police, but he didn't seem to care. We both knew his G-man badge would buy him a free pass to push the limits, if necessary.

I chain-smoked, sweated, and tried to relax, scanning one of the red rags scheduled for delivery to Majestic. It didn't work. After reading only a few disgusting paragraphs attempting to indoctrinate and agitate the masses, I wadded it up into a tight ball and tossed it out the window.

We finally wheeled through the airport front gates and followed the signs directing us toward the Amphibian Air Transport Company's seaplane base. It was located at the far end of the airfield, but within sight. Most of the more prosperous airlines at the little mom and pop airfield employed hangers and elaborate outbuildings serving as comfortable terminals for their passengers. The less fortunate, however; erected converted war surplus prefabricated Quonset huts and a smiling promise from the front desk staff for a safe flight.

A fat Grumman "Goose" and two Sikorsky S-43 flying boats stood about on the landing strip in front of A.A.T.'s little Quonset hut building, like big clumsy overstuffed birds anticipating the holiday axe to fall. The white

"Goose" with an impressive decorative go-fast racing red paint job and sporting twin Pratt & Whitney Wasp engines, looked the most distressed. The propellers were already spinning and it appeared to be warming up, poised to flap off at any moment. Just looking at that seagoing crate vibrating its rivets loose made me nervous.

The lot near the prefab building where we parked was lightly occupied. I pointed out Murphy's dark blue Mercury sedan with the California license plate 3K 66 30. It was parked off to the side, as if abandoned. We jumped out and examined the vehicle. The right front fender and bumper were both severely damaged as I'd expected from the sideswipe.

I hailed a passing airport police security officer sweeping through the airport's perimeter parking lots. He looked lost … I was wrong. There was an "All Points Bulletin" broadcast on the airwaves from the Long Beach P.D. They were searching for a high-speed, dark Ford sedan wanted for every traffic violation ever written. Glancing over at Canyon's Ford, brought stars in his eyes, but then so did Canyon's Special Agent Federal badge and a brief version of our mission.

It was already hotter than hell outside and we knew we couldn't leave the loser in the stifling trunk. Instead, we turned him over to the airport police security officer, with instructions to have him collected and booked by the local police department for his involvement in an illegal counterfeiting operation. That would be further explained, when more formal charges were filed, later. His involvement with the commie connection wouldn't apply … yet. I also requested that the Mercury on the lot be impounded as evidence in a hit-and-run accident in Los Angeles's Laurel Canyon the night before.

The airport officer complied with our situation immediately, calling for assistance from the police department, while we rushed inside the Quonset hut to collect two seats on a flying boat hopefully to Catalina Island.

I wasn't looking forward to a seaplane trip anywhere. But was more worried that Murphy had slipped through my fingers already and was already on his way south with McCullen.

An attractive, perky ticket agent decorated the front desk and greeted us wearing a funny little navy blue, beanie shaped like an inverted cupcake liner, a snappy navy blue blazer with a gold propeller lapel pin, and matching navy blue skirt. She flashed us a glistening toothy smile, as expected, and showed me the flight schedule to Catalina.

It was now 9:15 a.m. The next flight was scheduled for 9:30 a.m. We'd made it just in time. After that, the next flight wouldn't be until 11:30 a.m. and then nothing more until the afternoon, unless we commandeered a plane.

It was already boarding and would normally cost $5.75 each, for the one-way trip. Our I.D.'s bought us a free pass. The twenty-six-mile, junket out into the Pacific Ocean was supposedly the shortest, safest, and fastest United States commercial flight at only 15 minutes. The red-lipped doll gave me a last-minute, pep talk about their "Safe No-Crash to Date" sales pitch, tailored to build my confidence. I wasn't sure whether it was more for her benefit or mine. I hoped she was right on the flight time anyway. Even 15 minutes was too long in my book.

She optimistically suggested two round-trip tickets. Good anytime, just in case we couldn't pull ourselves away from the island paradise and insisted on staying longer, she advised. Canyon sensed my nervous reservations about taking that kite and just smiled.

We reserved the last two open seats. Before we departed, I asked for the passenger list on the earlier 8:00 A.M. flight. Sure enough, there was no Frank Murphy, but instead, a John Smith was listed. That would be good enough.

We climbed aboard and I prepared for the worst. Especially, after listening to the noise from the twin engines, the vibration rattling the windows, and observing several other passengers gripping the edge of their seats in panic.

Naturally, it was over almost before it started, gliding smoothly up to a landing barge secured to the end of the pier in Avalon Harbor. I breathed a sigh of relief, unbuckled my seat belt, grabbed my crime-busting hardware in the case and we deplaned before the kite sank…now, in search of bigger fish.

Chapter Twenty-Seven

I looked around, but didn't spot McCullen's big Matthews powerboat sitting idle at the harbor dock where our seaplane just landed, as I expected. I couldn't see it tied up on the other pier either. Canyon and I looked at each other, worried.

Both piers jutted out from the semicircular sand beach fronting the center of the small seaside village and were easy to survey. Normally most all private boats, unless loading or unloading heavy and bulky items were tied to buoys in the harbor. They were accessed by either personal launch or one that was provided and operated for a small fee by an island employee. It circulated on a random schedule around the anchored and moored boats for passenger pickup or drop off from shore and could be seen offloading a couple onto their private sailboat moored close to shore.

From where we were standing near the beach, it wasn't possible to identify McCullen's boat if it was buried amidst all the others scattered across the bay on mooring buoys. Maybe we were too late and McCullen had already left. We'd have to check with the Sheriff's office first anyway and get him involved, before trying to locate the boat with the harbor master.

The island was already bustling with a few sleepy residents and mostly tourists who just landed from the mainland by seaplane, a small cruise liner, personal power and sailboats. Vendors were hawking souvenirs up and down the warm sand beach selling nothing special, the usual tourist junk you didn't need. The public beaches were already beginning to fill up with sunbathers in bright colored swim suits, picnic baskets, too many children and excessive amounts of paraphernalia.

I nudged Canyon in the ribs and pointed with a nod saying, "Catch the doll over there walking along the shore line."

He followed my gaze and said, "The blonde walking barefoot wearing the red short shorts and the white sleeveless blouse?"

"Yeah…isn't that vision worth the trip over, chum? She looks like a suntanned mermaid out of the water, doesn't she?"

He wasn't interested. I said I wasn't either… at least not just then anyway.

It was going to be a sweltering day, with only a slight balmy breeze to ward off the humidity. Canyon and I were overdressed for the little casual island and wanted to tear off our suit coats. We were also both packing sidearms and didn't want to draw undue attention, so we nixed the idea. Instead, we loosened our neckties and sweated out the couple of blocks to Sheriff Dan Blair's hopefully cooler office.

It was located just off Sumner Avenue, a short walk inland from the beach. Housed in a squat blocky one-story, whitewashed stucco building, it contained a combination courthouse, police station, and city library. I looked up and down the narrow street and noticed only a handful of automobiles brought over from the mainland. Except for a few birds disturbing the peace from somewhere in the background, it was quiet, nice, and unhurried. Soaring mature King Palm trees dotted the streets. Brown parched hills inland were still home to the abandoned relatives of buffalo herds leftover from the silent movie era that continued to roam in peace. The hills towered in the distance over the rest of the town's few commercial and scattered residential buildings like an immovable painting backdrop and were still thankfully undeveloped, unlike the rest of southern California.

It was a peaceful little town and a good place to live unless you were McCullem and his gang who were about to be either captured or buried.

"Dan Blair? Jesus, what the hell happened to you?" I said entering the Sheriff's office as he struggled up from his desk chair and grabbed his crutches. He hobbled over to greet me, one broken leg in a heavy plaster cast.

"Matt Thornton? Yup, I know it looks bad, don't it? I broke it falling off my horse Pinto Beans, you remember her, don't ya? Happened just last week.

I was riding over to a little inland shack at the other end of the island by Two Harbors to check on another domestic quarrel between a couple of alcoholics. Wanted to arrest'm both for making me ride all the way over there, too. Happens every few months or so. I guess when the moon gets full, they start getting morose, drink'n too much and fight'n. Their neighbor always calls me. It was get'n close to dark and hard to see. Old Pinto Beans just stepped in a gopher hole. She broke her leg and so did I, fall'n off, except she had to be shot, poor old girl."

I thought he was going to burst into tears telling me this story and I really wasn't interested. I looked over at Canyon and neither of us wanted to go down memory lane with this guy telling us about his old nag. I started to say something. Before I could open my mouth, he just cleared his throat and finished his train of thought.

"Instead, they had to call for help and I got rescued instead. Very embarrassing for me and sad for my old horse, she was only 25 years old. Had maybe another good ten left, I'll bet. I felt like shoot'n those two God-damned drunks instead of my horse, but didn't."

Canyon and I couldn't help smiling at that.

"Next time I get the call, they'll both be eat'n dust—for good." He sighed, shaking his head in regret he didn't kill them both. "Now then, what are you doing over here so soon? I just left you a message about McCullen's boat arriving during the middle of the night, didn't you get it?"

"That's why I'm here now and with a friend. He's a "Special Agent" with the Federal Government," I said introducing him to Wes.

Wes pulled out his badge. Blair whistled, impressed with the shiny government shield and I.D.

"What's going on here gentlemen? Why does the federal government have an interest in my small, quiet, little slice of paradise? Has this to do with that McCullen discussion we had, Thornton?"

"Afraid so and some of his associates. One in particular, by the name of Frank Murphy who attempted to kill me last night."

"Oh, no."

"Sheriff, it looks like our friend McCullen's not the mild-mannered well-heeled businessman he pretends to be. He's been masterminding a counterfeit money operation and laundering it through a communist ring in and around Los Angeles. There's a trail of death that's been connected to this rat too and baffling authorities all over Los Angeles."

"And now he's here and the trap is about to spring?"

"That's about it. We trailed him here. I think his printing operations were set up here on the island and after making several hundred thousand dollars peddling it to the Communist conspirators who financed his plan, he's planning to fold up his tent and move south, until the heat's off. These thugs are dangerous killers. They won't surrender easily, if at all. I've been hot on their trail investigating several connections to missing and murdered individuals and Wes has joined me as he also has a personal stake in these characters related to the murder of several close fellow agents. The trail ends here on Catalina."

"I'd like to help, but as you can see, I can hardly walk around and my one deputy is in bed with the flu."

"We didn't see his boat still tied up to the pier. It's possible he and his gang are still on the island and his boat is moored or at anchor, someplace. It's also possible he already shoved off. We followed Frank Murphy over on one of those flying kites. His was an earlier 8:00 a.m. flight and ours was the 9:30 a.m."

"I don't like those shaky birds. I wouldn't get on one if you paid me. Too damn dangerous, I hear."

"My sentiments exactly, Dan. What about the other two guys that came over with McCullen? Did they stay on the island or did they leave right away?"

"I had my daughter keep an eye out for them as you requested. Guess they're still here as they went off with McCullen right after he landed."

"Ah- nice professional surveillance team you've got there, Sheriff," I said, grinning.

"It's usually quiet and peaceful around here, until you show up, Thornton. While you hotshot private dicks and cops usually beat up the troublemakers on the mainland. We just brush off the sand fleas, give'm a night in the cooler to sleep it off, and turn'em loose the next day. Makes everybody happy, all right?"

I followed his eyes as he glanced over at a framed photograph on his desk. It was a beautiful smiling blonde in her twenties wearing a small two-piece, flower-printed bathing suit with a red hibiscus in her hair. She was standing on the beach with the ocean in the background and looked familiar.

"*That's* your daughter? She's beautiful. I think I might have seen her somewhere before," I said, regretting I'd made a flippant comment about this knockout.

"Yup, that's my surveillance team all right," he said. "I hope she hasn't seen you, Thornton. She deserves better than a shady shamus. If you hang around here long enough though, you might be lucky enough to meet her." he added, beaming at the thought of his gorgeous daughter.

"Okay, okay- you win, Blair, forget I mentioned it. Let's see if McCullen's big Matthews is still on a mooring or at anchor someplace else. Let's call the harbor master's office."

Blair dialed up the harbor master's number at his beachside command post overlooking the entire bay and briefly explained the situation with the Special Agent and the P.I. in pursuit of dangerous criminals and their mission to apprehend McCullen and his crew.

The harbormaster described to the sheriff who relayed the conversation turning towards Thornton as it unfolded, repeating it with his hand cupped over the mouthpiece, "He said he saw McCullen and three of his men drive by earlier with a large quantity of supplies loaded in the back of a small pickup headed toward pier A. That's the other one closer to the big casino building where he must have the *Sundancer* tied up. You missed it, must have been hidden behind one of the large cruise ships. He said it looks like they're still there and preparing to leave. If you need to stop them you better step on it."

Blair turned back and said to the harbormaster. "Mac, get my patrol boat ready, I can't go out as I'm still on crutches, but I'll direct them to where it's tied up and they can use it, if necessary."

He turned back toward us again and repeated the harbor master's last comments, "He said okay, it'll be all set." And then hung up. "Maybe you two can overtake them before they leave, if not, the boat will be warmed up and ready to go. And … good luck."

"Thanks, we'll need it."

He filled us in on the dock location and his personal 29' custom speed boat built by the Catalina Speedboat Company in Wilmington.

"You're familiar with the *Miss Catalina* series of speed boats the city uses to take tourists on hair-raising rides around the island at over 50 mph?"

"Yeah, mahogany beauties, so?"

"The city decided to refurbish the last one for a patrol boat instead of scrapping it when a replacement was ordered. It's now like new and faster than hell with her Liberty Aircraft V12 cylinder engine. A real monster, with over 400 horsepower. This one now has a forward deck and an open utility configuration for my purposes instead of three separate cockpits for passengers and the driver. I renamed her *Avalon*, after my baby over there, too," he nodded proudly toward his daughter's photograph.

She's the fastest patrol boat on the Pacific, gentleman. Take good care of her."

I smiled at Canyon and said to Blair with a grin, "If we can't nail them at the dock, we'll run them down at sea."

Canyon was serious. "I'm looking forward to nailing those bastards too, Thornton. Let's hope we can take McCullen alive. I need him to testify in front of a congressional committee before he's jailed or buried."

He was getting a little ahead of himself, but he was at least on the right page following me over here so far. I had other plans for those crumbs and would take them out any way I could, beginning with Frank Murphy.

After shaking hands with Blair and thanking him for the speed boat, we borrowed more. He offered his Chevrolet station wagon. We loaded that up with his 30-06cal. Browning Automatic Rifle and a couple of loaded magazines, a 12ga. shotgun with 00 buckshot shells, my 45cal. Thompson trench sweeper I'd picked up after that warehouse fire, more ammo for our sidearms and we raced over to Pier A.

Chapter Twenty-Eight

Pier A was on the other side of the harbor near the round multistory casino building. I had hopes of catching McCullen and his gang before they shoved off. Approaching the pier cautiously and concerned about the citizens milling about close by, we were disappointed to see the Matthews pull away from the dock at a leisurely pace. They were as unconcerned with their departure as if they were going for a Sunday picnic on the end of the island.

"Damn it, we were close, but it was too crowded by the beach anyway," said Canyon, rationalizing our miss. We stood far enough off to the side on our approach, so looking back they wouldn't spot us.

"Yeah, we'll still get them though. See, that's McCullen there at the helm," I said, pointing him out to Canyon as his big yacht slid by the other moored boats in the harbor and began to swing south headed toward open ocean and probably Mexico. Canyon squinted, trying to see better with his hand shielding his eyes. I pointed out more. "That other guy coiling the lines and hauling in the rubber fenders? That's Frank Murphy. I can't wait to put a bullet into that bastard. And those other two weasels in the background just standing there?" "They're the two crumbs that work at the Pike in Long Beach that McCullen's been using as a crew. From what I can see they look pretty worthless, here too."

Canyon nodded he'd been following my directions so far, although the boat occupants were quickly becoming small unrecognizable specs.

I said, "I'd hoped the bums from the Pike weren't gone or slipped past us on the return flight back to shore. I doubted McCullen would have left them behind on the island. It looks like they're on board too.

"I want the whole damn gang Canyon. Now we're going to get them all wrapped up in one nice floating birthday cake and I'm looking forward to lighting their candles."

"They think they're going to get away and enjoy themselves built on everyone else's misery, don't they?" he said, a frown creasing his face seeing the boat disappearing in the distance.

"Looks like it, but it doesn't work that way, chum. At least not in my book. They're going to find out that scum like them get what they deserve. When I'm finished, the sharks will be feeding for weeks.

"See, they're so cocky they're just cruising off half throttle. They still don't know we're onto them yet. Let's go get Blair's speed boat and surprise those bastards before they get any further than the end of the island."

We piled back into the station wagon and I drove slower than normal because of the foot traffic. Weaving carefully around the tourists crossing the street to the beach, I maneuvered towards the main pier at the other end of the crescent beach without clipping anyone. We slid into a "Reserved for Sheriff" parking space and jumped out carrying, an armload of arsenal. I spotted Jeb MacGruder the harbor master standing further out on a dock spur reserved for city-owned boats. He was standing sentinel over the already warmed up sheriff's speed boat and helped us load our gear on board as we dropped in.

Canyon flashed him his Federal shield, he already knew me. "Showtime," I said, giving Mac a thumbs up. He waved good luck while I revved up the big engine a couple of times and I slipped her into gear as we cast off.

Blair's *Avalon* was an impressively powerful 29' sleek beauty all right. I looked over at Canyon with a grin feeling the massive horsepower underneath us, pulsating like a thoroughbred anxious to get out onto the track and get turned loose. She came fully equipped with a deck-mounted windshield, a chromed police siren, a chromed searchlight, and port and starboard police interceptor signal lights. The front separated cockpit contained the steering controls, room enough for several passengers, and a split center padded seat to allow access to the fully open rear cargo area, with only the cowling covering the huge inboard aircraft V12 Liberty engine in the center.

After creeping past the moored boats and the others gently bobbing at anchor in the shelter of the harbor, I poured on the power and blasted out to sea. The sound of the massive engine deafening our ears. We swung south towards McCullen's boat, already a fading dot in the distance. His Matthews was still just loafing along, nonchalantly taking it's time, unconcerned. They were still unaware of our presence. We skimmed and bounced over the choppy wave tops, the speedometer reading a neck-snapping 45 mph. The Matthews sport fisherman would be no match for us in pursuit. We'd have not trouble catching up.

Our best tactic would be to hit them hard, fast, and with deadly fire, if they didn't surrender immediately. I was sure they had disassembled their printing machines and had crated them for transportation and storage somewhere else until it was time to begin operations again. Canyon wanted those machines as much as I wanted those losers. Our strategy was to herd them as close to shore as possible in case we sunk the Matthews where anything of value could still be salvaged in the shallower water. We swung wide and decided to hit them on their port side driving them toward the island.

The further away from the shelter of the island we were, the rougher the sea became and I cut back on the throttle. By now we were almost even with McCullen, but approximately 200-300 yards away. His boat headed due south was between our patrol boat and the island. He hadn't reached the end of Catalina yet and I'd make sure he wouldn't get much further.

Unfortunately, we'd been spotted, and it appeared that McCullen was now trying to make a run for it. He began increasing speed on the big sport fisherman, but it wasn't going to buy him anything. Where they thought they were going to evade capture was uncertain, but they were probably trying to formulate a plan while they armed themselves to fire on the powerful, intruding speedboat they could see headed their way.

I slowed down, switched seats with Canyon, and worked my way back to unpack Blair's BAR 30-06cal light machine-gun rifle with several 20 round magazines and my 45cal. Thompson sub-machine gun with its 50-round drum. We were prepared for attack.

I shouted, "Time to hit'm…and fast."

With Canyon at the wheel, we charged the Matthews broadside at full speed like an apocalypse from hell. The noisy unmuffled V12 engine was in its glory roaring like a herd of stampeding elephants as we bore down on them. With a massive ocean water rooster tail trailing in our wake, Canyon added to the chaos with the deck siren blaring, interceptor red lights flashing and his voice shouting into the loud hailer announcing that they were under arrest, reduce speed and stand by for boarding.

Instead of playing smart and obeying our demands, we received a hail of bullets fired in our direction. The shots pinged off the water around us, smashing into the boat's windshield, wounding Canyon somewhere in the arm and another grazing me high on the shoulder. Canyon tried to ignore his hit and managed to steer an evasive zig-zag course as we closed in. At the last minute, we flared parallel to the big cruiser and powered by. I let loose with a broadside emptying a drum load on full automatic from the Thompson submachine gun sweeping the cockpit area and riddling the port side of the boat's hull at the waterline.

I could make out both Murphy and McCullen as they flew over backwards, hit during our attack. Still attempting to resist capture, they hunkered down in the open cockpit, continuing to shoot blindly in our direction from their ineffective cover behind the gunwale. It wouldn't save them. I couldn't see either of the other two losers from the Pike and assumed they'd either both been hit as well or were cowering inside, hoping this nightmare would soon end.

Mine was only a flesh wound and I wasn't bleeding much. I'd had bigger hits in the past and this one just made me mad as hell for getting nicked by those punks. I yelled to Canyon, who looked pale, "Sweep by one more time and closer, pal. I'm going to give them a taste of the BAR and sink those bastards."

I wrapped my mitts around the heavy automatic rifle and rested it over the edge of our gunwale for support. As Canyon circled again on the next pass,

I unloaded a 20-round magazine of the full metal jacket 30-06's through the hull and into the fuel tanks. We swung past at lightning speed, sweeping a heavy wave, rocking the big cruiser, and powered out of range. This time we reduced speed to idle and sat there watching from about 150 yards away. The big powerboat had now been literally stopped, dead in her tracks. She was finished and began smoking from the hits. Her big twin Chrysler engines were now silent and no more gunfire could be heard coming from within. As she drifted silently toward shore, she erupted first in a ball of flames fueled by the leaking 200 gallon, tanks of gasoline and then exploded. Scattered smoldering wreckage and a sheet of leaking burning gasoline and oil from the damaged hull, spread over the ocean surface surrounding the once beautiful vessel.

We slipped in as close as possible, keeping just outside of the burning slick, with our sidearms prepared, but they weren't necessary. As we watched, both Murphy and McCullen appeared out of the smoke and flames, fighting their way out of the burning inferno. Attempting to save themselves, they jumped into the water, struggling to swim through the engulfing flames. There was still no sign of the other two.

They thrashed through the burning surface in the direction of our idling patrol boat, but we were too far away and had to steer clear of the liquid inferno ourselves. They couldn't make it across the slick without their hair and skin consumed by the burning fuel, both burning as they thrashed through the water in our direction.

They reached the patrol boat at the same time with McCullen's blackened and charred face begging for assistance from Canyon's side and Murphy's roasted arms reaching up and his scorched face pleading on mine. I glanced over as Canyon, holstered his handgun. He was preoccupied attempting to hoist McCullen over the side, the flesh sliding off the counterfeiter's arms like slippery rotten meat.

I turned back to Murphy who was already burned toast, envisioning his attempt at killing Rhonda in a purposeful hit and run collision on a dark road at night. He'd left her in the crushed and battered car at the bottom of a ravine and she was now lying in a coma. I stuck out the boating hook, which he initially mistook as an assist to board. It was his ticket to a clam bake and he was already the clam. He struggled to within grasping distance.

Instead of receiving the tip of the pike straight into his cabeza, which by now would be softer than a rotten pumpkin and what he deserved, I didn't have to. Shoving him down deep into the Pacific as far as the pole would reach and holding it there until there was no longer any resistance, wouldn't be necessary either. He'd seen my face and read my mind. After a few more weakened strokes, this time backing away, he stopped thrashing and disappeared from sight in the burning gasoline-fueled flames, sinking into oblivion.

The beautiful Matthews gave a few final gasps and minor eruptions as the wreckage continued to burn on the surface for a while longer. She then sank below the surface to join the body of one of its passengers already precooked and halfway to decomposition for the fish to feed on.

I took over the wheel again as Canyon slumped down near the charred and barely alive McCullen lying next to him. The burning cruiser had been spotted from shore and rescue boats were dispatched immediately, but unnecessary. We returned the bullet-scarred *Avalon* back to a disgruntled Sheriff Blair and received a patch up at the Catalina medical clinic for our minor flesh wounds. McCullen's were so severe that he was transported immediately back to a Los Angeles hospital on the next flying boat flight of the day…escorted and under arrest by "Special Agent" Wes Canyon.

I stayed overnight on the island, met Dan Blair's beautiful daughter Avalon as promised, and returned the following day back to the mainland. This time…by slow boat.

Epilogue

D oris Fillmore's initial report on Carson McCullen was reasonably accurate in its findings. But, the overall scheme of events was much more complicated and verified by McCullen himself, who miraculously survived his Catalina Island boat explosion. He made a full confession to his counterfeiting scheme and connections to the communist ring leaders who financed it. After extended convalescing from his burns, he was eventually sent to federal prison where he died before serving out his sentence...

Carson McCullen lived beyond his means. He was broke both personally and his business was on the verge of bankruptcy as Doris and I surmised. He'd apparently been turned down by banks and other loan institutions all over town as he was already overextended on loans and his available credit lines were maxed out everywhere.

He began cultivating friendships with some of the Hollywood A-List crowd, hoping the big names with their wealth would lead him to more financing from somewhere. One of those connections was with Joey DeCosta a former known gangster and now the head of Majestic Studios. DeCosta was becoming a big wheel around town, known for his philanthropy and his charity parties. McCullen wrangled an invitation to several of these events and while there met DeCosta's beautiful twist, the Ava Gardner lookalike Erika Sherwood.

He and Sherwood hit it off immediately, especially with his disarming personality. He sold her on his persona as a big-time, manufacturing tycoon and she was hooked and wanted to know him better.

During some of his despondent hours, contemplating how he was going to resolve his financial debacle, he'd taken to hanging out in some sleazy dives around town and down by the Los Angeles harbor where he kept his expensive yacht over at one of the marinas. Shanghai Ruby's was out of the Hollywood mainstream, on the waterfront. It was one of his favorites and so he coerced the beautiful Sherwood into going there for drinks and entertainment. Naturally, he had more in mind and their secretive relationship grew close one night ending back at the Blue Parrot, which he was familiar with as it was located close to his company. She always drove her own car to *Shanghai Ruby's* and told him it was only a short drive back to West Hollywood where she supposedly lived in an apartment but was vague as to the address.

They continued to meet back at Shanghai Ruby's, but after one of their nightly trysts, she didn't show up again. And he never saw her after that. Afraid to tackle DeCosta and ask her whereabouts, he fruitlessly scoured the apartment area she'd mentioned in West Hollywood, but couldn't find her. Eventually he had to give up, except he knew it was only a matter of time before DeCosta and his gangster association uncovered their relationship. He had to do something. That's when he panicked after he spotted her photograph in the newspaper and in desperation, hired me to find her fast but with a slightly different twist to his story

* * *

In the meantime, the clock was ticking on his outstanding and rising debts. With the war, just a fading memory, and his profits dwindling from manufacturing questionable aviation instrumentation, he was in deep trouble.

Right about that time, his wife told me, he received a letter from one of his old friends left behind in Europe during the war. They apparently corresponded regularly and this time the letter contained something that piqued his imagination and appeared like a light at the end of his dark financial tunnel. His letter, written in German, contained the usual gossipy bits of everyday happenings, but this time it included something special. It was a crisp, never been used, folded, washed or wrinkled newly minted Deutschemark. At that stage, it was completely worthless as currency. It was sent more as a light-hearted reminder as to what the old country's plans for world domination were than as funds for spending. She remembers him turning it over and over, holding it up to the light, and mumbling about something with a big smile on his face.

He stuffed it into his wallet and didn't mention it to her again. But an idea was born. If the German war machine could crank out impressive-looking currency like that, why couldn't he do the same here in the States? He knew how to build large paper printing machines; it would be easy to build something smaller, but with more detail. He just needed someone that had the right artistic expertise to design the plates he'd need for printing. He could do the rest and could procure inks, paper, and any other equipment and supplies under the guise of his huge company. But where to find such an individual? He'd mull it over for a while, but not too long.

Back at *Shanghai Ruby's* slumming again one evening after work and still brooding over his dilemma, he was knocking down one shot of booze after another, when a tough local dock worker with tattooed forearms sidled up to the neighboring barstool and ordered a cold brew. McCullen glanced over at this character and remarked about the intricate designs he had plastered on his arms. The guy smiled proudly and said there was only one guy in town, a new guy that could create those designs with such accuracy. And that guy, Frank Murphy worked at Archie's Tattoo Shop there in Long Beach. McCullen bought him another round or two, got the exact location, and slid off the barstool, another germ of his plan, now maybe planted.

One trip to Archie's, was enough to get him started. Archie, himself an ex-con with a sketchy past and a thirst for dough, was reluctant to give out any personal information about his employees, but with a short stack of sawbucks staring at him across the countertop he opened up about his pal, Murphy also a recent con and best detail man in the business. He'd apparently learned from some of the best tattooists while he was serving time in the joint. Several of them had also cut their teeth in the counterfeiting business, before being sent up to the big house and were pros at designing very intricate and detailed designs whether on skin or on etched plates, but now only for the other cons on their bodies. That was all McCullen wanted to know and arranged to meet Murphy with the intention of having him design the plates he'd use in his machine, if he was that good.

He convinced McCullen he was and they hit it off, followed by a plan now set in motion to begin the counterfeiting scheme.

McCullen began designing a small press that he could have fabricated in his own shop, right under the eyes of the unsuspecting, disguised as a new prototype press for small business use. Murphy had connections for some labor, Archie and his other two tattoo artists. Two others to help McCullen out when needed were suggested by Murphy's blonde girlfriend Gina Slade, now working at the Pike Amusement park running one of the concessions. She'd been waiting for his return from jail, but in the meantime, unbeknownst to Murphy, she'd also struck up a relationship with one of the Pike workers, a tough psycho named Chester Pruitt, who'd eventually get even with Murphy for reclaiming Slade.

Everything was moving forward with the equipment construction, a small truckload of printing supplies on order, and Murphy's printing press counterfeit plate designs. When after a few trial runs to see if the public was falling for it, several small-time low-life handlers got picked up all carrying some of the fake cash in identical serial numbers and the Feds. were tipped off. Snooping around for answers regarding the fake dough, they stumbled into a hornet's nest one night in a bar near the Santa Monica Pier where Chester and his pal from the Pike, Roy Stryker were boozing it up with some other bums. Pruitt and Stryker took it upon themselves to snuff out the two unidentified Feds and carelessly dumped them in an alley.

Then one night shortly thereafter, during Erika Sherwood's final meeting with McCullen at *Shanghai Ruby's,* she met the beautiful blonde Gina Slade who was with Murphy that evening. The blonde clung to Murphy like a wet dishrag and Sherwood could see that the girl had as much potential as any of the others at Majestic to be on the big screen. But she said she was apparently stuck in a dead-end job at the Pike and didn't make much money, yet. Slade admired Sherwood's ankle bracelet and while McCullen and Murphy were huddled together over at the bar drinking, smoking cigars, and discussing business, she took off her ankle bracelet and gave it to her, but told her not to talk about it because it had been a gift from McCullen. She was going to break it off with McCullen anyway afterwards, as it was getting too dangerous with her mob-connected jealous lover DeCosta breathing down her back. Gina apparently repeated her safety concerns to Murphy who repeated them to McCullen after she'd dumped him.

Note: Upon further questioning, Joshua Keys remembered seeing both women that night sitting by themselves at the same table in a serious discussion, exchanging something shiny, which the blonde placed around her ankle.

McCullen told Murphy to meet him back at the shop later that evening after he and Sherwood had parted, but Murphy wanted to take Gina to a motel somewhere first. McCullen suggested the Blue Parrott as it was close to his factory. Murphy agreed and left with Gina.

Unbeknownst to Murphy, they were being followed by a jealous Chester all the way to the Blue Parrott. He waited somewhere inside and found out where their room was. Murphy and Gina spent an enjoyable interlude making love. Afterwards, they just lay there, he smoking one of McCullen's gift cigars and she puffing on a cigarette, while they discussed a better future with some of the fake dough he said was a bonus for working for McCullen on some vague machine shop project. After a while, he noticed the time, dressed quickly, gave her a parting kiss, and said he'd be right back soon after a short get-together with McCullen at his company around the corner.

While he was at McCullen's office that night to discuss details about making more plates with different serial numbers, Murphy couldn't resist lifting the pawn ticket from McCullen's desktop slipping it into his breast pocket, intending to find out what it was of value that he'd pawned.

Blondie was left there in bed waiting for Murphy's return. A little while later, she was surprised when instead of Murphy knocking on her door, a frustrated Chester burst into the room instead. Standing there half-naked wrapped only in a handful of hastily grabbed clothes and shocked, she tried to scream, but he covered her mouth with one hand, threw her on the bed, and roughed her up. He wasn't finished. Grabbing her panties off the side chair, he wrapped them around her throat, strangled, and raped her, thinking the finger would be pointed only at Murphy. Then he wiped up any tell-tale fingerprints of his and scooped up her purse so that it looked like a robbery, and fled.

When Murphy returned later, he found her dead on the bed. Who had done it, he didn't know, but it looked like the motive was rape and, robbery. Being out on parole, he figured he'd be the prime suspect, even if he called the police. They'd registered under a phony name and now he didn't want to be involved in murder. He nervously looked around in panic, didn't see anything significant to worry about, she'd already hidden the money he'd given her in the Bible before answering the door and saw only that the money and her purse were missing. So, he pulled out his handkerchief from his breast pocket, dropping McCullen's swiped pawn ticket, wiped up his fingerprints, left her as he'd found her, and slipped out a side exit door, relieved that he was in the clear and the blame would be elsewhere.

Note: The witnesses at the Blue Parrot in the room next door to the crime both originally had conflicting descriptions of the man going in and out of the room. They both had made their observations at different times and were actually describing two different men, which at my suggestion to the P.D. matched the descriptions of both Frank Murphy and Chester Pruitt.

That scheme would eventually backfire on Chester, as Murphy wasn't stupid. What Chester didn't know was that Gina had already confessed to Murphy, before the Blue Parrot evening, about her affair with Chester while he was in prison. He didn't like it and beat her up. She swore she'd be faithful from then on, but wasn't and continued to see Chester on the side. Chester didn't fall for the double-timing and planned to kill her slowly with light doses of rat poison, while he continued to use her for his own selfish purposes. A box of arsenic was eventually uncovered by the P.D. in his Long Beach apartment containing his fingerprints.

When she was strangled at the hotel, Murphy immediately suspected that the killer was her former lover, Chester. He'd learned to be patient in prison and waited until the right moment for revenge. It finally occurred on McCullen's boat escaping from Catalina Island. With the boat under fire from the pursuing sheriff's patrol cruiser, Murphy blasted back with his own automatic pistol and ordered the other two crew members Pruitt and Stryker below to grab firearms and help defend their escape. Murphy then seized his long-awaited, opportunity. He locked and barricaded the salon door preventing them both from escaping as the boat began smoking from a ruptured gas tank. The two losers from the Pike were now trapped below as the smoke turned to flames and then to a fireball explosion. It consumed the burning boat, which sank from sight taking them and the counterfeit producing machinery and engraved plates with it. Salvage operations would recover all, which would be used as evidence in final convictions of those arrested for complicity in the related crimes.

Note: L.A.P.D. homicide detective Tank Sherman almost had McCullen tagged for killing Gina when he finally located the jewelry store that sold the ankle bracelet and the tobacco shop identified his photo as the customer who usually bought those expensive cigars. Several of my "stupid" questions about the cigars though were the clincher and Sherman finally caved in and looked elsewhere for the killer before finally closing the case.

I explained to Sherman that McCullen was a gentleman from the "Old School in Europe". Old habits are hard to break and how you smoke a cigar is one of them. Most Europeans remove the cigar band before smoking. The one found at the Blue Parrot was left on like an advertising sign. It was also smoked down to the stub and snuffed out in the ashtray like a common cigarette. All would be considered "poor form" by any experienced old world, cigar smoker. There was more and the evidence just piled up excluding McCullen; the end had been bitten off instead of snipped carefully, cardboard matches had been used instead of wood or a lighter, as I'd seen him use and all the ash was just crumpled and not rolled as it dropped off into the ashtray. All the evidence pointed to another smoker from the cruder "School of Hard Knocks." Ergo...that smoker was anybody other than Carson McCullen.

As for the ankle bracelet, I would also explain to Sherman how Gina Slade had acquired that piece of jewelry from Erika Sherwood.

* * *

His connection to the commies in Hollywood was well paved. It looked like all roads led back to *Shanghai Ruby's* again. McCullen's connections through DeCosta's social affairs were beginning to pay off, this time in another way. One night while he was still plotting his counterfeit schemes with Murphy at a side booth in *Shanghai Ruby's,* several men entered. A couple he recognized as high-level producers at Majestic Studios. He'd met them and many others at one of DeCosta's fundraisers organized to finance one of his movies, with money from the attendees, including himself.

They apparently asked for Black Jade and were seated at a private booth on the side opposite. Soon they were joined by Black Jade and deep in serious discussion. Murphy a communist party member since his jailhouse days was also a long-time San Francisco associate of Black Jade's, before Shanghai Ruby was killed. He said he'd seen the men before with her discussing the communist movement now actively in play on the West Coast, from San Francisco to Los Angeles. He told McCullen she was one of the party leaders representing the Chinese community and the men were part of a discrete communist Hollywood set poised to either takeover or topple the movie industry.

McCullen suggested they join the gathering and see if they couldn't do a little business with them. McCullen's suggestion to help finance their cash-strapped social movement, for a fee, with some of his "special high quality, counterfeit banknotes" which could be easily turned for a big profit. After much discussion, his offer was accepted. Especially, after Black Jade disclosed the Chinese community would also be in agreement to share in the same proposal. The plan was to launder the counterfeit dough through the Chinese Tong controlled community's illegal gambling operations and merchandise sales, the profits split between the commie party leaders and Black Jade's associates. The transaction was guaranteed to be harder to trace in the tight-lipped, oriental community than selling illegal Moonshine on an Indian reservation.

Note: The commie leaders had a silent partner in the deal. So silent he was kept in the dark on their real plans. Joey DeCosta's movie financing wasn't doing as well as his gangster friends had envisioned and they were all getting nervous. He feared the commie sympathizers in his studio were either going to make or break his business. Threats and begging weren't working. Once he suggested bribes, he was on to something. For a certain sum, which they used unbeknownst to him as their chip to buy into the counterfeit scheme, they would minimize but not eliminate, disruption on his sets and keep their creative writing, producing and directing talents within acceptable limits so as to avoid scrutiny from the political machinery and political watchdogs in Washington.

Murphy and his pals would discreetly handle the transfer of funds in Chinatown's *Full Moon House of Pleasure*, a questionable massage parlor run by Black Jade's sister, Apricot Blossom. As an added incentive, McCullen agreed reluctantly that he would also print up several issues of an underground commie newspaper on some of his other equipment for the party leaders at Majestic with news of their social agenda, which they would distribute. This they also liked and agreed to provide him with some newsworthy articles to print up.

There wouldn't be many issues, but just enough to get them started and then they could find another printing source.

* * *

Shanghai Ruby's and the Full Moon House of Pleasure were shut down with the arrests of both Black Jade and her sister Pearl, the Apricot Blossom. After confessing before the HouseUn-American Activities Committee in Washington, D.C., acknowledging their major connection to the communist party in the states and back in China, including the communist ringleaders employed at the Majestic Studios, they were also tried, convicted, and served time in Federal prison for conspiracies to overthrow the government using the finances from the shared counterfeit currency scheme.

They were eventually deported back to China as undesirable aliens…their ultimate fate is unknown.

***

The Gang of Eight, the communist ring of writers, producers, and directors, led by producer and director Milo Dimitrius and all employed at the Majestic Studios, also testified before the HUAC. Dimitrius fingered the unwitting DeCosta in the counterfeit financing scheme and he also sank with the rest of the party members. They were all found guilty of similar crimes in Federal court as the two Chinese women and sentenced to stiff fines and even stiffer terms in federal prison.

Upon eventual release, they were all also blacklisted for life from the movie industry in the United States, many returning to Europe, struggling to survive in the foreign film business.

In addition to DeCosta's stiff prison sentence, he also had a lifetime "contract" bulls-eye pinned on his back. The mob connections that had elevated him to movie mogul status in the first place had been stiffed by his bungling studio operations and needed to collect for damages. While in prison, he mysteriously hung himself, supposedly despondent over declining health.

No one attended his funeral.

***

The Majestic Studios struggled for a while under new leadership and decided to drop the "Swords of Dawn" project, as maybe it wasn't that good after all. Hemingway got to keep his money even though the movie had been shelved, which he was informed was only temporary, but it was never filmed. All the actors involved, excluding Wes Canyon who disappeared back into the Washington bureaucracy after his acting cover was blown, were reassigned to other projects under the direction of an entire new cast of writers, producers and directors or loaned out to other studios for a fee…

whichever was more profitable.

* * *

Hemingway didn't return to Southern California. He thanked me indirectly for my efforts by eventually sending a short chatty letter regarding another novel he'd written. He never mentioned the mess at the Majestic Studios except to comment, "I knew you guys were up to the task." And that was all. Maybe he knew more about what was going on there than I realized. Smart to stay out of it, if he did.

He made a "let's do lunch sometime" offer to visit him if I ever traveled to Cuba. I never did and never saw or heard from him again, except one other time when I was traveling in Spain years later

* * *

McCullen's original story initially presented in my office contained some validity of truth buried beneath the pack of lies he'd fabricated to throw me off balance. He told me he suspected his wife was having an affair with someone unknown. He should have hired me to find out what that was all about, as she actually was…with his next door, neighbor.

That man's wife finally succeeded in committing suicide in despair over her husband's infidelities. Right after McCullen was sent to prison for a long, long stretch, his wife eagerly divorced him and married her next door, lover.

* * *

The seaplanes were just as dangerous as I'd imagined. On August 16, 1948, shortly after I crossed to Catalina, one of the Sikorsky S-43 flying boats developed engine trouble and crashed at sea halfway to the island, landing in heavy swells. Luckily, none of the passengers were seriously injured.

All were rescued by a coast guard cutter dispatched from the mainland

and the flying bathtub was towed back to Long Beach's Terminal Island for repairs.

* * *

A search of McCullen's estate on Catalina Island turned up more of his printing machines and supplies which were added in evidence to the salvaged engraved plates and other equipment he'd taken on board the sunken Matthews sport fisherman.

* * *

Doris Fillmore at the *Los Angeles Herald Examiner* was, in spite of her protests, taken off the crime beat and kicked "upstairs" to become the newspaper's assistant editor. She told me she'd gotten too close with some of her stories finger-pointing in the direction of several well-known celebrities in L.A. that had friends in high places on the newspaper. Much to her disappointment, she was no longer collecting the city's dirt first hand, but recycling the stories other reporters were having fun collecting.

Only her bank account wasn't protesting.

* * *

Jean Spangler, the chorus girl, part-time movie extra, and girlfriend of Rhonda's at the Florentine Gardens never did return. She mysteriously disappeared with only a cryptic note written to a "Kirk" somebody, left in her tattered purse that was found in a remote section of L.A.'s Griffith Park by a massive search party.

The case remains unsolved to this day.

* * *

My call to inform little Candy stuck north of Los Angeles with Joshua Keys and his relatives in the desolate town of Val Verde had another pitch. Much to my relief, the phone at Shampy's Saloon was answered this time by the pink-haired doll instead of Juba. She informed me that even if the coast was clear with those punks from the Pike gone, she had a job in the bar. She'd rinsed out the pink hair color in favor of her natural blonde and picked up a couple of new names. They were now calling her "Sweet Pea" and "Foxy Baby" and she decided to stay there a while longer with Joshua.

I wished her good luck, told her maybe I'd see her again sometime, to hang onto my card, and to give my best to Joshua for taking good care of her and his Aunt Juba, if she still remembered my name.

I hung up shaking my head and smiling.

* * *

Rhonda finally made a full recovery and aside from a few tell-tale marks here and there, was anxious to return to her normal life. She wasn't up to the whirlwind engagement tour Grant had envisioned before the accident. Instead, she needed time to recuperate. While she was convalescing, Lili St. Cyr returned to L.A. at the *FlorentineGardens* and stole her bathtub striptease act. Rhonda wasn't happy with that and decided to put her own performance on the backburner for a while. She was more comfortable just knocking about with me in the detective business during the day, at least for a little while longer. That was fine with me, as she would have been hard to replace anyway.

As a reward for her assistance on my last case and for taking the beating in my Buick in Laurel Canyon that was meant for me, I took her on that once in a lifetime trip to Paris, France. I let her soak up the ambiance in person that she'd only been dreaming about back in L.A. and she couldn't have been happier.

I was getting restless for more action than cocktails and accordion music near the Eiffel Tower, but the trip wasn't for me anyway and that would have to wait.

* * *

After we returned from Europe, one of the first callers to my P.I. office was from a showbiz friend of Rhonda's. It was the funny little red-haired comedian with a penchant for insulting the wrong guys in the audience at the *Florentine Gardens* night club. Red Burns was desperate, scared, and calling from a hideout cabin; somewhere up by Lake Arrow Head. He wasn't on holiday. He was on the mob's hit list for witnessing a murder he shouldn't have and needed my help. Why wasn't I surprised?

Now things were back to normal again.

A Note from the Author

My characters, novel time period, settings, and genre choice were influenced by memorable detective/mystery/crime stories by James M. Cain, Carroll John Daly, Cornell Woolrich, Raymond Chandler, and Mickey Spillane as well as numerous film noir masterpieces including *Out of the Past*, *The Big Heat*, *The Asphalt Jungle*, and *Laura*.

Acknowledgements

Many thanks to Verena Rose, Shawn Reilly Simmons and Harriette Sackler, the editors and publishers of Level Best books for their wisdom in carrying on the tradition of publishing private detective novels reflecting the golden age of noir crime/mystery fiction.

A special mention of my wife Darquise, a true inspiration for several characters appearing in my Matthew Thornton P.I. novels. In addition, her many suggestions and comments regarding various 1940s era details of culture, clothing styles and the entertainment industry have been invaluable.

Congratulations also, to my historical research partners, D. Quelle and S.W. Thompson, regarding suggestions and details of mid-century Los Angeles with its shady characters, gangster and criminal activities, places of illegal business, flashy night clubs and scenic descriptions of surrounding neighborhoods and the community of Val Verde, at that time.

About the Author

David R. Thompson is a former international business executive, managing manufacturing operations at companies in the United States and Canada. He is a graduate of Arizona State University and was on the board of directors of the Algonquin College Industrial Technology program in Ottawa, Canada.

He's been an active outdoor sportsman, hunting and fishing in Canada, Alpine skiing in Switzerland, Mohave Desert motorcycle racing in the Adelanto Grand Prix, and participating in California skeet shooting and archery tournaments as well as ocean sailing on his 40-foot black ketch, the *Belle Darquise*, aka the *Black Swan*.

He's written numerous short stories, and several historical/adventure stories regarding world explorer Thor Heyerdahl (Kon-Tiki & RA expeditions) & western writer and big game fisherman Zane Grey.

His new series of noir era Matt Thornton private detective/crime/mystery novels begins with *Pandora's Box*, and continues with *The Blonde with the Ice-Blue Eyes*. The novels take place in the Los Angeles area during Hollywood's post-war golden era.

David resides in Huntington Beach, California, with his wife Darquise. He is a member of the Private Eye Writers of America.

Visit David's website www.davidrthompson.com for details on the Matt Thornton P.I. novels.

9 781953 789921